CELEBRATION

Rosie Thomas is the author of a number of celebrated novels, including *Bad Girls, Good Women*, *A Simple Life* and the Top Ten bestsellers *Every Woman Knows a Secret*, *Moon Island* and *White*. She lives in north London, and when not writing fiction spends her time travelling and mountaineering. Her most recent novel *The Potter's House* is now available in Arrow.

Acclaim for Rosie Thomas:

'Rosie Thomas writes with beautiful effortless prose, and shows a rare compassion and a real understanding of the nature of love' *The Times*

'Compelling ... a master storyteller' *Cosmopolitan*

'A story full of passion ... will keep you reading long after bedtime' *New Woman*

'Honest and absorbing, Rosie Thomas mixes the bitter and the hopeful with the knowledge that the human heart is far more complicated than any rule suggests' *Mail on Sunday*

'A special talent' *The Times*

D1343567

Celebration

Rosie Thomas

ARROW

For CK, CMK and SS, with gratitude

Published by Arrow Books in 2002

1 3 5 7 9 0 8 6 4 2

Copyright © Rosie Thomas 1982

Rosie Thomas has asserted her right under the Copyright, Designs and Patents Act, 1988 to be identified as the author of this work

First published in the United Kingdom by Fontana Paperbacks 1982

Arrow Books
The Random House Group Limited
20 Vauxhall Bridge Road, London, SW1V 2SA

Random House Australia (Pty) Limited
20 Alfred Street, Milsons Point, Sydney,
New South Wales 2061, Australia

Random House New Zealand Limited
18 Poland Road, Glenfield
Auckland 10, New Zealand

Random House (Pty) Limited
Endulini, 5a Jubilee Road, Parktown 2193, South Africa

The Random House Group Limited Reg. No. 954009

www.randomhouse.co.uk

A CIP catalogue record for this book
is available from the British Library

Papers used by Random House are natural, recyclable products made from wood grown in sustainable forests. The manufacturing processes conform to the environmental regulations of the country of origin

ISBN 0 09 940642 X

Printed and bound in Great Britain by
Bookmarque Ltd, Croydon, Surrey

CHAPTER ONE

Love divine, all loves excelling . . . sang the choir. The hot afternoon sun struck through the rose window and illuminated the little church, all along its length to the chancel steps. It rested on the bride in her froth of white tulle and silk as she turned to smile at her bridegroom, and made pink and purple diamonds on his black coat as he tucked her hand under his arm.

Two tiny bridesmaids in forget-me-not blue stooped to pick up the corners of the bride's train and the little procession moved out of the flower-scented brilliance of the church and into the dimness of the vestry.

The bride looked down and saw her left hand clenched around the bouquet of cream and yellow roses. On the third finger shone the plain, thin circle of gold, but she hardly glanced at it. She was much more surprised to see the tense whiteness of her knuckles. Very deliberately she made herself put the flowers down and pick up the gold pen. Her left hand smoothed the paper and the vicar's finger pointed to the place.

She wrote

'Annabel Elizabeth'

and then paused. The stuffy little room was silent, but outside she could hear the congregation crashing into the last verse of the last hymn. With an effort she concentrated on the register again and wrote her new name.

'Brooke'

There, it was done. But it was hideously wrong.

There was no such person as Annabel Elizabeth Brooke, and there never would be. Impatiently she shook off the vicar's hand. He was trying to take away the pen, but she hadn't finished. Underneath the non-person's name she wrote, in deep black letters that scored the page,

'this is all a terrible mistake'.

5

Then she turned and ran. She tore off the horrible, imprisoning white veil, twisted up the long skirts to show her pale silk stockings, and stumbled away. All the way down the chancel steps and along the nave, between the rows of gaping guests, she could hear Edward's voice calling after her.

'Bell! Bell! For God's sake don't go. Come back. Come back to me.'

Her face was wet with tears and sobs were bursting in her chest, but she would never go back. Never, never, never.

The dreamer rolled over and flung her arm up to protect herself. She opened her eyes and immediately felt that they were wet. She was panting, and the suffocating fingers of the bad dream were still trying to pull her back, but she was struggling free of it.

'It didn't happen,' she told herself in her calm daytime voice. 'It couldn't have happened.' But then why, why did these dreams keep coming back to haunt and terrify her? What was she so afraid of?

Bell Farrer wearily pushed back the tumble of dark brown hair from her face and looked around the room. It was daylight, but still very early. The tranquil, creamy colours of her bedroom reassured her and reminded her of the ordered efficiency of her waking life. While she was awake she had everything under control. It was only at night that her unconscious fears could billow out and smother her. In reality there was nothing to run away from and nothing to hide.

In any case, there wasn't anyone to hide anything from.

Bell looked down at the smooth pillow beside her own damp and wrinkled one. Edward wasn't there, of course.

They didn't live together any more, and he understood that she would never marry him. Just as he had always understood everything except the strange, perverse fear that had driven her to give him up. Yet he knew her better than anyone else in the world, knew the secret, vulnerable Bell that seemed well hidden from the rest of her friends. If she telephoned him now, she could tell him about the stupid dream, and they would laugh about it together.

Bell reached for the receiver on the bedside table, but then her hand dropped. She must remember that she was on her own now. She was living the life of the successful career girl, the life that she had always dreamed of, and there was no place in that scheme of things for ringing up Edward every time she needed comforting after a bad dream.

Instead she pushed back the covers and padded into the kitchen to make a big pot of coffee. Half an hour later, in her thinking clothes of jeans and the scarlet sweatshirt emblazoned 'Weehawken Majorettes' that Edward had brought back from a business tour of America, she was at her desk. On top of a pile of notes lay *Cocks et Féret*, the 'bible' of Bordeaux, and Michael Broadbent's *The Great Vintage Wine Book*. Bell opened the Broadbent and flipped through the pages to *Bordeaux*. Then she ran her finger down the columns looking for Château Reynard.

At twenty-seven, Bell Farrer was the wine and food editor of a national daily paper. She had worked her way up from being the most junior of trainee reporters. Her editor, hard-nosed Henry Stobbs with his determinedly northern antecedents and loathing of the London smart set, had taken a lot of convincing that his paper needed a wine and food writer at all. But Bell was quite out of the ordinary run, and Henry Stobbs was always good at spotting talent. Bell's name was becoming familiar to her own generation who had money to spend and no patience with outmoded conventions. They read what she wrote, then ate at the restaurants and ordered the wine that she recommended.

They also bought her newspaper, so Henry Stobbs was happy too.

At her desk, Bell found what she was looking for and began to read a list of dates and tasting notes, frowning with concentration. Tomorrow was the start of her biggest single assignment, and there was a lot of homework to be done first. Bell had been invited to spend a few days at Château Reynard in the Haut-Médoc, to write about the making of one of the world's greatest wines. As she thought about it, she felt a nervous churning sensation in her stomach. Baron Charles de Gillesmont, her host, had a reputation for being withdrawn and difficult, as well as very hostile to the press. Bell had been flattered and excited when the invitation arrived exclusively for her. None of her press colleagues had been invited, yet now she began to wish that she was going with the usual cheerful set of wine writers for company and camouflage. She squashed the thought at once.

'Come on,' she told herself impatiently. 'This is a *coup*, so make the most of it. They can't eat you, it's only three days, and somehow you must make some copy out of it that Stobbs will approve of.'

She bent over her book again, but the phone rang beside her.

'Hello. Tell me if this isn't a welcome call and I'll hang up right away.' Bell's face split into a smile that showed the dimples at the corners of her mouth.

'Edward. Do you know, I dreamt about us?'

'Oh.' The voice was guarded, the response of someone who had been recently hurt and was quick to defend himself. Bell winced, then let the words tumble on.

'I'm sorry, it doesn't matter. What are you doing, this lovely Sunday?' Outside her window she could see the summer sunshine catching the tops of the trees in Kensington Gardens.

'Wondering if we should see each other this evening before you go off on your travels. I could come round and have a quick drink with you, then take you to Les Amoureuses. Mary and Elspeth might join us.'

'Fine,' said Bell, a little blankly. She remembered his voice calling after her in the dream. *Don't go. Come back to me.* But she had wanted her freedom, wanted it so badly that she had hurt them both in disentangling herself. Now she was free, and she had no claims on him any more. Certainly no right to his exclusive attention. But she missed it, even more than she was willing to admit. An evening sharing him with their friends would be better than not seeing him at all and staying in alone.

'See you about seven, then?' He rang off.

Bell tilted backwards in her chair, chewing on the end of her pen. When she felt confident, being alone suited her.

At the best of times she was sure that she could take on the world and win, single-handed. She loved her job, and she had plenty of friends. She had planned it carefully, imagining herself getting steadily more successful, travelling and writing and meeting new people. There would be lovers along the way – yes, of course there would. But she was sure that she didn't want a husband. Her thoughts shied away from that ominous truth. She didn't want to think about why, not just now. It was too bound up with her guilt about her panicky retreat from Edward, and the fears that gave her those horrible dreams about weddings. And with other things, too.

Work was the thing to concentrate on. Her career was what mattered, after all. Just so long as she could keep going. Keep doing it right. Keep writing what they wanted to read.

Bell pressed the heels of her hands into her eyes. She was scared today, and lonely. She hadn't reckoned with that, when she had blindly broken away from Edward. Sometimes life was very bleak. There were empty weekends when everyone she knew seemed to have gone away for a few romantic days *à deux*. Parties she had to go to alone, and then escape from in a solitary taxi. And days like today, when she needed a shoulder to cry on, and then someone to tell her that of course she could confront the baron in his château and carry off the role of the calm career woman that she had imposed on herself.

She sighed. Sitting here feeling sorry for herself wasn't going to help her to do what had to be done at Château Reynard.

She turned to her work again, her determination doubled.

She worked hard for the rest of the day, keeping her attention fixed on the pages in front of her. At last she felt that she had boned up on all the background she could possibly need. She gave a decisive nod and fanned out her sheaf of notes, then snapped them together into a neat pile and clipped them to her list of questions. She would need those to act as a prompt in case she dried up in her first interview with the baron.

Bell looked at her watch. An hour before Edward was due to arrive. Plenty of time to change and then do some packing. Les Amoureuses was a newish supper club with a tiny dance floor, and good French food. It would be hot and crowded.

Bell put on a pale lilac round-necked shirt and a pair of narrow-legged trousers in exactly the same shade. On top went a loose violet linen jacket. She brushed out her hair until it made a glossy frame for her high-cheekboned face, and stroked a careful glow of amethyst shadow on to her eyelids. She was ready. Bell pulled a workmanlike canvas bag out of her cupboard and turned back to the wardrobe. Her job meant a lot of travelling, and she was beginning to feel that her clothes would be a credit to any magazine feature on capsule wardrobes. Plans for a few days' stay in a Bordeaux château with a baron for company required a little more thought than usual.

Moving quickly, she laid out her travelling-wine-writer's outfits – mostly carefully chosen separates in soft shades, but all spiced with other bits and pieces in her favourite colours, periwinkle blue and violet. Last of all she pulled out a well-loved evening blazer, the grey and violet stripes shot through with multi-coloured threads and lines of gold. Bell knew that it suited her and she smiled with satisfaction as she smoothed the lapels. She was getting used, these days, to her reputation preceding her when she went to interview people. But she was feminine enough to enjoy their surprise – especially the surprise of middle-aged Frenchmen – when they actually saw her. She was so much younger and better-looking than they expected.

She shook the folds out of her blazer and held it up against herself with a little surge of excitement. Perhaps this trip would be fun after all. The blazer was the last item. Bell was noticing with satisfaction that the little collection would fit easily into the canvas bag when the doorbell rang. Edward didn't have his own keys any more.

She opened the door and stood there smiling at him, framed in the doorway like a picture.

Just as he always did, Edward thought how striking she was. Not beautiful exactly, more interesting than that. She was almost as tall as he was, and thin enough to look rangy. Tonight her hair was loose, waving frivolously around her narrow face. Her eyes were an extraordinary blue-green mixture that changed with the light. Aquamarine.

'Come in,' she said softly. 'It's lovely to see you.'

He kissed her briefly on the cheek and followed her into the familiar room. They had furnished it together, bidding for the furniture at auctions and picking up the other things in country junk-shops. In one corner a palm tree flourished luxuriously in a green and gold jardinière. He stared at it, trying to dam up the memories that came flooding back.

'What would you like to drink?' Bell repeated.

'Oh . . . white wine?' he said, vaguely. His eyes went to the windows, to the familiar jumble of rooftops and chimney stacks and the greenness of the park beyond. Bell put a cold glass in his hand.

'Sancerre,' she said. 'Tell me what you think of it.'

They had been together all through Bell's steady climb up the ladder towards the success she had set her heart on. He had shared the special bottles and the celebration meals, advising her and encouraging her.

Their eyes met at last, and she smiled awkwardly at him.

'Edward, I . . .' but he put his hand to her lips to stop her saying any more.

Instead he guided her to the rocking chair in front of one of the windows, and sat down beside her. They sat in silence, staring out at the view, exactly as they had done hundreds of times before. Her fingers wound and knotted themselves in his hair.

'I feel so . . . sad today,' she said at last. 'I keep remembering all the things we used to do together. How hopeful and excited we were. What a waste.' Her voice was full of bitterness.

'No, not a waste. You learnt something about yourself. I discovered a lot too. You were right, Bell.' He was talking quickly, urgently, trying to convince himself as well as her. 'You couldn't have married me, and we wouldn't have made each other happy. Not in the end.'

She nodded, hoping that he was right and grateful for his generosity.

'It would be sadder still if we didn't miss each other at all,' he reminded her.

'All those years.'

Four years, to be exact, before she had felt the terror of

commitment closing around her. Four years before she had realized that if she didn't escape now she never would. A long time to get used to having somebody so close. Long enough to become dependent on him. Almost too long.

'Do you remember,' Edward said into the silence that had fallen, 'the first time that we came into this room? We'd only known each other a few weeks, but we were quite sure that we wanted to live together. Happily ever after.'

Bell laughed, remembering. 'I loved you desperately. I couldn't believe that I could be so lucky. As soon as we got the keys we dashed up here with an armful of books, that potted palm . . .'

'. . . and I grabbed you and we made love on the bare floorboards.' Bell leant her head back against the cushions and closed her eyes.

'I know we're only remembering the good things, but it was wonderful. All those Sundays when we stayed in bed until lunchtime . . .'

'. . . and then had kippers and a bottle of Chablis . . .'

'. . . and then went out for a walk in the park . . .'

'. . . and then out to see a film and have a pizza.'

'It wasn't always a pizza. Sometimes a curry.'

They had met at a party, an ordinary, crowded party in someone's flat with beer spilt on the floor and a girl in a long skirt crying on the stairs. Edward was in his first year out of Oxford, bored with his job and irritable with the confines of London. He was, without realizing it, very lonely. Then he saw Bell.

She was stretched out in an armchair with an untouched glass of murky red wine in her hand. Edward could see that she wasn't listening to the man who was perched on the arm of her chair, although he was leaning over her and shouting above the blare of the music. Even in the dim light Edward noticed her intense blue-green eyes, fixed far beyond the tawdry party.

Bell felt even more cut off than Edward. She was just back from a year in France, and was, she told herself, buckling down to real life. It was just that real life seemed to add up to nothing more than a very junior job in the subs' room of a newspaper. She knew that she was lucky to have even that, and saw clearly that to get a better job she had to do this one as well as she could, but she still felt impatient and restless.

She sighed in the sagging armchair and rotated the sticky glass gently in her fingers. Her eyes flickered over the man, still talking, still straddling the arm of her chair. At twenty-two Bell knew surprisingly little about men, but she knew enough to recognize that this one was planning to sleep with her. She frowned at the thought, knowing that she would fend him off by pretending to be coolly surprised. It always worked. Inside she was puzzled, nearly always shy and unsure of herself, but she was getting better and better at hiding it. The more she played up her natural reserve, the more people mistook it for calm confidence.

That was easy, but it wasn't at all easy to escape from behind her own defences. She wasn't really aloof or cold, even though people often thought she was. It was just that as far as love was concerned, even demonstrative affection, she was not even in the beginners class.

Bell's mother had died when she was eleven years old, leaving her in the care of her father. She had no brothers or sisters, and her father was too shattered by his own grief to help his bewildered child.

She had had a solitary, bookish adolescence. When she was sixteen her childish gawkiness had disappeared almost overnight, but by then she was too used to being alone to know what to do with the young men who started to swarm around her. She kept them at bay, politely but definitely, and stuck to her books. She had enjoyed university and had emerged with an excellent degree and several very close friends. But she had never been in love. She had no idea how it happened to other people.

Bell thought, afterwards, that it was in answer to her unspoken question *how*, that Edward pushed his way across the room and stood in front of her. She saw a man with a quick smile, brown eyes and silky, almost feminine hair pushed back from his forehead. He was nodding at her glass.

'Can I try and find you a glass of something else?'

She stood up and put the tumbler down carefully on the mantelpiece. Staring straight into Edward's eyes, she answered. 'I don't think there is anything . . .'

'In that case,' he said decisively, 'I shall have to take you away from here.' He took her hand and guided her across the room. Bell heard the stream of anxious talk from the armchair stop in mid-sentence.

'Bell? You're not going, are you?'

'Yes,' she whispered, not loudly enough for even Edward to hear.

'I think I am going.'

Out on the shabby landing they stood side by side, staring into the kitchen where a beer barrel was dripping on to a carpet of newspapers. An array of green and brown wine bottles stood in a litter of French bread and cheese. Their eyes met, and they smiled at each other.

'Have you got a coat?'

'On the bed, in there.'

The bedroom door was locked now and he retrieved it from the pile that had been flung out on to the landing floor. They picked their way down the stairs, past the girl in the long skirt, and out into the street. To Edward, for the very first time, the thick London air smelt clean and invigorating.

He took Bell out to dinner and then back to the door of her flat.

He saw her every day for a week before he kissed her, and it was a month before he felt he was even beginning to know her. Every time he saw her he was surprised by the way her beauty unfolded. At first he had seen her simply as an attractive girl with unusual eyes, but gradually he noticed the luxuriance of her dark hair, the fragility of her long neck and the bloom of her skin, and the vulnerability of her mouth.

Her face kept changing.

For Bell they were weeks of enlightenment. Slowly she discovered that Edward could be trusted not to disappoint her. He was never dull, never at a loss. To her delight she found that if he wasn't beside her he was a step ahead, waiting for her to catch up. She found that she could be herself with him, as with no one else. She began to show him aspects of herself that she had buried deeply years ago, when she was a little girl convinced that her mother had been taken away from her to punish her own wickedness. Not even her closest friends knew about her spurts of temper, or her bleak fits of pessimism. Bell stopped hiding them from Edward, and her feeling for him quickened when she saw that he accepted her faults as gratefully as her merits.

The habits of years fell away as she accepted the rhythm of life with him. She began to think in the plural after what felt like a lifetime of solitude.

One evening, Edward brought her home as he always did. They had been to see a film, and then for a meal at the tiny restaurant around the corner. Bell had watched the candlelight making black shadows in the hollows of his face as he talked and she had realized, with a little shock, that she knew the contours of it as well as she knew her own face. She was faintly surprised when she remembered that she was still keeping part of herself from someone so well-loved.

In the deserted flat Edward took Bell in his arms to kiss her goodnight.

'Don't go,' she had said, in a small clear voice. 'I'm sorry it's taken so long, but I'm ready now.'

There was no need to say any more. Edward put his hand on the catch of her bedroom door and it swung open. They stepped into the dim warmth of her room. With infinite tenderness he took off her clothes and knelt beside her.

'Are you quite sure?'

Her eyes were luminous as she answered, 'Quite sure. I love you, Edward.'

He had been astounded by the depth of her passion. It was as if she had flung herself blindly into an uncharted sea, and found that she could swim like a fish.

They had been very happy, Bell recalled. Until their need for each other had become claustrophobic to her, threatening rather than secure. Until she had begun to have dreams about being trapped underwater, or about failing to rescue him from burning tenements. Or about jilting him. She remembered her early-morning dream, the feel of her billowing wedding dress gathered up in her fists to leave her free to run, and her mouth went dry.

It had been painful, and it still was, but she had done the right thing. She wished that there had never been any nagging sense of something missing, so that she could have been happy with Edward for ever. But it was not to be, and now even in her loneliest moments she delighted in her freedom. It had been hard to win, this independence, and now she had it it felt like a prize.

Suddenly she felt a suffocating wave of affectionate tenderness for him. She bent forward and wrapped her arms around his hunched shoulders, rubbing her cheek against his hair.

'Thank you,' she said. 'It's helped, sitting here remembering all the good things. It seems less of a . . . waste. And it's made the bad bits easier to contemplate.' Edward stood up and pulled Bell to her feet. The wine bottle was empty, and she knew that it was time to go and meet their friends. He raised his eyebrows and she nodded, half smiling.

'I'll go and get my things.'

Edward watched her go. In an automatic gesture she stretched out her fingers as she passed to feel the dampness of the earth in the potted palm. Instantly the memory came back to him. He smelt the dust and her perfume, saw himself lying in her arms and felt the drooping palm fronds brushing his skin. Suddenly he longed to take hold of her again, to feel the softness of her against him one more time. She was standing in the doorway again, turning up the collar of her jacket.

'Let's go and eat,' he said, in a voice made rough with desire. She heard it at once, and her eyes jumped to the palm. How well we know each other, he thought.

'Yes,' she said softly. 'I think we should.' She took his arm and the door closed behind them with a neat click.

Every table in Les Amoureuses was taken, and the bar and dance floor were packed. Edward and Bell peered through the smoky atmosphere, trying to see some faces in the crowd.

'Table in the corner,' Edward mouthed at her and they

squirmed past the crammed tables. Three people looked up as they arrived, large blonde Mary and little dark Elspeth with half-moon glasses, and Marcus who was Edward's best friend. He had straw-coloured hair and a rubbery, mobile face.

'Oh good, the fun people. Bell, darling, how chic you look. Now, press yourselves in where you can and I'll see if I can conjure up some glasses.'

Edward kissed the two girls and they sat down. It was, thought Bell, going to be an evening exactly like hundreds of others.

Odd that life was such a combination of the frightening and the absolutely, routinely predictable.

'. . . going well in the world of high finance?' asked Mary.

'Oh, just the same as always,' Edward answered, evasively. He worked, very successfully, in a City merchant bank, but considered it something to be hushed up as far as possible.

'Bell's the only one who ever does anything interesting. You should see her diary. Bordeaux tomorrow, next week California.'

'California?' Mary and Elspeth looked at her with such open envy that Bell felt herself blushing.

'All thanks to Marcus,' she said quickly. 'I'm going to stay with a friend of his, researching a series for the paper on West Coast life. Wine, food, people. I suggested it ages ago to Stobbs and he liked the idea, then came up with a budget that would have kept me alive in San Francisco for about twenty-five minutes. So Marcus suggested his rich friend who lives in the Napa Valley. He responded with true Californian hospitality, and I can afford to go after all. I've never been to the West Coast, and I'm longing to see it. It'll be hard work, too,' she finished defensively.

'Work?' Mary was derisive. 'Who is this friend, Marcus? Got any others to spare?'

Marcus finished his mouthful deliberately and then flattened his features to produce a wide, toothy American smile.

'He's always glad to offer a bed to an English chick. Specially one with an ass like yours, Mare.'

Bell said, 'Marcus, you didn't tell me that.'

Marcus winked at her. 'Don't worry, you'll like him. He's larger than life in every respect. Maverick, almost certainly a con-man. You could fill all your articles with him alone.'

'Anyway, Bell,' Mary put in, 'who could be better equipped to deal with someone like that than you? Just give him your ice-maiden act.'

Into the little silence that fell around the table, Edward said, 'Shall we have a dance, Bell? I think there's a spare foot of space on the floor.'

'And pardon me, too,' said Marcus. 'I'm going to the boys' room.'

The two women were left alone at the table. Mary lit one of Marcus's cigarettes and blew the smoke out on a long breath. She was watching Edward and Bell dancing, forced close together by the press of other dancers.

'I think she'll regret it in the end,' she said.

'What?' Elspeth sounded resigned.

'Edward, of course. He's still in love with her, poor sap. And Bell Farrer is going the right way to end up with nobody. One of those lonely, successful women with nothing to talk about but her work. Why does she bother? Edward's going to be very rich one of these days.'

'Mary,' Elspeth protested, 'Bell wouldn't have cared about the money. She's just not like that. Don't you think it's possible that she just couldn't love him as much as he needed? Whereas you could, of course.'

Mary chose to ignore the stab.

'Entirely possible. I don't think Bell is capable of loving anyone except herself. She couldn't possibly be so cool and efficient and successful if she didn't devote all her attention to number one.'

Elspeth laughed. 'I know what you mean, but I think you're being a bit hard on her. Everyone likes her, after all, except perhaps you.'

'Oh, I like her too. I just don't believe in her. She's too good to be true, that's all.'

'You're jealous.'

The other girl stubbed out her cigarette and turned to stare at her friend. 'Of course I'm jealous. That's just the point.

However likeable she may be, if everyone she knows is jealous of her she'll end up alone and unhappy. You have to be vulnerable to get human sympathy, and do you think Bell is vulnerable?' There was no answer, and they both looked across at the knot of dancers. Neither of them had ever seen Bell crying, or ill, or apparently unsure of herself. No one had, for years, except Edward.

And now she didn't have Edward any more.

Bell would have laughed, unbelieving, if she could have heard their conversation. She let herself lean against Edward, feeling the familiar contours of their bodies fitting together. It felt very secure. Temptingly secure.

Yet tomorrow she had to go to France and face up to the intimidating French baron, alone. Not only face up to him, but impress him enough to make him talk about his château as he'd never talked to any other journalist. She didn't want to go, but she couldn't stay where she was either.

Bell knew that she was in a mess. It would have amused her if she could have known that anyone envied her at that moment.

The evening came to an end at last. They all stood outside the door of the club, hugging each other affectionately. The two women and Marcus wished her bon voyage.

'If we don't see you before, send us a postcard from San Francisco,' said Elspeth. 'Have a wonderful time.'

'Give my love to Valentine,' Marcus called. ''Byeeee.'

Edward slammed the door of his battered car and reversed recklessly down the street before glancing at Bell.

'Cheer up,' he advised her. 'You are quite lucky, you know.' She bit her lip. Guilty of self-pity, as well.

He left her at the door of her flat and drove away with a cheerful wave and his habitual three toots on the horn.

Bell let herself in and wandered into her bedroom. Her packing was done, and she wasn't sleepy yet. A nightcap, perhaps. She sloshed a measure of brandy into Edward's empty wine glass that was still standing on the coffee table, then went over to her dressing-table to look at the open diary.

The square for the next day read '10 a.m. Wigmore & Welch. Plane 12.30'. That meant a wine-tasting first at an old-established firm of merchants, always worth a visit, and straight from there to the airport. The next three days were crossed through with neat diagonals and the words 'Ch. Reynard'. The second of those days was to be her twenty-eighth birthday.

The realization made Bell smile ruefully and she sat down to examine her face in the mirror. Not too many lines, yet, and the ones that she could see were all laughter lines. Automatically she picked up her hairbrush and began to stroke rhythmically at her hair. The one hundred nightly strokes was a habit left over from childhood and she clung to it obstinately, as a link with her dead mother.

In one of Bell's last memories of her she was standing at her side with the identical blue-green eyes fixed on her own in the mirror.

'A hundred times, Bell,' she was saying, 'and your hair will shine like silk.'

That was it, of course.

The thing she was really frightened of, and the thing she wouldn't let herself think about. Except at times like now, when she was alone with a brandy glass in her hand and the memories were too vivid to suppress. She had seen it all through the agonizingly clear eyes of childhood. Her mother had died, and she had watched her father disintegrate. Day after day, year after year, defencelessly turning into a wreck of what he had once been.

Bell didn't think she was remembering her very early years with any particular romantic distortion. Her parents had very obviously been deeply in love. They had been quite satisfied with their single child. Bell had the impression that her father didn't want her mother to share out her love any further. He wanted the lion's share of it for himself.

Selfish of him, probably, but he had suffered enough for that.

There had been very good times, early on. Her father was a successful stockbroker in those days, comfortably off. There had been a pretty house in Sussex, French holidays, birthday parties for Bell and the company of her witty, beautiful mother.

Joy Farrer had probably never been very strong. Bell remembered the thinness of her arms when they hugged her, and the bony ridges of her chest when she laid her head against it. Sometimes she had been mysteriously ill, but Bell remembered those days only as brief shadows.

Then, with brutal suddenness, she was gone.

One night when Bell went to bed she was there, reminding her not to skimp on the one hundred strokes with the hairbrush. In the morning she had disappeared. The house was full of whispers and strange, serious faces. Her father's study door was locked.

It was several days before they told her she was dead, but she had really known it from the moment when she woke up on the first morning. The house had smelled dead. Something in it had shrivelled up and vanished overnight. A housekeeper arrived, but Bell did her crying alone. The sense of loss suffocated her, and at night she would try to stifle herself with her pillow to shut out the misery. She was convinced, in her logical, childish mind, that her mother's death was her own, Bell's fault.

She had rarely seen her father in those first months. She learned from an aunt, years later, that he had taken to going out all night and driving his car round the Sussex lanes. Round and round, going nowhere. With a bottle of whisky on the seat beside him. By the time he was convicted of drunken driving Bell was away at boarding school and knew nothing about it. He simply stopped coming to pick her up from school at half-terms and holidays, and she travelled on the little local train instead. All she did know was that he was getting thinner, and an unfamiliar smell emanated from the well-cut grey suits that were now too large, creased, and slightly stained.

Her once-handsome, assured father was turning into a grey-haired stranger who behaved peculiarly.

It was in the middle of the summer holidays when she was fourteen that Bell realized that her father was an alcoholic. She found the plastic sack of empty whisky bottles in the garage when she was looking for the turpentine. She had been trying to brighten up the dingy kitchen with a coat of white paint.

That was the day Bell grew up.

She understood, in a single flash, how badly he had crumbled after the death of his wife. At the same moment she accepted another weight on to her burden of guilt. If only she could have compensated him in some way. If only she had been older, or more interesting to him. If only her mother and father hadn't loved each other quite so much, and she herself had been more lovable. If only.

Her father had died when she was seventeen. Cirrhosis of the liver, of course. Bell looked down at her empty glass. It was ironic that she should be making her living now by writing about drink. She toyed with the idea of pouring herself another brandy, but it was easy to decide not to do it. No. Whatever else might happen to her, she didn't think that was going to be her particular problem. It was enough to have watched it happen to her father.

'Well now.' Bell looked at her white face in the mirror. 'While you *are* thinking about this, why not try to be totally honest?

'Is it that you are scared of Edward being hurt like that one day if you disappear? You're trying to protect him, in your heavy-handed way?

'Well, yes . . .

'Or are you really much more frightened of it happening to you? No commitment, therefore no risk?

'Yes.'

Bell folded her arms on the dressing-table in front of her, laid her head on them and cried.

If someone else had told her her own story she would have dismissed it as too neat and pat. Incapable of loving, of marrying, because of her parents' tragedy? Cool and collected outside in self-protection, but a guilty mess inside? Surely human beings were more complex than that?

'This one isn't,' said Bell, through the sobs.

At last the storm subsided. She snatched up a handful of tissues from the box in front of her and blew her nose. A red-eyed spectre confronted her in the mirror.

'What you really need,' she addressed herself again, 'is to look a complete fright tomorrow. That will give just the important, extra edge of confidence. Come on, Bell. What's past is past, and the only thing that you can do now is carry on. At least you seem to understand yourself quite well.'

She put her tongue out at herself and caught the answering grin. That's better.

She leant over and stuffed her passport and tickets into one of the pockets of her squashy leather handbag. Then she zipped and buckled the canvas holdall and stood the two bags side by side next to the door.

Notebooks, traveller's cheques, file, tape recorder . . . she counted off in her head. All there.

She was ready to go, whatever might lie ahead.

CHAPTER TWO

'Hello, gorgeous.' The voice had an unmistakable Aussie twang. 'All dressed up and somewhere to go? Not with me, as per usual.'

Without looking round, Bell knew that it was Max Morgan, wine correspondent of one of the local radio stations. She always felt that he only refrained from pinching her bottom because she was big enough to pinch him back. Still, she turned and smiled at him. His aggressiveness was redeemed by his raffish cowboy good looks, and she liked him well enough to ignore the challenge he invariably dangled at her. It was just a little harder to take than usual at five to ten on a Monday morning.

'Hello, Max. Thank you for noticing the extra polish on my turnout this morning. As a matter of fact I am winging my way direct from here to Château Reynard itself.'

Max rolled his eyes and pursed his lips in a silent whistle of mock amazement.

'Comment? Ze baron opens sa coeur to ze jolie Eenglish scribblaire?' The parody French accent overlying the rich Australian vowels made Bell dissolve into laughter.

'Something like that. It should be interesting.'

'Too right. See if you can sweet talk him into getting out a bottle of the '61. Haven't tasted it myself, but I hear . . .' He bunched his fingertips and kissed them extravagantly.

'Mmmm. Shall we get on?'

They were standing at one end of a long, narrow room in the rear of Wigmore & Welch's St James's Street shop. The summer light was bright, and reflected off the white cloths spread over two long trestle tables down either side of the room. Along the length of the table, open bottles and rows of glasses were lined up. Down the centre of the room stood four waist-high metal cylinders, spittoons. Wigmore & Welch, wine merchants, were holding a press tasting for the publication of their latest list. Bell picked up a tasting sheet. Each wine was listed with blank spaces next to it for her comments.

'Forty-seven wines,' she remarked to Max. 'Too many for me this morning. I'm just going to look at the clarets.'

'Attagirl,' he responded with his Wild West smile. 'See what they've got that beats de Gillesmont.'

She walked the length of the room to where the line of high-shouldered bottles glowed against the white cloth. Wigmore & Welch prided themselves on their clarets, and today they were offering for comment a dozen fine wines from the sixties and seventies. Several of them would still be too young for drinking, but Bell was eager to see how they were developing, quietly sitting in their bottles. Her eyes flicked along the row of labels, then she picked up a bottle and poured an inch of wine into a glass. Quickly she held the glass up against the white cloth background to see the colour, then bent her head over the rim of the glass and sniffed sharply. Only then did she take a mouthful of wine, rolling it gently on her tongue and staring absently into the middle distance as she did so. Finally she twisted round and spat the mouthful into one of the tall metal spittoons.

Frowning with concentration now she scribbled on her tasting sheet 'good colour. Still closed in on the nose, but developing. Plenty of fruit and some oak.' It was a special vocabulary, almost shorthand, but when Bell came back to her notes in a year, or two years, or whenever she tasted that particular wine again, it would be enough to trigger her memory.

Slowly she moved along the line of twelve bottles, tasting and spitting out a mouthful of each, writing quickly on her tasting sheet, talking to no one. Then she went back and tasted from three of the bottles again.

At last she pushed her hair back from her face and folded up her notes. The fine concentration needed was tiring, even after only twelve wines, and all round her people were working their way through forty-odd.

Across the room Max caught her eye and winked. Bell blew him a kiss, spoke briefly and in a low voice to two or three of the other tasters and turned to go. She would have to move quickly to get to Heathrow in time for her plane. At the door she met Simon Wigmore, scion of the family and latest recruit to the company of pinstriped well-bred young men who staffed the shop and the offices. His pink face brightened when he saw her.

'Bell! Not going already?'

'Yes, Simon, I'm sorry. I've got a plane to catch so I only had time to look at the clarets. The La Lagune is spectacular, isn't it? Thank you for the tasting – I must dash.'

Simon Wigmore turned round to watch the tall, slim figure taking the steps two at a time. He sighed. Somehow he never seemed to be able to pin Bell Farrer down for long enough to . . . well, long enough for anything.

Out on the pavement Bell spotted the yellow light of a taxi and waved energetically.

'Heathrow, please,' she said and slammed the door behind her.

'Right you are, duck,' responded the driver, pleased. Bell stared out at the West End traffic and sighed with relief. At least she was on her way.

Three hours later Bell was ensconced in her window seat aboard the Air France 707, staring out at the curve of the French Atlantic coast as the plane dipped to meet it. At the same moment Baron Charles de Gillesmont sat facing his mother down the length of highly-polished walnut dining table. He was peeling a peach, using a tiny mother-of-pearl handled knife to make a little unbroken whorl of golden skin. Hélène de Gillesmont's mouth tightened with irritation as she watched him.

'Charles,' she said sharply, unable to bear the tense silence any longer, 'you do not even do me the courtesy of listening to what I have to say.' The baron looked up, laying down the peach and his knife as he did so with a gesture of infinite weariness.

'I am so sorry that I can't make you understand. I can't bear to see you go on hurting yourself, and us, like this. God knows we have talked about it enough. There is no possibility,

I tell you, none whatsoever, that Catherine and I can be together again. Too much has happened for us to be able to go back and take up the same old reins. And, as you know perfectly well, she is happy in Paris. And I . . . I am busy with what I have to do here. I don't wish to change things, Hélène.'

The baronne clicked her tongue sharply. 'I can understand that you are still grieved, shocked even, but defeated? My son? If only you would bring Catherine back here, make her stop all this Paris nonsense. You are her husband, after all. Then give her another child, and . . .'

Charles pushed back his chair with a savage jolt, knocking the table so hard that his glass fell over. A few drops of pale gold wine ran out on to the polished wood.

'Why can't you be quiet?' His voice was barely more than a whisper and his face was dead white. Hélène faltered for a moment and put up a hand to adjust the smooth coil of grey-blonde hair. Her eyes avoided her son's face until he spoke again, in a normal voice now.

'Will you excuse me? I have to go and check whether Jacopin has left for the airport.'

'And why,' his mother called at his departing back, 'must we have some foreign girl that none of us know in the house now, of all times?'

In the doorway Charles looked back, a tired smile lifting the corners of his mouth.

'Mama, this time is no different from any other. This is what our life is like, now. Nothing is going to change so you had better accustom yourself to it. You still have me, and Juliette, after all.'

This time the click of Hélène's tongue was even sharper.

'And a fine pair you are. My beautiful children, the envy of everyone, and what have you grown up into? One stubborn, cold, living like a monk, and the other no better than a *hippy*.'

But Charles was gone. He walked briskly down a flagged corridor to a heavy oak door. Inside, the little room was a comfortable clutter of papers, dusty bottles with torn labels, maps and rows of books. In the middle of the room, on a square of threadbare carpet, was an elegant little desk that might have been Louis XVI with an ancient black telephone perched on the top. Charles dialled a number and spoke at once.

'Pierre? Has Jacopin taken the car to meet the young lady?' Evidently satisfied with the reply he replaced the receiver and briskly took up a pen and a sheaf of account sheets. For a moment or two he stared intently at his work, then shrugged and leaned back in his swivel chair. From his window, at the extreme corner of the front façade of the château, he could see a sweep of manicured lawn and the curve of the gravel drive. Uncomfortable memories tugged at his consciousness as he stared unseeingly out, but he refused to admit them. Not worth starting work now, he told himself. Miss Farrer will be here within the hour, and the rest of the afternoon must be devoted to her.

He picked up a copy of *La Revue de France Vinicole*, tilted his chair so that he had a clear view of the driveway, and settled down to read.

Bell passed the trio of smiling hostesses at the aircraft door and stood at the top of the steel steps. Somewhere out there, underlying the airport smells of oil and rubber, she could detect the real smell of the country. It was earthy and sensuous, but clean and natural too, made up of damp leaves and rich food and woodsmoke. Even here in the airport chaos there was a feeling of calm, fertile prosperity. It was good to be back.

'*S'il vous plaît, madame*,' murmured a portly French businessman behind her, nudging her slightly with his briefcase. Bell started and hurried down the steps. She was waved through customs and her canvas bag rolled out on to the carousel within minutes. An excellent omen for the visit, she told herself, as she made for the barrier. As soon as she was through into the crowd of waiting faces, a hand touched her arm.

'Mees Farraire?' She turned to see, at shoulder height, the wrinkled, nut-brown Bordelais face of a little man in blue overalls and a round blue hat. She smiled down at him, feeling like a giantess.

'That's me.'

'Not too flattering a photograph, if I may say so, but good enough for this purpose.' His French was heavily-accented to Bell's Paris-educated ear, and she looked down half-bewildered at the magazine he was brandishing. It was a piece she had contributed to *Decanter*, decorated with a large snapshot of herself smiling rather toothily into the camera. It amused her to see it in such incongruous surroundings.

'Where on earth did you get that?'

'Oh, monsieur thinks of everything. You'll see. This way to the car, madame. My name is Jacopin, by the way. Welcome to Bordeaux.'

Baron Charles's car was a capacious brand-new grey Mercedes, veiled with a thick layer of whitish dust. Jacopin tossed her case into the boot and she sank into the passenger seat with a sigh of pleasure. The car swept along with the tiny man craning disconcertingly to see over the top of the long bonnet. Bell glimpsed the ugly, modern outskirts of the old grey town and then they were purring north-westwards into the fabulous country of the Haut-Médoc.

Under her breath, like a litany, Bell found that she was repeating the sonorous château names as they passed. From here, from vines growing in this flat, undistinguished countryside, came the most famous, elegant wines in the world. To the right and left of the road stretched the green sea of vines, all carrying their precious bunches of grapes peacefully ripening in the August sun. Occasionally she glimpsed the bulk of a château behind its wrought-iron gates, or screened by a protective belt of trees. Sometimes the flat gleam of the River Gironde appeared to their right, reflecting the hard blue of the summer sky. It was a peaceful, unspectacular, almost deserted landscape at this time of year, turning inwards to soak up the sun before the feverish bustle of the vintage when the grapes would be picked.

Jacopin shot a glance at Bell.

'You know our country well?' he asked, conversationally. Bell wrenched her attention from the clustering châteaux around the town of Margaux to answer him.

'Not well. I've been a visitor three or four times, but always in a party of other journalists. This is my first visit to Château

Reynard, and my first chance to spend a little time looking closely at the workings of a single château. I'm looking forward to it enormously,' she added, truthfully. Jacopin nodded sagely.

'Of course,' he murmured, as if he could imagine no better place for her to be.

They drove on. Past the villages of St Julien ('Ducru-Beaucaillou, Léoville-Barton, Léoville-Poyferré . . .' murmured Bell), the landscape began to swell a little, rising to rolling mounds that were the closest that this open countryside came to hills. At last they were driving through the *commune* of Pauillac towards the little hill where Château Reynard dominated the surrounding acres of vines. Bell, still counting off the names, knew that they were almost there. She craned forward to catch her first glimpse of the buildings, and was rewarded by a flash of sun reflected from the rows of windows. The wrought-iron gates were open and the car shot straight through into the driveway, slowed between the expanse of lawn, and drew up at the château steps.

Bell opened her door, slowly, and tilted her head to look up at Château Reynard. It was classic late-eighteenth-century perfection, from the steeply-pitched slate roof pierced with the discreet row of dormer windows, down through the two rows of tall windows framed in their wooden shutters, to the double flight of stone-balustraded steps running up to the heavy double front doors. Two wings at either side, each with its own narrow-pitched roof, framed the symmetry of the main façade. Bell had seen it in pictures many times, but she was unprepared for its exact simplicity, and its air of authority.

As she stood with Jacopin waiting patiently at her side, her bag in his hand, one half of the massive double doors swung open.

Bell saw a tall man, dressed in a formal, dark suit. For a second or two he stood staring expressionlessly down at her from the height of the terrace. Then he walked slowly down the right-hand flight of steps and came towards her. Bell's heart sank.

The baron looked even more formidable than she had expected. He was younger than she had imagined, only in his mid to late thirties. He had an aristocratic face with a high-bridged nose, the face of a man who was used to deference. His sun-bleached fair hair was brushed smooth to his head and his eyes were slightly hooded.

The complete autocrat, thought Bell.

There was only the ghost of a smile around his mouth, and none at all in his eyes. He held out his hand and she shook it firmly, putting all the warmth she could muster into her smile.

She wouldn't be here, after all, if he hadn't invited her.

'Welcome to Château Reynard, Miss Farrer,' he said. 'I am Charles de Gillesmont.' *Yes. I don't think I would have mistaken you for the butler.*

'Will you come this way? Jacopin, I will take the luggage in for Miss Farrer. I am sure that you have other things to do. Jacopin is our *maître de chais*,' he told Bell. She looked back at the little man with new respect. As cellar-master, his responsibility for what appeared in the bottles labelled Château Reynard would be almost as great as the baron's. Jacopin winked at her and settled himself back into the big car. Regretfully Bell watched the car disappear round the corner of the house in a spurt of gravel.

Then, feeling just as if she was tiptoeing into the lion's den, she followed Charles de Gillesmont into his château.

When they stood side by side in the stone-flagged hallway, Bell saw that he was much taller than her. His eyes were very dark blue with darker rims to the irises, almost navy in the dim light.

Before he spoke again she noticed that his mouth was full, the top lip deeply curved.

'Marianne will take you up to your room,' he said. A thin dark girl in a maid's uniform came out of the shadows towards them. 'I am sure you will need an hour's peace and quiet after your journey. Do come down when you are ready.' He nodded, formally, and strode away.

Bell obediently followed Marianne. A huge stone staircase edged with intricately wrought iron curved upwards, and as Bell's eyes followed it she caught the gleam of a gilt and crystal chandelier hanging over the stairwell.

'This way, madame,' the girl prompted and turned to the

right at the top of the stairs. The wide corridor was lit at either end by tall, narrow windows. Heavy oak chests stood at intervals with high-backed chairs in dark, carved wood between them. It was very sombre and completely silent except for the sound of their footsteps on the thin matting.

'Here we are,' said Marianne, opening a door at the end of the corridor. The big room was in one of the narrow wings at the side of the house and it had windows in three walls. It was very sunny, clean and bare. Marianne pushed open another door and gestured inside.

'Your bathroom, madame. Is there anything else you need?'

'No, this is perfect, thank you.'

As soon as she was alone, Bell crossed to the end of the room and stood looking out of the middle window. From the first floor, and with the height of the little hill beneath her, the view was commanding. She could see the river, with the town of Pauillac and the huge oil refinery on the near bank. In the distance the scene was built up, almost industrial, but in the foreground were rolling masses of vineyards, bisected by tracks and the white, dusty road.

The right-hand window looked across the golden stone face of the château to the identical opposite wing. A slight woman in a navy blue pleated dress with a bow at the neck strolled across the lawn from the front steps. A fat dachshund waddled at her heels.

'Now that,' thought Bell, 'must be the baroness dowager. I wonder where the young baroness is?' Still musing, she turned to the left-hand window and immediately forgot the mysteries of Charles's family. Below her were the working buildings of the château, the long, low *chais* with tiled roofs and lime-washed walls grouped around a cobbled yard. Blue-overalled men were crossing the yard and Bell could see Jacopin standing in the open doorway of a barn, deep in conversation with a fat woman in a white apron. The sight reminded her that she was there to explore a living vineyard and make a story out of it, and she felt an immediate surge of energy.

Abandoning the view she made a quick survey of the room. It was almost bare except for a high brass bed with a well-laundered plain white cotton coverlet and the traditional long, hard French bolster. There was a pretty chest of drawers, a tall mirror in a gilt frame, the glass flecked with dim spots, a pair of spoon-backed armchairs upholstered in pale blue moiré silk, and a tiny pale blue rug with a faded pattern of rosebuds beside the bed. The rest of the floor was bare, highly polished, dark boards.

'The baron is evidently not investing his profits in domestic comforts,' Bell murmured to herself, but a glance into the bathroom surprised her again. It was the last word in luxury, with a deep bath and a separate shower, a thick carpet and a cane armchair piled with fluffy white towels. A long white robe hung from a hook and a case of heated rollers stood on a glass shelf next to an enticing row of crystal jars. The gentle smell of expensive French soap filled the room.

The contrast between the stark bedroom and the sybaritic bathroom pleased and intrigued Bell, and she found herself wondering if Charles was responsible for it.

Oh God, Baron Charles. She must think about getting down to work, however much the chilly Frenchman disconcerted her. She went into the bathroom and splashed her face with cold water, combed her hair and then went to unpack her tape recorder.

Here goes.

Charles was sitting in an armchair in the dim hall, reading. He stood up as she wound down the grand staircase and watched her impassively. There was still no smile, but Bell thought that the lines of his face looked less taut.

'If it suits you, Miss Farrer, I thought we might have a talk now about the château and the way we run it. Then perhaps you would like to spend tomorrow seeing it all from the practical point of view.' Bell nodded, and as she moved her head she thought she saw Charles looking coolly at the curve of her cheek. Then their eyes met, and there was a second's silence.

'That sounds fine,' she said quietly. 'And won't you call me Bell?' They were speaking French, as they had done ever since she arrived, and the crisp English monosyllable sounded suddenly incongruous.

'Bell?' The blue eyes met hers again, and she suddenly heard her own voice and knew that she was talking too quickly.

'I was christened Annabel but somehow it doesn't suit . . .'

'No,' he said. She noticed with astonishment that his eyes were crinkled with amusement. He went on in English. 'Bell it shall be. I am just plain Charles.' The way he pronounced it, with the soft ch and the rolling r, it sounded anything but plain to Bell. She laughed back at him and held out her hand. He shook it gravely, then seemed to remember something and withdrew his hand.

'Won't you come this way? In my study we won't be disturbed.' He led the way to the little, untidy room and closed the oak door firmly behind them.

It wasn't exactly an easy interview.

Charles de Gillesmont answered her questions about grape varieties, hectares and mechanization punctiliously. He could quote the recent figures fluently and he was careful to explain to her the particular problems and advantages he faced at Reynard.

It was all information that she could have found herself in the reference books. Most of it was in her notes already.

He definitely did not want to talk about the glamorous aspect of being a French baron and owning one of the most famous wines in the world.

Bell had a sudden mental picture of Henry Stobbs swivelling round in his editorial armchair to give her one of his famous beady stares. He would tap her neatly-typed copy and say, 'Dull. Bloody dull. We didn't send you out there to get five pages of figures, sweetheart. Where's the story? Where's the juice?' Henry believed that his readers were 'people people'.

Bell gritted her teeth. Somehow she would have to break through this man's polished reserve and winkle out what Henry called the human interest angle. She leaned forward slightly to adjust the position of the mike on the table between them, and gave the baron a disarming smile.

'There have been de Gillesmonts at Château Reynard for centuries, I know . . .'

'Four hundred years.'

'Thank you, yes. What about the continuing tradition? Do you and your wife want your children to carry on as you are doing?'

She was certain that he was married, she had checked on that, but the blue eyes snapped at her, icy cold and offended.

'Forgive me, I thought you were a wine writer? That is what your editor told me when he wrote to ask if you could come here.'

'My editor wrote?' Light was dawning. She hadn't been given her exclusive invitation to Reynard because Charles had seen and admired her work. Silly of her to imagine that she had. It was just one of Henry's schemes.

'Of course. I would normally have refused but he happened to enclose some of your cuttings. I was impressed by your unusually sensible approach to the subject.' Well, that was something. 'Which is why I am surprised to hear you asking questions like a gossip columnist. How many of your readers could possibly be interested in my wife? And children?'

Bell went scarlet. She was stung by his tone into a quick retort.

'Of course I'm a wine writer. I'm a good one because I know what people want to read. In this case, that means you, not just the wine. I have to do my job as well as I can, otherwise I'll find myself without it. And what you've given me there,' she pointed at the cassette in the recorder, 'doesn't exactly sizzle.' She looked up at him, ready to go on defending herself, but she was amazed to see that he was laughing.

It transformed his face, rubbing out the severe lines and making him look almost boyish.

He's got a very sensuous mouth, Bell thought irrelevantly, feeling a tiny constriction in her throat.

'Must it sizzle?' Charles was asking her.

'Yes,' she said, defiantly.

He bent forward to the low table and pressed the 'off' button on the machine.

'You care about it, this job, don't you?' He was looking at her differently. As if she was a person and not a prying journalist.

'Yes,' she answered, and then, to her surprise, 'it's all I've got to care about, now.'

Why on earth had she said that, to a frosty, upper-class stranger? Something about him had caught her unawares. His stare was serious now, with a distinct edge of sympathy. He glanced at the recorder as if to make sure that it was really switched off, then said softly, 'We have that in common, then.'

He stood up and rummaged in a cupboard, then produced a pair of champagne flutes. As he put them on the table he added, 'My wife and I are separated.' It would have sounded like a casual afterthought if Bell hadn't seen the pain and bitterness in his face. The disdainful self-assurance had gone. For that brief instant, he was just an unhappy man. 'Excuse me.' He walked out of the room, but Bell barely had time to gather her thoughts after the bewildering change in his manner before he was back, carrying a bottle. It was Krug, connoisseur's champagne, 1964.

He opened the bottle deftly and let the wine foam into the thin glasses. He handed one to Bell and then raised his own.

'To you, Bell. And to the success of your assignment.'

They drank, and for the moment Bell forgot everything but the reviving fizz of the wonderful wine in her mouth. When she looked back at him Charles was watching her with clear approval in his face.

'Thank you,' she said, meaning for his good wishes as well as the champagne. He made a tiny, mock-formal bow and leant back against the mantelpiece. The room was very quiet, and warm with the early evening sunlight.

'Yes,' Charles said almost to himself. 'My wife and I are separated. Divorce is not a possibility, so . . .'

Bell frowned and then remembered. Of course, the aristocratic de Gillesmonts would be devout Catholics.

'. . . you see, I can't predict for you or for your readers what will happen here in the future. That will depend on who takes over after I am gone. Whoever it is, it will not now be a child of mine.' Charles had gone very pale, and his voice was so low that Bell had to strain to catch the words. She didn't know what to say, and after a moment he collected himself and went on.

'All I can tell you is that so long as I am breathing, it will stay exactly as it always has been. In that, at least, there is some permanence. Not very fashionable, I know, when everyone else is rushing headlong to get rid of the old ways. You are welcome to write that about me, if you think anyone would be interested. More champagne?' A little of the suave gloss was beginning to creep back. Bell held out her glass as she answered.

'I'm sorry, I had no intention of prying. Put it down to vulgar journalistic curiosity.'

He was watching her speculatively. 'I don't think, somehow, that vulgarity is one of your faults. I was watching your face when we had our disagreement a moment ago. It upset you. That sort of sensitivity can't be a very helpful trait, for a journalist.'

'This is all wrong.' Bell tried to laugh, casually. 'I'm supposed to be interviewing you.'

'Well, perhaps it would be more amusing to turn the tables. I could try my hand at a profile of you, and risk a few personal questions. Let me see . . . perhaps you are suffering from a newly broken heart?'

Bell looked into his dark blue eyes with a jolt of surprise. This was ridiculous.

She felt uncomfortable under his stare, but at the same time there was something about him that made her want to go on talking to him. It was as if he was familiar in some way that she couldn't quite identify.

'No,' she said at last. 'Not a broken heart, exactly. More a sad, wasteful mess that I'm ashamed of. He – somebody else – got more hurt than me. I wish it had been the other way round.'

'Yes,' he said drily. 'One always does. So, what now?'

'Oh, becoming the greatest wine writer in the world.'

'Of course. Impossible for me to stand in the way of that. We shall have to cook up something between us that will satisfy your editor.'

Charles glanced down at his watch and frowned.

'Nothing would give me greater pleasure than to sit here with you like this all evening.'

That was conventional French *politesse*, but Bell caught herself hoping that there was a whisper of truth in it.

'But I think I should take you to meet my mother. She will be waiting for us. She always sits in the salon before dinner.'

Charles drained his champagne glass and picked up the half-empty bottle. Bell stood up too, and then glanced down at her bare, suntanned legs.

'Perhaps I should change?'

'Oh, I don't think so. There will be just the three of us. My sister Juliette is away until tomorrow.'

He was holding the door open, looking a little impatient. Bell followed him obediently.

Across the hallway a pair of panelled doors opened into a long, graceful drawing-room.

It struck Bell as exquisitely French and at the same time very feminine. The spindly chairs and chaises longues were gilt and upholstered in faded, rose-coloured silks. Panelled walls were painted the palest duck-egg blue and hung with gilt-framed landscapes and clusters of miniatures.

Charles's mother was sitting to one side of a creamy marble fireplace, leaning over an embroidery frame. As they came in her eyes went straight to the champagne bottle in Charles's hand.

'Charles,' she said in a high, clear patrician voice, 'couldn't you have found a tray and a napkin?' Bell thought that he stiffened as he set the bottle carefully down on an inlaid table.

'Mama,' he said, 'this is Bell Farrer. Bell, my mother – Hélène de Gillesmont.' Mother and son were very alike, except that the baroness's face was more deeply etched with lines of pride and hauteur.

Her cold eyes travelled over Bell's plain blue linen shirt and very slightly creased skirt, and the pale eyebrows arched upwards a fraction. Bell's hostess was wearing a pale grey silk dinner dress with couture written all over it and a triple rope of pearls.

She held out a reluctant hand. There was a huge emerald in the ring on her third finger.

'How do you do, Miss er . . . Won't you sit down, and my son will pour you another drink?' She spoke English, perfectly, sounding like the Queen.

Bell perched on the nearest fragile little chair and sighed inwardly. Black mark to the grubby English journalist. She guessed that she was going to have to work very hard indeed to keep her end up this evening. Perhaps it would help if she showed off her own almost equally perfect French.

'What a beautiful room this is. It feels so restful.'

Back came the reply, still in English.

'Yes. My daughter-in-law and I planned it together.' It was a deliberate snub, and Bell felt a flash of irritation. She looked at Charles but his face was turned away from both of them as he stared out of the window.

It was going to be a difficult evening.

It felt to Bell like about five hours later when they filed back into Hélène's salon for coffee.

The meal had inched past punctuated with long frozen silences. The food had been simple and perfect – spinach soufflé, chicken, fresh fruit – but Bell had eaten her way cheerlessly through it without tasting a mouthful. All she remembered was the fine Château Carbonnieux in her glass The only time Charles had looked directly at her was when she tasted it, and she had signalled her approval with an infinitesimal nod. Hélène, she was sure, would have condemned it as appallingly vulgar to discuss either the wine or the food. Now they were sitting in the salon again, drinking strong black coffee from tiny gold cups.

Bell wondered a little desperately how soon she could plead tiredness after her flight and escape to bed.

'Your room is quite comfortable, Miss er?'

'Bell Farrer,' said Bell, deliberately stressing the syllables. 'Yes, thank you, quite comfortable. Is that beautiful bathroom new?'

'Catherine, my daughter-in-law, designed it.' Hélène was looking sideways, towards her work-table, and Bell followed her gaze. There was a photograph in a silver art nouveau frame, carefully angled to catch the light from a rose-shaded lamp. Under a smooth cap of dark hair the girl's face was pale and grave. She was looking down, so that her eyes were hidden by a sweep of dark lashes, but there was a determined point to her chin. Clasped around her long, fragile neck was what looked like a collar of diamonds.

Catherine. Charles's wife, thought Bell, fascinated. She looked delicate but very beautiful. Bell glanced quickly across at Charles. All evening he had sat unsmilingly at the table between his mother and his guest. He had led the stilted conversation with polished politeness, but he had gone back to being the formal stranger she had met on the steps outside.

The strange moment of intimacy might never have happened.

Now Bell thought that an atmosphere of uneasy tension was creeping into the frigidity of the evening. Charles was sitting tautly in a small armchair, squeezing his little gold cup as if he wanted to crush it into fragments.

Hélène had picked up her petit point and she was stitching with studied calmness. She was still talking in her high, grand voice.

'We plan to put in new bathrooms throughout the house. It's surprising how Catherine's ideas have always coincided with mine.' She gave a tiny resigned sigh. 'Unlike Juliette and me. My own daughter is a mystery to me nowadays.' Bell was still watching Charles, noticing how the tiny blond hairs on his cheekbone glinted in the pinkish light when he clenched his jaw muscles. Moving very slowly, as if he found it an effort to control his movements, he leant forward and put his cup back on the tray.

Bell sensed that something in him was vibrating, ready to snap.

'As soon as Catherine returns from Paris.' Hélène's voice rippled on and Bell listened in puzzlement.

Charles had said that they were separated. Weren't they, after all?

'She has been ill. She needed a long rest, and a complete change, but now she is well enough she will be coming home. Then we . . .'

With a sudden movement, as lithe as a cat, Charles was on

his feet. In a split second his dark figure was towering over his mother. Bell saw that his fists were clenched.

'Mama,' he hissed, 'you will stop this pantomime. Now.' Hélène shrank backwards for an instant and then the lines of her face hardened in defiance.

'It is your pantomime,' she breathed back at him. 'You are a fool, and not only a fool but a destroyer. Of my life, as well as your own.'

Bell longed for the floor to open up and swallow her. They were oblivious of her presence now, but later they would remember that she had been there and they would find it difficult to forgive her for that.

Charles's face was grey and he seemed to be struggling to breathe.

'Your life. I don't care about the pretence and sham that life means to you. You know nothing about human emotion. Love or hate, so long as appearances are preserved.'

Hélène snatched up her embroidery frame and held it against her as if to shield herself.

'You talk to me of love and hate? You are hardly better than a murderer, and you . . .'

Bell sank in her chair as she saw the expression in Charles's eyes. His fist swung up, and then dropped again, leaden, at his side. Hélène's voice faltered as she saw him.

'You know I didn't mean . . . I just meant that you would have let Catherine die of grief and done nothing . . . it was left to . . .'

'Will you be quiet?' Charles spat out the words as if they were poison.

Hélène stood up. Her head barely reached his shoulder and she had to tilt her face to look up into his. She looked years older, and racked with bitterness.

'Why must you humiliate us, in front of . . . this girl?' Her hand waved towards Bell. 'A stranger. I am ashamed of you. Ashamed.'

She turned away and crossed the room without a backward glance, walking slowly as if her body ached. The door shut fast behind her.

Bell swallowed, dry-mouthed, to ease the tension in her

throat. She stared down at the pattern in the rug, wishing she was anywhere else in the world. The scene had been so unexpected and so shocking. So pregnant with things that she didn't understand. Didn't want to understand. Whatever it was that had happened at Château Reynard, it had shattered the lives of both Hélène and Charles.

Then a tiny movement made her look up at Charles. She saw horror and bewilderment in his face, as if he was staring into a black pit that had opened at his feet.

Bell recognized that expression. And she knew in the same instant why Charles had struck that odd chord of familiarity deep inside her.

Her father. That aloof assurance belied by the loss, the pain showing in his face.

Oh, God.

Without giving herself time to think she went to Charles and put her hands on his arms. This time at least she was old enough to understand, even if she was powerless to help. For a moment the man looked down into her eyes, bewildered. Then, with a low groan, his arms went around her and his head dropped on her shoulder.

Bell had no idea how long they stood there. She felt as if all the blood had drained out of her head and body and she struggled to stay upright, supporting what felt like the entire weight of Charles de Gillesmont.

At last he looked up, shivered a little and let her go.

When he spoke, his voice was thick.

'I am ashamed too. Bell, I'm sorry that you should have had to sit through that.' He made a visible effort to pull himself together and Bell saw the ghost of the elegant baron reappearing in front of her.

'As you see, this isn't always the happiest of households. It's one of the reasons why we don't entertain many of your profession. I'm glad it was you here, tonight.' He was trying to make his voice light, but he meant what he was saying.

Bell nodded. It had been shocking, but somewhere inside her head she was glad that she had been with him too.

'I think we need a drink,' he said. 'Let's get out of this room.'

In the comfortable clutter of his study he said, quickly as if he wanted to get it over with, 'You must be wondering what that was about. My mother is not an easy woman, but she has had too many disappointments. She was close to Catherine and she misses her badly.' He rubbed his hand over his eyes. 'It was unforgivable of me to have given way like that. Sometimes I . . .'

Bell shook her head. 'No. Please, there's no need.'

She recoiled from the idea of hearing their secrets. She could guess enough, and she had no desire to reawaken the pain she had seen in Charles's face. It was too close to home.

Charles looked relieved. He sat down in a leather armchair and Bell found herself cross-legged on the floor, leaning against the arm. She had often sat like that with Edward, and she remembered with a sad little smile. He seemed very far away now.

Charles murmured, 'Talk to me about something else, then. Anything so long as it has nothing to do with Château Reynard. Tell me about Bell Farrer.'

Haltingly at first, then more fluently under the pressure of his gentle questioning, she did. She felt that there was no need for self-protection after what she had witnessed tonight. It should have felt incongruous, sitting there telling her private thoughts to Charles de Gillesmont who she had known a bare few hours.

Yet it didn't.

Charles sat motionless in his armchair as she talked. His eyes were fixed on her profile, and on the shadow in the hollow of her cheek.

It was very late when Bell stretched and turned to smile at him.

'That's all. I know where I am, now. At least, I think I do.'

'You think you do,' he agreed, smiling back at her.

They stood up and with his hand on her arm he guided her across the dark hallway to the curving stone stairway.

'Goodnight,' said Bell. She wanted to tell him that it was all right, that she would forget what she had heard tonight, but she couldn't find the words. 'Thank you for asking me to Château Reynard,' she said, simply.

The baron made a quick movement in the dimness and for an electric moment Bell thought he was going to kiss her.

No, she thought. Not yet. Then he took her hand. The blond head bent over it and he kissed her knuckles. When he looked up again their eyes met and laughter bubbled between them.

'If one is going to be a French baron,' he murmured, 'one might as well behave like one. You would have been disappointed if I hadn't kissed your hand.'

'Bitterly disappointed,' said Bell.

He let go of her fingers and she turned to climb the shallow stairs. When she reached the top and looked down he was still standing there, watching her.

Bell woke up to a morning that was all brilliant light and dancing shadows. From her three commanding windows she could see that the blue sky was dotted with fast-moving puffs of cloud and a strong breeze was rustling the leaves of the elm trees that fringed the château lawns. The vague feeling of apprehensiveness that had weighed on her when she opened her eyes was dispelled by the beauty of the day. It was impossible to feel anything but lighthearted.

Bell hummed softly as she showered and dressed. Jeans and a T-shirt were the best clothes for touring cellars and vineyards, and she topped them off with a brilliant blue ciré jacket that made her eyes look more blue than green.

Marianne tapped on her door.

'Monsieur le baron asks if you will join him for breakfast?'

'Right away,' said Bell, and ran lightly down the stairs to find him.

In the early sunshine reflecting off the length of the polished table and without Hélène's chilly presence, the dining-room seemed smaller and more inviting.

Charles was standing between the long windows, a dark figure between the shafts of light, waiting for her.

'Good morning. You slept well, I hope?' Calm, polite and self-assured again. Very much the baron in his château, conventionally concerned for his guest's comfort.

'Very well, thank you.'

44

'Excellent. Marianne, we are ready for our coffee now.'

As soon as she was gone, Charles smiled his rare smile and pulled out a chair for her.

'Today will be our day for business. If it suits you, I will take you round the *chais* this morning. Unfortunately I have to do some other business at lunch and for a while this afternoon, so I will leave you in Jacopin's care.'

'That will be fine.'

'Then, this evening, perhaps you would like to meet my sister, Juliette?'

'Very much.'

Marianne brought in the coffee, and he poured Bell's himself into a deep porcelain bowl decorated with harebells. As he handed it to her he said, 'You will see that life at Reynard is not all unhappiness.'

Bell opened her mouth to say she hadn't imagined it was, but a glance from Charles told her that she should leave the topic closed.

Over their croissants and coffee they talked about the hopes for the vintage. The summer had been long and hot, and all over Bordeaux men were praying now for a few days of gentle rain to swell the grapes before the picking in October. With a little rain and then a few days more sunshine it could be a magnificent year.

Later Charles and Bell walked together towards the *chais*. The gravel crunched underfoot as they skirted the end gable of the house and followed the sweep of the driveway towards a stone arch. The archway framed a cobbled yard and the barn-like doors beyond like a picture and Bell paused to admire the view.

Jacopin popped up beside them like a rabbit.

'*Bonjour*,' he said, the brown skin wrinkling all over his face.

'Jacopin,' Charles told him, 'Miss Farrer will want to see everything.'

'Of course,' the little man responded, beaming at her with pleasure.

Together they walked over to one of the long, low buildings and Bell lost herself at once in the heart of the château.

Hélène's frigid domain with its gilt chairs and silk cushions, on the other side of the wall, was forgotten. This was the real Reynard, where Charles was the king of these rows of barrels, fermenting vats and massed ranks of bottles.

The tour of the *chais* with Charles at her side did remind Bell of a royal progress. Blue-overalled men straightened up from their work when they saw him and waited for him to speak. Bell saw that his cool glance missed nothing. It was plain that he ran his cellars with old-fashioned discipline. Charles's men were hard at work scrubbing out the great fermenting vats ready to receive the new vintage. As soon as the grapes were ripe, some time over the next few weeks, they would be picked and brought by the lorry-load to be crushed in the huge, old-fashioned mechanical crusher. Then they would be allowed to ferment, at carefully controlled temperatures, into wine. All had to be spotlessly clean before the harvest, the focus of the year. Bell noted the clean bare walls and well-swept floors, and the men with their steaming buckets, with approval.

But one thing she saw even more clearly. The primitive machinery was beautifully, lovingly maintained, but it was antiquated. Charles was making no effort to bring in the technological advances that were slowly creeping into the cellars of the greatest châteaux. For a little while yet, Bell thought, he would be able to hold his own. But, in the end, his refusal to march with the times would tell against him. Already, Bell knew, there were whispers in the trade that Château Reynard would not hold its top position for ever. She remembered quite clearly what he had said last night. *Here, at least, there is some permanence.* Bell understood, but she knew that he was wrong. If Charles clung for too long to the old, slow ways he would destroy Reynard.

How could anyone tell that to a man like Charles de Gillesmont? Bell glanced at the beaked profile beside her, remembered the arrogant set of his mouth, and shuddered at the thought.

Jacopin was ushering them into the next section. Along the shadowed walls, reaching up to the low arched roof, were rows of stacked-up oak hogsheads. Each one had a loose glass plug in the top and a primitive spigot in the side. They contained last year's wine, soon to be pumped into barrels to make room for the new vintage.

Jacopin produced a candle, lit it, then stuck it into a little clawed holder on the front of one of the hogsheads. He watched with Bell as Charles bent over the nearest dark wooden shape and ran some of the wine off into a little shallow silver cup. He handed it to her and she held it to the candlelight. The wine was inky-dark with the bright silver barely gleaming through it. Bell sniffed and then took a mouthful on to her tongue, sucking air over it through her clenched teeth. The new wine was cold and bitter, dumb and full of tannin, but somewhere lurking beyond the immediate unpleasantness was the sinewy promise of a great claret.

Bell rolled the wine around her mouth once more to detect the last nuances and then spat it out on to the sawdust-covered floor. Charles's face was in deep shadow but she knew that he was waiting. She gave him a quick, confirming nod but there was admiration in her eyes. Château Reynard was still, just, one of the greatest of the great. Satisfied, Charles led her on down the length of the *chais*.

At midday they came out into the cobbled yard again, blinking in the light. Charles consigned her formally to Jacopin's care and strode away. At her side the little man blew out his cheeks in a sigh of relief and winked at her again.

'Come with me,' he invited, all smiles.

For lunch she shared a coarse *cassoulet* with Jacopin and his gang of broken-toothed and Gauloise-redolent workmen. They sat in the richly-smelling kitchen that linked the *chais* with the main house, hung with shiny copper pans and strings of hams and onions. The château's chef, Madame Robert, ladled the steamingly fragrant stew out on to thick white plates and put a basket of roughly chopped French bread in front of each person. The conversation, not always intelligible to Bell, eddied round the scrubbed oak table and was punctuated with roars of laughter. Jacopin obligingly repeated some of the politer phrases for her, and she joked back in her educated Parisian French which made them laugh even louder.

As they ate, the men gulped down tumblers full of coarse new wine as if it was water. This was the thin everyday drink made specially each year for the grape pickers and the workmen, and it was as different from the nectar in Charles's cobwebbed bottles across the yard as lemonade is from vintage champagne.

Bell enjoyed her lunch enormously, particularly when she remembered the stilted formality of dinner the night before with its clink of fine china and the patball of polite conversation. She was just reflecting, as she failed to catch the punchline of a joke that sent everyone else off into gusts of laughter, that she definitely belonged to what Hélène probably called the common herd when Jacopin tugged her sleeve.

His eyes were still streaming with tears of laughter, and his little hat was pushed right to the back of his head.

'You enjoy yourself with us?' She smiled her answer. 'Good, good. Mademoiselle Juliette, too, often comes to have her meal in here. Then you should hear the jokes!' Bell began to look forward to meeting Charles's sister. Jacopin lifted up his half-full glass and drained it, then mopped up the last of the juice on his plate with a ragged hunk of bread.

'Now,' he went on, 'are you ready for a long walk? We will look at the vineyards.'

The afternoon, spent walking between the rows of rustling vines and breathing in the clear air, was as enjoyable for Bell as the morning had been but she was heavy-footed with tiredness when at last Jacopin led her back towards the château. As they rounded the corner of the house Bell saw a girl running down the steps from the front door. She saw a mass of blonde hair exactly the same colour as Charles's and heard the little man exclaim with pleasure at her side.

'Mademoiselle Juliette is back!' A moment later Juliette was standing in front of them, a huge smile showing her even white teeth. Bell thought that Charles had inherited most of the beauty in the family, but his sister radiated more than her share of warmth and good nature. Dark blue eyes the same colour as Charles's met Bell's, with a long, clear-sighted stare.

'Hello, Bell,' she said at last, shaking her hand hard.

48

'*Ça va*, Jacopin?' She patted his shoulder and he grinned with delight.

'Mees Farraire took your place at *déjeuner* today,' he told her, 'and we gave her a real taste of Reynard, I can tell you.' Juliette chuckled as she watched him heading back towards the *chais*.

'Baptism by fire? Well done. You don't belong at Reynard until they've taken you to their hearts in the kitchen.'

'I don't think I understood more than half of it, but the other half I did enjoy.'

Juliette nodded vigorously so that the tight blonde waves bounced over her shoulders. 'Shall we go inside?'

She took Bell's arm and steered her firmly towards the steps. Bell let herself be propelled along, fascinated and amused by the difference between this lively, friendly girl and her reserved brother.

There seemed to be nothing of Hélène in Juliette, either. Bell noticed that the sleeve of the girl's grey sweater was matted with little blobs of what looked like plaster, her fingernails were short and blunt, and her freckled profile was bare of make-up.

No wonder the two women didn't get on.

Juliette crackled with good humour and directness. Bell didn't make new friends very quickly, but she warmed to Charles's sister immediately and without any reservations.

When they reached Bell's room, Juliette swung her legs up on to the white bedcover, obviously settling down with relish for a long talk.

'Tell me what you've been doing here since yesterday? I'm sorry I wasn't around last night. Missed a really jolly time, I hear.'

Bell stopped short, remembering with a kind of happiness that surprised her.

'Charles and I – sat up and had a long, long talk.' She smiled suddenly at Juliette. 'I haven't done that for ages, not since university, practically, after just meeting somebody. We were both upset,' she finished, candidly.

'Yes. Charles told me about him and Mama having a scene. It must have been horrible for you.'

'Not nearly as horrible as it was for them.'

Juliette groaned and ran her hands wildly through her hair.

'What can I do? They love each other, but Mama goads Charles until he can't control himself any longer. Then pouf! Explosion.'

Bell sat down in front of the dim mirror and began to put her hair up. She needed something to do with her hands, and even more she needed somewhere to look that wasn't into Juliette's eyes. They were searching Bell's face with unnerving thoroughness, and they seemed to see something that Bell herself wasn't even properly aware of yet.

'Has it been like this for very long?' she asked.

'Since Catherine went away.'

Juliette's openness touched Bell. The other girl began to talk about her mother with affection and exasperation in her voice.

'She's very lonely. And getting older. And as she gets older her dynastic instincts get stronger. She loved my father very much, threw everything in with him here although her own family lived quite close. At a rival château, in fact. Then Papa died, but Charles was just married and she thought that there would be children. Lots of them, the family going on, you know. The château, the business, tradition. Everything she and Papa had cared about.'

Bell listened, imagining the older woman's fading dreams and feeling her first dislike tinged with sympathy. Reflected in the mirror she could see that all the merriment had drained out of Juliette's face, leaving it pale and, without her smile, quite plain.

'Catherine was perfect in her eyes. Aristocratic, of course . . .' the corners of her mouth turned down in a wry grimace, '. . . very correct, and clever too, in a domestic way. Charles met her and married her almost at once. I know him better than anyone,' Bell heard the note of pride in her voice and guessed that she must love her brother very dearly, 'and I thought from the beginning that it was a mistake. Charles is cool, but only on the surface. Underneath he is fiery and he needs someone tough and straight, and as hot-blooded as he is. Catherine is outwardly pliant, which is wrong for Charles, but inside she has a little, steely core. And that's wrong for him too. He's very traditional, you see. Has to be, *au fond, le maître*.'

Bell nodded, understanding as she recalled the defiant tilt of the chin in Catherine's photograph.

'Then why did they marry?' she asked.

'Oh, they were in love, no doubt about that. But as soon as they were married, the discoveries started. I don't think things ever went right. In bed, even,' she added very softly. 'Terrible rows began. Really agonizing rows. Hélène bore it very discreetly, but I couldn't stand it. Went to live in Bordeaux.' Suddenly Juliette bent her head so that her face was screened by the mass of hair. One hand picked at a thread in the white cotton coverlet.

'Then. Then something . . . tragic happened, and instead of it bringing them together it drove them even further apart. They were making each other so unhappy. At last Catherine just went away. Packed a few clothes into her little Renault and just vanished.' Juliette paused for a moment, her eyes looking out at the sweep of gravel driveway. 'It was courageous of her, don't you think? Since then Charles's life has been pretty empty, but at least not as painful as before. I came back here to keep him company. He needs it.'

There was a long silence before Bell spoke again.

'What will happen now?'

Juliette shrugged and pulled again at the loose thread.

'Nothing. Things will go on just as they are.'

Bell felt a small, unpleasant shock as the words sank in, then wondered half-consciously why.

Divorce is not a possibility, Charles's voice came back to her.

'Can't they divorce?' she asked Juliette, knowing the answer.

The other girl looked at her, unsurprised, before she answered.

'No, Bell. Charles is a religious man. It's part of him, unchangeable. Catherine is his wife, and always will be his wife before God. They can't live together, but they can't be freed from each other. Ever.'

Bell closed her eyes for a second. She saw Hélène's face and the bitter lines etched around her mouth. How painful it must be for her, sitting here in her empty château, alienated from her children and denied the chance to see her grandchildren growing up to inherit it all.

Bell put down her hairbrush and turned to face Juliette.

'I'm just going to change . . .'

The other girl, sensitive, saw at once that she wanted to be left alone. She got up quickly and then turned back in the doorway.

'Don't worry too much about changing. Mama always stays in her rooms the day after a scene. You know,' she added, 'your hair suits you like that. Shows off the lines of your cheeks and neck. Beautifully modelled.' Bell waved her away and she went, calling back from down the corridor, 'I am a sculptor, you know. These things are not lost on me.'

Bell was frowning as she took off her jeans and stepped carefully into a soft crêpe de chine dress patterned with tiny wildflowers.

Something awkward and unexpected had happened, and she had to force herself to face up to it.

Charles de Gillesmont had stopped being just someone she had to interview for the paper. He was a man, and he attracted her. More, she knew intuitively that he was drawn to her too.

But that must be all. Nothing else could happen. Nothing should happen. It was sad, but that was the only sensible answer. Charles was irrevocably married. He had told her that himself, and so had his sister. And he lived in a world totally apart from her own.

What's more, what about her own determination to make her way alone? Charles de Gillesmont was altogether too powerful to fit into the category of lighthearted love-affairs along life's wayside.

Bell went over to the window to look out at the rich acres of Charles's vineyards. She rested her forehead against the cool glass and laughed at herself. English Cinderella falls head over heels into life in an exotic French château and succumbs within minutes to the mysterious baron.

No, not quite like that. Worryingly, it went much deeper.

Bell's smile faded.

Charles fascinated her. It was his combination of natural power and the right to command, bred back over the centuries, coupled with the glimpses of human hurt that drew Bell. She was hungry to know him better. She wanted to go on admiring and being in awe of him, and at the same time she wanted to comfort him with her own hard-won understanding.

Impossible. Romantic dream.

Worse, there was something else about him too. The arrogant sensuality around his mouth, and the way that his eyes held hers, commandingly, for just a second too long.

With a little lurch of her stomach, Bell recognized that she was physically drawn to him too.

Impossible.

She musn't think about it any more. Not give herself time to. *That's all.*

Bell's fragile resolution slipped away as soon as she found the brother and sister, sitting side by side on one of the pale blue sofas in the salon. Charles was laughing, they were both laughing, and when she came in they jumped up at once to draw her into the warmth of their company.

Bell's heart started thumping in her chest when Charles took her hands and kissed her on both cheeks in greeting.

She did want him, there was no use pretending. It was impossible, but it was possible. Oh no.

Yes.

The evening was as different from the one before as it could possibly have been. Juliette and Charles complemented one another perfectly.

They had been close all their lives, as irresponsible children scampering about in the draughty passages of the château, and then as adolescents becoming aware of their position in the world and the world's expectations of them. Juliette had defied those expectations as well as those of her parents. She had chosen to become a sculptor and had gone to Paris to a famous *atelier*. Her allowance had gone, and she lived on what she could earn as a waitress in her spare hours. For Charles escape would have been still less easy, even if he had wanted it. Wine-making and Château Reynard were in his blood, and he gave himself up to his heritage without complaint.

Juliette and her bohemian way of life remained a treasured alter ego for him. Bell could only guess at the closeness of the tie that held the two together but she saw at once how much they meant to one another. With his sister Charles was gentle, and almost frivolous.

The three of them sat until late at one end of the long table. The last of the wine glowed ruby-red in the decanter. It was Château Reynard 1961, and Bell understood that in giving her his best wine Charles was giving her something of himself.

After the pudding, rich little heart-shaped *coeurs à la creme*, Charles poured pungent cognac into more glasses. Bell began to see the room through a hazy golden glow of happiness and good wine.

Deliberately, she pushed back the doubts and questions that hovered at the brink of her consciousness.

Opposite her Juliette was sitting with her chin in her hands. They had been talking about family likenesses and Juliette had insisted that she and Charles were different because of their different star signs.

'Me, I'm Libra,' she said, 'Queen of the Zodiac, of course. Now Charlot – I'm sure you can guess what he is.'

'I don't think so,' said Bell diplomatically.

'Scorpio. Moody and difficult, but . . .'

'For God's sake, Juliette, don't bore us with all that nonsense.'

'Very well, but I was just getting to the flattering bits. What about Bell? I'd guess that you are . . .'

'Leo,' she put in, hastily.

'Ha! The extrovert with the vulnerable heart.'

'All wrong,' Bell smiled. 'I'm outwardly vulnerable, but my heart is really reinforced with pure steel.'

Across the table Charles studied her for a moment, his eyebrows raised a fraction. Bell went slowly, dully crimson.

There was a tiny silence before Juliette spoke again.

'Leo, eh? Then your birthday is soon.'

Bell looked from one to the other. There was no reason, after all, why she shouldn't share her birthday with friends, however new they were.

'I'm twenty-eight tomorrow.'

'Tomorrow?' Juliette leapt to her feet. 'Your birthday? This is a fine time to tell us. But we must certainly have a party. Charlot – mustn't we?'

'Only if Bell wants it.'

'Of course she does. Don't you, darling? I must telephone, and see Madame Robert . . . oh, what fun. Mama will be appalled.'

Dancing with excitement Juliette planted a kiss on top of each of their heads and whirled away.

Charles put his hand out to cover Bell's.

'Do you mind?' he asked, softly.

'No.'

The room grew very quiet as they sat and looked at one another. Bell saw that there were gold flecks in the dark blue irises, and noticed a tiny pulse jumping at the corner of one eyelid.

Charles was afraid of something too, she realized.

Bell wanted to stay suspended within that moment for ever. They were equals, waiting to offer each other something precious. She was still, for those last seconds, free and in command but the world seemed full of promise and enchantment.

Very slowly Charles reached out and with a fingertip he traced the outline of her mouth. Then he pulled the combs out of her hair and let it tumble down in a thick mass around her face.

'My English Bell,' he murmured. 'You are very beautiful, and very unusual.'

Then he was holding her hands, pulling her to her feet and into his arms. She let her face fall against the soft dark cloth of his jacket but his hand went to her chin, turning her face up inescapably to meet his. She glimpsed something then in his eyes, a shadow, but then their mouths met and they clung together.

Bell was rocked by a current so strong that it threatened to carry her away.

Time stopped moving for them both, questions went unanswered and fears disregarded.

At last Charles led her up the shallow stairs under the huge chandelier. They stood in front of her door, not speaking, their eyes still locked together.

Charles's hand rested on the catch.

'Not yet,' breathed Bell. 'Please. Charles, I must think.'

His mouth was set and she saw the shadow, guarded, in his face before he replied.

'I know. Tomorrow, Bell, we must talk.'

Then he turned away abruptly, and was gone.

'Tomorrow,' Bell said into the darkness. Then the memory of something that Juliette had said came back to her. It had been nagging at her subconscious all evening, and now it surfaced.

'Then something tragic happened,' she had said. Her face had been hidden by her hair, but the fingers plucking at a thread in the white coverlet had betrayed her anxiety.

Tragic? Something that affected Charles?

Tomorrow.

CHAPTER THREE

Light filtered in through the blinds, defining the outlines of pieces of furniture that only minutes ago had been vague shapes of denser blackness. Valentine Gordon, lying on his back in bed with his hands clasped behind his head, breathed out sharply in irritation. He rolled his head to one side to look at the green numerals of the digital clock. It was 4.23, and he hadn't slept at all. He turned his head the other way, towards the tangle of white-blonde hair and the exposed shoulders and neat breasts of the girl sleeping beside him. Her breathing went on, as even and deep as it had been for four hours, ever since he had rolled away from her and begun his long stare up into the darkness. He put his hand out to touch the tanned skin, thinking he might as well wake her up and make love to her again. Then he frowned and jerked his hand back. He knew that she would be instantly responsive, yawning and kittenish, and the idea bored him.

Instead he swung his legs out of the bed and groped for his bathrobe. He felt sticky, in spite of the cool air-conditioned room, randy, and irritable. He wanted something, or somebody, but it definitely wasn't Sam. If he left her asleep at least she wouldn't follow him around talking and giggling. He wrapped the robe around himself and walked away from her, treading very softly. It was dark in the corridor outside but he moved faster, very sure of his surroundings, through another doorway and across a big room to a wide expanse of curtained window. He pressed a wall switch and the curtains slid back, letting the room fill with the dawn light. It was getting brighter every minute. The touch of another switch set up a tiny humming noise and the long panels of glass glided away. The air that flooded in from the verandah was perfumed and still warm from the heat of the day before, but at least it was fresh. Valentine stepped outside and leant on the white-painted rail to stare out at the view.

Immediately below him three white steps ran down from the raised wooden verandah to the wide circle of well-watered lawn. Beyond the grass, with its fringe of cedar trees, was the low wall which separated the garden of Valentine's house from the focus of his attention. He was looking out at the vineyards, a sea of grey-green foliage, that swept away from him across the valley floor. Behind the house the sun was well over the horizon and the sky over the steep hills enclosing the valley was beginning to turn the electrically bright blue of the Californian August. It was very, very quiet.

Most of what he could see, including the impressive wood and stone winery just visible along the track to the left of the house, belonged to him but the knowledge didn't give him, any more, the frisson of pleasure that it once had. Instead one half of his mind mechanically listed the jobs he must attend to today while the other nagged around a deeper, uncomfortable awareness. Valentine knew that he was bored, and he knew that boredom dragged a different, dangerous Valentine out into the sunlight.

He turned sharply away from the beauty of the Napa Valley, intending to go inside and mix a big Bloody Mary to take the uncomfortable innocence off the day. Then the ache between his eyes reminded him of the night before, and instead he flopped down on one of the cushioned loungers that lined the verandah. This side of the house faced west and was pleasantly shadowed, and the leaves of the bougainvillea festooning the fretted woodwork waved in a light, warm breeze. Valentine pulled off his robe and dropped it beside him, rolled over on to his stomach and stretched naked against the cushions. Seconds later he was asleep.

At nine o'clock it was already hot and the breeze had dropped. Sam came out of the open glass doors carrying a tray with orange juice and a pot of coffee. Valentine was still asleep, one arm dangling off the lounger and the other cradled under his head. The girl bent to put the tray down beside him and noticed that there were two or three silver hairs in the crisp blackness over his temples. Her eyes ran over his body. Valentine Gordon was thirty, she knew that he ate and slept too little and drank too much, but he still had the physique of a twenty-year-old athlete, broad-shouldered and narrow-hipped. Sam knelt beside him and kissed the small of his back, letting her hair brush his skin. He stirred at once, then rolled over with sleep still clouding his blue eyes. He didn't smile, but she was used to that.

'Coffee first, Sam.'

She poured him a cup and he drained it thirstily. Then he pulled her down beside him, unbuttoning her loose shirt and sliding his hands over her small breasts. Sam closed her eyes.

He made love expertly, apparently giving it all his attention, but as the girl moaned and whimpered beneath him Valentine's ears were full of nothing but the birdsong in the garden. Afterwards he disentangled himself from her arms and lit a cigarette. At last he was looking straight at her.

'Sam. I'm sorry, but it's over.' He clenched his teeth as he saw her pansy-purple eyes fill with tears. There would be no platitudes, no talk of how it would be best for both of them. At least he owed her that.

'Valentine,' she was saying, softly and unbelievingly, shaking her head to and fro so that the tears rolled. 'Oh, Valentine, please, no.'

Halfway across the world, in the formal splendour of the big drawing-room at Château Reynard, another woman was saying his name.

'In the Napa Valley,' Bell Farrer said brightly, 'with Valentine Gordon, of Dry Stone Wineries.'

As she spoke, Bell was thinking that it had been the strangest, happiest birthday of her life.

At breakfast-time she had found the brother and sister waiting for her in the sunny dining-room. Bell was relieved to see that there was still no sign of Hélène.

'Happy birthday,' carolled Juliette. Charles was standing in his accustomed place between the tall windows and his face was in shadow. Bell felt rather than saw that he was watching her intently.

Juliette was pouring orange juice out of a glass jug and Bell saw it was foaming.

'Mmmmm. Buck's Fizz. A real birthday breakfast treat.'

'Now,' said Juliette, 'this is from me.' She pointed to a shape swathed in blue tissue beside Bell's plate. Bell peeled the paper away and stared down at the miniature sculpture resting in her cupped hands. It was the head and shoulders of a little girl, modelled in reddish clay, and the features were so full of life that Bell thought she could almost hear the child's piping voice. The face was impish, unmistakably French.

'Juliette, how beautiful. Is it yours?'

'My work, yes. Now it's yours to take home and remind you of us.'

'Who is she?'

'The child? She is the daughter of . . . Catherine's sister. The same age as . . .' There was an abrupt movement from Charles and Juliette faltered. Then the words came tumbling out again, too fast. 'Well, no one that you would know. I did a lot of studies of her at one time, much bigger than this. Yours was a preliminary maquette, but more successful somehow than the bigger pieces.'

'I shall treasure it,' said Bell simply, and hugged her.

Charles stepped forward. The sunlight caught the blondness of his head as he put his hands on Bell's arms and kissed her quickly on each cheek. The brush of his skin reminded Bell of the night before and she caught her breath.

'And this is from me,' he told her.

It was a smaller package, this one wrapped in white tissue paper. Bell held it for a second in her fingers, unable to think of anything but the closeness of Charles himself.

'Go on, open it,' prompted Juliette. 'I want to see what it is, too.'

Charles's present to her was a narrow ivory bangle, intricately carved with wreaths of vine leaves and bunches of grapes. Bell turned it to and fro under his gaze, marvelling at the delicacy of the workmanship.

'Phew,' said Juliette. 'Clever you, Charlot.'

Bell slipped the little, creamy circle on to her wrist and stretched her arm out to admire it. At last she looked up at Charles.

'Thank you,' she said. 'It's exquisite. Whenever I wear it I will think of you.'

'That was definitely the intention.'

How sexy, thought Bell, is the combination of those formal manners with the set of his mouth and the look in his eyes.

He made her feel like a girl again, a little in awe of him, fascinated, bewildered and entranced.

Later, he had said, 'May I take you into Bordeaux for lunch? There is a restaurant I think you will like, and it will give us a chance to talk.' Bell had nodded, not knowing whether to feel excited or apprehensive. Her own thoughts were in an impossible whirl, and she found it was beyond her to gauge what Charles was thinking.

Charles had driven her into Bordeaux in the grey Mercedes, leaving the streams of Citroëns and Renaults almost standing behind them. He looked relaxed at the wheel, evidently enjoying the speed, and Bell was content to sit in silence, watching the vineyards flashing past. They drove into the middle of the handsome city and Charles eased his car into a space in the broad Alleés de Tourny. He took her arm and guided her through the traffic, then led her down a narrow side street lined with tall, blank-faced houses.

Bell had been to Bordeaux often before, but this time she looked at it through new eyes. It was where Charles belonged, amongst the elegant eighteenth-century architecture and the calm, discreet prosperity.

A few more steps brought them to a nondescript green-painted door. Charles opened it for her and they walked into a little square hallway where a grey-haired woman in a black dress sat at a desk.

'Ah, Baron Charles, *bonjour*,' she said at once, adding '*et madame*' as her eyes travelled over Bell. Charles bent to kiss the woman's hand.

'Madame Lestoq,' he murmured and Bell could not help turning to stare in surprise. Charles acknowledged her look with a flicker of one eyelid, almost a wink, as they followed Madame into the dining-room.

There were only ten tables, all but one of them occupied,

and they were separated by what looked like yards of carpet. Bell said nothing until they were sitting facing one another across the starched white cloth and glistening silver of a corner table.

'So this is Chez Lestoq.'

'Of course. Where else, on your birthday?'

Bell knew that the food in this tiny restaurant was legendary, almost as legendary as the difficulty of securing a table. She suddenly remembered that Charles had only heard about her birthday a matter of hours ago. He must wield impressive influence to arrange for her to sit so casually in the best corner of the room.

'Well,' she said, laughing, 'I don't think I shall be able to match the splendour of all this with much brilliant conversation. I want to concentrate on every miraculous mouthful.'

'I will make do with just looking at you.'

Bell had wanted to read the menu syllable by syllable, but Charles waved it away and ordered, quickly and decisively, for both of them. Bell opened her mouth to protest, and then thought better of it.

The food, when it came, was perfect, of course. But afterwards, when she came to try and recall what she had eaten, the memory of the meal was just an exotic blur. She remembered the facts of truffle soup under a fragile golden pastry dome, their shared lobster in its veil of piquant sauce, pink lamb redolent of tarragon and a perfect concoction of summer fruits in a silver dish. Yet all she could really recall was the pleasure of being with Charles.

As they ate he told her about his childhood, and Juliette's, at Château Reynard. He described the old baron, a fierce and stubborn disciplinarian with the roll of the seasons from vintage to vintage in his blood.

When he died he had entrusted Reynard to Charles, and his son had accepted the charge proudly. To Charles, that meant keeping the property as his father had left it.

Bell asked gently whether for the good of the château Charles might not adopt some of the new, labour-saving technology. She meant that perhaps his father's wishes could be more liberally interpreted.

The blue eyes snapped with sudden anger and his mouth tightened into a hard line.

'Never. We have made some of the greatest wines in the world in exactly the same way for hundreds of years. Why should I imagine that I have the right to change everything, for the sake of a few extra bottles or a few more francs?'

Bell looked down at her plate. Charles de Gillesmont was not the kind of man who would suffer an argument about his heritage.

Then, seeing her discomfort, he reached out and put his hand over hers.

'You are such a child of the twentieth century, Bell. You have so much . . . freedom, to be the kind of person you want. But can't you understand how it is for me?'

Bell nodded. Yes, in a way she could, and she could sympathize. Yet – beyond that – with Charles's deep-rooted certainty and her own needle-sharp newness, what a team they could make against the rest of the world.

'I do understand,' was all she said.

Charles lifted her hand, turned it over and kissed the palm in a gesture as openly sexy as if he had reached across the table to unbutton her dress.

'You do understand,' he breathed. Around the room the eyes of the other diners returned discreetly to their plates.

Afterwards, outside the unmarked green door, they turned without speaking and strolled towards the Quai des Chartrous.

The watery, dockside tang of sea air penetrated the pall of exhaust fumes, and food smells from the clustering restaurants, beckoning them on.

Beside the oily, grey-blue water they fell into step, still in silence.

When Bell glanced at him she saw that Charles was frowning. When the sensuality of his mouth and the humanity in his eyes were masked, he looked as cold and aristocratic as the profile on an ancient coin.

At length he turned to look at her.

'I seem always to be asking you to understand things, Bell. I know you can, and will. That's why I feel myself drawn to you, as I haven't to anyone else . . . for years and years.'

Bell was watching him, waiting. He took a deep breath.

'Do you understand what it means, being a Catholic?'

So that was it. She had known it all along, really.

Yet Bell listened in silence as Charles talked about his faith, knowing that he was offering her a rare confidence.

As a child, he told her, Catholicism had seemed the simplest, most natural thing in the world. As much a part of life as eating and drinking. God had been safely in his heaven, watching and knowing and forgiving of the little, innocent childhood sins. The faith had seemed to Charles, as a small boy, like a magic talisman with its comforting, opaque rituals.

It was only with adulthood that the tests had come.

Then Charles, made aloof and lonely by his upbringing except for the closeness of Juliette, had fallen in love. Or thought he had.

He was nineteen years old.

Jeanne was older, the daughter of a baker. She had a pale, ethereal beauty that was utterly at odds with her robustly passionate nature. They had become lovers almost at once.

Charles was enthralled but at the same time tortured with guilt. Jeanne had had her sights set firmly on marriage, but Charles even at the height of his passion knew that that was impossible. For weeks he had wavered, tasting the illicit delights that Jeanne was only too pleased to share with him. He stayed away from church, promising himself that each time they made love it would be the last.

Then he had steeled himself to make his confession.

His priest had told him exactly what he had known all along. There must be no more Jeanne.

She had fought to keep him, using every weapon in her armoury, but he had kept faith.

Then he had missed her, achingly, month after month.

Almost ten years later he had met Catherine, who had the same dark beauty as Jeanne. The moment he saw her he was reminded of his old, agonizing love. Yet here was Catherine whose family was as old as his own, and she was young, rich, and a virgin.

She was perfect.

Charles, at his most imperious, had swept her off her feet. Within weeks they were married with the full panoply and the blessing of their Church on their heads.

Once again, devastatingly, Charles had made the mistake of confusing sex with love. His faith was about to be tested as it never had been before.

Bell and Charles had stopped walking and were leaning on a low stone wall. In front of them a forest of fishing smacks, festooned with drying nets, was bobbing on the water. Charles went on talking in a low, husky voice that told Bell how painful these memories were.

His marriage to Catherine had broken down almost before it had begun, in a cruel flood of disappointment and mutual destructiveness. In the confusion of all the terrible things that had happened over those months Charles had almost abandoned his faith. Then, in despair, he had snatched at it again. He had found that it held, and it became the centre of permanence in his life. His belief remained, even though he was left with nothing else. And by a bitter irony that very faith kept him married to a woman he could never live with, and from whom he could never be free.

Charles's dark gaze travelled over Bell's intent face and stopped at her mouth. Through the blood rushing in her ears she heard him say. 'For so long, it's been all that I have – except for Juliette. It just isn't possible for me to pretend, to you or to myself, that I'm not married. Even to kiss you, as I did last night, even to think about you as I have, is . . .'

'A sin.' Bell finished the sentence off for him. 'Charles, I am an outsider. I can only admire the strength of your faith without understanding it. But how, why, is it wrong for us to feel as we do, to want to know each other better, provided that it doesn't hurt anyone else? Does God want you to go on being alone, denying yourself the . . . the comforts of human relationship because of one honest mistake?'

She saw that there was amusement in his face and felt a prickle of irritation.

'So, I sound naïve. I don't know the priestly language to dress up what I want to say. But must there be so much difficulty? Why can't we just . . . see what happens?'

Charles took her hand in his.

'You are innocent, Bell, and so free of feminine guile that I could almost forget you are a woman. Don't run away with the impression that I am a monkish recluse. Nothing would please me more than to take you to bed, now, at once, and I think we would match each other to perfection. But . . .' his face darkened, 'it would be going against my faith, and every principle that I have tried to live by. Up until today.'

Bell nodded, her heart already seizing on the glimmer of hope that he held out in the last three words.

'Yes, I see that. Charles,' she said impulsively, not giving herself time to remember that what she was saying ran contrary to all her own considered thoughts, 'this has happened so quickly, but I know it's more important than anything that has ever happened to me before. Time doesn't matter to me. Won't you just think about what it means? Ask for . . . spiritual advice?'

His stare was speculative, almost calculating.

'I can hardly ask you to wait,' he said coolly, 'while I tussle with my conscience.'

Bell raised her face to his and kissed him.

'Yes,' she said. 'You can ask me. I want you to, and you can trust me to wait for as long as it takes. Whatever it costs.' For an instant Bell listened to her own words in stunned disbelief. No, wait . . . she wanted to say, as the realization dawned on her that she was giving away her precious, hard-won prize of independence. Then, following the uncertainty, came a wave of absolute conviction. She was coming home, home to the man she wanted. Why should she ever again crave independence? When Bell looked back at Charles there was no trace of doubt in her smile. There was surprise, disbelief and the beginning of a kind of happiness in Charles's face as he wrapped his arms around her.

The three deckhands in stained blue overalls who were watching from one of the cargo boats whistled and catcalled, but neither Bell nor Charles heard anything.

*

He drove even faster on the way back to Château Reynard, and with only one hand on the wheel. The other hand held Bell's, their fingers tightly laced together. Juliette came bounding down the steps to meet them as soon as the car skidded to a stop on the gravel sweep.

'Lunch? You didn't say that you were going to vanish for practically a weekend. I've asked people for six-thirty and Mama is having the vapours because she thought you wouldn't be back in time. Not that she wouldn't be having them anyway, giving a party at a day's notice.'

Then she looked sharply from one face to another. Her tone changed. 'Oh, I see,' she said softly. 'I see.'

Her broad, freckled face was full of concern, but there was no surprise in it. She took Bell's arm firmly and led her up the steps.

'You must change,' she told her. 'We only have an hour . . .' Once they were inside Bell's room, Juliette shut the door firmly behind them.

'Look,' she said, some of her habitual cheerful confidence having drained away. 'May I say something?'

'Of course.'

'If you and Charles are falling in love, will you try to be careful? Of yourself, of course, but of him too? It won't be easy for either of you, I am afraid, but Charles has been so much hurt . . .'

Bell loved her for her concern for him.

'If I can make him happy,' she answered, 'I will.'

'Yes. I think you will, too. Now, hurry.'

Bell was ready within minutes. She picked up the flamboyant violet and gold jacket and slipped it on. Her eyes were very bright, and there was a warm blush of colour over her cheekbones.

'You look,' she told her reflection, 'like someone who has just fallen in love. What madness, after all the decisions you have just struggled to make. But, ohhhh . . . how wonderful.'

Bell danced down the stairs towards her birthday party.

She met Marianne crossing the hallway with a loaded tray of champagne glasses.

'Monsieur le baron?' asked Bell.

'In the *grande chambre*, madame.' Marianne indicated with a tilt of her head.

'Thanks. Oh, is there anything I can do to help?'

The little maid looked shocked.

'But no, madame.'

Bell pushed open another pair of double doors, then gasped. Under a pair of glittering chandeliers was an expanse of brilliantly polished, inviting bare floor. The room ran the whole length of the main wing of the house, and the row of windows reaching from floor to ceiling looked out over the lawns at the back to the circle of trees beyond. Charles was standing alone in the middle of the room, his blond head on one side. He was listening to the music that filled the magnificent room.

His eyes widened when he saw Bell, and then he smiled.

'Every time I see you again, you look more beautiful.' He held out his hands.

'Shall we dance?'

Bell stepped into his arms and he swept her away across the gleaming floor. His dancing was just like his outer self, dominating, assured and accomplished. Bell had always been forced to be the man at dancing classes, and usually she surrendered herself to being led with the greatest difficulty. Yet now she closed her eyes and let everything slip away except his arms, his mouth against her hair, and the music. The sound rippled around them and they moved faster, tracing arabesques over the shining floor. They might have been a single body, Bell thought, as they swept in a wide arc and Charles's arms pulled her closer and closer. I'm here, now, she told herself. I'm so happy. I don't want this moment ever to end.

'Charles? What can you be doing?' The voice from the doorway was Hélène's, of course. The dancers sprang guiltily apart and turned to watch her as she glided down the room. The dowager was wearing a stiff little blue satin dress, and her neck and fingers were loaded with diamonds. Hélène's eyes missed nothing, and she made Bell feel uncomfortably aware of the absence of a bra under her own pale violet shirt.

'I understand that I am to wish you a happy birthday, Miss er.'

'That's right.' Bell smiled, undeterred.

'That's right,' said Juliette, coming in to join them. 'And we are going to have a brilliant party to celebrate it.'

Then the doorbell, a real bell that swung at the end of a system of levers, clanged sonorously across the hall.

'Hooray, people,' said Juliette, and danced away to open the door.

Soon the guests were pouring in in what seemed like throngs. Bell recognized several wine-trade faces, and spotted the gossip-column good looks of a raffish playboy who owned a nearby estate. Juliette's friends in jeans and dungarees surged in amongst them, mingling with the dark suits of the wine shippers and the haute couture of their wives.

It was an impressive achievement of Juliette's, thought Bell, to do all this at less than a day's notice.

The volume of noise and laughter swelled to fill the grand room, competing with the soft music and the clink of glasses.

Bell stood in the middle of it all, thanking everyone for their birthday good wishes, sipping her champagne, dazed with happiness. She tried to stop her eyes from following Charles around the room by concentrating hard on the talk around her.

'How enchanting that you are so knowledgeable as well as so decorative,' said the playboy. His wife, a leggy blonde draped in Missoni, smiled indulgently.

More champagne, and the music throbbing louder.

'. . . this vintage. Another month like this, and . . .'

'. . . with three blue blobs in the middle of the canvas. What could I say?'

'. . . Bell, I want you to meet my friend Cecilie . . .'

'. . . did you say twenty thousand? . . .'

'. . . absolutely impromptu of course, like everything my daughter does, but rather fun, don't you think? . . .'

Then two or three couples started to dance, and more and more joined in.

Charles materialized at her side and she slipped gratefully back into his arms as if she belonged there.

Bell began to feel dizzy, with surprise as well as with champagne. She had been so utterly sure that she never wanted to fall in love again.

She had torn herself away from Edward, and dammed up the flood of fear that had threatened to engulf her. Bell nodded, dreamily, her head safely on Charles's shoulder. She had been right to be afraid. Edward had been the wrong man. Now she had stumbled miraculously, thrillingly – into the arms of the right one.

There were no doubts this time, and no fears. So she could use all her strength, her certainty, to help Charles.

The waltz rippled on and they clung together, oblivious of Hélène's stare and the smiles of the other dancers.

'There's only one thing,' she whispered to Charles, 'to spoil it. Having to leave you tomorrow. There's still so much I want to know about you.'

He answered, fiercely, 'As soon as the vintage is over, we will be together again. Somehow. I promise.'

Later, on Charles's arm, Bell found herself in the supper room. There was a group of people sitting at a round table. Afterwards Bell remembered the playboy and his wife, Hélène and Juliette, a red-faced jolly man who was introduced as a Bordeaux *négociant*, and Jacopin leaning over to fill glasses with yet more champagne.

'Tell me, Miss Farrer,' said the jolly man, 'after you have summed up Château Reynard, where do your travels take you next?'

So Bell, with everyone's eyes on her, was saying *It's very exciting. I'm going to California, to the Napa Valley. To stay with Valentine Gordon, of Dry Stone Wineries.*

After a tiny, horrified gasp from Juliette a frozen silence seemed to radiate outwards from Bell to seize the whole room. It stretched on and on. Bewildered, Bell glanced from face to face and they all seemed to stare straight back with hostile eyes.

Then she turned helplessly to Charles but he wouldn't even look at her. Instead he stood up stiffly and walked away.

A second later Juliette and the playboy started talking, both at once and too loudly.

Bell couldn't speak. She pushed her chair back with a clatter, excused herself and began to look wildly around for Charles. He had gone, but another hand caught her arm. It was Juliette.

'Leave him, Bell.' She was pulling Bell away, away from the stares and whispers.

'Come with me. There's something I have to tell you.'

Bell followed her upstairs with leaden feet. They sat down facing each other in the spoon-backed armchairs. Juliette wrenched the cork out of a cognac bottle and slopped the brandy into two glasses. Her speech was already slurred and she was frowning to keep the room in focus, but she said defiantly, 'I've got to have a drink before I can face talking about it all again.'

Bell sat frozen in her chair, unable to imagine what horrible story she could be about to hear. Dimly, as if from another life, she heard the music stop abruptly as the party came to an end downstairs. She closed her eyes but her head swam sickeningly and she opened them again to see Juliette's white face.

What had happened?

'Charles and Catherine had a child,' she said abruptly, not looking at Bell.

'A boy, Christophe. He was perfect and we – all of us – adored him.'

Bell waited, her heart thumping, dreading what Juliette was going to say. She was horrified to see that huge tears were pouring down her friend's face and splashing down on to her fingers clasped around the brandy glass.

'He died. Just after his second birthday. Oh, *Bell*, he was so innocent – to have died like that. He was blond, you know, just like us. His head was covered with little flat gold curls like . . . like wedding rings.' She was sobbing now, her shoulders heaving. Bell knelt beside her and took her in her arms.

'Juliette, I'm sorry, I'm sorry,' she whispered helplessly into the mass of blonde waves. Juliette took a deep breath,

71

blinked, then rubbed at her face with a screwed-up handkerchief.

'I won't cry any more. Now I've said it. It was meningitis, you see, and he was just too small to fight it.' She took a huge gulp of her drink and managed to smile into Bell's worried face.

'What I'm going to tell you doesn't reflect well on Charles, but I think it will help you to understand him better. Because of . . . what is happening between you it's important that you should know, and he will never tell you himself. So here goes.'

Bell slipped back to her chair and waited.

'I told you that they were never really happy together, right from the beginning. But they tried hard, to start with, and although there were terrible arguments, there were reconciliations too. A pattern was established. Charles managed to live even more inside his own head – and he's always been good at that – and Catherine involved herself with the domestic life. She and Mama became very close, and of course the baby was on the way. Then, when he was born, the delight of having a son and heir transformed them both. They took such pleasure in him, it formed a real bond between them. I think, then, I started to believe that it might all work. I wasn't living here, but I stayed often and they seemed to have come to terms with their differences and to be living amicably side by side. Not together, exactly, but at least in partnership. There were two happy years. Then – so suddenly, he died.

'Catherine's grief was terrible, paralysing, but it was immediate. She abandoned herself to it, which was exactly what she should have done. Mama helped her, I did what I could, and her own family too. Her sister's child, Laure – the child of your sculpture – was born at almost exactly the same time as Christophe and her sister understood better than any of us what she was going through. But there was none of that with Charles.

'Of course Christophe was his child too, the same loss, but he seemed to draw back from Catherine's grief as if it disgusted him. And she needed him to help her, to share the sorrow but he wouldn't – as if he couldn't – have anything to do with her. For what seemed like months he went on, mechanically doing his work, not speaking, barely eating, recoiling from us all as if we were contagious. I think it was the way that he removed himself during those weeks that killed Catherine's feeling for him. Slowly, she began to get over Christophe's death, to be almost her old self again, but I knew that their marriage was over.'

Juliette poured herself another drink but Bell shook her head when she waved the bottle in her direction. It all fitted in. She could imagine how Charles would withdraw, sealing his own misery up inside him and hating the show of it in others.

'And Charles, all this time, was grieving in his own way?' she asked gently. Juliette nodded. 'In his own silent, self-punishing way, yes. I'm sure that there was blame in Charles's heart, to be doled out as he sat there on his own, brooding. To all of us, probably, but most of all, most bitterly, to himself. And to God, I think, which must have hit him hardest of all. He couldn't explain to himself why God should have taken such an innocent, blameless little thing, let him die so painfully, unless it was as a punishment. And punishment for who else but he and Catherine? Either there is no God and his son's death was tragic chance, or it was . . . divine retribution, I suppose?'

Bell understood. So, by seeing the tragedy of his son's death as punishment, for whatever sins he and Catherine were guilty of, Charles kept the fact of his faith alive. Yet he lost his wife, and at the same time locked himself in a marriage that denied him the chance of future happiness. With another woman, and another woman's children, thought Bell bitterly.

Juliette was staring down into her glass, wrapped up in her own memories.

'So Catherine left him?' she prompted, with a trace of impatience, not understanding how the sad story had any bearing on the frozen ending of her birthday party three years later.

'Oh no,' said Juliette at once. 'Not then. Something else

was happening. You know that Château Larue-Grise once belonged to my mother's family?'

Bell shook her head, surprised by the abrupt change of subject. Larue-Grise was a once-prestigious property a few kilometres from Reynard. It had been going downhill for fifteen years, but had changed hands a few seasons ago, and now there were excellent reports of it.

'No,' she answered, 'I didn't. I do know that it's owned now by an American consortium who are investing large amounts of money, replanting and putting right the neglect . . . I'm sorry, that doesn't sound very polite to your mother's family.'

'It doesn't matter. There was no money and – well, the family sold out, as you rightly say, nominally to an American consortium.'

'Nominally?'

Juliette smiled without any trace of amusement.

'Oh yes. The real power behind the paper title is your new friend Valentine Gordon.' She held up her hand. 'Don't protest yet. There's no doubt that he will be a new friend. He's very charming. Very attractive. We all liked him, except for Charles who would have nothing to do with him from the very beginning. Too different, you see, too radically opposed on every possible point. Well, Valentine came from California to live at Larue-Grise, supervising the facelift. He was admirably thorough – not only must the vineyards be restocked, the *chais* kitted out with all the latest technology, but the château itself must be restored to its former glory. Naturally, he came to see Hélène to find out what he could about the old ways. We all became friends – at least, we women did. This was a little while before Christophe died.'

Juliette was looking at Bell now, candid and direct, her forehead wrinkled with the concentration needed to tell her story clearly against the effects of what she had drunk.

'I liked him especially,' she said, after a second's hesitation. 'He's very powerful, very good at getting what he wants, but it's all done with a . . . recklessness that makes you feel he doesn't really care about anything. It's a fatally appealing combination.'

74

Bell raised her eyebrows, not needing to put the question into words.

'No,' responded Juliette, 'although I would have, with pleasure, if I hadn't been occupied with someone else during those months.'

Bell was beginning to see.

'Then there was Christophe's illness. Afterwards, for a time, Valentine proved himself to be a real friend. He wasn't part of it, not family, but he was always there when one of us needed to get away from this. I cried in his arms enough times, and Catherine did too.'

Bell's suspicion became an unpleasant conviction.

'He seduced her?'

'Yes. He wanted her, and he saw his chance. He didn't intend to take her away from Charles. He didn't want to be responsible for her, or help her recover, or anything noble like that. He just wanted to put her notch on his belt.' There was a dark red flush of anger over Juliette's face and neck now, and her fists were clenched.

'He was a bastard. I watched it happen, and I saw poor Catherine beginning to cling to him. She was getting better, coming back to life, and she needed love more than anything else. Valentine Gordon was hardly the man to give her love, of course, but she didn't understand that. He was just warm, and full of life, and touchable. Of course she compared him with Charles, always silent, with that terrible, set, disgusted face.'

The rest of the story came out in a rush, as if she couldn't wait to get it over and done with.

'Then the inevitable happened. Valentine gave a party, to celebrate the end of the vintage. He always does – did. Catherine wanted to go and – oddly, I thought, although I understood later – so did Charles. There was a great deal of drinking. There always is, when Valentine is around. Then,' Juliette sighed, and shrugged, 'Charles saw them together, somewhere. Not in bed, I don't think, but I suppose doing something that turned his suspicions into certainty. Instead of confronting them there and then, in private, he slipped away and waited until they came back to the party.'

She put her hands over her eyes as she spoke, as if she couldn't bear to remember the scene.

'Then, in front of what felt like the entire population of the Médoc, he stood up and accused Valentine of stealing his wife. And challenged him to a duel.'

Bell's mouth fell open in amazement.

'A duel?'

'That was more or less Val's reaction. In fact I can still hear exactly what he said into the awful silence in the room. It was "Jesus Christ, a fucking duel. This is the twentieth century, Baron. Why don't you just come over here and smash my face in?" Charles didn't, of course. I wish he had. Instead he turned around and walked out, leaving Valentine standing there with Catherine like a ghost beside him. Val tried to laugh it all off, rather shakily, but I think he was wishing then that he had taken up the challenge.'

Bell said sharply, 'Not all that reckless after all,' and Juliette smiled at her.

'It's quite right that your sympathy should be with Charles, but you mustn't assume that it was cowardly of Val to refuse the pistols at dawn or whatever crazy idea it was that my brother had. He just thought it was irrelevant. Not the way to solve a problem.'

Bell knew that she was right. But the vivid image of Charles waiting to fight in the grey light of some misty-wet meadow excited her, perversely. Suddenly she wanted him very much.

'Then what?' she asked Juliette dully.

'After the party, the next day or the day after, Catherine packed up her things and went away. We saw no more of Valentine, and I heard a little later that he had gone back to California. That's all, Bell.'

'And you hate him.'

Juliette smiled at her again, a resigned, crooked smile that surprised Bell.

'Hate Valentine? No, he's not the kind of man that you can hate very easily. And what was happening here was nothing to do with him, really. He just treated Catherine as he treats all women. As he will certainly treat you.' Juliette's face darkened at the thought. 'But Charles hates him. Charles is a passionate man, and is capable of passionate extremes. Val Gordon is clever to stay away from him.'

Juliette stood up, swaying a little. 'Now do you understand tonight?' Bell nodded dumbly. 'Then I must go to bed. I'm drunk, and I can't bear to think any more about Christophe.'

Bell lay down wearily on the white bed and let the held-back tears come. Poor Charles. Poor Charles and poor Catherine. That life should be so cruel. No wonder the pain in his eyes had reminded Bell so sharply of her father. It was the old pain of inconsolable loss, the pain that frightened Bell herself so much.

Oh God, how could she have been naïve enough to think that she could warm that hurt away? She had failed once in her life, and this time all she had had was three pathetic days. And at the end of those she was going away to Valentine Gordon.

It was the cruellest, bitterest coincidence. No wonder. Oh, no wonder.

At last Bell fell asleep with the jaunty striped blazer all wrinkled up underneath her and the ivory bangle digging a red weal into her wrist.

She was woken up by the sun pouring cruelly in through the undrawn curtains and the sound of someone tapping at her door. It was Marianne, with a breakfast tray. She stopped dead when she saw Bell, her eyes and mouth wide open with surprise.

'I must have dropped off,' Bell said feebly, trying to raise a smile.

'*Oui, madame*. Monsieur le baron, he asked me to say that there is not much time. The airport . . .'

'I know. Thank you.'

The coffee was hot and mercifully strong. Bell gulped it down as she packed her bag. A hot shower helped her headache, and clean clothes made her feel almost human again. But her face was dead white, with all yesterday's pink, happy glow gone.

At last there was another knock at the door.

'Charles . . .' He was standing there, looking as distant as when he had first greeted her on the château steps. 'Charles,

77

I'm sorry. I'm so sorry, about it all. About everything.' She buried her face against his chest, and then felt the blissful relief of his arms going round her.

'Valentine Gordon is a dangerous man,' he said stiffly, and she felt a little clutch of apprehensiveness at the weeks that lay ahead. How could she go out there, alone?

'I won't go, I won't go,' she told him in desperation. Stobbs didn't matter. Her job didn't matter. Nothing mattered except Charles.

'Of course you must go. The greatest wine writer in the world, you told me.'

That sounded more like the Charles that she thought she knew. Bell smiled, in spite of herself, relieved.

'When will we see each other again?'

'When I have picked my last grape, and when you are safe back from California.'

His voice was light and deliberately non-committal.

Safe?

It came as a bitter wrench to leave Reynard. Bell could almost have clung to Hélène's cold fingers as she said her formal goodbye in the salon. Juliette was outside, leaning against the Mercedes. She was tracing idle arabesques in the dust on the bonnet as she waited for them. The women hugged each other, wordlessly, then Juliette whispered, 'Remember. I told you that it wouldn't be easy. But he needs you.' Louder, she said, 'Come back to Reynard soon, Bell.'

Bell nodded, swallowing at the lump in her throat. Then she was in the car, craning backwards for a last glimpse of the sun flashing off the rows of windows.

All the way to the airport Charles's eyes were on the road. Bell watched the Greek-coin profile hungrily, trying to fix it in her memory. Then, too soon, they were there. Charles walked beside her into the sticky, malodorous air of the terminal building. Flight AF2192 to London Heathrow was already being called.

The uniformed man at passport control looked at them incuriously, waiting. Bell realized that the barrier into the departure lounge and boarding gates was blocking her path.

It was time to say goodbye.

Deliberately she turned her back on the man and looked up into Charles's face. Once again she saw the gold flecks in the dark blue irises and the promising curves of the top lip, and once again she failed to fathom his expression.

He lifted her hand and kissed the knuckles.

'Don't tell me you wouldn't have been disappointed,' he reminded her.

'You could never disappoint me. And Charles . . .'

'What is it?'

'I won't disappoint you, either.'

There was a long pause. With a little twist of foreboding Bell realized that he had shut off the intimacy that had warmed his eyes. In front of her was the elegant, formal and remote Baron Charles de Gillesmont. The baron made a little, polite bow.

'Well. We shall see.'

With the taste of bitterness in her mouth Bell turned away. The douanier flipped through her passport and waved her on. She pressed blindly through the gate. Charles stood watching her until she was out of sight, but she didn't look back. A little tic was pulling at the corner of his mouth.

The plane taxied to its place in the queue for take-off and Bell turned away from the little window. There was no chance of a glimpse of the car park, and logic told her that Charles would have driven off long ago. She looked down at her hands instead, clasped over the buckle of her seatbelt, and with a quick movement she slipped off the ivory bangle. She put it away in her handbag, out of sight.

Two days later Bell was sitting at her desk, staring blankly at her typewriter. The piece on Château Reynard and Charles de Gillesmont was proving to be the most difficult she had ever tackled. She kept hearing his voice sardonically reading out the slick phrases as she typed them, and the memory of his voice made her long for the touch of his hands and mouth. She missed him, achingly. Sadly Bell went back to her work. Everything she wrote seemed either to mean far too much or else nothing at all. In real journalist fashion she had put off the job until the last moment, and now it had to be done. Tomorrow she was flying to San Francisco.

She was just stabbing her forefinger at a row of Xs to obliterate yet another hopeless sentence when the telephone rang. It had been ringing non-stop, uninterestingly, ever since she had been back and she picked it up now with an irritable sigh.

'Bell Farrer?'

The voice was unfamiliar, American, warm and lazy.

'Speaking.'

'This is Valentine Gordon in California.'

Just for a moment Bell was nonplussed. Valentine had become such a dark figure in her imagination that it felt quite wrong to be casually talking to him on the telephone, just like anyone else.

There ought at least to have been a clap of thunder and a puff of black smoke to herald the entrance of the villain. Bell smiled at the thought and then heard him say into the transatlantic hum, 'Are you still there?'

'Yes.'

'Well that's good. Are you arriving tomorrow?'

'Yes.'

'Not giving much away, are you? How about telling me your flight time, so that I can be there to meet you?'

Bell collected her thoughts with an effort and reached out for the Pan Am ticket folder on her desk.

'Seventeen-fifteen your time. But there's no need to worry about meeting me. I'll make my own way out to you.'

She heard a low chuckle at the end of the line.

'I admire the pioneering spirit, but it really isn't necessary. It suits my own arrangements for tomorrow quite well to be there to meet you.'

Bell frowned. She didn't want to feel taken over by him.

'I want to hire a car, and I might just as well do that at the airport.'

'No need,' he said easily. 'There's a spare car here that you are welcome to use.'

It would be easier and quicker to capitulate, she thought.

'Okay,' she said briefly, and he told her cheerfully that he would be waiting for her flight. Just as she was going to hang up he said something else.

'You'll be disappointed if I don't say it. Have a good day.' There was a click, and she was listening to the dialling tone.

The memory of Charles kissing her hand came painfully back to her. Quite a coincidence that they should use the same words, she thought, the same mockery of their own stereotypes. It occurred to her at the same time that Valentine didn't sound like a villain at all.

Bell pressed her fingers to her temples, trying to clear her head. She couldn't think straight. She was numbed with missing Charles, bewildered at the intensity of feeling that had erupted so unexpectedly.

Concentrate. Get this work done. It was the only thing she could do, now.

By shutting her mind resolutely to all the other thoughts that crowded in as she pounded the keys she managed to type the first draft straight off. Four hours later she was putting in the minor amendments. Then Bell wrote a note to Henry Stobbs and clipped it to the typed sheets. She decided that she wouldn't give the piece a last read-through in case Charles's French-English voice intruded again. She pushed it all into an envelope and dialled for a messenger.

That was one job done, and the next weeks, after all, were only another assignment. Thoughtfully she picked up the Pan Am folder and tucked it into her bag.

CHAPTER FOUR

The jeep was painted bright mint green, and on the sides the words 'Dry Stone Wineries' were emblazoned in big white letters.

As Valentine Gordon eased the vehicle out of the underground parking lot at San Francisco International Airport and into the dazzling late afternoon sunshine, Bell noticed that the windshield was dotted with the exploded remains of fat insects. The air was hot, and sticky with humidity. Bell sank back into her seat with a small sigh, grateful for even the dusty fume-laden wind that blew back over her as they gathered speed. Valentine looked sideways at her, sympathy showing in his face.

'Bad flight?' he asked.

'Not terrific,' she answered tiredly.

It had lasted an interminable eleven hours and she hadn't even managed to doze. Dehydration made her skin feel as if it was too small for her face, and there was an ache between her eyes that shot jagged light whenever she moved her head too quickly. She had expected to be excited by her first glimpse of the West Coast, but she felt too jet-lagged now to take in any of it. All she was aware of were streams of traffic, towering advertisement hoardings and a long straggle of unprepossessing concrete and glass buildings.

'Napa will soon put that right,' he said cheerfully. 'It's a longish drive first, though. Do you want to stop and eat or shall we get straight on?'

'Straight on,' she said, thinking longingly of a cool dark room, and bed.

Valentine pressed his foot down and they shot forward. The padded seat was surprisingly comfortable, and as they nosed out on to the freeway the wind blowing over her face grew cooler.

Valentine looked sideways again and saw that her eyes

were closed. Her face was white and she was still frowning, but her fists looked less tightly clenched. He began to whistle soundlessly as he pulled across into the fast lane.

'I wonder,' he mused, 'what's bugging this lady?'

He had been agreeably surprised to see her coming through the arrivals gate and making straight for him. Or rather straight for his Dry Stone sweatshirt. Somehow he had expected a dumpy girl with glasses and an attaché case, yet here was this tall, slim brunette in baggy bright blue cotton pants and a rainbow-striped T-shirt. Her eyes were the most astonishing shade of blue-green he had ever seen, although there were unhealthy dark smudges underneath them.

'You must be Valentine Gordon,' she had said in that Jacqueline Bisset voice.

'Yes, I must,' he had agreed reasonably, thinking that there was more coolness in her greeting than jet-lag warranted. 'This way, madam.' Still, she's got a great figure and long legs, he added to himself as he took two battered canvas holdalls out of her hands. And no fancy luggage either. He liked that.

So here they were, bowling along towards Dry Stone and a couple of weeks of each other's company. Valentine loved new people and new things, but he hoped that this time he hadn't landed himself with an uptight English girl who would be a wet rag to his more exotic plans. He braced his arms straight to the wheel like a Grand Prix driver and sliced past a cruising Merc. Now that he had disentangled himself from Sam – and he scowled as he remembered the scenes – he felt like whooping it up a little. Whatever the English girl thought.

Beside him Bell dozed intermittently. She didn't feel like shouting over the wind and the engine noise, and Valentine seemed ready to let her sit quietly. When she drifted into wakefulness again she noticed the intermittent soft phut as another insect smashed into the windshield, and the whiff of cooking and gasoline from the roadside pull-ins. Telegraph lines were strung against the blue sky. It occurred to her that it was all exactly as she had imagined it, or perhaps as she had seen it in countless movies.

She fell asleep again.

The next time she jolted fully awake she saw that they were in the Napa Valley. Valentine nodded amiably at her.

'Just come through Napa itself,' he said. 'This is the vineyard road, St Helena Highway. Dry Stone is about fifteen miles up ahead.'

Bell sat up straight and looked around. The valley was very beautiful, rolling green and fertile on either side of the highway. but with that touch of parched brownness that spoke of a long, hot summer. They passed Yountville and the road swung to the left to skirt the little outcrop of the Yountville Hills. Then, with the flat valley beginning to narrow and the steep wooded slopes that enclosed it beginning to march closer, they were in the vineyards.

Past Oakville Bell craned sideways to catch a glimpse of the Robert Mondavi winery. Dusk was falling, and lights were beginning to show on the slopes and along the highway. At last Valentine swung to the right up a narrow road, and then down another road guarded by a pair of tall white gates.

'Home,' he said, and stopped the jeep in front of a long, low white house with an arched verandah running round it. With the jeep's engine quiet at last, Bell felt that she could almost touch the silence. Then she became aware of the sound of running water and a faint shrilling of cicadas. The air was still heavy, but as clear as glass. Suddenly feeling better than she had done since Heathrow, she followed Valentine up the verandah steps and into the house.

He showed her to her room, put the bags down and stood smiling at her with his hands in his pockets.

'I'll be in the room down at the end,' he pointed, 'if you want anything to eat or drink, or just some conversation before you go to bed. 'Bye.'

She nodded, and bent to unzip one of the cases. She had planned to go straight to sleep, and stood for a moment looking longingly at the big bed with its crimson-covered duvet. Then she changed her mind. She would unwind a little from the journey first, or else she would find herself lying in the darkness with her thoughts racing. As she combed her hair and dabbed cologne on her temples, her mind was busy with Valentine. She liked his loose-limbed, relaxed style but she felt her own response to him being choked by what she knew. Even the simplest words had other meanings, the shortest sentence layers of intonation . . .

She kept seeing Charles's face and hearing his voice. And then she saw Catherine, in the silver-framed photograph on Hélène's work-table, and imagined her turning up that pale, delicate face to answer the American's friendly drawl.

Bell bit her lip and slammed the cologne bottle down on to the table. If only she didn't know any of this. She wanted to get on with her work and she hated the way the clear-cut issues of life were being clouded with emotions. Then she smiled at herself, remembering that she hadn't felt the same irritation at Château Reynard. Which goes to prove, she thought, that Charles de Gillesmont is someone very special. Another less appealing idea came hard on the heels of the first. Had she just convinced herself that he was very special? In her imagination she saw the thousands of miles of land and sea that separated them. Charles was a very long way away, and the distance diminished his power. Already she felt a slight bewilderment when she recalled what had happened.

Exasperated, Bell saw that she was mooning in front of the mirror like a schoolgirl. And she had prejudged Valentine Gordon in a way that was hardly likely to make the next few weeks any easier. With that thought she squared her shoulders and went off to look for him again.

When she found him, in the big room that took up the whole of one end of the house, she stopped short in surprise. Her own room was comfortable but non-committal, lined with matt white-painted tongue-and-groove cupboards with inset brass handles that gave it a vaguely nautical look. There was a table and a leather swivel chair, a big bed and a chest with a mirror beside it. The colours were plain navy, dark red and white. She had noticed nothing unusual either on her way to the door of this room, but now she stood on the threshold fascinated.

The room was full of *things*, thrust together it seemed at random by someone with an eye for unusual and beautiful junk, as well as an eclectic appreciation of valuable antiques. Meissen figurines rubbed shoulders with Victorian fairings; a piece of white driftwood carved by the waves into the shape of a nude torso sat beside a shallow, fragile Chinese bowl filled with polished pebbles and a row of early Georgian rummers, each one different.

In the middle of the room stood a huge library globe mounted in a brass and mahogany frame. The seas and continents were dark olive green with age, and rubbed shiny with use. Persian rugs, overlapping haphazardly, lined the floor. In this hot, open countryside the effect ought to have been dusty and contrived, but the height of the room – open to the rafters and painted palest cream – made it cool and airy. The furniture, in pale wood and cane, was modern except for two dark Elizabethan oak chests and a nineteenth-century rocker.

Valentine was sitting cross-legged on the floor in front of the huge open fireplace of unplastered stone. English fire dogs stood in the empty grate. On the chimney breast hung a big Hockney swimming pool picture, the light reflecting from the ripples almost strong enough itself to brighten the room.

The effect was intriguing, casual and – against all the rules – successful. Bell longed to look around, and her fingers were itching to pick up all the pieces and examine them one by one. She was enchanted, and it showed in her face.

'That's better,' drawled Valentine.

But Bell was looking out through the wall of glass at the far end of the room. It was too dark now to see the view, but the lights were reflected off the inky black ripples of a pool. She turned to Valentine.

'Could I have a swim? Just a quick one?'

He nodded. 'Of course.'

'I'll just go and get my . . .'

'There's no need,' he said drily. 'You'll find a towelling robe in the verandah locker just outside there. And I won't look. If that bothers you.'

There was, she recognized, a taunt in that. As if it was stuffy and English of her to be concerned about baring her body. She didn't rise to the bait, and he leaned over to press a button in the panel beside the chimney breast. The glass doors slid back.

Bell stepped out into the scented night air, sensuously letting its velvety warmth wrap around her. Then, quickly, she groped in the locker and found a thick towelling robe. She walked down the three steps to the edge of the pool and stripped off her clothes, leaving them in a heap beside the towel. Then she slipped into the water. It was blissfully cool, and felt like silk over her tired limbs. She swam a couple of leisurely lengths, letting the tension ebb out of her body, and then rolled over to float, motionless, with her hair fanning out around her. Above the sky was velvety dark, the stars unusually bright. She had been awake for almost twenty-four hours.

Bell came back inside wrapped up in the white robe. Valentine was still sitting in exactly the same position, a book open on his knees. She grinned at him, rubbing at her hair with the deep collar of the robe.

'Just what I needed,' she said.

'Good. What about something to eat?'

She shook her head and a shower of fine droplets spun into the air. Bell wrapped the robe tighter and laughed.

'Sorry. Like an airedale shaking water all over the place. Nothing to eat, thanks. I feel as though I've eaten a kilo of polystyrene today already.'

'I know the feeling. You should take your own food,' he said seriously. 'Never eat anything provided by the airline. Well, have one of these at least. Full of wonderful calories without the bother of having to eat them.'

He poured her a tumbler full of a thick, reddish-brown brew and she sipped it warily. It was tomato, peppery and lemony and with – she suspected – beaten raw egg and a hefty slug of vodka.

'You like my room?'

'Yes. Yes, very much. It's not very – American.'

'I'm not sure that that's at all flattering, at any level. I have been to other places, you know. Here and there. I even lived in France for a while.'

'Yes, I know.'

It was out before she could stop it, and if she had let it pass

87

casually he wouldn't have noticed. Instead she was blushing and he was looking curiously at her.

'Do you?'

It was too late now. She would brazen it out.

'Yes. I've just been staying at Château Reynard. Researching an article. They told me you had been a neighbour.'

'I'm sure,' he said quietly, and stood up to refill her glass. Neither of them mentioned it again and half an hour later, suddenly overcome by enormous stifling yawns, Bell went to bed.

She slept for fourteen hours.

When she woke up again the room was filled with the rosy glow of sun filtering through the red curtains. They were thick, she recalled, so it must be very bright outside. Her watch, inexplicably, told her that it was ten past three. Morning? Afternoon? For a moment a panicky disorientation gripped her until she forced it back by rolling out of bed. She pulled back the curtains and saw the sun high over the eastern rim of the valley. So it was morning. Not early, but at least still some time in the morning. She saw that the watch had stopped.

Bell rummaged in her bag for her tiny white bikini and put on a plain white T-shirt dress with deep side slits. She brushed her hair thoroughly and pulled it back into a loose knot, picked up her sunglasses and a floppy white cricket hat with the brim lined in green, and strolled out on to the verandah. Beyond the circle of garden, men and tractors were at work between the opulent rows of vines, and as she stood watching a crop-spraying helicopter hummed busily up the valley, swooping among the vineyards with a trail of spray suspended beneath it like a cloud.

To her left loomed the stone bulk of the Dry Stone Winery, with huge external hoppers and enclosed conveyor belts like diagonal smokestacks for carrying the tons of grapes up from the harvesting lorries into the winery. A big silver bulk tanker truck was parked in the shade of the building.

Bell walked on round the verandah, looking at the

comfortable padded chairs arranged in sociable groups and the tubs of brilliant red and pink flowers. She made an almost complete circuit of the house, and finally came out at the south end beside the pool. Valentine was in the water, streaking up and down in an effortless racing crawl. Drops of spray caught the light behind him in rainbow colours.

On the verandah stood a white table with a loaded tray on it. Two chairs had been placed ready at either side of the table. There was a beguiling smell of coffee in the air.

In the middle of a racing turn at the far end of the pool Valentine saw her. At once he levered himself out of the water in a single smooth movement, and Bell saw that he was naked. Every inch of skin was deeply tanned, and with the mat of curling dark hair on his chest and his white teeth he looked almost Mediterranean. He came towards her, shaking the water out of his hair and smiling his challenge. Bell's smile was inward as she nodded coolly at the table.

'Breakfast poolside, I see.'

'Naturally. No waffles or hominy grits, I'm afraid, just coffee and eggs. Shall I pour?' He was casually wrapping a small red towel around his middle.

They sat down just at the edge of the shade so that their bare legs were deliciously dappled by the sun. Bell became aware that he was staring appraisingly at her.

'You look very pretty. No dark rings under your eyes this morning. But you've still got too many clothes on. This is California, you know, not Fulham.'

She couldn't help laughing. Was she so much of a type?

'Kensington, as a matter of fact, but you're close enough to home.' She pulled her chair fully out into the sun and then peeled off the scrap of white dress. She settled back into her chair, closing her eyes with a sigh of pleasure.

'Better,' he murmured. 'Much better.'

'I'd love some coffee now, please,' she said carefully, 'and what's the time?'

'Here. It's nearly midday. A whole day of sun and fun lies ahead of us. What would you like to do?'

She had chosen a guided tour of the winery building. At

once Valentine had agreed and his habitual expression of lazy detachment had been replaced by one of alert interest.

'Must get dressed if we're going to the office,' he had said, and five minutes later had reappeared in banana yellow jeans, a sweatshirt and sneakers. 'As the boss I have to preserve a touch of formality,' he had said seriously as they set off along the track that led to the big building.

Dry Stone was a showcase for all the latest, most rarefied technology in wine production. Valentine took her proudly into his computer room, where two boys who both looked no older than about seventeen oversaw the delicate machinery that controlled the temperature of the fermentation vats. The little room was warm, and they were dressed identically in nothing but cut-off jeans and flip-flops. Bell began to understand what Valentine had said about formality.

'Bit of a bind with the "malo" in seven . . .' one of the boys was saying, and at once Val was all attention. Bell was well aware that the secondary, or malolactic, fermentation was a vital part of the magic that transformed grape juice into wine and she stepped back to let Valentine concentrate on his job. He gave a string of decisive instructions before steering Bell over to another piece of gleaming hardware.

'This is our information storage bank,' he said casually. 'Every fact and figure about every vintage, combination of weather and soil, cuvée, opening price or what-have-you is stored in here. Then all we have to do is tap out the question here,' he indicated a keyboard, 'and the answer pops up here.' This time the screen of a visual display unit.

'Very neat,' said Bell, but he corrected her.

'You mean real neat.'

Bell had a sudden vision of the equivalent arrangement at Château Reynard. It consisted of a pile of leather-bound ledgers, inscribed with a succession of spidery brown hands and going back to the middle of the last century. The newest volume was Jacopin's, even more illegible than its predecessors.

No wonder the two men, Charles and Valentine, didn't understand what the other stood for.

They were moving down from the control floor to the

arched fermentation rooms, and Bell put the thought of Charles firmly out of her head.

'They are both graduates of the oenology department at Davis,' Valentine was saying. 'Bright boys, and with a useful qualification in computer science.'

Bell doubted that Jacopin had ever heard of computer science. With an effort she wrenched her attention back to Valentine and concentrated hard on what he was saying. Big stainless steel vats with winking dials and levers gleamed at her in the subdued light. He was running his finger down the columns of a computer print-out and explaining how he had designed the set-up inside the winery to bring the best out of the varieties of grapes peacefully hanging in the sun outside.

'I've got about forty-eight per cent Cabernet,' he told her, 'and twenty per cent Zinfandel. The rest is roughly equal proportions of Chardonnay, Chenin Blanc and Petite Sirah. I did have Pinot Noir, but I replaced that. Never had enough success to warrant keeping it.'

In California vineyards are differently organized from those in the Old World. For Bell, touring Dry Stone was like seeing half a dozen French properties rolled into one. Valentine made huge volumes of both red and white wine, most of it table wine made from a blend of his own grapes and those of neighbouring growers. This ordinary blend was made very quickly and either put into litre bottles at his own bottling unit, or else taken away. in tanker trucks to be commercially bottled elsewhere. It was a giant operation, run with the precision of any successful big business.

Valentine had every reason to be proud of it, but Bell discovered that he was much more interested in talking about his fine wines. These were made from single grape varieties with just as much loving care as Charles de Gillesmont lavished on his Cabernet Sauvignon grapes from the vineyards of Reynard. In Bordeaux or Burgundy Charles and his compatriots of the famous estates concentrated on growing just one or two grape varieties and on making the finest possible wine from them, year after year, battling against the unreliable weather that could wipe out a whole harvest almost overnight. In the Napa Valley, Valentine could bank on months of uninterrupted warmth and sunshine, commercial success was guaranteed by his reliable table wines, and he could concentrate on his fine wines almost as a hobby.

'It's the variety that keeps me going,' he told Bell as the doors of the fermentation chamber closed behind them. 'And the thought of winning a reputation for my Cab as good as any of your top clarets.' Dry Stone Cabernet Sauvignon was the star of Valentine's show. His first vintage from the grape was now eight years old and Bell had recently tasted a bottle in London. She remembered it as only just coming into its full glory, perfumed and fruity and as subtle as any of the great clarets. Dry Stone Cabernet Sauvignon was already a sought-after commodity in the world wine markets, and the new vintages were snapped up as soon as they became available. It was an impressive success story for a self-made man who was still only thirty years old.

'I'm sure you'll achieve that,' murmured Bell tactfully, although privately she thought it unlikely that California Cabernet Sauvignon would ever carry the same cachet as Château Margaux, at least while the old French wine *snobisme* still lingered on.

'And this,' said Valentine, flinging open a door to show a brightly-lit white room, 'is the lab.' Benches against the walls were crowded with formidable-looking gadgetry, and a stocky sandy-haired man in a white coat was bending over a row of tubes in the far corner. The tubes were filled with varying amounts of a red liquid that might almost have been wine.

'Hi, Bob,' said Valentine. 'Bell, meet Bob Cornelius, my right hand – *both* hands – man. Bob's a chemist,' he added, superfluously. Bob looked up, showing Bell a round, serious face and short-sighted brown eyes behind green-framed glasses.

'Glad to know you,' he said cheerfully. 'Read some of your work. Matter of fact I told Val he ought to have you out here to see what we're doing. As good as anything else in the world,' he finished, with conviction.

'I know,' said Bell simply. 'Tell me, you've been making a

big study of barrel-oak, haven't you? Can we talk a bit about that?'

Bob's face lit up. 'Sure, if you've got the time. It's a little complex if you really want all the details.'

'Yes please,' said Bell, taking out her notebook.

For almost an hour the talk was all of pH levels, critical temperatures, chemical volatility and abstruse formulae. Bell kept her end up without difficulty and Valentine watched her admiringly. At last they stood up to go. In the doorway Valentine asked him, 'You're coming with us to Don and Marcie's this evening, aren't you?'

'Yeah,' said Bob. 'Wouldn't miss it for the world. See you there, Bell,' he called after her.

'Tonight?' Bell asked Valentine as they made their way back to the house.

'Oh, yes. A little party in your honour. Don and Marcie Klein live up the valley a little way. He was a music producer in LA until they dropped out and came up here. They're growers, in a small way, but what they really do is give parties. You'll like them.'

'Oh good,' said Bell, but the dryness was lost on Valentine.

They ate lunch together in the shade of one of the cedar trees. The food was simple, salad and cheese and fat juicy peaches, but the wine was Valentine's Chardonnay, as full and buttery as any grand white burgundy from the Côte d'Or. Afterwards they sat drowsily watching the light change over the hills. Occasionally Valentine looked sideways at Bell's calm profile, admiring the way her hair curved at the high cheekbones and was then swept back to reveal the vulnerable lines of her jaw and throat. She was very classy, he thought. Much cleverer than he had expected, and good-looking in a way that was steadily growing on him. The suffocating boredom that he had dreaded was drifting away. Instead he felt agreeably ready to meet the challenge that Bell would offer. He knew that it was going to be a challenge, but he never doubted that he would win out in the end.

Suddenly the restful quiet was ripped apart by the sound of a small, high-revving motorbike travelling too fast along the road towards the house. The bike and its rider came into view and there were a few more ear-splitting revs before the engine coughed and was allowed to die into silence.

Valentine sighed. 'Here's Joannie. I taught her to ride that machine myself, but she does me no credit. She's my . . . domestic help,' he explained. 'She comes in now and again to do some cleaning and cooking when – ah – I'm on my own here.'

Bell indulged herself with a quick mental picture of the Californian version of a grey-haired English charlady with a knot of dusters and a cross-over print pinny. Then Joannie came sprinting across the lawn towards them and Bell had to bite the inside of her cheeks to stop herself laughing out loud at her mistake. Joannie was no more than seventeen, and she was dressed in the smallest pair of denim shorts and the tightest boob tube that Bell had ever seen. She was all pliable golden curves, and her china-blue eyes were fixed on Val with melting adoration.

'Sorry I'm so late,' she panted. 'I had to shop, and then the bag burst in the middle of the highway and some guy stopped to help, but he turned out to be a real weirdo . . .' She turned her blue eyes to the heavens and burst into infectious shrieks of laughter.

Valentine winked at Bell. 'No problem, honey,' he said. He introduced the girls and the three of them strolled across the grass to the house.

'I'll vacuum,' said Joannie, 'and I'll dust, and I won't smash a thing, Val darling, I promise. What about dinner? Bell, you choose what you'd like from the freezer and I'll fix it. I'm a pretty good cook, aren't I, Val? Well, at the plain things at least,' she admitted disarmingly.

'Don't worry,' Val said gently. 'We're going to the Kleins'. Will you be there?' Joannie pouted adorably at him. 'You know I can't go. Dad's so stuffy, he'll never take me up there. What can it be that you all get up to?'

'Oh, you'll find out when you're grown up,' said Valentine airily. He patted the rounded curve of her bottom. 'Off you go now, and don't rush about like a buffalo.'

She took one last backward glance at him before she went, and Bell saw that there was a longing invitation in her eyes that couldn't have been more grown-up. Valentine turned to Bell and returned her stare with a crooked smile.

'I know,' he said ruefully. 'I think I've got a problem there. But I've known her since she was three and a half, and her father's one of my oldest friends. She's quite safe with me, for God's sake.'

Bell didn't return the smile. It doesn't stop you encouraging her, she thought sharply. I know what you are. One of the kind who can't resist exercising his charm on anything female between fifteen and fifty. Not that the charm, in your case, isn't very considerable indeed. *But you needn't think it's going to work on me, Mr Gordon.*

'Oh dear, don't take it all so seriously,' Valentine was saying. 'Look, I've got to do some work before this evening. Can you look after yourself for an hour or so, or shall I call Bob over to keep you company?'

Bell protested that she had plenty to think about.

'Good. We'll leave for the Kleins' at about seven. Oh, and don't bother . . .' the bright blue eyes were sparkling with amusement, '. . . to dress up.'

Then he was gone.

In the event it was eight before they were ready to set off. Valentine was late emerging from his workroom, then he had had a swim and fixed them a drink apiece. Then, glass in hand, he sat down in the rocking chair to listen to a Mozart sonata. The music rippled beguilingly through the exotic room and he leant back, eyes closed, apparently listening intently. Bell stared at him, perplexed. At last she said softly, 'It's nearly eight. Shall we ring your friends to say that we're going to be so late?'

The blue eyes snapped open and he was laughing at her. 'Relax. It doesn't matter when we get there. Have another drink.' Bell noticed that he was appraising her from head to foot, quite openly, as she stood in front of him. She had chosen a short, swirling Jap dress in a brilliant jungle print, and she had arranged her hair to fall around her face in a tumble of glossy curls. The effect was vivid, Gauguinesque. She did a little twirl to offer him a back view as well, but he was unabashed.

'You look great,' he said, suddenly serious. 'And very touchable. May I?' Before she could dodge he stood up and kissed her fleetingly on the corner of her mouth.

'No, you mayn't,' she said humorously. She was well used to fending off approaches much less graceful than Valentine's had been.

'Well in that case we might as well hit the road.'

In the big garage next to the house a dark blue BMW saloon was gleaming next to the jeep.

'I think we should travel in style tonight,' he said, 'but first let me show you the real loves of my life.' Bell blinked and looked around in the gloom for a giggling cupboardful of bronzed Californian lovelies. Then she saw that he was rolling the covers off three huge motorbikes. He ran his hand over the fuel tank of the nearest, a black and silver monster with a crown of dials between the handlebars.

'BMW, 750cc,' he said. 'This one is a Kawasaki, the newest, biggest and best. And here is something really special. A vintage Vincent one thousand. British made, of course, like all the best bikes used to be. One of the most beautiful things on wheels.' There was more warmth in his voice than she had heard there before, as well as a caressing throatiness that made the skin prickle at the back of Bell's neck. There was no doubt, she thought, that he got some kind of bizarre kick out of these machines. He looked sideways at her in the gloom.

'I'll take you for a spin, one of these nights,' he promised. Bell sidestepped the double entendre, if that was what he had intended.

'Okay. But not in my party frock.'

He opened the door of the BMW saloon and helped her inside. As they purred north-eastwards along the St Helena Highway Valentine stabbed a button on the tape deck and *Hotel California* burst out of the speakers.

'Oldie but goldie,' he murmured. 'D'you know, I feel just like a party tonight.'

Bell thought that he looked keyed up. His eyes glittered in the headlights that swept past them, and there was a spot of 'colour high on each cheek. She wriggled her bare toes in answering excitement. As always, the prospect of new faces and new encounters sent an anticipatory frisson down her spine.

'Me too,' she murmured.

The Klein homestead was a blaze of light when they arrived. Don Klein was standing on the porch. Bell caught a glimpse of a mane of greying hair, tinted spectacles and the obligatory West Coast tan as he enveloped Valentine in a crushing bear-hug.

'Val, baby, glad you got here. And this is the lady herself? Come on inside.'

Bell was hugged in turn and they were propelled at bewildering speed into a room full of people. It seemed as if they all turned round at once to wave and call affectionate greetings. The men, like Don and Valentine, were all wearing brightly coloured jeans and open-necked shirts. The women were in anything from Bill Blass to faded denim, and all levels in between. A small, plump woman in a long pink dress came out of the crowd and took Bell's arm. She was in her forties, with shrewd kindly eyes under a blonde hairstyle that was slightly too young for her face.

'I'm Marcie – welcome. Make yourself at home because there's no ceremony here. We all just pitch in together. Now, you're the celebrity. Everyone wants to meet you, so come with me.'

Bell wanted to meet them all too; there was an atmosphere of informal friendliness in the room that made her feel relaxed at once. She accepted a glass of white wine – everyone was drinking wine – and followed her hostess into the throng.

The guests all seemed to be involved in the wine business, as growers or winery bosses or shippers, or all three at once. Flatteringly, most of them seemed to know who she was and were eager to talk about their properties. It soon became obvious to Bell that it was a man's world. The women, immaculately turned out in their chosen styles, and with bright, appraising, bird-like eyes, were friendly and hospitable but each one asked her about the pressures of being a career woman. Each one asked her if she was married. Each time she said no, she wasn't, she noticed a flicker of surprise and then a glance that darted from her face to Valentine, wherever he was in the room. Bell knew what they were thinking and it amused her. It amused her even more that her secret was immunity to what was evidently regarded as Valentine's fatal charm. But she had Charles, and no one else could touch her now.

Bell's pocket diary began to fill up with invitations to lunch, poolside drinks, dinner, Sunday brunches, and with arrangements to tour vineyards and wineries. She began to see, with a sense of relief, that there would be no shortage of material to fill her articles.

There was no need for her to try to circulate. New people kept coming up to her to say welcome, you must come over and see us, you must tell me what you think of my Chardonnay, I'll send a case over to Dry Stone.

She met Joannie's parents in the rotating circle. Her mother was an only very slightly older-looking version of her daughter, and her father had patrician features that looked odd over a shirt left unbuttoned almost to the waist to show a fat gold medallion.

'You must come over, and bring Val of course,' said Joannie's mother. 'Joannie will be thrilled. She adores Val.' She frowned a little, which made her look even more like her daughter. 'In fact sometimes I think her hero-worship of him goes a bit too far . . .'

Bell glanced across to where Valentine was sitting between a pair of long-legged girls. She was beginning to realize that his was the kind of face that was difficult to conjure up in his absence. Put together, feature by feature from memory, it was handsome but blank. It was only when you saw him again that you remembered the animation that lit his face up from the inside. He was full of life. Bell smiled unconsciously as she watched him, sprawling loose-limbed and at ease between the two prettiest girls in the room. He was omnivorous, probably unscrupulous and more than a little dangerous, but she couldn't help liking him more and more.

'. . . what do you think?' Joannie's mother had said, and she was staring at Bell now, obviously waiting for an answer.

'Oh, I don't know,' she responded vaguely. 'There's probably nothing to worry about.' Bell couldn't really tell her that if she was Joannie's mother she wouldn't let her within a mile of Valentine Gordon. It could only be a matter of time before he started to regard those peachy-gold expanses of flesh as fair game.

When they regrouped once more Bell found herself talking to a tall black man with horn-rim glasses. He was the most conservatively-dressed man in the room.

'Jim Taylor,' he said pleasantly. 'Oenologist, from Davis.' Bell was impressed. The University of California at Davis was a Mecca for the study of wine, and she wasn't going to pass up the opportunity to ask a few questions.

'I met a couple of your graduates over at Dry Stone this afternoon,' she said, slipping her notebook out of her bag as unobtrusively as she could. She was helped by the arrival of Bob Cornelius who stood beside her beaming and blinking through his glasses.

'Met Jim, have you? Good. Knowledgeable guy.'

For a few moments the talk was all of micro-climates and soil analyses.

'Dry Stone is a useful place to be,' Jim Taylor told her. 'Valentine is one of the best wine-makers in northern California. He's a hard-headed businessman, of course, but he has something else that even we scientists can't quantify. A real gut feeling for wine. He seems to know what to do instinctively, and no amount of money or studying can buy that.'

Bell felt an arm slip round her waist and she stepped sideways to escape. It was no surprise to see Valentine.

'I just came to see if you would like some food. Don's barbecuing like crazy outside.'

With Jim Taylor and Bob beside her she followed him out on to the patio. The inside of the Kleins' house was done up in what Bell was to come to recognize as West Coast Opulent. The keynotes were discreet Italian furniture upholstered in pale leather or creamy wool, hand-loomed rugs in bright, assymetric designs, and expensive modern paintings. It made Val's room look like an alchemist's den. The exterior followed the same pattern. There was a broad, flagged patio with a big barbecue built at one end and groups of sun-loungers shaded by umbrellas. There was a pool just beyond the patio, with its own circle of loungers. The whole scene was lit so brightly with lamps on the house wall and in the trees that it was almost daylight.

Valentine handed Bell a plate with a thick steak and a bowl of beautifully-made salad. They sat down together with a group at one of the patio tables. Everyone was drinking red wine now, made from Don Klein's Cabernet grapes as Bell's neighbour informed her. Bell tasted it carefully and noted that it was fresh and fruity, but it lacked the grace of Valentine's Dry Stone vintages. She felt, surprisingly, ridiculously proud that his wine should stand out head and shoulders above its rivals.

Music was starting to ripple around them now, and Bell saw that two or three couples were already dancing inside. Beside her Valentine put down his glass.

'Shall we have a stroll around before the fun really starts?'

'Fine,' she responded, neutrally. He put out his hand to help her up from the low chair but he dropped it again as soon as she was on her feet. He pointed down the patio towards the corner of the house.

'This way.'

They strolled along together in silence. The house faced east and west, like Valentine's, and as they came round to the southern end Bell saw that the patio continued here, but broader. The house stood on a rising slope and in daylight there would have been a commanding view right down the valley. All they could see now were necklaces of lights and the occasional arc of a car's headlights on the highway.

In the middle of the paved patio, right in front of them, was a little circular pool. It was screened from the house by a waist-high semicircle of smooth cedarwood but the front of it was open to the panoramic view beyond. Bell could see that there were three or four people in the pool, and she heard a girl laughing over the splash of water.

'Jacuzzi,' said Valentine beside her.

'I know what a jacuzzi is,' said Bell briskly, knowing what was coming, too.

'But have you ever tried one?'

'Well, no,' she had to admit.

'Then what are we waiting for?' he asked, and although this end of the patio was less brightly lit Bell could see the challenge, mocking, in his eyes.

Well damn you, she thought. I might just surprise you. The idea suddenly appealed to her and she moved quickly. She leant over the wooden screen and asked, softly, 'Do you mind if we join you?'

'Come right in,' said a man's voice.

Her eyes met Valentine's and held them defiantly. Slowly she unbuttoned her dress and let it fall to her feet in a multi-coloured heap. The wisps of underclothes dropped beside it and for a second or two she stood stock-still in front of him. The light shone on her smooth skin and cast shadows in the secret curves and hollows of her body. There was surprise as well as admiration in Valentine's stare and he breathed out a long, audible breath. Then, abruptly, she turned away from him towards the jacuzzi.

'In Kensington,' she whispered over her shoulder at him, 'we are brought up to believe that it is rude to stare.' Then she plunged out of his sight down the steps into the bubbling water.

It felt delicious. A broad seat ran round the wooden tub and she sat down, submerged up to her shoulders in the hot water. Two men were sitting opposite her talking about real estate in low voices, and their wives or girl-friends were discussing clothes. They might have been at a cocktail party except that they were all undressed and there was this lovely, gentle erotic swirl of hot water all around them.

Bell threw her head back against the wooden headrest and laughed out loud. Above her the stars gleamed in the dark blue sky and music throbbed in the still air.

'. . . a cool two million dollars,' said the naked man beside her, while the women stared in polite puzzlement at the English girl. Laughter kept fizzing up inside her as the hot jets of water caressed her skin and the steam drifted away on the night air.

'Glad you're enjoying it,' said Valentine as he stepped in beside her. 'Here. Bubbles for inside too. Californian, of course.' He handed her a champagne glass then raised his own and drained it at a gulp. His head sank back and he closed his eyes with a sigh of pure pleasure. Suddenly, electrically, Bell became aware of every muscle of his body stretched beside her. She closed her eyes but the image was still there on her eyelids. He was motionless, taut, and very close to her. She stirred a little, uncomfortably, and the water went on licking insistently at her. She felt herself yielding to it in slow waves. Then, so gently that for an instant she thought it was still only the water, he laid his hand on her thigh. His uncurled fingers traced tiny circles only an inch away from the dark triangle of hair. She sat transfixed, barely breathing, aware of nothing but the water and his fingers and the music, swirling louder and louder around them.

Then, too soon, his hand was gone. Bell bit her lips to stifle a cry. More guests were squeezing in, laughing and joking as they surrendered themselves to the fizzing warmth. It seemed so natural, Bell thought dreamily, all these fit, bronzed, unclothed bodies tumbling about together. She rolled her head sideways to look at Valentine and caught the flicker of triumph in his face. It was like a cold douche poured over her and she sat up at once, hot with annoyance and a sense of violation. He saw the change in her immediately and the triumph was masked.

'What we need now,' he said calmly, 'is a quick swim and then some dancing. Okay?'

They stood up, gleaming like fish in the lights, and made for the pool. The water felt icy after the jacuzzi and Bell gasped as she hit the water. But after two brisk lengths she was glowing and tingling.

Valentine bent to help her out but she swam past his hand and swung herself out, panting. Without another word he wrapped her gently in a huge towel and showed her to a changing cubicle. He grinned at her over the door.

'Save the first dance for me.'

They were still dancing when the dawn came and Bell begged to be allowed to rest. The party showed no signs of coming to an end, but exhaustion had hit Bell like a sandbag. Valentine looked down at her.

'Home?' he said, and she nodded dumbly. Minutes later they were in the BMW, purring back down the St Helena Highway in the pearly light of the new day. Bell rested her head against the cool glass of the window and tried to think. She had had a lot to drink and her head was beginning to ache, but she knew that she had to make a very firm resolve. Valentine must come no closer. She had been dangerously close to yielding to him tonight, so soon and so easily, and she would have to fight extra hard now. Beside her he was humming softly, arrogant and sure of himself. Her resolve strengthened.

Outside the door of her room she stood with her hand on the latch.

'It's been a wonderful evening. Thank you.'

His arms came around her, roughly, and he bent to kiss her. She turned her head away so that his lips could only brush her cheek. There was a ripple of irritation in his voice when he spoke.

'Are we really going to live here, side by side for days on end, and not know each other any better than this?'

'Yes,' she said, in a small voice. 'That's right.'

His arms dropped to his side. He was angry, and the bright blue eyes were hooded. All the easy amiability was gone.

'How stupid,' he said, 'and what a waste. What is it, promised to a nice young man in Kensington?' There was a sneer in his voice now.

'No,' she said truthfully. 'I just don't want to go to bed with you. Not now. Not ever. Goodnight.' There was only one person she wanted, and he was half a world away.

Bell fell into a dreamless sleep as soon as she had pulled the crimson duvet up over her head.

A few yards away Valentine lay on his bed, wide awake, staring up at the ceiling. Again and again he saw her standing beside the Kleins' jacuzzi, beautiful and sleek yet somehow fragile. But it wasn't her body that he remembered. He had seen innumerable others, some of them even prettier than Bell's. What kept coming back was the expression in her eyes, the defiance mingled with uncertainty, and the glimmer of reckless resolve that had made her taunt him with her nakedness. She interested him more and more, so he wanted her more and more. He groaned with exasperation and rolled over, trying to squash the desire that was beginning to chafe him.

'Not now. Not ever,' he heard her say. Not now, perhaps. But ever was a long time.

Bell's days at Dry Stone settled quickly into a comfortable pattern. She would swim and then eat breakfast with Valentine on the shady verandah. Then she would climb into the mint green jeep and drive along the valley with the sun on her shoulders and the wind blowing her hair back. She would visit the other big wineries and listen carefully as the owners talked about their properties and their plans. Day after day she rolled the gulps of fruity Cabernet and intense Chardonnay around her mouth and scribbled on her tasting sheets. Outside she watched the tractors trundling to and fro between the rows of vines and chatted to the men who tended the fat, ripening grapes. These men were calmer than their counterparts in Bordeaux, sure of the sun that blazed down every day to reward their efforts. There was no fear of a sudden, vicious spell of weather that could wipe out a whole year's patient watching and waiting.

Then Bell would go on to lunch somewhere else, sitting at a scrubbed kitchen table or on a patio with a circle of cheerful new friends. It was the most hospitable place she had ever visited.

In the late afternoons she would drive back to Dry Stone and sit beside Valentine's pool, tapping out her notes on his portable typewriter and shaping them into articles to be mailed regularly back to London. In the evenings they usually drove out to dinner with Valentine's friends, or to homely little restaurants with checked tablecloths and liberal jugs of local wine. Two or three times Joannie, true to her promise, cooked them a steak or grilled some fish and they ladled thick American ice-cream on to their plates straight from the plastic freezer boxes.

Bell knew that Valentine was watching her carefully as the days slid by. She often looked up to find his eyes on her, thoughtful, and then he would smile and look away. He touched her often too, dropping an arm casually around her shoulders or reaching out to touch her cheek affectionately. After one or two particularly happy evenings he kissed her goodnight, quickly, and she didn't try to turn her mouth away. But he never pressed her again, and neither of them ever referred to her first refusal.

Yet she didn't feel at all secure. She was convinced that he was just waiting for something, coiled up and ready to spring as soon as a crack appeared in her defences. She was always on her guard. When she thought about it, she realized that it gave their days together an extra tantalizing tingle of excitement. And Bell was fully aware that she did find his company exciting.

There was the unpredictability that lay behind the easy charm, and a determination to have his way that challenged her own. She liked Valentine Gordon, often liked him very much. Sometimes, in spite of herself, she found herself responding physically to him as she had in the jacuzzi. Valentine was aware of those moments too, and she would look up to see him watching her with his clear blue eyes and waiting. Then, invariably, the memories of Reynard would come back and she would turn abruptly away from the American to lose herself in her longing for Charles.

When Bell had finished her exploration of Napa she turned her attentions further afield. She drove across to Sonoma, and then up to Santa Rosa and the string of wineries along the Russian River. On these longer expeditions she took Valentine's BMW, revelling in the surge of the engine's powerful acceleration along the open freeways.

Another time she drove right away from the coast to the fertile flatness of the Central Valley. She stayed away for three nights, each of them spent with friends of Valentine's in the wine townships of Fresno and Modesto. When she drove the BMW back at last along the track to Dry Stone she found him waiting for her, leaning over the verandah rail in the early dusk. When she saw the dark head and the familiar lean figure, her pulse quickened and she braked unnecessarily hard in front of the steps. He swung his legs over the rail and leaned down to open the door for her.

'Good trip?' he asked casually, and she stared up into his eyes. There was a glimmer of amusement behind the conventional Californian welcoming smile, and she stiffened.

'Yes, very useful.'

'Oh, jolly good,' he mocked her. 'Listen, Joannie's parents have asked us over to dinner. Which is why I was looking out for you so anxiously.'

I see, she thought, and why should she feel disappointed?

'Could you bear it? They have been looking forward to seeing you again, and you have such a busy schedule.'

They walked inside together.

'Of course. Just give me time to have a quick shower.'

Joannie sat across the table from Valentine and it seemed to Bell that her eyes never left his face all evening. He teased her like a schoolgirl, but Bell thought that there was another, less innocent level to the good-humoured banter. It was as if Val was testing the girl, gauging coolly whether her reactions to him were those of a child or a woman. Usually she blushed and giggled her response, but occasionally her eyes blazed and she ran her tongue over her lips with obvious, adult hunger. Then Valentine's voice would deepen and he would look away, making a casual remark to one of the others.

Joannie's parents seemed oblivious, but Bell felt disapproving and schoolmistressy. It was as if Valentine couldn't help himself. As if it was second nature to him to try to attract even a half-child like Joannie.

When they were sitting side by side in the car on the way home she turned to him sharply.

'Do you know what you're doing to Joannie? You said you knew you had a problem, and you seem to be doing everything you can to make it worse. Isn't she just a little young for you?'

His voice was just as sharp in response.

'Doing? Absolutely nothing. And she's not as innocent as you think, Bell. She's just a normal, carnally-inclined American teenager.'

'I don't care. I didn't like you much this evening,' she answered, slowly. 'You were leading her on. Turning her on, right in front of her parents. And me.'

'Crap,' he said, with the sneer in his voice that she had heard once before.

'Anyway. I need some kind of feedback after being stuck with you, my English icicle.' He gripped the wheel harder and shook it so that the car swerved alarmingly. 'How do you think I feel, Bell? Do you think it's easy for me, watching you trailing yourself in front of me day after day, and having to act like I'm in a straitjacket?'

She turned her head away wearily.

'Grow up,' was all she could bring herself to say. 'This is one lollipop you can't have.'

They drove on in silence to the white gates of Dry Stone. Valentine stopped the car at the verandah steps to let Bell get out and then swung round towards the garage with an angry screech of tyres. Bell hesitated in the deep shadows of the verandah, her irritation with him slowly evaporating. When the roar of the engine died the quiet night soothed her, and she listened absently to the rustle of leaves and long grass. Then the soft pad of Valentine's footsteps came back across the lawn and she stepped out into the porch light to meet him. She saw that he was frowning, his eyebrows meeting in a dark line across his forehead. Bell put out her hand to touch his arm, but his expression didn't change.

'Valentine, I'm sorry,' she said softly. 'It's not for me to criticize how you act with your friends.'

'No,' he agreed curtly. 'It isn't.'

Bell sighed. 'And the other thing . . . I did try to make it clear, from the very beginning, that I didn't want to sleep with you. Would it be better if I moved out? I could easily stay somewhere else.'

After a moment's silence Valentine shrugged dismissively and walked past her into the house. Only when the darkness inside had swallowed him up did she hear him say, 'No. I don't want you to move out.'

Bell listened to him going down the corridor and into his room, and then she leant on the verandah rail to look out at the lights on the opposite hillside. Suddenly she shut her eyes tightly to close out the sight and wished, as she did a hundred times a day, that she was safe with Charles at Château Reynard.

CHAPTER FIVE

As the hot days slid by Bell felt more and more at home on the West Coast. Nothing ever seemed to happen by arrangement. The happiest parties were the most impromptu ones, the busiest and most successful days always turned out to be the ones she had made no plans for. In Valentine's company it was easy to live for the moment and to enjoy every hour as it came.

At one of a dozen barbecue parties Bell met the editor of a local paper.

'Great!' he said, grinning at her in the brilliant light reflected off the pool. 'What about writing me a nice piece on the French châteaux? You know, the really big names, with lots of behind-the-scenes stuff and not too much technical talk?'

'Yes,' Bell grinned back at him. 'I could have a go at that.'

As soon as she sat down at her typewriter she wished that she had refused the assignment. Every word brought back the Médoc, and every château name reminded her of Reynard. And Charles, whose absence made a dull, cold place in the middle of all this pleasure and sunshine, seemed further away than ever. Over and over again as she worked she relived her last morning with him.

When you are safe back from California. Safe? From his enemy Valentine Gordon? Bell smiled briefly. She was safe, although Juliette had been right in her prediction. Valentine was a new friend, and she did like him. Yet she could see, all too vividly in her imagination, that same smiling face bending to kiss Catherine de Gillesmont's pale mouth, those strong arms pulling her to him just as he had tried to do with Bell herself. Then she would hear his lazily drawling voice mocking Charles's passionate, anachronistic challenge, and anger with him would prickle along her spine. She had seen Valentine work his magic on Joannie, and on the girls who flocked around him at parties and dinners, but her promise to Charles was her own talisman against it. That made Bell smile again, ruefully now. She needed that talisman. It wasn't easy to go on fighting against Valentine's open belief that they should enjoy themselves in bed as well as out of it. It would have seemed natural to Bell too, in that Californian atmosphere, to seize whatever fun the moment offered. But she had promised Charles, beside the calm water of the Gironde, that she would wait. Wait? For him to square his need for her with his conscience? With his threatening, baffling, vital Church? Bell sighed. How long? Months or years? And even then, what would she have won? A man scarred by tragedy and disappointment, and encased in an impervious armour of self-protectiveness.

It saddened her that the more she thought about Charles, the further he seemed to slip away from her. She couldn't see his face, only sometimes the navy-blue depths of his eyes, or the deep-etched curves of his mouth, or the blond stubble glinting on the high bones of his cheeks.

And then the doubts would come. It had been three brief days. It had happened thousands of miles away from this sunshine. Sometimes, when the memory of him caught her unawares, the muscles of her stomach would clench like a fist and she would be left gasping. Yet when she tried deliberately to recall his presence, the certainty that she had felt when their eyes locked together, there was only blankness. Exasperation would overtake her, with a bleak amusement at the romantic cliché of her predicament.

This is you, Bell Farrer, she would murmur. Out here in California, being wined and dined, meeting dozens of nice people, doing everything that you love best. Yet you are pining in your secret heart for an unattainable man that you hardly know. It chafed her to realize that if she had never met Charles, these gilded days would have been golden. She would have met Valentine head-on. Yes, she thought, she would have gone to bed with him, and would have luxuriated in the pleasure that his body would have given her. She would have made it happen on her own terms, and she would have kept her inner self apart and intact. Then, at the end of her stay, they would have gone their separate ways happy and satisfied. They would have stayed firm friends, having dinner together from year to year in London or Los Angeles. Now, she thought regretfully, their friendship would always lack the equilibrium of the kind that has been tested by loving. And she was here now, watching every reaction that she made to him and distancing herself with a kind of prissy coldness that gave the lie to her true self.

But the spell that Charles had cast wouldn't go away. Nor did she want it to. He drew her like no man she had ever met, even through the veil of cool reserve that he used to protect himself. Bell saw that veil, and understood it. Just as Charles understood that she protected herself in the same way. Her heart quickened when she thought of it. They were the same, and they lived by the same standards. Those were the times, remembering, when she felt closest to him. Whatever difficulties lay between them, their understanding was shared. And the memory of him went on pulling her, to his way of life and the traditions he stood for. Bell wanted to be part of it more than she had ever wanted anything else. Compared with that longing, her enjoyment of California and Valentine's easygoing attraction seemed ephemeral. Impatiently, Bell realized that there was nothing she could do but cling to her promise and wait. Wait until she was safe home and Charles had harvested his last grape. Then, she resolved, she would go and find him.

At this point she would be consumed by a boiling irritation that made her want to throw all her papers up in the air, or run as fast as she could, or drive eastwards at once without stopping until she found him again.

In the grip of such a mood one evening she flung herself off her bed and banged blindly through the door. She had intended, without thinking about it, to throw herself into the pool and swim up and down until tiredness drove the itch away. Instead Valentine caught her by the elbows and twisted her round to face him.

'Hey, what's the matter?'

'Oh, I don't know. I feel – so restless. I can't keep still.'

It sounded so feeble, but she could think of nothing else to say.

'Then let's go to Vegas.'

'Las Vegas?'

'Of course. Right away. It's the best cure for restlessness in the world. Pack your bag and we'll be off.'

'What about . . .?'

'Don't argue.'

There was no more to be said. Tingling with anticipation in spite of herself she stuffed a few clothes into her canvas bag. Almost before she was ready Valentine was hooting the horn outside.

'Don't you need to pack anything yourself?' she gasped, as she scrambled into the car and they shot forward.

'You don't need anything in Vegas. Except the ability to stay awake.'

That drive, for Bell, was the essence of all the road movies she had ever seen distilled in one night. They drove through the dark like a whirlwind. Neon signs shouting EATS or THE BIG BURGER flicked past them. Their headlamps picked up towering roadside hoardings for Marlboro or Coke and then let them fall into blackness again. Valentine unwrapped sticks of gum for them, handing hers over with the merest droop of his eyelids indicating that he was enjoying playing the part as much as she. When they stopped for petrol – gas, she corrected herself – she climbed out and leaned against the car with her hands in the pockets of her jeans, chewing the gum and watching the attendant in his white overalls. He sponged the insects off the windshield and winked at her.

As they drove on, Valentine told her the stories of his other trips to Vegas. When he was much younger, he said, he had come alone. His game was poker and he needed to win, in serious games that went on for days in curtained rooms behind the flashy façades. Later he had come, bored, with gaggles of forgotten friends. The men had played blackjack and tried to date the dancers, while the women had lolled by the hotel pools, only moving to feed piles of dollars into the fruit machines or to catch Sinatra's act at Caesar's Palace. Once or twice, as now, he had taken a girl there.

'Are you a gambler, Bell?'

'No. Well, horses sometimes.'

'Oh really?'

'Cheltenham, Gold Cup Week. The Derby.'

'Ah, that kind of horses. Top hats and binoculars.'

He was laughing at her again.

The highway wound on, black and almost empty in the dead hours of the night. Bell had a sudden sense of the vastness of the country stretching east in front of her, and of themselves as a tiny speck crawling along under the limitless heavens. Perhaps Charles was right. Perhaps, in the overall scheme of things, the minuscule sum of individual human emotions mattered less than the continuity of faith. The promise she had made to Charles shrank in significance until it seemed small and petty. Did any of it matter, after all? Bell shivered a little. At once Valentine's hand reached out and covered hers and she grasped it gratefully.

'Why don't you have a sleep?' he suggested softly.

'No. I don't want to sleep,' she said quickly. She wanted to keep her eyes open and keep the thoughts at bay. 'Talk to me. Go on telling me about what you used to do.'

'I've told you a bit. Now it's your turn. What happened to you, to make you the way you are?'

It was the first time that Valentine had ever wanted to know more about her than she had chosen to tell him, and it surprised her. For a man who lived so much in the present, the past must seem an irrelevance. *Made me the way I am?* Bell thought. No, I don't want you to know anything about that. You don't belong in that part of my life. Stay here, in California, please. Yet for a moment she longed to tell him about Charles. It would have been such a relief to talk about him to someone. Anyone. Even to Valentine. But she bit back the confession and turned sideways in the leather seat instead to stare full at him. Her answer deliberately headed him off.

'You mean what has made me impervious to your considerable charm?' He chuckled, entirely at ease and seemingly unaware that she was keeping him at bay.

'Of course. It wouldn't have done either of us any harm,

you know. No strings, if that's the way you prefer it.'

Bell hesitated, choosing her words carefully.

'No, you see, it isn't at all the way I prefer it. You were right, in a way, when you made that jibe about being promised to someone else. Although it isn't in the way that you probably imagine.' She paused again, still thinking very carefully. 'But I like you very much. As you've probably guessed. If things had been different – well, they would have been different, that's all.'

He stared back at her for a second before jerking his attention back to the road.

'Now, that's very feminine, and not very like you. You're too clever to think you can hide your real motives behind some half-assed romantic secret. But, if that's the way you want it . . .'

She didn't answer and for a while they sat in silence, busy with their separate thoughts. Then Valentine said, very softly, 'Look.'

Ahead of them, rising out of the black desert like a mirage, was a many-faceted blister of light. Behind Las Vegas the skyline was turning from dark to pale grey to rosy pink.

Bell breathed out a long sigh.

'That is romantic.'

As they drove into town the brilliant ribbons of neon were beginning to fade in the stronger daylight, but every hotel and gambling joint was still bursting with life. Bell gaped in astonishment as they cruised past the tinsel frontages along the Strip.

'Which one?' asked Valentine. 'Not that they aren't all identical. Come on, my fingers are itching.'

'All of them. One by one. No, wait. The Pink Slipper, please.'

In slow motion a huge flashing green champagne bottle was tipping a stream of sparkling gold light into a fluorescent pink slipper. As they watched the bottle tilted upright again, then swung forward to start the process all over again.

'The Pink Slipper it shall be.'

The foyer was like no other hotel foyer Bell had ever seen. It was lined with a winking, purring battery of fruit machines, each with its acolyte stationed in front of it. The players were machine-like themselves, feeding in the coins and pulling the levers like so many robots. Bell turned to share her astonishment with Valentine, but he was registering at a circular reception desk upholstered entirely with deep-buttoned silver plastic. The receptionist was a slender six-foot redhead in pink satin shorts. Bell glanced down at her own creased jeans and suddenly felt that she was all wrong for Las Vegas.

'I must,' she murmured as Valentine rejoined her, 'either find some satin shorts, or,' indicating the players at the fruit machines, 'a wash'n'wear pants suit.'

'You know what to do when in Rome,' he reminded her humourosly. 'When in Plastic City – wear plastic. Here's some plastic money to be going on with.' He pressed a pile of fat pink squares into her hand. Each one was stamped $50 PINK SLIPPER.

'Now, let's get to it.'

The inner hall was windowless. Except for the tiredness etched into the face of the man in a sequined jacket crooning into a mike, and the glassy, exhausted smiles of the croupiers, it could have been any hour of the day or night. More leggy girls in the ubiquitous pink shorts swayed to and fro bearing little trays of drinks, sandwiches or hamburgers. On their feet were high-heeled pink satin slippers.

Fanning out like the spokes of a wheel from the stage at the centre were the tables. A glittering chandelier loomed over each one. When the singer at last bowed to a faint patter of applause, the dominant sound became the rattle of roulette wheels.

Valentine guided Bell towards two empty seats at the nearest table. The croupier smiled at them automatically and said, 'Welcome.' She was wearing a pink plastic heart, inscribed 'CINDY', pinned to her bosom. The other players at the table didn't even look up.

Following Valentine's lead Bell slid one of her pink chips on to a numbered square and watched the hypnotic blur of the wheel as it spun the ball.

She soon discovered that she wasn't a gambler. It was

boring, and repetitive, rather than exciting. And as soon as her pile of chips had grown a little she began to feel absurdly protective of it. She worried about giving exactly the right number back to Valentine, and she shook her head when Cindy raised her plucked eyebrows at her for the next bet. Beside her Valentine played and lost steadily. At last she leant against him and whispered, 'I'm going to stop now. I'm sleepy.'

He pushed his remaining chips into place and watched impassively until Cindy had raked them away. Then he took out a key with a dangling pink plastic slipper for a tag and handed it to her.

'Crazy. You're into a winning streak. Well – I'm going to find myself a game of cards. Oh, and we'll have to double up in a suite. Only one left. Sweet dreams.' Bell was too tired to argue.

He kissed her forehead briefly and she smiled at his retreating figure with a tenderness that would have surprised her if she had been aware of it.

The suite he had booked them into was pink, in every possible variation of shade and texture. In the bedroom were two huge double beds swathed in shocking pink nylon ruffles. When she pulled back the covers of one Bell groaned aloud at the sight of pale pink satin sheets.

The window was muffled in slippery pink drapes that were obviously not meant to open. At last she found a corner and pulled it up, then prised apart the slats of the venetian blind behind it. Peering downwards she could see, many storeys below, the turquoise shimmer of a swimming pool. It was a lovely idea but she had to sleep first. Closing her eyes firmly on the pinkness she lay down and rolled over into oblivion.

When she woke, she lay for a few seconds blinking in bewilderment at the nightmarish decor. Then, remembering, she looked across at the next bed. Valentine was asleep. The incongruous sight of his lean, suntanned body half wrapped in pink frills made her smile, and she propped her head up on one hand to look at him more comfortably. He was frowning in his sleep and there were two deep vertical clefts between his black eyebrows. One arm was flung straight out and the other was curled over his head, as if to protect himself. Without the light from his bright blue eyes his face looked darker, almost saturnine. Bell felt very close to him. It was as if she knew him very well, yet – tantalizingly – didn't know him, and he was a man she would really like to know. With a sense of shock she realized that it would have felt quite natural to have woken up and found his warmth next to her. It would have been very easy to turn inwards to that warmth and let it dispel the uncertainties that engulfed her. Deliberately, as soon as the thought came, she made her mind go blank. Then she shut her eyes and replaced the image of Valentine's sleeping face with Charles. She saw him as he had been at the airport, pale and wary, and understood at last what he had been afraid of. He must recognize Valentine's magnetism all too clearly. He had seen him use it once before. No wonder Charles hated him. Quickly Bell leant over to her bag, lying open beside her bed. She groped for a second and then her fingers closed around the hard shape of the ivory bangle. She slid it out of its hiding place and grasped it until the carving bit cruelly into her fingers. Only then did she turn to look at Valentine again, and as she moved her head she saw that the low cabinet that separated their beds was almost covered with a drift of hundred-dollar bills. With another shock she realized simultaneously that the blue eyes were wide open, watching her unblinkingly.

'Hello,' Bell said. 'Did you rob a bank?'

He groaned.

'If only,' he said thickly, 'I could play poker without drinking whisky. I'd be a rich man. Well, at least my eyeballs must harmonize with the decor. Be a darling and go next door. Get me a glass of Perrier out of the fridge, plus whatever crummy complimentary hooch they provide.'

Bell went, glad of the long T-shirt that she was wearing in place of a nightdress. She brought him a tumbler of water and a glass of white wine well laced with soda. He drained both in two long draughts. Then he leaned up and caught her wrists, pulling her down beside him. She put her hands over his forehead and he moaned softly.

'How cool and soothing. Just like the rest of you must be.'

His eyes were open and he was gazing directly into hers. She recognized that they held not arrogance or challenge now, but the ancient simple appeal of a man to a woman.

'Won't you take that thing off and lie down beside me?' he whispered.

Bell's heart was thudding in her chest. It would be so easy, so easy that it frightened her. The fear made her voice high and unnatural as she answered.

'No. No, I won't. Please don't spoil things. I can't.'

'Can't, for Chrissake. Aren't you too old for cockteasing?' His eyes were sparking with anger and frustration. 'Listen to me, then. I'm through with begging you for it. It isn't my style. But I know you want it, darling, just as much as I do except that you're not honest enough to admit it. Remember that when the time does come, you will have to ask me. Right? Now go outside while I get dressed. Otherwise I might offend your maidenly modesty.'

Bell picked up her canvas holdall and closed the bedroom door behind her. For an instant she felt angry at being dismissed so abruptly, but the anger quickly subsided. The pink sitting-room looked very empty, and there was no sound from behind the bedroom door. Bell remembered that all Las Vegas lay beneath their windows, and crossed the room to peer through the blinds. She had imagined seeing it all with Valentine, and without him the prospect was dauntingly lonely. Damn. Bell frowned. He annoyed her, and he didn't play according to the rules. Yet, despite herself, he had slid under her skin, and now she realized that she didn't want to spend the day without him.

Well, that was too bad. She would go out on her own anyway, and leave him to his own devices. Quickly Bell pulled on her clothes and then stepped silently out into the anonymous hotel corridor. She looked left and right, trying to remember the direction of the elevator she had taken on the way up, and then almost ran down the dim peachy-pink tunnel towards it. She had no idea where she was going, but it was imperative to get away from Valentine for as long as it took her to regain some self-possession and to think two or three things out.

Bell took the elevator to the lower ground floor. When the doors rolled open she saw, across a paved area dotted with pink-shaded tables, the blue of the swimming pool. It was almost empty, winking invitingly in the late afternoon sun. Within minutes Bell was in the water, slicing through the lengths faster and faster, punishing herself and her whirling thoughts into exhausted submission. When she could swim no further she hauled herself out and lay gasping on a sunbed. The sun burnt two dull coppery discs on to the retinas of her closed eyes, and still the questions came flooding back. Charles, Catherine, Valentine. Valentine, Catherine, Charles. How had she got caught up in all this?

Bell sat up. She was, she realized, very hungry. She promised herself that she would eat first and think afterwards. A waiter in a pink jacket was passing.

'Can you bring me something to eat out here?' she asked him.

'Sure.'

'I'll have – oh, a chicken sandwich on rye, lots of mayonnaise, and a salad on the side with french dressing. Two apples, and a big glass of milk.'

While she ate Bell distracted herself by watching the other guests around the pool. They were mostly carefully-presented women well into middle age. Their eyes were hidden behind saucer-sized sunglasses and only the slightest movements of their heads gave away the fact that they missed none of the comings and goings between the pool and the tables.

The other sunbathers were young men. Their smoothly-oiled bodies were conspicuous among the ranks of minutely corrugated older flesh. The boys mostly wore very thin nylon racing trunks, and they strolled to and fro unselfconsciously with their towels and combs and packs of cigarettes. As Bell watched, one of them bent and flicked a lighter for a red-lipped woman in a turban. The muscles in his legs tautened and then relaxed as he moved. Bell was smiling inwardly when a shadow fell across her sunbed. It was cast by a fair-haired giant with small eyes and a mouthful of very white teeth. He winked at her.

'Hi there. Mind if I join you? You look kinda lonely.'

Bell frowned. She could think of nothing that she wanted less.

'I'd rather you didn't. I have some thinking to do, and I always think better alone.'

'Aw, don't be like that. I'll buy you a drink. What's that, milk for Chrissake?'

'Please go away. I don't want to be picked up.'

He grinned down at her, unabashed.

'Suit yourself. See you around,' and he strolled away.

Bell sighed and closed her eyes, tight. Now she would have to think. Valentine, upstairs or wherever he was at this moment, had shot his little dart home. Cocktease he had called her, and it rankled. She prided herself on being too direct, and too liberated, for games like that. But she also knew that he was partly right. Bell was angry with him for the assumptions that he had made about her, and for the situations that he had manoeuvred her into. She counted them off in her head. First, when they had barely met, challenging her with his nakedness. Then sexy jets of hot water in the jacuzzi. Then a double suite, and the calculated vulnerability of him asleep in the next bed. Then the guileless, straight-from-the-heart appeal he had just made. He had manipulated her, and it angered her even more that he had done it successfully. She felt hot and uncomfortable, and she recognized the signs. It was barely-suffocated desire. It was no use pretending, she did want him.

But if he had manipulated her, she had been aware that she attracted him – and had enjoyed it. She had played herself up for him. Subconsciously, or even consciously, it didn't really matter. Could she blame him for responding to that, or for his openly-admitted aims? Not really.

Well, what to do about all this, she asked herself coldly. This was America. Nevada, California, strange places, a month out of her real life. It was a little capsule of quite clearly defined time, more than half over already. Ahead of her lay the certainty that she must go to Charles. She felt the pull of him like a magnet. Yet now, in the meantime, why not a kind of celebration? As a farewell to the independence she had fought for. It was, after all, the end of her uncommitted life. From now on, after California, she would belong to Charles – just as she had promised.

But, here and now, there was no denying the strength of her attraction to Valentine. It was beginning to be irresistible. As soon as she let herself admit it Bell felt a lead weight lifting from her shoulders. She thought quickly. Couldn't she give herself, out here in this unquestioning New World, to an attractive man – without it meaning a betrayal of Charles? Their two worlds couldn't be further apart, and neither of them need overshadow the other.

And yet, and yet.

Valentine wasn't just any man. He was Charles's enemy. That mattered. It was that, and not the bare fact of sleeping with another man, that was destructive.

Bell stared down the length of the pool. The young men were still strolling up and down, enjoying the display of their own bodies. The women watched them, smiling and appreciative. One dark-haired Latin-looking boy bent down to whisper something to a heavily-oiled middle-aged woman and she nodded with pleasure, then laughed.

It doesn't matter to any of these people, Bell thought. Sex is just another pleasure, like eating and sunbathing. Just as it is to Valentine. Should it matter so very much what I do now, in these days before I go to Charles? Yes, came back her conscience's answer, but the rest of her disagreed. Go on, she told herself, take what you want from Valentine out here. Think of it as a celebration, if you like, of finding out at last what it really is that you want. Then go home and leave him behind you.

Bell nodded slowly. She knew how it should be with Valentine. Clean, cathartic, no strings attached, and to their mutual satisfaction.

Yes. She would do it. In this little bubble of unreal time, it could hurt no one.

Bell turned over to let the sun warm her back and smiled blindly into the stuffy canvas headrest.

It would be a relief to turn from quarry into hunter. She would enjoy that as much as she would enjoy confronting

Valentine with a different Bell. Oh yes, she would enjoy it. But she would have to choose her moment carefully . . . the right time and the right place . . . drifting comfortably between fantasies and sleep Bell lay and luxuriated in the sun.

When the sun dipped down towards California and slipped behind the tallest hotel block, Bell sat up again and stretched. She was determined to avoid Valentine for a few more hours. In her present mood, solitude suited her. So she swung her legs off the sunbed, picked up her holdall and went to look for somewhere to change. The ladies' room on the ground floor was an empty expanse of pink marble and mirrors. She washed, pinned up her hair and made her face up carefully. In her bag was a plain cream dress, cut like a collarless shirt. She put it on with a pair of high-heeled bright blue strappy sandals and pulled a length of soft blue leather tight around her waist. With a dab of *Chloë* at her throat she was ready to see Las Vegas.

The ivory bangle glowed against her tanned forearm as she hoisted her bag over her shoulder and walked out into the foyer. As an afterthought she stopped to buy a large gin and tonic in the bar, then pushed through the Pink Slipper's revolving doors and out on the Strip.

Night was coming with desert-like suddenness. Almost as she stood there the light softened, dimmed and ebbed away to the west. Garish neon sprang out to replace it and the pulse of the city quickened. The snarls of traffic were thickening and horn blasts cut through the different levels of tinny music pouring out of the hotels. Bell began to idle along the sidewalk, peering in the windows of the junky souvenir shops and wondering who would want a plastic roulette wheel ashtray mounted on a mock-onyx stand.

Everyone else was walking quickly, intent on getting somewhere else fast, and no one even glanced at her.

Las Vegas turned out to be a very easy place to be alone.

Bell slipped unobtrusively in and out of a row of identical flashy hotels. She sat on bar stools sipping drinks and watching the dancers high-kicking through their various routines. There were cow-girls in silver fringes twirling silver pistols, girls in tiny stars-and-stripes suits with top hats and canes, girls with tall feathered headdresses and almost nothing else. In between the dancers came singers and comedians in velvet or sequined tuxedos. No one looked at any of them. All eyes were on the rotating drums of the fruit machines, on the ball trickling around the slots of the roulette wheels, or the cards slipping out of the dealers' black shoes.

By about ten o'clock Bell was on her sixth drink. She was beginning to feel very slightly lonely, and sorry for herself. It occurred to her that she might just as well turn back to the Pink Slipper and find Valentine. Then, whichever singer it was at whichever hotel she was in, began to sing – badly – 'The Green, Green Grass of Home'. Bell knew that it was ridiculous, and part of her was already laughing sceptically at her sentimentality, but in spite of that the tears began to prick behind her eyelids. The green, green grass of home meant England to her, damp and misty in September and redolent of leaves and woodsmoke. It was so far, so very far away. What was she doing in this horrible place anyway?

It was too late to stifle a sob, and the first two tears were already hot on her cheeks.

'Well,' a voice drawled beside her, 'it doesn't look as though thinking agrees with you.'

It was the tow-haired giant from beside the swimming pool. Immediately Bell screwed her face up to dam the tears and sniffed, once, hard.

'I told you. I don't want to be picked up. I'm – with somebody.'

'And I told you that you could suit yourself. But I don't like to see a pretty girl crying on a bar stool all on her own. I'm just about to take a break and go for a pizza. You want to come and tell me all about it?'

'No, I don't. Oh, *shit*. All right.' She might just as well, as sit here alone.

He put out a huge freckled hand and helped her down from the stool. And so Bell found herself sitting in a rustic pizza bar where all the wooden decor was made out of plastic, and everything else was red and white checks festooned with empty chianti bottles.

The giant sat opposite her shovelling triangles of pizza into his mouth and nodding encouragingly as she told him everything. Charles, Valentine, Catherine, Juliette, Hélène. Catholicism, jacuzzis, divorce, promises and compromises all came tumbling out. The good-humoured face beamed at her as she finished and he crammed the last of her untouched pizza into his mouth.

'So what's the problem? You've got the bad guy out here, all nice and tidy, and once you've got him out of your system, back you go to Bord-oh or wherever it is and the good guy. Simple. Only wish my life was like that.'

'You really think so?'

'Sure. Trust your own instincts, baby. Don't screw things up by making them too complicated. All this uptight talk about guilt and betrayal is garbage.'

Bell grinned back at him, and his hairy paw, matted with coarse blond hairs, swamped hers.

'Thanks. You helped a lot just by listening. I don't even know your name. I think I must be a bit drunk,' she finished lamely.

'Jim.'

Two cups of greyish coffee arrived and Bell seized hers gratefully.

'Do you live here? What do you do?'

'Yeah. I'm an actor, but I have to fill in a little with other things from time to time. This and that; bartending, lifeguard jobs, you know.'

'Yes I do. I saw you this afternoon, remember? What's it like?'

The heavy face reddened slightly and Bell wished she had kept quiet. But the little scenes that she had watched beside the pool fascinated her.

'Sorry. I didn't mean to pry.'

'That's okay. And don't knock it. Some of those ladies are harmless, lonely, and it helps them. I'm good, you know.'

Bell was sure that he was. Even if only as a very good listener. She drained her coffee and stood up.

'Look, I must go. Thanks, Jim, for this evening. Let me at least pay for us. Over there?'

'I've paid,' he said briefly. Then he added, almost inaudibly, 'I suppose you don't feel like getting laid?'

She did, but not by any king-sized professional. She said, gently, 'Well, no. Thanks, anyway. What would you have . . .' but he cut her short.

'Jesus, nothing. Are you kidding? With someone like you?'

'I'm flattered,' she said, meaning it. 'Goodbye.' She reached out to touch his hairy arm, and then pushed her way out through the plastic doors.

It seemed a long way back to where the champagne bottle was still pouring golden light into the fluorescent slipper. When she reached the pink suite it was empty, but the frothy pink covers on Valentine's bed were tossed and rumpled. Beside the bed there was an ashtray half full of lipsticked butts. Bell picked up the ashtray, biting back her distaste, and tipped the whole thing into the wastebasket.

I suppose I asked for this, she thought. But that doesn't make it any pleasanter. She shut the door resolutely on the sight of the unmade bed and went off to find him.

It wasn't difficult.

He was playing roulette at the same table. In Bell's seat beside him was a plump luscious-looking girl with a petulant expression. They glanced up at her simultaneously, and she saw at once that Valentine was drunk. The usually clear whites of his eyes were bloodshot and his stare was glassy. The girl slid off her seat immediately. She put her hand out, calmly picked up half of the pile of pink chips from in front of Valentine, and snapped her handbag shut on them.

''Bye, honey,' she said. 'Thanks for everything.'

Valentine didn't even look at her. To Bell he said, 'Have a drink? Join me. I'm having a wonderful time.'

Bell shook her head.

'Let's go upstairs. Get some sleep and then get out of here.'

'Upstairs, eh? Sounds wunnerful. Lead on, Lady Macbeth.'

As soon as they were back in the pink suite, he seemed to sober up effortlessly.

He stood for a moment staring contemptuously at the rumpled mess of his bed, and then at the smooth surface of

Bell's. When she came out of the bathroom, ready for bed, he shot her a single cold glance.

'Somehow this room doesn't appeal any more. I'm going to sleep on the couch in there.' He jerked his head. 'Goodnight.'

Bell watched him go, smarting under the icy sneer in his voice. Perversely, the coldness in him drew her even more, making her want to follow him and try to dispel it. She thought suddenly that the sharpness might be his way of hiding hurt, and the realization gave a new dimension to her view of his familiar charm. If the hurt was her fault, then she wanted to ease it, for friendship's sake. Then Bell remembered with a tinge of bitterness that they didn't seem to be friends any more.

They had left Las Vegas without regret.

Over a sketchy, almost silent breakfast in the Pink Slipper Coffee'n'Do-nut Bar, Valentine had dropped something on the plastic table top with an unpleasant clatter. Bell saw the blue-and-white quartering of his key fob and looked at him in surprise. He was pale and tired.

'You drive,' he said, and she had pocketed the car keys without asking any questions.

They had barely spoken again until Las Vegas was way behind them and the car was beginning to wind up to the brown heights of the Sierra Nevada. Bell was absorbed in her driving, enjoying the vicious thrust of the acceleration and the snaky challenge of the road as they climbed steadily westwards.

Valentine said, 'You're good. There's something very sexy about a woman who drives like a man and enjoys doing it.'

Bell beamed at him, forgetting the tense atmosphere between them.

'Thanks.'

'We'd better have our spin on the bikes soon. Can you ride? You'd enjoy it.'

'I'd rather be your pillion passenger.'

'We'll go up the coast, perhaps, in a couple of days.'

'Yes, let's do that.'

After another silence he said, 'I can't say that I'm sorry to be getting back. At least tell me that the trip has cured your restlessness.'

She smiled at him. 'It's cured my restlessness.'

It was two days later that Bell was sitting in the rocking chair amongst the fantastic clutter of Valentine's room. The crevices of china shepherdesses and the smooth planes of metal sculptures were all gleaming, free of the pervasive white dust of summer. Joannie had obviously been hard at work. Bell rocked contemplatively to and fro, her eyes wandering in amusement from piece to piece. She felt very tranquil and sure of herself. Their days since Vegas had been a kind of truce. Valentine had disappeared to the winery for long hours and Bell had written one and a half columns. When they met they had been polite and considerate to each other.

Now, Bell thought, it was time for her celebration.

Valentine came in with a pitcher of fresh orange juice. In his thin white shirt and blue jeans he looked almost as young as the boys in the winery. He handed her a glass of juice, and their fingers touched. For a second, neither of them moved.

'I have recovered from my wounds a little,' he said at last. 'Let's go to a party tonight. It's on the coast, north of the Bay. Old friends of mine from Berkeley. What d'you say?' Their eyes still held each other's, waiting.

'Yes. Let me drink this, then I'll go and change.'

'Dress warm,' he called after her. 'We'll go on the bike.'

When she came back in her bright blue clown's trousers and a low-buttoned scarlet shirt that clung to her figure he raised an eyebrow.

'You look like something out of a painting. Lautrec, I think.' She noticed that there were fine creases at the corners of his eyes. Why had she never seen them before? Because he had never looked at her in precisely this way?

'. . . but I did say *warm*.'

She held out a scarlet zippered tracksuit top and he took it from her. When she had slipped her arms into it she leant back against him and his arms came around her shoulders. She felt the warmth of his breath in her hair. Neither of them spoke until he turned her firmly around to face him.

'Would you rather stay here?' he whispered.

She found that her voice came out husky, quite unlike itself.

'Take me to the party. I'm looking forward to the ride.'

He drove very slowly on the big black and silver Kawasaki. She clung with her arms around his waist, learning how to lean her weight with his as they cornered and straightened. She loved the breadth of his shoulders sheltering her from the wind and the rich night scents that rushed past her. It was nothing like riding in a car.

Nor was the party like the gatherings they had been to in Napa. The people were much younger, long haired and dressed with echoes of hippiedom. The rooms in the little house were crowded and redolent with the sweet-musty smell of marijuana. The music, deafeningly, was Fairport Convention as well as Bruce Springsteen.

'Pretty laid back, wouldn't you say?' whispered Valentine.

Unusually, he never left her side all evening. They danced a little, ate some food, joined a circle out on the porch who were passing joints around. As always, Bell found that it gave her pins and needles and then made her feel sleepy. The evening trickled on and she began to feel stifled by the conscious gentleness of it all. There was an itch under her skin that was getting harder and harder to ignore.

Beside her Valentine was laughing lazily and lighting up another joint.

'Relax,' he told her. 'You wanted to come.'

'Now I want to go. Please. There are too many people here, and it's you I want to be with.'

His face was expressionless behind the smoke, but his eyes were watching her avidly.

'Are you asking me?'

Valentine wanted his moment of victory. Bell shut her eyes. In a second it would be too late.

Charles. No, not at this instant. She would think about him later.

'Yes, damn you. *I'm asking you.*'

Roughly he pulled her to her feet.

'God help you if you change your mind now.'

Then they were on the bike again, moving fast, and she was

pressing her face blindly into the leather shoulder of his jacket. He was pushing the machine to its threatening limit. In front of her his dark shape was crouched so low that she was no longer sheltered. The speed tore her hair back from her scalp and scoured the tears out of her eyes.

Faster and faster. The lights along the highway ran together in a blur and she was gasping for breath. She ground her teeth and prayed, wordlessly, for him to stop. But they screamed on through the night encapsulated in their solitary speed. They swooped so low on the bends that Bell's eyes screwed shut and her hands dug into his jacket in her certainty that they would hit the road. She saw against her eyelids the huddled shape of her own body on the gravel and the blood and grit cloaking it. *Stop*, she moaned, but the word was snatched out of her mouth and lost in the hurricane. Oncoming headlights dazzled her for a split second and were gone. As they howled past other cars she caught the brief, dim blasts of their horns before distance swallowed them. She wondered, giddily, just how fast they could be going. It was faster than she had ever believed possible, and faster, until the wind was smashing against her like a solid wall. Fear engulfed her in terrible sick waves, and somewhere knotted up with the fear was excitement, salt and physical. It came with an unformed wish that must have been a death wish that the machine would explode in a roar of sparks, and that she and Valentine would explode with it.

Once, only, his head jerked round to look at her and she saw in terror that there was a kind of craziness in his streaming eyes. Then there was only the crest of his black hair blown backwards. He flung them over to the left, right again, upright for a blessed instant and the whiplash kiss of an insect exploding against her cheek, then cornering again and the road slicing up to meet the pitiful fragility of her bones and skin.

Then, unbelievably, he was slowing down. With a wrenching turn they were bumping down a track and she could smell the salt in the air. The ocean, somewhere up ahead. She was trembling; her arms felt so weak that she was afraid that she couldn't cling on any more. They were on sand and Valentine's arms were braced to keep the front wheel from losing its purchase on the shifting surface. The bike bucked and slithered and Valentine cursed softly.

At last there was coarse grass brushing around their thighs. With a quick jerk of his right arm Valentine closed the throttle and the roar of the engine died into a gentle throb and then silence.

Bell let her head fall forward against his shoulder and tears ran down her cheeks. The ringing in her ears slowly subsided, and she could hear the sound of the surf, very close at hand.

'You bastard,' was all she could say, and her voice sounded like a feeble gust of wind in the seagrass. She wanted to rain punches on his face and chest, but her arms felt so leaden that she couldn't have lifted them. The terror had wiped all other sensation out of her.

Valentine's arms came around her and he lifted her effortlessly off the bike. With the tips of his fingers he brushed the tears away from her cheeks. His mouth found hers and for a second she hung motionless in his grip, her head forced back by the pressure of his kiss.

Then, into the vacuum left by the ebb of terror, a different sensation started to flow. It came in liquid waves, rolling from the centre of her physical being and drowning everything, until the whole world except her need for Valentine was submerged and forgotten. With a stifled gasp she let her hands reach up into his tumbled black hair. She pulled his face down to hers so hard that their bones jarred and the stubble of his beard rasped her lips. Her mouth opened to his searching tongue, hungry for it.

At the moment when she knew that she could stand up no longer, Valentine reached out to one of the bike's sleek panniers. He shook a blanket out on to the soft sand and she sank down on to it, pulling him down beside her, careless of everything but his nearness.

His hands were shaking as he unbuttoned her shirt. His fingers slid over the planes of her ribcage and, at last, the roundness of her breasts. Bell's body convulsed in a grinding ache of longing as his mouth came down on her nipples, teasing and circling. Her teeth clenched and her hands went to the belt of his jeans. She had to touch him, discover him for herself. For a few seconds they were caught in the prisons of their clothes. Then, freed at last, she felt the hard maleness of him lying all along the electric sensitivity of her skin. She moaned, once, afraid that she could hold on no longer. Her hands went down to try and guide him into her but he arched himself away.

'Please. Oh, please,' she whispered, her mouth against the curves of his closed eyelids. Her throat was dry with fire.

'Wait.'

Then his mouth was slipping away, down over the smoothness of her belly to the heat and wetness of her longing for him. Again his tongue was probing, caressing her closer and closer to the brink of the explosion. Her fingers knotted in his hair and her back arched. Her eyes were staring sightlessly at the wheeling stars in the thick sky.

It was too late. She was crying out, helpless, but then his mouth was on hers again, slick and salt, and he was inside her. Their bodies bucked in unison, clung and rolled and stretched again. Valentine's groan came from deep in his chest and was drawn out through the warm night. For Bell, the sky exploded into a million fragments of black and silver light, reflecting the bursting dam and then the delicious waves of release that tore inside her.

Valentine shuddered into stillness and his head flopped damp against her breast. Beneath him Bell lay blind and transfixed, her fingers unconsciously circling in the white sand. It seemed hours before the stars reassembled themselves into the familiar constellations and she blinked at the reddish moon hanging on the horizon of her field of vision. Sound slowly seeped back into the world. There was the shush of the warm breeze in the grass and the muffled roar of the surf ahead.

She shivered involuntarily and Valentine rolled, slipping away from her, to cocoon them in the weight of the blanket. They lay in silence, staring into each other's eyes, mouths almost touching. Bell listened absently to the breaking waves. The night was calm and utterly, luminously peaceful. One star, brighter than the rest, caught her attention. She whispered, almost to herself, 'The moving waters at their priestlike task . . .'

Valentine leaned over her once more, blotting out the sky. He kissed her eyebrows and her cheekbones.

'. . . of pure ablution round earth's human shores,' he finished for her, and then stopped the surprise with his mouth before she could utter it. Gratefully she abandoned herself to him. This time their love-making was infinitely slow. They explored the recesses of each other's bodies with tongues and fingertips, as if they were blind. This time the silence that had hung between them was dispelled. They murmured to each other their needs and sensations as honestly as children. Bell found that he was gentle in coaxing her body, steely in his control of his own. When at length he entered her again, it was to move maddeningly slowly, drawing shuddering thrills through her as he withdrew to the very tip and then pressed inexorably back again. The rhythm grew faster and he drove deeper until she cried out, once, at the very threshold. His own low moan answered her and, through her own intense pleasure, she felt him pulsing deep inside her.

Afterwards an extraordinary languid sweetness engulfed her. All the tension that had vibrated between them was gone. She fell asleep in his arms, her hair dampened with their sweat tangled across his face.

'Wake up, darling,' he said at last. 'I want to take you home to bed. The open air is all very well for the young . . .'

Bell laughed softly, stretching luxuriously as she remembered, and his fingers spanned the taut skin over her ribs. The surf was still pounding over the beach. Bell stood up, supple in the moonlight, and he gazed up at her.

'Let's swim first,' she said. 'Come on.'

They ran towards the water, their heels kicking up plumes of fine sand as they went. The sea was creamy-white with foam as they plunged in, gasping at the cold and shouting with laughter. They rolled and dived in and out of the waves and then he grappled her and they fell sideways in the spray, wrestling each other's slippery limbs. Bell wriggled free like an eel and ran away back up the beach, with Valentine stumbling after her. They reached the grassy hollow where the bike was parked, panting and exhausted. There were no towels so they rubbed each other in turn with the coarse blanket. Bell's skin tingled and glowed as he helped her back into her crumpled, sandy clothes. He wrapped his leather jacket around her and zipped it up to the chin.

'It'll be cold on the way back,' he said.

She looked up into the blue eyes. The familiar sparkle of challenge had given way to a relaxed gleam of triumph but she couldn't find it in herself to resent it. It had been a kind of victory for Valentine, but it was partly hers too – although he wouldn't guess that yet. Her subconscious told her that she should regret nothing, but she didn't let herself think beyond that now. And he was a fantastic lover. She would make the most of it, her celebration, in the days that were left.

'What a strange mixture you are,' was all she said. 'On the way here you nearly killed us both, now you worry about me catching a chill.' Her eyes softened. 'And you take my favourite lines from my favourite poem right out of my mouth.'

Valentine swung his leg over the bike and kicked it into a deafening roar. He jerked his head for her to climb on behind him. She did so, and wound her arms tightly around his waist.

'Don't you know that extremes of sensation heighten one another?' he asked wickedly.

'I didn't, in practice, but I do now,' she shouted back over the throb of the bike's engine.

'And you don't have a monopoly on sensitivity. Or romantic poetry. In fact I can lay claim to a whole lot of things that you wouldn't give me credit for. But we'll see about that.' He eased out the clutch and the bike began to slither away across the sand.

'Please drive slowly,' she begged, and his head nodded.

It felt the most natural thing in the world to slip beside Valentine into his king-sized bed back at Dry Stone. She noticed that his night-table was piled high with books, with a 200-capsule size phial of sleeping tablets on top. The room itself was bare, and restful like her own guest room, but the curtains were heavy to keep out as much as possible of the bright Californian light. On the wall opposite the foot of the bed was a water-colour of a château. It was less formally grand than Reynard, and without Reynard's commanding position, but the colour of the stone and the architectural similarity was unmistakable. It must be Château Larue-Grise, once the home of Hélène de Gillesmont's family and now owned by Valentine's consortium.

Bell turned her head away deliberately.

Valentine was lying on his back beside her and he stretched out his arm companionably to draw her closer. She rested her head on his shoulder and studied the angles of his face.

'You sleep badly?'

He shrugged.

'Sometimes. Who needs it, anyway, when there's so much else to do in bed?'

'Like reading biographies?' She nodded at the pile of books.

'Well no, not altogether like reading biographies. Care for a demonstration?'

'Tomorrow.' Bell stretched to turn out the light and then curled back against him so that her body fitted smoothly into his. 'Goodnight.'

Yet it was Valentine who drifted into sleep first. The warm weight of Bell's body beside him was soothing and for a few hours the nagging restlessness that kept him awake was gone. Somehow this English journalist pleased him and entertained him in a way that dozens of other girls hadn't. She needled him, and her occasional sharpness stimulated him. Valentine was smiling faintly when sleep overtook him.

Bell lay motionless beside him until his breathing slowed and deepened. Then she inched away from his arms until she was lying in her own space. She stared through the darkness towards the spot where the little painting hung. Everything about it, from the colour of the light playing on the stone to the steep slope of the roof pierced with its row of little windows, brought back the smell and taste of Reynard. Part of her leapt to blank that memory out, suppress it utterly before she had to think about the place, or any of the people who belonged to it. Charles seemed impossibly far away from her now, but still guilt and regret were beginning to dull the happy satisfaction of her night with Valentine. Yet in spite of herself and what she had let herself do tonight, Bell clung to the image of Charles that lived endlessly inside her head. She went on reiterating the wordless promise she had made to him in spite of the flesh and blood of the man sleeping beside her. Already she knew Valentine Gordon much better than the enigmatic and tortured Frenchman, but it was Charles that she wanted. The American even surprised her with flashes of another, hidden Valentine quite unlike the one the world saw. But still, inside the little room where her real self lived, only Charles could come.

It was a long time before she could give herself up to sleep and all too soon afterwards she became aware of someone nudging her back into consciousness. Bell's dream of Hélène sitting at her salon work-table with Valentine's picture in the silver frame receded slowly. It was daylight. Bell found herself looking up into the face of the real Valentine.

He looked rested, relaxed and infuriatingly cocksure.

'Welcome to my bed. At last. Don't you think we should make up for lost time?'

She wound her arms lazily round his neck and pulled him down to her.

'Mmmm. Maybe we should, at that.'

He began kissing her again, expertly and thoroughly, and she fell back against the pillows with a small sigh of pleasure. Then, over Valentine's shoulder, she saw the bedroom door swing slowly open. Joannie was standing there with a tray in her hand. A little pot of coffee, one cup and saucer, one glass of orange juice. There was an idiotic feather duster tucked under one arm and she was wearing nothing but a tiny bikini. Breakfast for her hero and then perhaps a little romp afterwards.

When she saw them her face went white and her eyes and mouth widened into three perfect circles. Valentine felt Bell stiffen underneath him and glanced round.

'Jesus Christ, Joannie, will you get out of here?' She dropped the tray and ran away without a backward glance.

'Oh shit,' groaned Valentine. 'Trouble.'

'You asked for it,' Bell said calmly. 'Does she always bring you breakfast wearing practically nothing but an expectant smile?'

'Don't be a bitch,' he said shortly. 'It doesn't suit you.' He pushed the covers back, pulled on a bathrobe and crunched over the china and spilled coffee in the doorway. 'I'd better go and see that she doesn't do anything else stupid.'

That's right, thought Bell. Try to keep them all happy. She felt obscurely irritated by the little scene. And perhaps a trace of jealousy. He ought to be here with her, not running around the verandah after some teenager just because she had the hots for him. Then Bell caught herself up short. Wrong, she told herself. Not at all what you should be thinking. Clean, clinical, cathartic and then all over with, that's what this affair is. Meditatively she put on her own robe and went to see what was happening.

Joannie had flung herself face down on one of the cushioned loungers on the verandah. She was sobbing uninhibitedly when Valentine padded up and put his hand on her shoulder. She whirled round at once.

'You don't understand, do you? I love you, Valentine. You're the only person in the world that matters to me, and you do this . . .' she waved her hand towards his bedroom window, '. . . all the time.' The sobs redoubled. 'I thought you cared about me. I thought that one day . . .'

Valentine caught her wrists and said, soothingly, 'Joannie, baby, I do care about you.'

'Because I'm such a nice little girl? I'd die for you.'

She threw herself back on the cushions and cried even harder. Valentine looked down at her, exasperated.

'Oh God, what nonsense. You've imagined all this.'

Bell came towards them along the white-painted boards.

'Why don't you leave me with Joannie for a bit?'

He went, with obvious relief. Joannie's voice was muffled but defiant.

'Go away.'

Bell sat down beside her and said, as gently as she could, 'Horrible, isn't it? I'm sorry you had to see that in there.'

The girl looked round at her now, her face reddened and her eyes streaming.

'Sorry? Why should you be sorry? You've got him, haven't you? The only man I'll ever care about . . . ohhhh, Valentine.'

Bell put her arms around her and rocked her to and fro as if she was a child.

'I haven't got him, Joannie. He makes his own rules, and we should do the same. Be a bit prouder of yourself. Give yourself a chance to see some more of life before making all-or-nothing choices. I know it sounds like a lot of preachy crap, but I have got ten years' experience on you, remember. Honestly, you'll still be falling in and out of love when you've forgotten all about Valentine Gordon.'

Joannie shook her head, quite certain.

'Oh no. There'll never be anyone like him in my life. He's so funny, and clever, and sexy. The others are just kids.'

What about vain, and self-centred, and arrogant too, thought Bell, while we're listing his qualities. As well as absurdly generous, unpredictable and inventive.

'Yes, he's all those, but he's other things too. Nobody's ever perfect. Try to see all round him, instead of just loving an idea.'

There was lots more in the same vein. They sat talking for an hour and then Joannie followed her inside when Bell went to shower and dress. She was mollified now, trying out a wounded but calm dignity that looked very comical on her round, smiley face. When Bell came out of the bathroom, she found her twirling the ivory bracelet round and round in her fingers.

'Pretty.'

'Yes. It was given to me by a man that I love. And can't have. Yet, anyway.'

The girlish heart-to-heart must have affected me too, thought Bell.

'Wow. What's he like?'

'Oh, clever and sexy. Funny, sometimes. Also hurt and lonely and difficult. He's a very long way away, and I wish he wasn't.'

'Wow. What're you doing with Val, then?'

Good question.

'Ummmm. Well, sometimes it's easier, and more en-

joyable, to swim with the tide rather than make a big deal out
of a refusal. So long as you keep your own rules straight in
your head, and don't go about hurting people gratuitously.
Can you understand that?'

'Yeah, I think so. Look, Bell, I've got to go home. Will you
come with me to say goodbye to him?'

Joannie had put a T-shirt and a knee-length skirt on over
her bikini. She looked positively demure. They found
Valentine working beside the pool.

''Bye, Valentine. If it's okay with you, I won't be coming in
to clean up for a while. Exams, y'know.'

He smiled at her, all brilliant blue eyes and warmth. Bell
could certainly understand what the kid saw in him.

'That's okay, Joannie. See you around.'

'I don't think so.' Very dignified now.

They followed her around to the front of the house and
watched her ride the hiccupping Honda off down the track.

'Thanks, Bell. That was nice of you and I appreciate it.' He
took her hand and she squeezed it back.

'Be careful about her from now on?'

'Yes.' He sighed. 'I'll be sorry not to have her around the
place any more, though. She is such a peach. But talking of
which, before we were interrupted . . .'

Laughing, they went back into the house together.

The last week of Bell's stay in California was idyllic. As soon
as Valentine had got what he wanted, which was Bell in his
bed beside him, he was like a child with a lavish birthday
present. He couldn't do enough to make her happy. Bell made
a final round of interviews and winery tours. She sat in the sun
in the afternoons collating her notes and scribbling drafts of
future pieces. She and Valentine staged some impromptu
tastings for themselves, sipping their way down a line of
bottles, but not spitting out the luscious mouthfuls of
Californian sunshine. They would get slightly and hilariously
drunk together, splash boisterously in the pool, then make
inventive love in Valentine's wide bed. It was all exactly as
Bell had hoped it would be. Innocent, happy, clear-cut and
not remotely threatening.

One evening Valentine leant over her desk and found her,

guiltily belated, writing a pile of postcards. The one to Charles and Juliette, which read simply 'There's nothing and nowhere like Bordeaux, love Bell', was safely hidden at the bottom of the pile. On the obverse of an improbably bright blue picture of San Francisco Bay, Alcatraz in the foreground and the Golden Gate Bridge in the distance, Bell was writing a message to Phillippa Gregory, the fashion editor of her London newspaper. Bell and Phillippa shared an office, and always exchanged postcards. 'Everything in California much bigger and better than I'd expected. xxxxB.' Valentine burst out laughing.

'I should hope so, too.' Idly he picked up another card and looked at the address. 'And who is Edward Brooke?'

'Oh, just an old friend. Now.'

'I see.' He was looking at her speculatively, for once without the habitual ripples of amusement showing in his face. 'Considering that we're getting to know each other quite well, we don't know all that much about each other's lives, do we?'

Bell leant back in her chair and grinned up at him.

'Okay. History time. You go first.'

He obviously enjoyed telling her his version of his life story. He played down all the achievements to make it sound more like every American boy's progress. His childhood had been spent in Santa Monica where his father was in real estate. It had been a comfortably middle-class, comfortably happy home. He had three sisters, pretty, giggly and adoring, but Valentine had always been the clever one. The pride of his parents and the envy of his sisters' friends.

'Just like you've seen in the movies,' he told Bell. 'Soda fountains and baseball games. High school proms and drive-in movies. A life of uninterrupted and totally unquestioning pleasure. Then three years at Berkeley, majoring in women and wine with a little English literature and art history on the side.'

'Keats,' said Bell.

'Naturally Keats,' he smiled back at her.

After that had come his belated experience of adolescent anguish. He had assuaged it with two years wandering in

Europe. He had worked on farms, driven trucks, picked grapes in the heart of the Beaujolais. Then he had stumbled into Bordeaux. It had felt like coming home.

'I met a girl in a café. Marie-Claire. Round face, little round bottom. Pure French, wildly irritating and absurdly sexy. I still write to her. She's married to a farmer up in the Pays d'Auge. But it was the place that really turned me on. I felt that I was really alive for the first time in my life.' There was love and regret in his voice as he talked about the feel of the shallow, gravelly soil along the Gironde and the pearly seaside light. It wasn't just romantic affection. He recalled bitterly hard work, dark winters and the cold mists rising over the low land. And the wine, the wine.

'I remember,' he murmured, 'standing on the vineyard road in the middle of the Médoc, staring in through these rusty gates at a neglected property. The roof needed repairing. The vines should all have been grubbed up and replanted years ago. And I thought what a waste. If only it was mine. Then I thought, why not? Within a month I was back in LA. Doing business. My folks retired to Florida, my sisters were all married. I had some capital, bought myself in up here. I was lucky, it went very well. Five years later that château was bought by a consortium, headed by me.'

For the first time Bell noted a little echo of pride in his voice. Quite justifiable. He was still talking about his other French possessions, telling her that he now owned a little slice of Meursault and several hectares elsewhere along the Cote d'Or, but it was Bordeaux that she wanted to hear about. Curiosity overwhelmed her.

'That was Château Larue-Grise?' she interrupted innocently.

'Mmmm? Yeah. Of course, I forgot you'd know that. It was Larue-Grise, all right. One of the most beautiful, most productive corners of the entire world.'

'You sound as though you miss it.'

He turned to look carefully at her and Bell bit the inside of her lip. She mustn't let him guess from her face that this was anything more than a casual conversation.

'Yes. I miss it,' he said at last.

'Won't you go back there?'

Suspicion was beginning to glitter in his eyes.

'Why do you want to know, Bell? I'd forgotten that you had a little vacation chez de Gillesmont. You must have heard some kind of story.'

'Oh, just that you were friendly with the women, but that you and Charles . . .' There. She'd said his name. '. . . didn't hit it off.'

Valentine let out a snort of derisive laughter.

'Hit it off? Let me tell you, de Gillesmont is one hundred per cent unadulterated shit. Snobbish. Reactionary. Cold as the grave. Sorry if he's a pal of yours, but that's the honest truth.'

Bell breathed in and out evenly to stop the hot, defensive words from tumbling out of her mouth.

'I like him, yes. I like them all. Even Hélène.'

Valentine was smiling sardonically to himself, obviously remembering something. He poured himself half a tumbler of whisky and sat down in his rocking chair.

'I'll tell you about it. It isn't a particularly pretty tale, but something tells me that you've heard more than half of it already. You might as well have my version as well. Who was it, by the way? Jolly little Juliette?'

'Yes. She told me how much she liked you.'

He nodded, unsurprised. There was just enough complacency in his face to irritate Bell. She looked away and out of the long window to the view of the hills. But she was listening carefully.

'Well. Bob Cornelius and I were there at Larue trying to sort things out. There was a hell of a lot of work to be got through. I knew what had to be done to the land, that was no problem, and in the *chais* we got rid of all the antiquated presses and vats and shipped in all the very newest stuff. That was frowned on by our neighbours for a start, not to mention all the rooting up and replanting that was going on under their noses outside. It's still too early to tell with the new vines, of course, and two poor vintages in succession haven't helped, but I'll be proved right in the end.'

There was a new, hard note in his voice. Bell remembered

Charles's reticence about his plans for Reynard. Recalled all the outmoded equipment in his *chais*. She saw quite clearly that Valentine would be proved right. The golden reputation of Château Reynard was a little dimmed already, and positive whispers were circling in the trade about the new regime at Larue-Grise. Damn Valentine.

She went on staring out of the window, trying to look impassive. Valentine took a gulp of whisky.

'I wanted to set the house to rights, make it look like it used to. Naturally I went over to see Hélène de Gillesmont and ask some questions. We got on like a house on fire. I flirted with her a little, ribbed her about all that gracious baronial living . . . you remember, gold cups and silk wallpaper? . . . In no time we were making little trips together to the salerooms in Paris, picking up an escritoire here and a piece of Sèvres there. She's very knowledgeable, and she taught me a lot.'

He waved at some of the delicate bits and pieces scattered incongruously around his California room. Bell understood where they had come from.

'Catherine came with us once or twice.'

'What's she like?' Bell couldn't help herself, but he seemed not to notice the tremor in her voice.

'Very beautiful, immensely chic. Outwardly sweet and docile, pure steel inside. More than a match for that cold fish of a husband. I thought she was fascinating.'

'Really.'

Oh no, not cold, not the way he had touched her and looked at her. Bell was sure of that. But a man with high expectations, of himself and of other people. And awkward morals. Happy, impulsive Valentine Gordon could never begin to understand that.

'Not in the way that you think,' he went on. 'Not then, anyway. As it happens I don't make a habit of screwing other men's wives. Unless they make a particular bee-line for me, in which case that's their own decision. I was interested in Catherine as a specimen of a certain class and culture. Almost extinct. Very European and exotic to a boy from Santa Monica.'

Oh, come *on*, Bell was thinking. You're a red-hot

businessman, an ace manipulator and as sharp as anyone I've ever met. One thing you aren't is a down-home boy from the far West. But still she said nothing.

'No, as a matter of fact it was Juliette I made a little play for. But she was occupied with someone else, so I diverted myself elsewhere too. For a while all was calm and cosy. Except that le baron Charles and I had less than no time for each other.' He drew out the long *Shhh* and rolled the *rrrr* until it sounded ridiculous. 'He hated everything I was doing, just on principle. He even hated me for being American, for Christ's sake. I just thought he was a prick.'

I bet you did, thought Bell, and closed her eyes. Valentine was silent, solemn. They both knew what was coming next.

His voice was much lower when he started talking again.

'Then their kid died. He was terrific, and I'm no great admirer of little children. I can see him now, running down the château steps and shrieking Mama! Papa! when we all got back from somewhere. He had very formal manners, like all those French kids, but he was a mass of mischief and nonsense too. Well, he died. As you know. It all happened in one week. Catherine nearly died too, did die inside her head for a while. And that bastard walked around like he was set in cement. He did nothing for her. No tenderness, no sympathy, no support. She was his wife, remember, with a dead child.'

'He had lost his child too,' Bell said softly. But yes. She could see how hard he must have seemed. Even though her sympathy was for Charles in his own despair and bewilderment, she wished he could have found it in himself to help Catherine.

'Yeah. Well, I expect Juliette told you the next bit. Catherine started coming to see me. Me, almost a stranger. I did what I could, and that meant letting her cry, talking to her about the kid, telling her that it wasn't her fault. I'd put my arms round her. Stroke her hair. Try not to think about ripping all her clothes off, which wasn't easy. One evening she drove over after dinner. They'd had a fight, I think. I kissed her and she responded quite deliberately. So I took her to bed and made her forget everything for an hour. She enjoyed it, Bell. The way she thawed out, it was a miracle. We did it again, the next day. Often, after that, and she started to come back to life.'

Quite the healer. But Bell knew in her heart of hearts that she couldn't condemn him for it. He had done the right thing in his own view.

'So that was how things went on right through the summer. Charles didn't notice anything, or anybody, and Catherine went on getting over it all. At the same time she realized that her marriage was over. I don't think that was anything to do with me, except as a catalyst. She asked me what I thought she should do, but I wouldn't tell her. In the end she decided for herself that she would leave him and go and try to start afresh in Paris. Then, like in all good melodramas, came the showdown. You heard about that, of course?'

'Tell me,' Bell said briefly, not wanting to say any more.

'I gave a party for the vintage. All the de Gillesmonts came, rather to my surprise, together with everyone else in the Médoc. I was, I'm not all that ashamed to say, drunk. And finding it difficult to keep my hands off Catherine. So I took her off into the library, which I'd closed to everyone else because the books are valuable. But, somehow or other, Charles must have seen us in there. He waited until we got back to the party, flushed and dishevelled as they say. Then he jumped up like somebody in a Regency novelette, accused me of stealing his wife and challenged me to a duel.'

He took a long gulp of his drink and Bell saw that he was angry now. His face had flushed a dull red and there were deep vertical lines beside his mouth that she had never seen before.

'This was in front of everyone, from the mayor of Bordeaux to my maître de chail. I just laughed. I thought it was something to do with me being drunk. You know, everything seemed distorted and I thought he was just extra distorted. I told him, into this terrible silence that had fallen, not to be a fool and just to come over and punch me or something. He just turned around and walked off. Very gradually people started talking again, pretending nothing had happened. But I think, and I can't forget it, that I saw surprise at me in their faces. As if they thought I should have accepted the challenge.'

Valentine suddenly leaned forward and buried his head in his hands.

'Jesus, I wish I had. I'd have welcomed the chance to have a crack at him, pistols at dawn or whatever shit he had in mind. Just for Katie's sake.' He sighed and looked up again, across the room to where Bell was still sitting with her head turned away from him. 'That's what happened. Catherine packed up and went. She didn't say goodbye to me. Or him, probably. I'd had enough of Bordeaux so I came home. End of story.'

Bell sat motionless. She felt utterly dislocated. Valentine had told his version so naturally that she was sure it was the real truth. Long, ominous rents were beginning to appear in the fabric of certainty that she had woven around Charles. She felt as though she was going down, very fast, in a dark lift.

The first thing she had to do was get away from Valentine without letting him see how much his story had disturbed her. She stood up, stretched, and feigned a yawn. Then she strolled over to him and kissed the top of his head.

'I don't think you did the wrong thing,' she told him, surprising herself with how casual she could make her voice sound. 'With Catherine, or about the stupid duel. One of you would have got hurt, and what good would that have done? It's just your macho pride that's suffering.'

He nodded, losing interest. 'Probably. Hey, what about going out for some food?'

'I've got a couple of things to do first, and I'm going to have a bath. Can we leave it for an hour?'

'Sure.'

She had escaped. She shut the door of her room behind her and lay down on the bed.

Think. She must think.

Just where did she stand, caught halfway between these two men who hated each other so much? She forced herself to go back, yet again, over what had happened at Reynard. Charles's coolness half-hiding flashes of fire. The way he had, somehow or other, cut right through to her inner self. Even though he had hardly touched her, even though she knew almost nothing about him except the ugly little facts she had just heard for the second time. Somehow she knew she needed him, and he needed her. She remembered the beauty and perfection of Reynard, with Charles as its autocratic master, and shivered a little. It was chilly now in its grandeur, but Bell knew she could change that. She wanted to share the magnificence with Charles, yes, but she wanted to make it a home for him again too. She would be a perfect mistress for Reynard. Their styles were complementary. Charles and she belonged together just as if they had been predestined for one another. Bell was certain of that.

Or, ominously, she had been certain. Charles seemed very dim and ghostly now, not a flesh-and-blood man. She couldn't recall exactly what it was about him that had drawn her so fiercely. And she knew that she didn't even like the man in the story that Valentine had told her.

Perhaps, perhaps. Perhaps it was all a mistake. What if she was quite wrong about both of them? There was a knot of fear and frustration in the pit of Bell's stomach. She wanted to cry, but her eyes stayed hot and dry. Feverishly she clung to the single thing that she was certain of. Valentine had come nowhere near as close to her as Charles. Although she had slept beside him night after night. Although he was just a few feet away, warm and vivid and flesh-and-blood, he mattered less to her than the mere memory of Charles. Maybe that memory was evaporating as fast as mist on a June morning. Maybe she was going to find out that she was horribly and humiliatingly wrong about him. But the memory of him was all she had to cling to in this mess, and cling to it she damn well would. Until Charles himself proved her right. Or wrong.

There was a knock at the door and Valentine came in. His hair was wet from the shower and there were still drops of water on his suntanned shoulders. Their eyes met and in spite of herself Bell felt the familiar tickling warmth begin to radiate through her.

Brutally, she shut off the stream of thoughts running through her skull and reached out to pull him down beside her. Before his own lust carried him away Valentine was surprised at the fever in her. She was writhing and scratching as if she was trying to fight him off, but all the time she was pulling him closer and closer.

'I'm going. Soon,' she whispered savagely. 'Then all this will be over.'

Her nails dug deep into his back. Valentine, misunderstanding completely, thought it was regret in her voice. He smiled his half-complacent smile into her hair and they rolled, locked together, across the crimson bedcover.

CHAPTER SIX

Sticky, late-summer London closed around her. It was suffocating. Bell felt unhappier than she had ever felt before, sickened at herself, and powerless to make the dull despair and anger go away.

Valentine and the golden light of California had faded together like a dream. Oh yes, the trip had been fun in its hedonistic way. Fun for as long as she had been able to stop herself thinking and abandon herself to Valentine's arms and mouth, and to his irresistible good humour. She couldn't help liking him, but as soon as she was apart from him, she felt amazed at what she had done. She had given in to him. What was he after all, under all that laughter and warmth, but a self-centred go-getter with so many notches on his belt that he must have lost count?

How *could* she?

Bitterly, Bell remembered how she had justified it to herself. As a celebration. Celebration *nothing*. A betrayal, that's what it had been. She had made her promise to Charles and then she had swanned straight off and broken it. Given herself to Valentine – *Valentine, of all people* – as thoughtlessly as if she had been handing him yesterday's newspaper.

And she had told Charles that he could trust her.

Charles, Charles. The name echoed inside her head but all it conjured up was more guilt, more bafflement. It hurt her sharply to realize that he had faded too, just like Valentine the interloper. She had fallen in love, she reminded herself. With what? A title, or a profile like a Greek coin?

Or a real man?

If he was a real man, where was he now? Why didn't he telephone, or write, or come and find her? And even if he did, how could she face him after what had happened?

So Bell would pace round and round her flat. It was dusty

and smelt stuffy, but she was too pent-up inside and too listless outside to do anything about it.

London had suffered a long, hot summer. September was dragging out its last days with the threat of a thunderstorm that never came to wash the stained streets. Every breath of air that Bell took tasted as if it had been used before, each Tube ride to and from the newspaper offices was a nightmare of heat and dirt.

Sitting in the office, Bell would alternate bursts of frenzied typing with long intervals sitting staring blankly at the torn calendar on the opposite wall. Even here, the atmosphere was uncomfortable as if another kind of storm was about to break. The paper's sales figures were plummetting and there were uneasy whispers about measures that would have to be taken to effect economies.

Bell barely listened. It was all she could do to focus on getting through the days. She was no more than dimly relieved when she heard that Henry Stobbs had been pleased enough with her California pieces, and her profile of Charles and Château Reynard had already appeared and been forgotten. It had been savagely subbed, but it was just about recognizable. Neutral, non-committal, superficial – it was the best she could have hoped for. Under the circumstances.

Now she was waiting through the slack time that always came at the end of the summer. With the first breath of autumn, there would be new restaurants opening their eager doors, the delights of weather cool and sharp enough to make eating a pleasure again – and the excitement of the vintage.

So Bell drifted through her first week back in London, mechanically going through the motions of life. She deliberately didn't telephone anyone to say that she was back. She didn't feel like talking to any of her friends, even Edward. Especially Edward, who knew her so well that he could see straight through her head and into all the things she was trying to hide.

The following Monday morning, Phillippa Gregory came back from holiday. Bell and the paper's fashion editor had shared a cubicle of an office since the last departmental reshuffle. Phillippa dumped her bulging tote bag on her desk, winked at Bell, and strode the two steps to the window. She clasped the vertical bars and shook them theatrically.

'Caged for another fifty weeks. Just look at it. For this I have left the golden beaches of Crete and the embrace of Nico? Or Piero, or whatever his name was.'

The window looked out at the bottom of a five-storey well. The view was of a litter of empty paper cups and cartons, well-shrouded with pigeon droppings. Phillippa sighed and turned back to her desk. Defiantly she zipped down the front of her jumpsuit to reveal yet more cleavage.

'Well, kiddy, how goes it?'

'Wonderful. Everything's great.'

'Oh Gawd, like that is it? What's up, didn't you enjoy the West Coast? Look at your tan, too. Wish I went that colour. Come on, tell aunty Phil. Mr Wrong again, is it? Edward?'

'No, not exactly.' Bell suddenly thought what bliss it would be to talk to someone sensible. She knew that Phil, for all her breezy manner, had the kindest of hearts.

'Will you look at all this crap? Two weeks out of the place, and it's an avalanche of bumf.' Phillippa stabbed viciously at the haphazard piles of paper stacked on her desk. 'Tell you what, I'll riffle through all this just for form's sake and make a few calls, then I'll take you across to the Blue Lion for a drinky. Yes?'

'Okay,' Bell agreed. Good idea. She couldn't go on like this for much longer.

Two hours later Phillippa held up her hand, all the fingers outstretched to show Bell that she would be five more minutes. Her telephone receiver was cradled under one ear and she was ripping open envelopes as she talked. Invitations to press parties for rainhats and knitwear ranges went fluttering into the wastebasket. 'Okay, yes darling, I know I okayed the contacts. But where did that final print come from? Yeah. Yeah. Next time? What next time? Yeah. Right. And goodbye to you too.' She slammed down the receiver.

'That is the last time I use him. He may be the prettiest boy in West One, but he's a bloody awful photographer. Now, let's be off.'

Phillippa shepherded Bell across the road and into the pub. The bar was crowded, mostly with the paper's reporters and printers, and it smelt of beer, cigarette smoke and cottage pie. It reminded Bell of a thousand other lunchtimes, and threatened several thousand more in the future. God, what a prospect. Had she ever really thought that it was a glamorous life?

Phil came back from the bar nursing two double gins and a pair of tired ham rolls. She took a gulp of her drink and sighed with relief.

'Well, that's one thing I'm not sorry to get back to. As far as I'm concerned you can keep your retsina.'

'I don't want it.' Bell laughed, for the first time in days. 'Philly darling, I'm so sorry to have greeted you with such a long face. It's just that life has got rather out of hand lately, and I haven't had you around to put all the little happenings into perspective.'

'Mmmm. Well, if it isn't Eddy boy, who is it? Somebody new?'

'Two.'

'Two? Jesus, and you're complaining? It's not a problem, pet, just give me whichever one you don't want. Any old Farrer throw-out, I'm not fussy. Who are they, anyway? Both of them . . .'

Bell was giggling now. 'Wait for it. You'll love this. One's a French baron and the other's a Californian millionaire.'

'Oh dear, this is so awful for you. What's the snag? One's eighty-five and the other's a hunchback? They're both eighty-five-year-old hunchbacks? Don't worry, you know I've always liked older men . . .'

Bell was still laughing, but somewhere inside she felt the nervous tension that had kept her going over the past days just snap. Her eyes stung and went blurry. Within seconds the tears were pouring down her face as fast as she tried to brush them away. Phillippa grabbed her wrist across the table top.

'Hey, stop. I've never seen you cry. If whatever it is is that serious, you'd better tell me. Look, here . . . tissues. Dry those tears up or you'll have Graham Tordoff over here trying to put his arm round you, and then where would you be. Two's company, but three – if one of those is Tordoff – is vaudeville.'

Bell scrubbed at her face and looked over at the bar. Sure enough, Tordoff – the most ineffectually predatory of sportswriters – stopped gaping and tried out a sympathetic smile.

Phillippa went over to buy two more drinks and mouthed *time of the month* over her shoulder at him on the way back, all exaggerated complicity. He went scarlet and turned back to his beer.

'Now then,' she said firmly, putting her glass in front of Bell, 'what is it that's bad enough to cloud the bliss of being in the Blue Lion on a clammy Monday morning?'

'You remember Château Reynard, Philly? And Baron Charles de Gillesmont.'

'Ah, that French baron.'

'I fell in love with him. Overnight, just like – catching something. I won't try and tell you what it felt like because it'll sound ridiculous. But I've never met anyone like him, and never dreamt that I could be so . . . overtaken. It was as if I'd known him all my life, and as if he knew everything there was to know about me without asking. I'm certain, Phil. I love him, and I need him. He's quite remote, in a way, but very . . . passionate, too. I think, I believe . . . he feels the same as I do.'

'And?'

'I made him a kind of promise. He's married, and separated, and he's been very . . . hurt. Their child died. And he's Catholic, fiercely Catholic, so he can't divorce. So I promised that I'd wait. While he . . . tried to set things straight.'

'Did he ask you to promise?'

'Nnno. But he accepted it.'

'Ah.'

'Then I went to California. It was as if I went mad, out there. The Californian millionaire, Valentine. I was staying in his house. He was all smiles and sunshine and wonderful company, and he kept trying to get me into bed . . .'

'Oh, the wicked devil.'

'. . . and I liked him, and something just got under my skin. I started wanting him, too. Not just sex, although it was

152

mostly that, to start with. But he was so open, uncomplicated, after Charles. I did like him, a lot. It was very physical, immediate, you know? So I gave in. No – didn't give in. Went for him, in return. I told myself that it was a celebration . . .'

'A celebration?' Phillippa looked surprised and Bell faltered, trying to straighten the tangle inside her head before explaining any more.

'Yes,' she nodded at last. 'Finally I knew who I wanted. The life I wanted. It was no more than to be with Charles at Château Reynard. Everything was right, you see. Charles himself, the way he lives . . . I felt that there would be no need for any more compromises. Then out on the West Coast, so far away, I justified my attraction to Valentine by calling it a last fling. Goodbye to all that – career, freedom, being uncommitted, everything. I was glad to say goodbye to it, but the end was worth celebrating with someone special. Or so I told myself. And Valentine is special.'

Bell stopped staring fixedly down into her glass and met Phillippa's eyes.

'Well, that's not so very terrible.'

'It's much worse. They know each other. They *hate* each other. Valentine . . . seduced Charles's wife, just after their little boy died. Charles challenged him to a duel . . .'

'Oh, Christ.'

'They didn't fight, but Charles warned me before I went out there. He said *Valentine Gordon is a dangerous man.* I thought he meant violent, you know . . . not . . . anything else. And I fell straight into the honey trap. Charles's worst enemy, no less, within days of promising him . . . Philly, I hate myself for it.'

Phillippa looked at her judiciously.

'And what have you told Charles?'

Bell was astonished. 'Told him? Nothing. We haven't spoken since I left Bordeaux.'

'You haven't rung him? Said Hi, here I am, back in town?'

'No. How could I?'

'There's a little red thing on your desk called a telephone. You pick it up and ask for International. I thought you told me you love him. If you do, surely you're not too proud to go and get him?'

'Not proud. Afraid.'

'Why are you afraid of him?'

'He's . . . formidable.' Bell frowned, trying to identify the feeling.

'He sets high standards for himself. It makes me feel that I want to . . . match them.'

'You haven't been very clever at that so far, then.'

No.

'Look, Bell. Talk to him. Stop moping about in the shadows like a Victorian heroine. Forget your American Don Juan – write him off as experience. If you're being honest – your usual, clear-sighted self – then you'll know that Charles is all that matters.'

She's right, thought Bell. Just to hear Charles's voice would make all the difference. She leant back in her plastic chair and smiled defiantly at Phillippa.

'I'll do it. This afternoon. Let's have another drink first and you can tell me about Piero. Or Nico, or whatever his name was.' They both laughed.

Alone in her office again, Bell picked up the telephone to place her call to Reynard. She felt reckless after Philly's gins at lunchtime, and breathless at the thought of talking to Charles in a few seconds' time. She pictured the cluttered comfort of his study, the ancient black telephone perched on top of the pretty antique desk.

Ah, there it was. After a succession of clicks came the burring of the French ringing tone. It had barely started before a curt French voice answered.

'*Oui?* Château Reynard.'

It was Hélène. Bell felt strangled. In her sudden excitement it had never occurred to her that it wouldn't be Charles answering at the other end.

'Oh. I'm sorry to bother you. This is Bell Farrer, calling from London.'

'Yes?'

'Could I speak to Charles, please?'

'I'm afraid not.' That was all. No explanation of where he was, or when she should call again. Bell clenched her teeth.

'Do you expect him back soon?'

'I'm afraid I can't say. I'm not generally privy to his movements.'

'Well, perhaps you could tell him that I called? I think he has my number.'

'Yes. Goodbye.'

Bell leaned forward very slowly and replaced the receiver. Then she just sat there, staring dully at it.

Phillippa came back. She looked shocked.

'Did you get through?' she asked, absently. Very obviously, her mind was elsewhere.

'What? Oh, no. Not to him. I left a message, with his mother.'

'Good enough. Bell, did you know just how bad things are here?'

'Bad?'

Phillippa sighed, marshalling her patience. 'Bad. Like, dreadful. Like closure time. Or, at best, redundancy time for quite a lot of the boys and girls. I've just been talking to Ransome . . .' Ransome always knew everything about everything, especially if it was bad news '. . . and he says that after the last set of figures the Group isn't prepared to put any more hard cash into keeping us going. The paper has to begin meeting the deficit itself. Or else.'

Bell rubbed her hand across her eyes. Another kind of anxiety, cold and uncomfortable, started to gnaw at her.

'No, I didn't know it was that bad. Can any of us do anything?'

Philly shrugged. 'Nope. Just fingers crossed, I think.'

Bell pulled her typewriter towards her and rolled in a fresh sheet of paper. Suddenly she felt panicky. What was the matter with her? Why wasn't she working? 'Fingers crossed, then,' she murmured and began to type an introductory paragraph. As if they were beyond her control, the black letters blurred and jumped on the page. Charles would be back, surely, in time for dinner. So she could expect his call this evening. Or tomorrow, at the latest.

Stop it.

Bell worked on, closing her mind. The words were coming out dull and lumpy, but at least she was doing something.

All evening Bell sat at home in her rocking chair. The telephone stayed brutally silent. When it got too dark to see the tops of the trees in the Gardens, she went to bed.

Charles didn't ring the next day, either, or the day after that. Bell felt numb with the tension of waiting, and too dejected to think beyond it. On the third day she stopped hoping and settled back into a dumb acceptance that even Phillippa couldn't joke her out of.

From the reports in the trade press Bell knew that France was enjoying an exceptional Indian summer after several days of rain. The conditions were perfect for a memorable vintage, and Bell was certain that Charles would be watching, praying and waiting for the right moment to begin picking the fat grapes. He was busy. Too busy to think about her. And he had warned her that they would have to wait *until after I have picked my last grape.*

It was painful, not knowing what he was doing or what he was thinking, but she would make herself hold on until then. No more phone calls.

The whole of Bell's world seemed to be waiting for something or other. Rumours of disaster came and went in the newspaper offices, and there was a series of heated union meetings at which the journalists discussed what was to be done when the bad news finally broke. Bell sat through the meetings, aware of the anxious atmosphere but stupidly unable to identify herself with the promised crisis.

She felt quite unlike herself – distracted, edgy and irritable.

One morning the phone rang on her desk. Bell had stopped gasping every time it happened and expecting to hear Charles's elegant French voice on the line.

'Bell Farrer speaking,' she said flatly.

'Hello again. What's new in Kensington?'

'*Valentine.*' Just at the sound of his lazy Californian drawl, the grey little office seemed to fill with sunshine. It all came flooding back, the shared jokes and the taste of the wine and the memory of his arms around her. Bell found that she was smiling. Phillippa had stopped poring over the fashion sketches that littered her desk and was staring at her.

'Valentine, where are you?'

'Napa, right now, but in three days I'll be at the Connaught.'

'The Connaught, London?'

'How many others are there? Yes, London. As you know, it's IWC time. I'm on the Committee, so I have to show up.'

The International Winemakers Conference. Of course.

'Bell? Are you still there? Listen, are you free on the twenty-eighth? I'll take you to the Committee Dinner and on to the Ball.'

'Well . . .' Frantically Bell tried to formulate an excuse. There must be no more Valentine. That was all over. But he sounded so warm and cheerful, and it felt so good to be asked. Yet if she did go, what if Charles heard, somehow, that she had been there with Valentine? The wine world was small enough and gossipy enough for the story to get back to him. Then with a tiny flicker of anger Bell remembered that Charles was a long way away, and hadn't even tried to call her. She realized how lonely she had been and how much, in spite of everything, she would welcome Valentine's company.

Well, why the hell not?

It would be fun to have an evening with him. If Charles heard about it – Bell's lips tightened – that was too bad.

'I'm not doing anything. I'd love to come.' The words tumbled out and Philly gaped before ducking her head back to her work.

After Valentine had rung off, the warmth that his voice had stirred up in Bell refused to evaporate.

I do like him, she thought. It's just myself that I can't stand.

'Philly,' she said irrelevantly, 'the International Conference dinner. And the Ball afterwards, no less. What am I going to wear?'

Phillippa shook her head in exaggerated bewilderment.

'You baffle me, you know. I thought this man was a libidinous monster, and now you're off to the ball with him like Cinderella and worrying about wearing the right gown. What's going on in that little head of yours?'

Bell nodded sadly. 'I know. I don't understand it either. I just wanted to go.'

The other girl shrugged and then her face split into a brilliant smile.

'I know. If you're Cinders then I insist on being the fairy godmother.'

Phillippa leapt up so fast that she sent her swivel chair spinning, and unlocked the long cupboard behind her desk.

Inside was a long, mysteriously swathed shape. From its layers of polythene and protective tissue she unveiled a ball dress. Over Bell's head she waved a ruler and crowed 'Cinders, you shall go to the ball.'

Bell gasped and then shook her head.

'I couldn't possibly wear that. I wouldn't dare even breathe in it.'

The billows of black taffeta gleamed sumptuously in the overhead light. The long skirts were huge, the bodice strapless and boned to a tiny waist. The dress was at once romantic and wicked.

'Designed exclusively for the rich and famous,' said Phillippa, 'and photographed by this newspaper for the grubby likes of you and me to gape at. Go on, borrow it. The model was only an inch or two taller than you, and you're just as slim. It'll suit you.'

Bell fingered the folds of fabric covetously. 'What if I spill soup on it?'

Phillippa winced. 'Just don't, that's all.'

Suddenly, there was something to look forward to. Bell smiled gratefully at Phillippa. 'I'd love to borrow it. I'll take great care.'

The other girl gave her a long look. 'You'd better. And I don't mean just the dress.'

Neither of them mentioned Valentine again.

For Bell, the days before Valentine's arrival trickled uneventfully past. London was still shrouded in dull, airless heat. On her way home from work Bell would walk across the park where the leaves hung dusty and motionless and the grass was burnt brown. As she scuffed along the dusty paths, she debated with herself whether she should put Valentine off, make some kind of excuse for not seeing him after all.

Then she thought, *why?*

She was looking forward to seeing him. And then accompanying him to a business dinner and a very decorous ball didn't present a threat of any kind.

Bell knew that she was making excuses, but there was something else that she was much less ready to admit to herself. She was stung by Charles's failure to respond to her call. It would have cost him so little, yet he must know how much it must have meant to her.

Well, he hadn't. She would wait, just as he had told her, but in the meantime she would have her evening with Valentine.

On the morning of the dinner Bell arrived late in her office.

She had been to have her hair done. The black dress would leave her arms and shoulders bare, and she decided that wearing her hair up would look too severe. So she had had it done in a mass of shiny waves and curls that swung to her shoulders, pinned back from her cheeks with a pair of mother-of-pearl combs that had belonged to her mother.

As Bell came into her office she felt pleasantly excited, more like the old Bell than she had felt since before Bordeaux.

The room was empty, but she saw at once that there was a message on her desk. It was in Phillippa's handwriting, on a sheet torn from one of her square yellow notepads.

It read 'Valentine Gordon rang. He will pick you up at your flat at seven.'

Underneath, in a different colour, Phillippa had written.

'Stobbs wants to see you this a.m.'

It was an unusual summons. Orders usually came down from on high via the features editor. Bell was frowning as she picked up the internal telephone and dialled the editor's secretary.

'Bell Farrer. Mr Stobbs wants to see me?'

'Oh. Yes. Could you come at eleven-fifteen?'

'Sure.'

Perhaps it was another of Henry's bright ideas for a food feature. He considered himself something of a grass-roots gourmet and was forever unearthing little restaurants in far-off suburbs.

At eleven-thirteen, Bell stepped out of the lift on the executive floor. There was wall-to-wall carpeting up here, and softer lighting. Stobbs's secretary was in the outer office, pouring coffee.

'Want a cup to take in with you?' she asked, pleasantly.

This was more than unusual, it was unheard-of. Bell began to feel dimly afraid.

'Yes please,' she said in an unnatural voice.

'Come on in.' Bell heard Stobbs's aggressive northern tones. 'Right then,' was his characteristic greeting. 'Sit down.'

Bell slid into the chair facing him. The office was lined with crowded bookshelves and piled-up wire baskets, but the desk was bare except for a little square of paper in front of Stobbs. The editor was wearing a dark suit, and a funereal tie, an unusual departure from his usual crumpled green corduroys. He looked a little like an undertaker, thought Bell, but at his first words her little inner smile faded and died.

'Not a pleasant task, this,' he told her. Bell sat frozen, suspended in the silence that followed his words. *Get on with it*, she heard herself thinking. *Only please don't say what I'm afraid you're going to say.*

'You'll know all about our problems with falling circulation and decrease in advertising revenue?'

Bell nodded dumbly.

'It's a problem we have in common with every other paper, and in the normal run we would have weathered this recession like every other. But last week the Group management executive informed me that their investment in this paper over the next year will be reduced to sixty per cent of last year's figure.'

Stobbs was talking curtly, the short vowel sounds even more pronounced than usual. Bell thought *he hates this. It diminishes his sense of being all-powerful.*

'Naturally, that will mean a very severe cutback in expenditure for us at every level, if we are to survive. And that includes staffing.'

Bell was beginning to feel sick. She knew what was coming.

'Across the board we must lose eighty jobs.' *We?* Bell doubted that Henry Stobbs's job was going to be one of the eighty.

'Ten of those must be journalists. I'm sorry, but there it is. In the present economic climate, this paper cannot justify a full-time food and wine correspondent. Your contribution in the past has been very valuable, but . . .'

Bell stopped listening as the rehearsed speech grated on.

Shock, disbelief, fear and anger raced through her in turn, but it was anger that got the upper hand.

'. . . hope that you'll be a valuable freelance contributor,' Stobbs was winding up at last. He looked down at the square of paper in front of him.

'I see that you have been with us for two years. Your redundancy payment has been calculated on this basis, and I think it's a generous settlement.'

Bell didn't even glance at the hateful figures. She was too angry, and her hands were shaking too much to pick up the paper. Instead she stood up and stared down at the little man. The light was reflecting off his glasses so she couldn't see his eyes, but she thought he looked surprised. No, she wasn't going to accept whatever it was he was doling out, being meek and mild and grateful. Was this what her two years' work for Henry Stobbs and his readers added up to?

'I don't want to see your settlement,' she told him, surprised at being able to suppress the tremor in her voice. 'I won't accept this. You can't do it.'

Bell was already in the doorway before Stobbs said, 'There are negotiations to be completed with the various union chapels, of course. But I think you'll find that you must accept it in the end.'

Bell stumbled through the secretary's office and out to the lift. Mercifully, when it came it was empty. She leaned against the steel wall and closed her eyes. The slow descent matched the sensation inside her perfectly. The anger ebbed with the adrenalin, leaving her numb and unbelieving.

Phillippa was back in their office. She stopped dead when she saw Bell's face.

'You too?'

'Yes. Me too.'

All Bell's tense self-control dissolved at the first sign of sympathy. She flopped down at her desk, buried her head in her arms and burst into tears. Other journalists began to gather in the office. There was a jabber of angry conversation and the air thickened with cigarette smoke. Phillippa had escaped the axe this time, she was saying grimly, but this was only the first round. She was counting names off on her fingers. The list came to ten. Just as Stobbs had said.

'We'll fight to the end,' said somebody. 'Chapel meeting at three.'

'Not one of these notices to quit is valid,' said someone else.

'This is a sell-out . . .'

'Treachery . . .'

'Concerted action . . .'

Bell looked round the room wearily. It was full of pugnacious expressions and fingers stabbing the air for emphasis. The smoke made her eyes sting.

All the anger and defiance she had felt in Stobbs's office had evaporated. There was no fight left in her. The strain of the last few days had drained all her resilience. What she wanted now was to get away. To crawl away into the pit of emptiness that suddenly gaped where her successful, happy, well-ordered life had once been.

'I think I'll go home,' she told Philly.

'Good idea. Then, tomorrow, we'll start the fight in earnest. Oh, and enjoy tonight. Try and forget this for a few hours.'

'Yes. Thanks.'

Bell knew already that she wasn't going to fight. She would go quietly. Just find herself another job, that was all.

She even had an idea. Only the seed of an idea, but it was beginning to take root.

Hardly daring to breathe, Bell slipped the dress over her head. The black folds rustled exotically as she zipped up the close-fitting bodice. The strapless boned top was cut so low that it exposed the swell of her breasts, and then tapered to a dramatically narrow waist. The dress fitted her so perfectly that it might have been made for her.

Bell glanced at herself in the long mirror, and smiled.

Impulsively she gathered up the swirling skirt and made a deep curtsey at herself. She did look regal, but at the same time intriguingly sexy. It was all that bare skin that did it, still pale gold from the Californian sun and set off to perfection by the rippling black fabric.

Bell arched her head to and fro so that the dark waves of hair fell away from her neck. It was delicious to feel so narcissistic.

What this dress really cried out for was diamonds, but that was just too bad. She would wear a chain of flat gold links that had been the last present from her father.

Valentine. Where was he? Twenty past seven. Bell knew that he was always late, but it irritated her to be kept waiting tonight.

She had made herself stop thinking about being sacked. Forced herself, by sheer willpower, to put it out of her head. She wouldn't even tell Valentine, until tomorrow. By putting on her make-up very carefully she had made herself look bright-eyed and glowing. There was no trace of tears or anxiety. It had been a supreme effort, and now she was all keyed up and ready for the evening.

And Valentine wasn't here.

The edges of Bell's careful façade of happiness were just beginning to crumble when the bell rang.

He was here.

As soon as Bell saw him her irritation was forgotten. In her narrow hallway he seemed taller and broader than she had remembered. There was the familiar, lazy smile, instead of an apology for being late. She had forgotten the way that smile illuminated the ordinary, handsome American features with its own peculiar teasing warmth.

Valentine was steering her back into the light.

They stood in the middle of the floor, staring at each other. Then he kissed her.

'You look . . . and smell . . . and taste . . . delicious,' he told

163

her. 'I think, in retrospect, I've missed you. Have you missed me?'

It wasn't really a question. It assumed the answer yes.

'Not a bit.' Bell grinned at him and stepped safely out of his arms. She had felt the old, familiar response to him begin to seep through her.

To her surprise, he looked good in his evening clothes. She had never even seen him in a tie before, yet here he was in his formal white bow tie and black tails. The sombre clothes made him look very tanned and fit, and made his eyes look even brighter blue. He brought a fresh tang of salt Pacific air into the staleness of London.

'Too bad. Shall we go?'

He held out an arm and they swept away together.

In the street was parked a long, dark blue Bentley with a uniformed chauffeur.

'Good job I didn't bring the bike. One breath of wind and you'd be blown out of that dress, and then we'd both be arrested.'

The chauffeur held open the door and they stepped into the car. They were both laughing delightedly.

The IWC Committee Dinner, the most formal event in the wine establishment's calendar, was to be held this year in Goldsmiths' Hall in the heart of the City of London.

Bell kept her head firmly turned away from the newspaper offices as they swept down Fleet Street and didn't lean back against the padded upholstery until the car was purring up Ludgate Hill. The dome of Wren's St Paul's towered over them with dark storm clouds massed behind it. The long-awaited thunderstorm was brewing. Bell shivered a little and then relaxed. She was perfectly cocooned against the elements in this sleek car with Valentine drawling companionably at her side. There would be no getting wet or standing in queues tonight. She might as well enjoy the privilege while it lasted, she thought, because tomorrow it would be gone.

Cinderella was about right, she reflected wryly. A borrowed dress, borrowed car, and a man borrowed back from a misbegotten celebration that was supposed to be over and done with.

Well, there were a few hours yet before midnight struck.

The car swished to a stop outside a grand urban-Palladian entrance. It was framed with a striped awning that beckoned at the edge of the pavement. Arm in arm, Bell and Valentine passed under the canopy and into the hall of the ancient livery company.

Following the directions of the flunkeys in their ceremonial dress they mounted a curving staircase and found themselves in a panelled antechamber under a huge dome. At one side the balcony looked down into the black and white marble-flagged hallway, and at the other was a pair of tall doors. Past the doors Bell glimpsed a long white table gleaming with glass and plate. Down the length of the white cloth marched gold candelabra blazing with candles.

Fervently, Bell thanked Phillippa for the loan of the dress. Amongst the other gowns in the antechamber were two definite Diors and a possible Balenciaga.

Valentine was greeting the other Committee members. They all looked at least twenty years older than him. They would be spending the next two days closeted together in conference, and Bell couldn't help smiling at the idea of Valentine's pungent American slang cutting through all these mellifluous, well-bred French and German and Italian voices.

François Pirron, august President of the Conference and one of the great names in the wine world, was welcoming them. He grasped both Bell's hands and then kissed her on either cheek.

'You must allow an old man,' he twinkled charmingly at Valentine, 'to admire from afar.'

Bell smiled downwards and blushed faintly. It was her practised response to gallant Frenchmen of a certain age. Out of the corner of her eye she was watching the arrival of another couple below. The man had a slight look of Charles, she thought absently.

She was used to heart-stopping moments when she thought

she caught a glimpse of him from the top of a bus as it pulled away, or in the back of a taxi speeding in another direction, or on a crowded Underground platform as the doors closed inexorably in her face.

It never really was Charles. She half glanced away from the newcomer and then looked back again.

Blond hair brushed sleekly to a finely-shaped head. A brooding profile, faint shadows under high cheekbones. Dark evening clothes of impeccable but unmistakably French cut.

It was Charles.

Oh, please God, no. Not to find her standing here with Valentine Gordon. Charles, coming up the stairs towards her. Juliette, all in scarlet ruffles, smiling beside him.

Bell was dimly aware of a flash of lightning that split the dark glass dome over her head with livid light. Almost at once a deafening clap of thunder boomed over London. The storm had broken.

Escape. Get away. Hide.

'Are you all right?' Valentine and François Pirron were gazing at her in concern.

She had gasped aloud in shock.

'Yes,' she managed to croak. 'A little . . . faint. If I could just . . .'

'Hey, hold on. I'll get a woman to take you. You, there . . .' Valentine caught the arm of a passing waitress. 'Find a rest room,' he ordered her. 'Give her some air, will you . . .' How brashly American he suddenly sounded.

Bell almost ran, the waitress anxious at her side. They reached the cloakroom together. It was all cold marble and polished brass taps and echoing drips. Rain was beating on a glass roof somewhere in the darkness overhead, and gurgling and splashing through long-dry gutters.

A fat attendant in a turquoise nylon overall began to cluck around Bell.

'Not this old storm is it, duck?' she asked. 'You're quite safe here.'

The waitress leaned against a door to watch, evidently glad of a five-minute break. 'She came over queer out there,' she explained to the attendant.

'All right, now,' Bell managed to tell them. 'I'd just like to be by myself for a few minutes.' The women drifted away, disappointed, leaving her sitting in her corner in the faded chintz chair they had pressed her into. The walls were mirrored and Bell looked up to see a hundred hunched Bells retreating into infinity.

Gradually her heart stopped pounding. She didn't think, after all, that she was going to faint or be sick. Philly's face, comically protesting, popped into her head. To throw up on this dress was, after all, unthinkable.

No. What she must do is get away, discreetly, before Charles could see her. Tell Valentine anything. Suddenly taken ill. A closer look in the mirror convinced her that that was the answer. Her face was so white that the careful make-up stood out like clown's daubs.

She would find Valentine at once and insist on being taken home. If necessary she would run away into the torrential rain.

But it was not to be.

The first people she saw when she slipped back into the crowded ante-chamber were Charles and Juliette.

Simultaneously, their eyes lit on Bell. Juliette was calling out to her.

'Ah, Bell, how wonderful.' They reached Bell's side together. 'We only got here this afternoon. We were going to ring you tomorrow. But how fantastic that you're here tonight. Charles has been co-opted at the last instant because poor Bressandes died so suddenly.'

Bell heard none of this.

She saw nothing except Charles in front of her.

He bent to kiss her lips, quick and cool, and murmured, 'You are ravishing.'

He was so strong now, so powerful and certain and inescapable.

'Charles. Charles.' Forgetting everything, Bell grabbed his hands and pressed them in her own cold fists. She was gabbling in her anxiety. 'I telephoned you. I wanted to talk. Tell you about something. Didn't Hélène give you my message?' As she spoke, she realized what had happened. Of course, Hélène, crabbed and bitter Hélène, hadn't told him. Why hadn't she thought of that? If only she had thought. If only. She wouldn't have been so hurt. She wouldn't have been here tonight with Valentine. It was the cruellest trick of fate, but she had no one to blame but herself.

Charles's eyes had gone dark. 'No, Bell, I didn't know.' His mouth loomed dangerously close to hers, sensuous and demanding. For both of them, now, there was no one else in the room.

In the world.

'Tell me,' he insisted, his voice very low. 'What is it?' Then he remembered, and gestured with impatience. 'Not here, I know. Tomorrow. Tomorrow we can talk. Bell, you know I need you.'

Frantically they feasted on each other's faces. Outside the thunder rolled and crashed in the veiled sky. Somehow, telepathically, he had caught her panic and his eyes devoured her face as if he would never see her again.

Bell knew that there could be only seconds left to her, tiny seconds of his affection and admiration before he found that she had betrayed him. Before he started to despise her.

Then suntanned fingers snaked out to grasp her wrist, vice-like.

'Met some friends, sweetheart?' Valentine's drawl was bland, but there were threatening notes in it that she had never heard before.

Charles's eyes left Bell's face at last and turned to the Californian. Passion and longing in his face were replaced by surprise, then the dawning bitterness of understanding. And that was chased away by cold, white anger. He looked as if he was carved out of ice, all sharp frozen angles, except for the living hurt in his eyes.

Bell knew that he looked as he must have done in the depths of his loss and despair. Her heart began to bleed.

She, Bell, had done this to him. The man she loved.

'You,' Charles said. He mouthed the single syllable at Valentine with all the force of distaste and mistrust. Then his glance licked over Bell and away again. He knew what had happened. He had seen and understood in a single glance.

'Yes, Baron, me.' Valentine grinned mockingly. 'All dressed up for the big night, with my girl on my arm.'

Bell caught her breath with horror but Charles had already turned away. He held out his arm to his sister. Juliette was standing a little apart, but she linked her arm with his at once.

She gave a tiny shrug at Bell, perfectly Gallic, resigned and disappointed.

The de Gillesmonts walked away towards the door where the majordomo was announcing the guests' names before they took their places at the table.

'Baron Charles de Gillesmont, Château Reynard,' he intoned, 'et Mademoiselle de Gillesmont.'

Valentine jerked his head abruptly at Bell. The smile was left stamped on his face and he was flushed a dull red under his tan.

'I told you that that asshole and I had no time for each other. Come on,' he said with an obvious effort to regain his equilibrium. 'Let's join the party.'

'Mr Valentine Gordon, Dry Stone Winery. Miss Bell Farrer.' The man even gave the name of her newspaper. Valentine must have told them. How American of him to have to reinforce her presence with a label. Bell felt an irrational sharp dislike for the culture that she had so recently thought warm and welcoming and natural. Well, Valentine had got it wrong. She was just plain Bell Farrer now, of nowhere very much.

With leaden feet Bell let him escort her into the candlelit grandeur of the Dining Hall.

Gold, silver, damask, crystal.

Elegant talk that she couldn't listen to, however hard she tried. Exquisite food that was dust in her mouth. The finest wines of each of the proprietors of the Committee.

Château Reynard '61 in her glass again. Bell swallowed and the room swam. Bitterly she recalled her last taste of the legendary wine. The three of them, complicit in laughter, in the pool of light around the end of the dining table at Reynard.

Several places away from her now, Charles's chiselled

profile was turned away. He never once looked at her. Juliette caught her eye just once, then glanced away again.

The dinner was interminable.

Beside Bell, Valentine was drinking heavily and with determination. By the time the table was cleared for the speeches and toasts he was talking volubly and joking, the witty centre of a circle of laughing faces, but Bell recognized the faint blurring in his voice that she had heard before, just once. In Las Vegas. Bell turned to her left to the portly German who, left without another plate of food to wolf down, was beginning to look round for conversation. Desperately she racked her brains for something to say to him.

Endless speeches.

Then one from Charles, short and graceful, thanking the Committee for the honour it had done him in inviting him to join them, and hoping that he would be able to serve the Conference as valuably as his '*chers collègues*'.

Bell's eyes clung hungrily to him. She wanted to remember every detail as currency to be jealously counted over in the bleak days to come.

At last it was over. How could she face dancing now, more people and more talk? Valentine gulped another brandy and escorted her firmly to the waiting car.

'The Dorchester, James,' he said thickly to the chauffeur. His arm went round Bell and his hand groped for her breast. She stiffened at once and shrugged him away, furious at his proprietorial manner. Her body didn't belong to Valentine. Nothing of her did, not an atom. Bell stared unseeingly out at the deserted streets, refusing to let her head turn towards Valentine. Raindrops splintered the light on the car windows and the windscreen wipers whisked hypnotically to and fro. Beside her his face was mask-like under the livid street lighting, but his eyes were fixed speculatively on her profile.

'Trouble, Bell?' he asked softly, slipping out of boozy abandon as easily as he had done in their Las Vegas suite. But when no answer came his mouth slackened again and he ran the flat of his hand appraisingly up her naked spine.

'This is the kind of dress,' he told her insinuatingly, 'that a man looks forward to taking off.'

Oh no you don't, Bell thought, dislike of him beginning to prickle through her.

'But first,' he went on, 'bring on the champagne and the dancing girls. We'll make the Dorchester jump tonight, eh? And after that . . .' he chuckled softly.

Bell shrank away from him into her corner. Eleven o'clock. How long until she could escape? An hour? Two hours?

Valentine gave every sign of being in high spirits as they arrived at the ball. He swept her on to the crowded dance floor and immediately gathered her up in a choking embrace. Bell could feel every hard line of him pressed against her, so familiar and now so unwelcome, and she shrank further and further into misery. The music pounded deafeningly, her head throbbed and she could only bring herself to respond to Valentine's stream of bright talk in whispered monosyllables. Their eyes never met, and so Bell missed the hard glimmer in Valentine's that belied his dazzling smile.

Bell was surprised by his popularity. There were waves and smiles at every turn. He knew everyone, and was greeted constantly. Bell saw with bitterness how the women invariably softened and fluttered as he kissed them, while their men stood by in beaming approval.

Valentine could do no wrong, it seemed.

All through it, whoever they spoke to, he kept his fingers firmly laced in hers and his arm around her waist. Whenever he swung her back into the dance his hands slid over her hips, always pressing her closer to him. As if he wants to show the world that he owns me, Bell thought. She longed to scream out *Stop. I can't bear this.* Yet all she could do was keep her face turned from him and her body stiff with rejection.

At least all the hundreds of delegates to the main conference and their guests were crowding the huge ballroom. With any luck she and Charles wouldn't have to see each other here. Perhaps he and Juliette hadn't even come to the ball.

'Valentine,' she made herself say at last, through stiff lips. 'I'm tired. Could we find a table and sit down?'

He glanced down at her briefly. 'But of course.' He found them a table at the edge of the floor and ordered champagne.

Inevitably acquaintances of both Bell and Valentine began to gather at the table. Girls buzzed around Valentine just as if he was a pot of honey, and he smiled through them at Bell with something like defiance. She looked away again and back into the mass of dancers, half longing for and half dreading a glimpse of Charles. Mechanically she drained her glass of champagne, tasting nothing, and leant to replace it on the table. Valentine's fingers caught her wrist.

'Shall we dance again? Or go somewhere . . . quieter?' Again there came the insinuating smile, overlaid with mockery now.

'No.' Bell groped to her feet and reached for her black silk evening purse.

'Will you excuse me for five minutes?' She would hide for a few blessed minutes in the cloakroom, and perhaps the solitude would give her the strength to make her escape.

'But of course,' said Valentine again. Despite the conventional politeness there was anger in his eyes, and even before Bell could move away he had turned to a bright redhead from the French Tourist Office.

'You'll dance with me, Princess, won't you?' Bell heard him say. Without a backward glance at her he was guiding the girl on to the dance floor, one arm already around her waist.

Bell walked slowly away, hot with anger at herself as well as Valentine. Home, she thought. I must get home.

Someone was blocking her path through the rococo pillars. It was Charles.

Gravely, he said, 'Will you dance with me?'

Too bewildered now to respond, Bell let him take her hand. His own felt very cool and dry.

The last time they had waltzed together. The empty, gleaming floor at Reynard and her own bewildered happiness.

Nothing left of that now, but the irony of his arms supporting her and his deft way of leading her, protected and apart, through the jostling throng of dancers.

'I owe you an apology,' she mumbled against his shoulder. He leaned away from her a little, cool and faintly surprised.

'An apology?' His eyebrows went up a fraction. It was as if

they had just been introduced. He steered her through an elaborate turn and back into the centre of the floor.

The words Bell had had mapped out in her head were hopeless. How could she remind this tall, aloof man of the things that they had said to each other beside the calm Gironde on her twenty-eighth birthday?

He wasn't even the same man who had whispered to her, only hours ago, that he needed her. The steel shutters had closed. Charles wouldn't permit himself the luxury of needing her any more.

Bell had lost him. Dully she recognized it and accepted it.

It was her own fault.

Fault, fault, fault. The music and her headache pounded together in her skull like a mad incantation.

At last Charles said, 'You don't owe me anything.' He was looking away from her, over her head and into infinity.

'Oh, God. Please listen, Charles. I promised that I . . .'

His gaze, pebble-hard, descended to her face and she faltered.

'Don't make any more promises. You aren't ready, Bell.'

Bell was silenced. She felt rebuked, like a child trying to meddle in grown-up affairs beyond its understanding.

There was no more to be said.

A moment later Charles was talking pleasantly about the prospects for the vintage. Their intimacy, so short-lived but to Bell so astounding, was over. He had asked her to dance because he was too much of a gentleman not to acknowledge her presence at the ball. He wanted to put a neat, social full-stop to whatever it was that they had meant to each other. It wouldn't have been his style just to cut her dead after seeing her with Valentine.

Charles de Gillesmont was too suave for that, too urbane.

No, instead of the drama of anger and hurt here was the polite trivia of strangers' talk. How enclosed he is. How self-protective. It was all so horrible. Wildly Bell thought of screaming, or pretending to faint – anything to shatter this distant calm. But she knew that it would do no good. Hysteria would only make him despise her more.

Charles was guiding her gently but inexorably back to the table where she had been sitting with Valentine. As soon as the band stopped playing he released her. Bell's arms dropped emptily to her sides. Charles bowed his formal little bow, and thanked her.

'Perhaps we will see you at Château Reynard again some day.'

Or perhaps not.

He lifted her hand and kissed it. The navy-blue eyes with the mysterious flecks of gold held hers for a second, then slid away.

'I'm sure your escort will be missing you,' he said softly. 'Goodbye, Bell.'

Then he was gone, a tall, elegant figure moving fluently through the crowds of revellers.

Goodbye. Bell's mouth shaped the word, but her heart numbly refused to accept that he had vanished. She stood rooted to the spot, staring unseeingly into the strange faces that weaved to and fro in front of her. She could no longer see his blond head above the sea of dancers. Gone.

Her body ached as if she had been beaten up.

Home. Suddenly all she could think of was the security and silence of her own room. She must go home at once.

There was no sign of Valentine at their table. The champagne bottle was empty, and the redhead's pink angora wrap was flung over her empty chair. Well, good luck to them both. Bell didn't want to see or think about Valentine Gordon ever again.

She turned away.

The Dorchester doorman in his top hat called her a taxi as she stood shivering on the steps. He even held an umbrella over her head to shield her from the torrential rain as she climbed in.

Not quite as humble an exit as Cinderella's, thought Bell, but her loss was greater. She had left no glass slipper in Charles's hand. And even if she had, he would have tossed it into the nearest waste bin.

The cab pulled away into the Park Lane traffic. Bell was too immersed in her own thoughts to see Valentine plunging past the startled doorman and calling something after her into the blanketing rain. Too late. He stood for a moment oblivious of the wet, staring after the red tail lights with a mixture of irritation and disappointment plain in his face. Then, slowly, he shook his head and retraced his steps into the bright lights of the foyer.

CHAPTER SEVEN

There was a bell ringing, somewhere.

Bell stretched out a hand to the alarm button, but the shrilling went on. Groggy with the sleeping pill that she had taken in the small hours, Bell reluctantly opened her eyes. The sight of the black dress shrouded in its protective wrapping over the door of the wardrobe brought it all back. A wave of misery hit her.

That damned bell. She must stop the ringing. She was aware now that it was the doorbell, and somebody must be leaning against it. She groped her way out towards the noise.

In the doorway stood a florists' messenger, half-hidden under a pyramid of red roses. He grinned cheekily at her.

'Customer told me not to go away until I'd delivered these. Personally.'

Bell sighed wearily. 'What time is it?'

'Nine.' He goggled at her. 'A.m. that is.'

'Thank you.' She shut the door and ripped open the white envelope that was pinned to the cellophane wrapping.

The note was on Connaught writing paper.

'I should have taken better care of you last night. When
I got back from dancing with that redhead you were
gone, and I don't blame you, but did you get home
safely?
And will you forgive me, whatever it is I've done?
V.'

The note fell from her fingers as Bell stared at the mass of flowers. They were long-stemmed florists' roses, thornless and somehow sterile. The colour reminded her of blood.

She sighed again and went into the kitchen in search of a jug large enough to hold them. She jammed the long green stems into the water without attempting to arrange them. She walked away and left the flowers on the tiled worktop without a backward glance, then picked the note up from the rug and dropped it into the wastebasket.

Valentine Gordon and his unwanted peace-offering were irrelevant.

Only one person mattered, and he was gone.

Moving slowly and deliberately, making tiny trivial decisions in order to occupy her mind, Bell got dressed and then made strong coffee and toast thickly spread with Marmite. She smiled crookedly at the sight of the homely plateful. It was what her mother had always made for her when she was ill as a small child, and the habit had stuck. She might as well look after herself, Bell thought sadly. No one else was going to.

Stop that.

There were things to be done, now, and wallowing in self-pity wasn't one of them. Even in the midst of today's unhappiness, Bell knew deep down that she was a survivor. She was used to fighting, and most of those fights had been to do with loneliness. But this time it was different because she herself had made a bad mistake, a horrible and disastrous mistake, and it had cost her Charles.

Don't think about that now. It was done. It had happened, and there was no changing it. Anyway, it all ended up the same, she thought, allowing herself the luxury of bitterness. She was on her own, and she would have to learn to live with it.

Ah, she had been right to be afraid. Afraid even with Edward that happiness was too good to be true. And now . . .

Be practical. She must be practical, tackle the things that she could actually hope to do something about. First, work.

With a show of briskness Bell dialled the newspaper and spoke to the secretary that she shared with three other journalists. She had some holiday due to her. She was taking it, as from this morning. She was sure that in the circumstances it would be understood, etc. etc. In the unlikely event of anyone needing her, she would be at home.

She hung up with a sigh of relief.

Now.

The tiny idea that had taken root in her head yesterday was still growing, putting out little shoots in every direction. She made herself re-examine it from all angles.

Last night had changed things, of course. It had changed everything except her imperative need to find a new job. And that was it. Her job had been the only thing that had held her in the last months, and now that it had been suddenly snatched away she didn't want to stay in London any more. Her life there had become meaningless and repetitive.

Before last night, she had been allowing herself to think that she might go to Bordeaux. She could feel the pull of the slow, prosperous city like a magnet.

Why not, even now? Bell asked herself deliberately. Bordeaux was one of the great wine centres of the world. With her fluent French and knowledge of the wine trade she could get some kind of job that would add another interesting dimension to her experience.

Hastily Bell took out a sheet of paper and divided it into two columns. PROS, she headed it, and CONS.

It didn't take long to put down the points in favour. Her French was excellent and she knew the wine business. Her shorthand and typing were just about good enough for her to be able to fall back on that if nothing better presented itself. It would be difficult anyway, in these hard times, to get another job in London as good as the one she had just lost, and what would be the point of staying on to do something less challenging? Going off to Bordeaux at least looked as if she was taking the initiative, and she was sure that she could improve her knowledge and develop new contacts while she was there. Besides, the way of life itself attracted her. Its calm sureness was just what she needed in her own uncertainty.

The list of cons took longer and she frowned as she wrote, forcing herself to be realistic. She would lose her carefully-constructed network of London contacts, and she would miss the friends who up until now had seemed so important in her life. Nor did she yet have a job, or anywhere to live, or enough money to keep her going while she looked for one. Then she crossed each of these out. She was independent, she would find a job and a room, and she had Henry's redundancy settlement.

Her pencil hovered between the two columns as she came to the biggest question of all. Yesterday she would have accepted it as the real reason for wanting to go. Today that was impossible, but she was no nearer to knowing whether it meant that she should stay away. Bell doodled impatiently on her paper, knowing that she must face up to her true motive for wanting to work in Bordeaux. It was where Charles belonged, and she remembered it with pleasure for that reason. But did it matter now whether she was to settle in Alaska or a mere thirty kilometres down the road from him? She was a stranger. No, worse than that, she was just an acquaintance. Yet, perhaps, if she was so close to him Charles might think about her sometimes? Perhaps even want to see her again? There would always be the chance of meeting him, and she would be with people who knew him and who moved in the same world. Bell saw that it was a fragile thread to hang her whole future on, but at least it offered a kind of hope. And even the faintest hope was better than nothing, better than staying on in London immersed in her own sense of loss.

Suddenly Bell scribbled under the pro column in heavy capital letters IT'S WHAT I WANT TO DO. That was it, then. Bell leant back in her chair and smiled with satisfaction at having made a decision. All she had to do now was to sort out the practicalities. Bell opened her contacts book and wondered where she should begin her telephoning.

Before she could start the bell rang again.

It was the last person in the world that she wanted to see. Valentine.

Bell felt herself freeze with icy resentment as he stood there smiling down at her. He was unscathed. He looked as clear-eyed and rested as if he had gone to bed at ten-thirty the night before with nothing more dangerous inside him than a cup of hot milk.

'I would have rubbed ashes in my hair,' he said, 'but all I could find at my hotel were Havana cigar butts.'

Bell's mouth felt stiff. It isn't funny, she wanted to say. Leave me alone, can't you?

Valentine's smile faded when he saw the coldness in her eyes. She looked tired and pale, and defenceless. He had never expected to see Bell, so crisp and sure of herself, look like that. He went to put his arms around her but Bell turned away before his hands could reach her.

'Can't I come in?' he asked, unnecessarily, closing the door behind him. 'I don't want to say this out in the lobby.' There was still no reply. 'Bell, what's the matter? Has something happened?'

She had no idea how to answer. She was still angry with him, and hot with resentment, and dangerously close to tears. But the unwelcome, undeniable charm of his presence was already beginning to work on her. She was torn between her need to say vicious things to him and hurt him just for existing last night, and her fearful wish that he would put his arms around her again.

'I'm sorry, really very sorry you didn't enjoy last night,' he was saying softly. 'And I'm ashamed of having been a boor. Isn't that enough?' He was coming towards her now, his eyes fixed on her face. Bell found herself backing away in the confined space, barely conscious that her hands were pulling her flimsy jacket tighter around her.

'Why?' she was asking, playing for time without really knowing what she was afraid of. 'Why did you have to act as though you owned me?'

Valentine stopped, and his face darkened. He looked threatening, and Bell saw that his fists were clenched so tight that the knuckles were white against the tanned flesh.

'Why? Well, why did I . . .?' He might have been talking to himself. 'I don't think . . . I ever understood . . . how much I hate that man. Your friend Charles. And I was surprised by how much I hated seeing you beside him.'

Bell felt the hair prickling all over her scalp and a cold finger of dread laid on her heart. She was caught between two men who hated each other with a dangerous, bitter hatred.

'He isn't my friend,' she whispered, with a bitterness that he couldn't hear.

Valentine turned abruptly and went to lean against the window. His eyes were on the trees beyond the rooftops.

'That marble coldness. That veneered hypocrisy. Christ.'

He was spitting out the words. 'It makes me boil up inside I want to rant, and wreck things, and be vulgar and violent.

There was a tiny, shocked silence. The words seemed to hang in the air between them like a curse.

Then Valentine shrugged and laughed softly, trying to dispel the effect of his outburst. 'In view of that, I did rather well to control myself. Don't you think?'

Bell searched frantically for some way of deflecting the talk away from Charles. So long as his name echoed in the room, she was afraid that she would give herself away. And Valentine must never, ever guess what had really been happening last night.

'Shouldn't you be at the Conference now?' she asked, lamely.

'Yes, but I'm here instead.' Valentine crossed the room in two strides and had caught her before she could slip away from him. His arms came around her, inescapably this time, and he pulled her close. He pressed her hips against his body and his mouth began to move against hers.

Bell closed her eyes. She felt as she had done after the crazy bike ride through the Californian night when they had reached the haven of the beach and heard the surf pounding ahead. Shock and fear were slowly ebbing away, to be replaced with a suffocating need.

Valentine lifted the heavy mass of hair away from her face and stared down into her blue-green eyes.

'Come to bed,' he said simply.

With a superhuman effort Bell broke away. She stumbled to her rocking chair and sat down in it, drawing her knees up like a protective barrier between them.

'No.' She shook her head to emphasize it. Valentine was watching her, half-annoyed and half-amused, but confident of his eventual power.

'I don't want to,' she told him, beginning once more to believe that she meant it.

'Something's happened, and I have to deal with it, and there isn't . . . room for anything else.'

Valentine came and knelt on the rug beside her. He wasn't listening.

'Look, Bell, I've got an idea. Bob Cornelius and I are going to Larue-Grise after this, for the vintage. Why don't you come out and join me? Write the vintage up for your paper?'

Bell started to shake her head, then her thoughts raced on. Larue-Grise? No. Impossible. It was the enemy's camp. Then, wearily, she reminded herself that the only person she had to consider now was herself. Valentine was a useful ally, she thought, trying to be hard-headed. Larue-Grise would be a perfect temporary base. Perhaps she could sell a feature on the vintage to one of the colour supplements . . . or one of the glossies . . . Somewhere, deep inside her, a little spark of enthusiasm flared. She would work. The loss of this job was just a temporary setback. She smiled gratefully at Valentine.

'I'd like that.'

'Wonderful.' He was all good humour now. 'If I'm not to be allowed to take you to bed, will you give me a cup of that coffee before I go and grovel to the Committee?'

Bell poured coffee into a mug and passed it to him. Carefully, she said, 'I wasn't at my best last night either. I lost my job yesterday. Got made redundant.'

Valentine's head jerked up. Surprise was followed by sympathy.

'Oh shit, Bell, that's bad news. What happened?'

She told him, reciting the bare facts unemotionally. When she had finished, he hugged her encouragingly.

'Well, you'll be able to get another job. No problem. God knows, you're sharp enough. Think big, this time. Start your own newspaper.'

'Yes,' she said sadly, 'I suppose I'll be able to get another job.' She lifted her chin and stared back at him. 'Anyway, I'll do some freelance work. Try and sell a piece on this vintage. I'll start at Larue-Grise.'

'You still want to come? Even though you can't write it up for your paper?' Bell recoiled. She felt exactly as if he had slapped her. Inside her head she was gabbling excuses to herself, frantically shoring up the crumbling walls of her self-defence. He didn't mean that, she told herself. He just means that you might be too busy elsewhere, looking for another job, perhaps. It didn't mean that he only wanted you because of who you were. Oh, of course, it would have been partly that. But not entirely. Definitely not entirely.

'Well,' she said aloud, trying to sound as if she was thinking it over, 'I don't know, at that. I haven't quite . . . finalized my plans yet. Better not to make any promises.'

He smiled at her. He's very handsome, and very generous, she caught herself thinking, but he's nobody's fool. He was kissing her again, and stroking her hair back from her hot face.

'You must do whatever you want, Princess,' he murmured. 'You know where I am, and if there's anything I can do . . .'

She shook her head and gave him a bright smile.

'Nothing. Really.' She felt so churned up inside that she was afraid that it was all going to come pouring out in a gush of tears and words that would give her away. She wanted him to go before it could happen.

'I must make some phone calls,' she prodded him. He let her go and glanced at his watch.

'Oh God, they'll probably blackball me or take away my ornamental tastevin and silk ribbon, or whatever dire penalty they keep up their sleeves for truants.'

He blew her a kiss from the door and then said, suddenly serious, 'I'm at the Connaught for another two days, and then at Larue until after the harvest. You've very welcome, Bell . . .'

Then, thank God, he was gone. She knew now that she wouldn't be going to Larue-Grise. Never, ever. The gulf between slick, street-wise Valentine and Charles, bred out of centuries beyond such considerations, had never seemed wider. Bell felt sure without a shadow of doubt which man she wanted. It was Charles, and all that Charles stood for. In comparison to that, and with last night's memory still smarting in her head, Valentine seemed a brash upstart.

Bell sat stock-still in her accustomed position for an hour, and then another hour, thinking. Outside it was still raining, and the temperature must have dropped by fifteen degrees. Great fat raindrops slashed against the windows and the leaves were whipped to and fro against the backdrop of leaden sky. Summer had turned into winter overnight.

At last she stood up stiffly. She was sure that she must get away from London, and France beckoned seductively. There was only one person she could talk to about it now, she decided. Edward. Edward would advise her honestly.

Bell dialled his number, the private line that rang straight through on to his desk in the mysterious depths of the City bank. She had rung him there only a handful of times in all the years that she had known him. Edward answered at once, sounding clipped and businesslike. When he recognized her voice he said, 'Bell? Is that you? How long have you been back?'

'Just a few days. Edward, I'm sorry to bother you.' Bell bit her lip. They had moved so far apart already. 'Something horrible's happened. Stobbs has made me redundant. I've got an idea about what I should do, and I need some advice.'

She felt on the edge of tears again, and she rushed on headlong. 'You're my best friend, after all, Eddie.'

There was a long silence at the other end of the line.

Then Edward said, 'You know I'd do anything I could, Bell. And I'm terribly sorry about your job. It's just that we're – I'm going straight from here to Gatwick. I'm going on holiday, just for a couple of weeks. As soon as I get back, I'll come and see you, and we can talk about this then.'

We're going on holiday, you were going to say, Bell thought. Go on, don't try to shield me from it. Who is she?

'That's nice. Don't worry about the stupid job – I just thought it would be a good idea to talk the possibilities over with somebody. Where are you going?'

'Italy. Not far from Naples.'

'Lovely. Who with?'

Again the silence. She knew that he didn't want to hurt her, even after everything that had happened. Don't worry, she wanted to say, I'm getting immune to it.

'Ah, I met her about a month ago. I don't know, yet, Bell, but it seemed worth going on with.'

'I'm glad. Look, I'll see you when you get back. Have a good time, okay?'

She hung up.

The knocks were coming thick and fast today.

Don't give in to it. Once you let the tears start, you won't be able to stop them. A walk. Some fresh air, that was the answer.

Bell found a pair of thick, green wellingtons at the back of a cupboard, and pulled on an old burberry. Her umbrella was a man's golfing one in bright primary colours, left behind by Edward, and she grasped the reassuring smooth roundness of the handle as she clumped down the steps. The protective clothes made her feel somehow protected herself, and she squared her shoulders ready to face the weather and whatever else the day might bring.

Bell walked along the streaming pavement towards the park. At the street corner something made her look back. She was just in time to see a yellow-oilskinned figure hesitating at the door of her block of flats, and then ducking inside into the lobby.

There could be no mistake. The long, fair hair was darkened with rain, and the oilskin collar was turned up to hide her face, but it was still Juliette. And she must be looking for Bell.

Bell's first instinct was to run away. She shrank from the idea of confronting Charles's sister and seeing the accusation again in the dark blue eyes that were so painfully like his. Then, almost immediately, a kind of wild hope began fluttering against her ribs. Perhaps she was bringing a message from him. Oh, what if she had missed her?

Bell began to run, back towards her own door. She was dodging the puddles and bumping into people coming towards her, and all the time hardly daring to hope that Charles . . . that Charles . . .

Juliette had half-turned away from her door when Bell came panting up the stairs.

'Hello,' she said simply. 'I'm glad you're here after all.'

'Juliette,' Bell gasped, 'Juliette . . .' The French girl took her arm.

'I think the rain might stop. Will you walk me through Kensington Gardens?'

They turned back downstairs together. Out in the street

Bell looked up at the sky and then unfurled the striped umbrella. They leaned together under its shelter, with identical red and blue shafts of light slanting obliquely across their faces.

When they reached the Gardens, Bell automatically turned along the path that she took on her way to work. The ground was dark and moist now, smelling richly of leaf-mould. The air was as clean as if it had been washed and the rain dripping through the leaves made soothing pat-pat sounds.

It was very quiet. The only sound was the hum of traffic along Kensington Gore, muffled by the thick damp air.

Juliette's grip on her arm tightened as if she was getting ready to say something.

Bell waited, her heart thumping.

'Don't run away,' she said at last, so softly that Bell had to strain to catch the words. 'He still needs you.'

Somewhere overhead a blackbird started singing, a full-throated river of sound. Bell's spirits lifted with it.

'Did he ask you to come?' she dared.

Juliette shook her damp blonde curls.

'No, Bell. He'd never do that. I came because I still think – because I still remember the way you looked at each other when you were at Reynard. Whatever's happened since. I think,' she went on simply, her freckled face shaded with shifting red and blue light as she turned to look at Bell, 'you could help him back to life.'

Bell winced. And instead, what had she done?

They walked on for another few paces, watching the raindrops spattering into the gravel. Then Juliette went on delicately, 'I know it isn't any of my business. But are you and Valentine . . .?'

Bell shivered. She didn't want to have to admit it to honest, loyal Juliette. She felt, more than ever, ashamed and angry with herself. But Juliette believed that he still needed her. She had said so. Bell steeled herself to tell her Californian story.

'I went out there expecting to meet a kind of monster,' she began.

Juliette laughed, a real laugh.

'Oh no. I told you. He's not that. Do you know, even when I saw him myself last night, I felt a kind of undertow of attraction to him? What's his secret, do you think?'

Bell joined in her laughter, and at the same time felt a surge of liking and gratitude towards Charles's sister. Intuitively, she had said something that made the recital of Bell's awkward story a thousand times easier.

Bell told her everything. Juliette listened carefully, nodding sometimes so that the blonde curls bounced over the collar of the yellow oilskin.

It was only when Bell started to describe how she had felt since getting back to London that Juliette turned to watch her. Sympathy combined with speculation in her face.

Their walk had taken them through into Hyde Park, and now they reached the coffee shop in the Dell. The white metal tables at the edge of the Serpentine were empty and pooled with water that reflected the grey-white sky. The rain had stopped so Bell fetched them plastic beakers of coffee from the kiosk and they sat down at one of the tables. The forest of rowing boats and little dinghies moored in front of them bobbed gently as a breeze began to lick over the water. Over to the west a tatter of blue sky appeared as the wind began to chivvy the tail-end of the storm clouds.

Bell was tracing rivulets of water across the table-top, her face drawn with anxiety.

'I'm not trying to excuse what happened at Dry Stone, but everything looked different out there. Juliette, I was missing Charles and he seemed so far away. I hadn't heard from him, and I needed to so much, and it had all happened so quickly at Reynard that I felt disorientated. I started to think that perhaps I'd misjudged everything, and that I was a fool to pin all my hopes on Charles. So I gave in to Valentine. It was no more than . . . fun, just something that happened and should have been forgotten as soon as it was over. Instead, it's led to all this. And it's made me see that I was right from the very beginning. I love Charles. He matters more to me than anything else in the world.' She was pulling at the rim of the plastic cup as she spoke, trying to tear it. 'Yet, do you know, I still like Valentine? I saw him this morning. He came to apologize, preceded by about a thousand red roses. I almost agreed to go to Larue-Grise with him.'

Juliette stiffened. 'No, don't do that.'

'I won't. It's odd, isn't it? How Valentine is unaffected by all the things that hurt the rest of us, yet remains so likeable? I wanted to be angry with him, but I couldn't be. He just made me feel angrier with myself.'

Bell smiled lopsidedly, then remembered the flash of rage and passion that she had seen in Valentine. He wasn't quite invulnerable.

'They hate each other, don't they?' she asked, feeling the cold touch of foreboding on her again.

'Yes, they hate each other. Bell,' Juliette said abruptly. 'What do you want to happen?'

'I want it to be a month ago. I want to be back at Reynard, just as it was. And I want none of this,' Bell gestured at the emptiness around them, 'to have happened.'

'That's no good,' Juliette told her gently. 'What about *now*?'

Bell's eyes dropped, but to Juliette there was no mistaking the passionate conviction in her voice as she answered. 'I want to be with Charles. I want to make it right again.'

Juliette gripped her wrist. 'Do it then.'

Bell started talking again, fast. 'Listen, Juliette, I've lost my job.' She brushed aside the other girl's startled exclamation of sympathy and rushed on. 'I've been thinking and thinking, ever since. I don't want to stay here. My life here isn't . . . important any more, for all kinds of reasons. My work, all the efforts to be successful and independent and free to live my own life – none of it matters.' As she spoke, a new certainty took hold of Bell. It was the utter conviction that she loved Charles, and there was a kind of comfort in that alone. Maybe he had rejected her, now, but no one could take away the pleasure of knowing that she had once mattered to him. She had broken through his aloofness and touched the real Charles – and she hugged that to her like a magic charm. Bell knew how isolating her own defences could be, and it gave her a heady thrill to know that she had penetrated Charles's. She pressed her fingers to her temples as if to fix the sudden certainty inside her head.

'All I want now is to be near Charles. To have the hope of seeing him sometimes, even if it's only the hope. I've got an idea. You might think it's crazy . . .'

'Go on,' Juliette commanded.

'I could come to work in Bordeaux. Find somewhere to live. Just be close, in case he does want me . . . Will you help?'

Juliette's eyes were shining. 'Yes. It will be all right, Bell. You'll see, it will.' Then a thought struck her and she looked serious. 'I . . . don't think I could ask you to stay at Château Reynard. There's Hélène, and Charles is still shocked, you see, and I am afraid that he is angry.'

'I know that,' Bell told her, remembering the steely formality of their dance together last night.

'He needs some time to think. But I could find you somewhere else, Bell. In fact,' she brightened up again, 'I know the very place. Perfect. In Vayonnes, between Bordeaux and us. It's an auberge, summer trade mostly, and Sunday lunches for fat Bordelais burghers. The Durands are friends of mine, and the food's good, and . . .'

'Is it expensive?' Bell asked, cautiously.

'Mmmm, not very. And they have a little cottage in the garden, a summer holiday house. I'll persuade them to rent it cheaply over the winter.' Juliette clapped her hands. 'You'll like it, I know. The auberge is called Le Girafe.'

'The Giraffe?'

'Oh, yes, it's such a sad story. It makes me cry every time I think of it.'

Juliette looked mournful. 'Some circus people from Paris went down to Africa – oh, two hundred years ago – to trap wild animals for their show. They captured a giraffe, the first any of them had seen. They walked it back, all the way up Africa and through Spain, over the Pyrenees and on towards Paris. Every night they stopped and charged the local people money to see this amazing phenomenon. The auberge at Vayonnes was one of the places, and its name was changed after the great event. The poor old giraffe died of cold and exhaustion before they got to Paris.'

Bell, in her heightened emotional state, felt the tears spring to her eyes at the thought of the wretched creature stumbling through the midwinter snow, every step taking it further away from its home.

'You see?' Juliette said, and there were tears in her eyes too. 'Isn't it sad?'

The two girls sat across the tin table from each other, laughing through their absurd tears.

A kind of bond had been forged between them.

Le Girafe, Bell thought. Well, why not? Something about it sounded right.

After that it had all happened surprisingly quickly. Bell had put her flat on the books of a letting agency. She had left the newspaper, depositing the redundancy cheque securely in her bank on the last day.

'Goodbye,' Henry Stobbs had said, holding on to her handshake for a shade too long. 'We're sorry to lose you, you know that? Anything I can do, personally . . .'

'Thank you,' Bell had said, wanting to get away.

With three of the other journalists who were leaving, she had thrown a farewell lunch party at the restaurant across the street. It had been a boisterous, surprisingly cheerful occasion.

Phillippa had said, 'Are you sure you're doing the right thing?' and Bell had thought, carefully, and then said, 'Yes.'

'Good luck, then.' They had kissed each other, and Philly had made another joke.

Bell had thought, *I'll miss some things*. Ordinary things. But she wasn't going into exile. She could always come back; it needn't feel like failure. Bell set off for France armed with a commission to write a 'mood' piece about the vintage for a glossy magazine, and a promise from one of the trade magazines that they would buy whatever she could send them from the spot.

It wasn't a lot to be starting a new life on, but at least it was something. The trip wasn't the most comfortable she had ever undertaken, either. Determined to eke her money out as far as possible, Bell had carefully worked out the cheapest way to travel. It had turned out to be via the overnight ferry to Dunkirk, and then by train from Paris to Bordeaux. It took twenty hours from start to finish, and she was loaded with unwieldy luggage. The connections were awkward, and the train crowded.

By the time the long, grey snake of SNCF coaches was crawling into the central station at Bordeaux, Bell was exhausted, lonely, and beginning to be terribly afraid that she had done the wrong thing. She hauled her bags down out of the high compartment, looking up and down the platform and then back towards the exit.

There was no sign of a familiar face. She admitted to herself that she had been hoping to see Juliette, but she wasn't there.

A taxi. She would take a taxi to Vayonnes, and Le Girafe. Outside the glare and bustle of the station the air of the early October evening was cold and thin. A few dead leaves were whirling on the deserted patch of bare earth under the plane trees. The boules players had packed up for the winter and were sitting morosely in the cheap cafés, listening to the ping and rattle of the pinball machines and the blare of the television over the bar.

The car at the head of the rank was an ancient Citroën with a driver who reminded Bell of an unsmiling Jacopin. Grumbling a little at having to take her so far, the man heaved her bags into the car and they set off into the gathering darkness. The road was the one that she had travelled with Charles, and Bell felt the frayed thread that drew her to him begin to quiver and tighten.

Vayonnes. Bienvenu. Bell glimpsed the road sign as it flashed past, and then they were slowing down in the middle of the village. It was like a thousand others, with little houses along the main street, their curtains already drawn for the evening. There was the charcuterie with the steel shutters down, and the boulangerie with its proprietor locking up for the night, the baguettes for his own family supper tucked under his arm.

The auberge was on the outskirts of the village, standing back a little from the road. It looked very old, with solid timbering and steeply pitched, tiled roofs. The taxi driver swung sharply to the left and pulled up in a cobbled courtyard. Bell sat quietly, imagining the giraffe swaying here above a gaping circle of rustics before being shut into some freezing barn.

'*Voyons, madame,*' the driver said sharply.

As Bell was paying him, the inn door opened and a shaft of warm light struck across the cobbles. A fat woman in a black dress was waiting in the doorway.

'*Bonsoir, chérie,*' she called, '*Soyez bienvenue . . .*'

Bell was flooded with relief. She was expected. She wasn't quite alone.

She followed the beckoning figure inside. The door opened straight into a big, welcoming room. There was a crackling fire in a stone fireplace, a group of fat armchairs with fringed covers protecting the backs and arms, and yellowing walls hung with bright copper pans. Through an archway, Bell could see tables with red and white checked cloths. There was a delicious smell of garlic, fresh bread and stewing herbs.

Madame Durand was wheezing and chuckling beside her.

'All the way from London today? You'll want to go straight across to the little house and settle in? It's all aired and ready for you.' Bell nodded gratefully and the woman took a huge black key from a hook beside the door.

'Here we are, then,' she murmured. 'We were so pleased when Mademoiselle Juliette told us that she would bring someone here for the winter. We're very quiet, you know . . . this way, *chérie.*'

They crossed the cobbled yard again. At right angles to the main building was what looked like a row of outhouses, with a little, whitewashed afterthought tacked on at the end. The tiny house had a tiled roof, two upper windows that seemed to be almost at eye level, and a lower window beside the doll-size front door. The red curtains were drawn and a light shone rosily through them.

Madame Durand opened the front door and Bell followed her straight into a little parlour. There was a log fire with an armchair drawn up to it, a stone floor covered with ancient rugs, and a flight of wooden stairs that climbed at a precarious angle to the floor above. A little round table was laid for dinner.

Juliette was sitting in the armchair beaming at her.

'Welcome home.' She waved around at the homely room.

'But it's so lovely,' Bell said, looking delightedly round at the miniature house. 'It's perfect. Like a house in a story.'

Madame Durand chuckled again. 'Well then, I'll leave you to your dinners. Mind you come straight over if there's anything you want. My little girl will come over in the morning to see if there's any shopping you want done. Goodnight my dears.'

She squeezed out through the narrow doorway and Bell heard her footsteps retreating over the cobbles. A dog barked somewhere close at hand and then silence settled around the house.

Bell danced over to Juliette and hugged her.

'Thank you, for finding this. It feels like home already. Can I look at the rest?' Juliette grinned. 'Can you? It's your house. I'm warning you, though, it's a little primitive . . .' At the back was a kitchen with a stone sink and an ancient oven. '. . . but Madame Durand says that of course you must eat *en famille* with them whenever you want, and when you don't she'll send your food over here.'

Bell was going to protest but Juliette waved her into silence. 'I'd give in gracefully, if I were you. She cooks like a dream. In fact she presented us with this for tonight . . .' Inside the oven was an earthenware marmite sending out the rich smell of a *boeuf en daube*.

The rest of the house consisted of a single bedroom, almost entirely taken up by a high bed with a picture of the Holy Family hanging over it, and a tiny bathroom.

The two girls edged back down the steep stairs, ducking their heads to avoid the exposed beams. Bell sank into the armchair with a sigh of pleasure, and noticed the high dusty shoulders of a claret bottle *chambréing* near the hearth.

Juliette followed her gaze and another smile lit up her freckled face.

'I wanted to come to the station to meet you,' she said, 'but something held me up. It was Madame Durand, ringing to ask whether our English guest would be in time for dinner.' She paused, obviously for effect, and Bell gazed at her.

'Charles took the call. So . . . I had to stay and explain.'

Charles. He would have to know sooner or later. But why did Juliette look so pleased about it?

'What did he say?' she asked, as calmly as she could.

'Oh, nothing. He was very grave.' Juliette made a serious face, and Bell was struck again by the mysterious family likeness that made them appear to be opposite sides of the same ancient coin. 'But he told me to make sure that you were comfortable, and he sent this for our dinner.'

She twirled the bottle round so that Bell could read the label. There was the familiar, discreet labelling and the steel engraving of Château Reynard. It was another bottle of the precious '61. A message of welcome to her more explicit than anything else he could have devised.

As she looked back into his sister's dark blue eyes, Bell knew that she had been right to come to Bordeaux.

Juliette stayed to share the wine with her, sitting in the firelight in companionable quiet, then slipped away into the darkness.

When the silence fell again it was broken only by the crackle of the new logs on the fire. Bell felt more at peace than she had done for weeks. She was where she should be.

In spite of all the uncertainties and problems that lay ahead, in spite of the incongruity of being here in a funny little house beside Le Girafe with no job and no real plans, she felt calm and strong. She could make it all come right.

Bell was suddenly seized with a desire to mark the bounds of her new territory. She put on her coat and boots, and picked up the big black key that Madame Durand had left for her. Then, smiling, she put it back on the table. Something told her that this was not the kind of place where people locked their doors against one another.

Outside the courtyard was lit only by the half-moon as it sailed briefly out from behind the thin clouds. Le Girafe was already in darkness. Country hours, thought Bell. She slipped round to the front of the inn and stood looking up at the weatherbeaten sign. The paint was flaking off the giraffe, and the colours were muddy with age, but the old house in the background looked exactly the same.

Bell began to walk meditatively up the little street and over the hump-backed bridge at the other end of the village. Shallow, running water splashed noisily in the deserted darkness. She leant on the little stone parapet and gazed upriver. This little stream would run into the Gironde somewhere up ahead, and the water would flow past Château Reynard on its way to the Atlantic. Bell breathed in deeply. The air was cold, and smelled thinly of autumn. The latent summer warmth had ebbed away, and in a matter of days bad weather would start rolling in from the sea. It was vintage time, time to bring in the sweet, oozing mountains of grapes before the icy rains came to slash the bloom off them.

Bell's thoughts turned irrevocably to the two men in their châteaux, only a few miles away from this peaceful village. They would both be ready for the harvest, their miniature armies of pickers ready to swarm at their command along the avenues of vines. She shook her head as she thought of them, and as the memory of their opposition came back to her.

Valentine? As always, when she was apart from him, she could conjure up the separate parts of him but the essence of him eluded her. She didn't want to think of the power he seemed to wield over her so casually. She had been weak, that was all, and he had outwitted her.

Yet it looked, magically, as though she might be given a second chance. As though her mistaken celebration with him might after all be blotted out.

It was unbelievable, but it might be true.

And Charles? Bell hugged herself inside her coat, hardly daring to think about him now. Yet he had sent her his wine. It was a welcome, she knew that, and she knew with just as much certainty that it was only a matter of time before he came himself. He would welcome her here, to the country he loved and which had supported his family for so many generations.

It was where she should be. If she belonged with Charles, if she could dare to hope that, it was where she belonged too.

Bell thrust her hands deeper into her pockets and turned back towards the old-fashioned high bed in the tiny cottage bedroom.

Back home.

CHAPTER EIGHT

Early in the morning, the cobbled courtyard was busy with comings and goings to the back door of the inn. The baker's van pulled in and a round wicker basket of bread was handed over, and then a white truck appeared, driven by a red-faced man in a long white apron. Madame Durand came out into the sunshine and began to sort critically through the gleaming fish in their white trays. The fishmonger was pointing with enthusiasm to his wares as Madame Durand shook her head and complained through pursed lips. Bell leant against the windowsill, watching the little pantomime with delight. It probably happened exactly the same every Friday. At last the *patronne* made her choice, and the van man weighed it up on a hanging scale that he produced from his cab. There was another little display of surprise and reluctance, then Madame Durand handed over the notes. She saw Bell watching, and beckoned her.

'You are quite comfortable?' she asked, 'and are you busy, or will you come in and meet my husband?'

Bell followed her through the empty dining-room and into the kitchen. At the big scrubbed table a thin brown man in a striped apron was slicing meat. He came round to shake hands, wiping them carefully on his apron first.

Bell glanced round and saw that the kitchen rafters were hung with hams and sausages, the enormous cooking range gleamed, and rank upon rank of saucepans and knives were hung all round the white walls.

'*Bonjour, monsieur*,' Bell said, smiling. As a couple the Durands looked just like Jack Sprat and his wife.

'Sit down, sit down,' they told her. Bell found herself ensconced at one end of the table with a big bowl of *café au lait* and a perfect brioche in front of her. Madame Durand was working on the dough for *pissaladière*, rolling briskly one way

197

and then the other. Magically, a perfectly even elastic sheet spread in front of her.

'Our busy time here is the weekend,' she was explaining. 'Thirty and forty people for lunches and dinners, and no chance of sitting around. But during the week in the winter – pffff – Durand and I have no one to look at but each other.' The couple were smiling affectionately at one another. Bell basked in the calm atmosphere. A healthy little business, the company of their children, and the occasional guest like herself for diversion. It wasn't a bad way to live, Bell thought, remembering her own solitariness with a tinge of sadness. Yet it would be difficult to feel lonely here. The atmosphere was too warm and welcoming.

'Are you a friend of the de Gillesmont family?' Monsieur Durand asked her, with evident interest.

'Juliette de Gillesmont is a friend of mine,' Bell answered cautiously, 'but I couldn't have wished myself on the family for a long visit.'

By the time she stood up to go she had promised to come back to share the family's early dinner. Madame Durand had also given her an assurance that nothing in the world was easier to make than brioche dough, and she was welcome to come and have a lesson in the morning.

The three of them walked back through the dining-room where a young girl was laying the tables ready for the evening's diners, and into the open area that served as reception hall and salon.

There was the sound of a fast car approaching, and then turning sharply into the courtyard. It was a grey Mercedes, thickly veiled with the rich Médoc dust. Bell herself had barely glimpsed the shadowed but unmistakable profile at the wheel when Madame Durand murmured, 'It's Baron Charles. He must be coming to see you.'

She sounded impressed. He's an important man here, Bell thought dimly. She felt as though the world had suddenly tilted and slipped back into slow motion. It seemed to take an age for Charles to step out of his car and start on the journey across the cobbles towards her. His fair hair lifted and fanned very slowly in the light wind.

She had time to think *I can't think*, and to realize that her legs felt shaky beneath her.

The world seemed to right itself again and speeded back to normality. Bell was in control once more and was waiting calmly to see what lay ahead. Charles came over and nodded to the Durands, then his eyes slid over Bell's face.

'I wondered if you would like to come over and look at the vineyards?' he asked.

'Oh. Yes. Why not? That would be very interesting.'

'We shall begin picking tomorrow or the day after,' he was saying coolly, 'and everything gets rather busy then, so now would be the best time.'

He said good morning to the innkeeper and his wife and held the car door open for Bell. She slipped inside, into the familiar leathery smell. Then Charles was beside her and they were driving, fast, down a lane that led nowhere near Reynard. It was a moment of perfection for Bell. She was with him and he was taking her somewhere, she didn't care where or why.

Charles was wearing corduroys and heavy muddy boots, and a thick navy-blue sweater. He looked less formal than she had ever seen him, as well as more approachable, and somehow younger.

'Where are we going?' she asked, still not caring.

He smiled. 'There have been so many obstacles, but still we are both here. And so, I think, we had better explain to each other. Before we lose each other again.'

One hand left the wheel and his fingers interlaced with Bell's.

'If I may, I will take you for a walk. We will have some peace there.'

Bell let her head fall back against the seat and she watched the trees and fences flash past through half-closed eyes. Their hands were touching, they were together, and that was enough.

Charles stopped the car in a gateway and Bell climbed out. They had driven inland, and the wind was stronger here. Bell shivered. She was only wearing a thin shirt. Her hair blew about her face and she reached up automatically to knot it behind her head.

'Here.'

He was holding out a dark blue sweater like his own. He helped her to pull it over her head and then bent down to kiss her lightly on the angle of her cheekbone. Then he had turned away and was unlatching the gate.

'This way.'

A path ran diagonally across a long slope of field, and disappeared into the dark ridge of trees that sat on the horizon like a crown. They started out together, side by side. The path was only wide enough for one and so Charles walked on the rough, tussocky turf with his hands pushed deep into his pockets. With his face turned gratefully into the wind and the fine hair pushed back from his forehead he looked, more than ever, the complete aristocrat.

Yet Bell wasn't afraid of him any more. They were here on equal terms now. We must both explain, she thought. We must understand each other.

'And so?' she asked, gently. Charles was looking steadfastly at the line of trees ahead.

'I was disturbed to see you in London,' he told her, 'with Valentine.'

Just that. Valentine. As if he was a friend they had in common who had made Charles angry. He made it sound no more dramatic or important than that. 'Seeing him after so long reminded me of those unhappy times. It brought back Catherine, and . . . all the damaging things that the three of us did to each other. I wanted you to be completely separate from all that.' There was a moment's silence before he went on.

'When you came here, Bell, you seemed to bring such happiness. I wanted you very much, but I couldn't allow myself to make you want me. I let you go – and it cost me a lot to do it – because I haven't got the right to ask you to stay. I can't commit myself to you. I'm already married, and,' his mouth twisted with bitterness, 'after one failure it's hard to think of beginning again. Perhaps to be alone is better after all.'

Bell instinctively grasped his hand to reassure him, but he disengaged himself gently. 'Wait, I didn't want to pull you into this. I felt that all I had to offer you was pain, and difficulties. I'm not . . . free to give you what matters. Then you told me that you knew Valentine. That you were going out to him in California. That, fantastically, you already were involved.' Charles nodded, as if confirming something to himself. 'You. Me. Catherine. Valentine. We are all part of something, God help us.'

Without knowing it, Bell was climbing faster and faster. She was waiting, boiling with impatience, for him to finish. Beside her, Charles lengthened his stride to keep up. 'All I could do was wait for you to come back from California. Wait to see just how far you were going to be drawn in. Just as I am still waiting now.'

All the way in, Bell thought. *So far in that I almost drowned.*

'Then, when I saw you at that dinner, I was amazed at my own relief. There you were with exactly the same smile, just the same Bell. And a second later it was all gone. There was Valentine beside you with his hand on your arm. In possession.' He shrugged, and Bell caught the glitter of recollected anger in his dark eyes.

'I made a mistake,' she told him evenly. 'I see that now. Isn't that enough?'

He smiled briefly. 'Oh yes. It doesn't matter, whatever happened then. What does matter is here and now. What you want. Whether you really understand what you are asking for.'

Bell stopped dead and turned to face him. The cold wind was whipping stray strands of hair around her face and she pushed them back impatiently.

'What about you and me?' she asked fiercely. 'What about you? Don't you understand that I'm here, on your territory, without any . . . without anything to support me?'

'Except my sister,' Charles reminded her, with the ghost of a smile.

Bell was still fierce. 'Except Juliette, then. But I have come to you. That must be enough to tell you what I want, and how much I have thought about it. If you have been waiting, so have I. Now you must include me, Charles. I want to know everything. I want to know about you. No more mysteries.' The wind was catching her words and whipping them away out of her mouth. Even though she was almost shouting, Charles had to lean forward to listen. She could see that there was wariness, and speculation, as well as a kind of amused detachment in his eyes.

'Mysteries? There are no mysteries, except human feelings.'

He turned her back to face the slope of the hill and, with his arm resting lightly over her shoulder, they began to trudge on upwards. 'Listen then,' he said, with his eyes fixed on the rough grass rolling away in front of them. 'Do you believe that it's possible for two people to love each other and yet not be able to be together without hurting one another?'

Bell nodded, knowing what was coming. Charles was going to talk about his wife. Yet he surprised her. As oblique as ever, he left that as if it was understood between them and went on.

'When my son was born, none of that mattered any more. To either of us. There was a reason for doing everything better, and that reason was Christophe. Oh yes, fatherhood aroused all my dynastic instincts, and I was proud to have brought a son to Reynard. But it went deeper than that. It aroused a new kind of love, that was what surprised me. The fiercest, most protective love, in which there was only tenderness. No subterfuge. No guilt.'

Oh, Charles. Bell stifled her response, but she was thinking. Adult love need not hold those things either. Fear, and loss, and pain sometimes, yes, but so much else too . . . Where had he been, all these years?

'Those were the happiest times.' He was smiling at the memory. 'Christophe was an engaging child. Catherine and I both loved him so much. Too much, I think.' The smile disappeared and was replaced by deep vertical lines of pain that ran beside his mouth. His voice dropped lower and lower. 'I sat beside his bed, in those last hours, watching him fight. Watching the sickness drain the life out of him, seeing the light fade in his eyes. If it would have given him even a chance, I would have gone to the rack. I would have died the most tortured death that could have been devised. But that was denied me. They took him away from us. Christophe's death took everything.'

Charles shrugged, his shoulders hunched like an old man's.

'Everything,' he repeated.

Bell tried to blink back the tears in her eyes, then turned her face into the wind to let it scour them away.

'After that there was just darkness,' he said.

'For Catherine too?' Bell asked. Christophe was her son too, she wanted to say.

'Catherine.' Charles said her name slowly, as if he was tasting it on his tongue.

'Christophe's death killed us, you see. Catherine wanted human consolation. Human explanation of what had happened, and understanding. I couldn't give it to her. I couldn't find it for myself.' He sounded hard now, and coldness had chased the pain out of his face.

'Why not?' Bell was deliberately challenging. 'As people, human beings, that's all we can do. Help each other, comfort each other. In marriage especially.'

Like my father and mother, Bell thought. It's what I was too little to do for my father, and it's what I knew I shouldn't try to do for Edward. *What I long to do for you.*

Charles looked at her for a long moment before he tried to answer. They were coming up to the protection of the belt of trees now, and the wind was dropping away.

'I wanted to, but I couldn't. I was lost. My faith, my son, the apparent reasons for life itself going on, had been taken away and I was drowning in resentment. Catherine was part of that bitterness. We had failed each other, our whole life was a failure. How could I comfort her, out of my own bankruptcy?'

'But Valentine Gordon could,' Bell said brutally. She wanted to push their new frankness to its limits. They would hide nothing, so there would be no shadows for new misunderstandings to brood in. To her amazement, Charles laughed.

'Oh yes, Valentine could. In his way. Have you ever thought that Valentine is a plunderer? He's like an ancient raider, riding up in the dark to snatch what he can from the land without the labour of growing and tending it. He came and took Catherine when the fences were broken. Yet, according to some crazy law of humanity, he helped her where I couldn't.'

No, Bell was thinking. He isn't just a plunderer. She had a sudden, vivid mental picture of Valentine walking between his vines at Dry Stone and bending down to pick up a handful of the gritty earth. He was letting it trickle through his fingers and telling her 'This is it. The heart of it. The bare soil, and that.' He pointed up at the sun in the blue sky above them. Bell remembered, as she had never been able to do before, the exact expression of laughter coupled with passionate involvement in what he was doing that shone in his suntanned face. No, Valentine did his share of tending and nurturing, as well as raiding through the broken fences. He was a maverick, quick to snatch an opportunity when it presented itself, but he was a lot of other things too. He hadn't snatched her, either. She had offered herself quite freely. She must let Charles know that.

'He has a lot of warmth and strength,' she began, carefully.

'I'm sure he has,' he answered. 'He has a large number of detestable attributes, and one or two admirable ones. Even though I distrust him, I can see that clearly enough.'

'When I was with him in California . . .'

Charles looked away. 'That's nothing to do with this, Bell.' He was telling her, firmly, that he didn't want to hear. She bit her lip and kept quiet. 'What matters is here and now,' he repeated.

Side by side they reached the first fringe of trees and looked ahead into the dimness. This was ancient woodland, unusual for this countryside, of beech and oak. The ground was matted thick with leaf-mould that muffled their steps. Bell felt the atmosphere of the place close around her head like a hood.

Charles led the way forward and they began to walk in silence like conspirators. Fallen trunks and branches were littered across the way, many of them thickly furred with moss. The world seemed suddenly drained of all colours except dim green and grey.

For a little way the ground still sloped gently upwards, then they reached the crest of the hill. A fat tree-trunk lay on the ground and Charles beckoned her to it. They sat down side by side, looking outwards down the opposite slope. The trees were thinner on this seaward side and there was a fine view through them over the flat landscape. Bell realized that they had climbed the low hill that backed the gravelly plain of the Médoc. She couldn't pick out Reynard at this distance, but she recognized the solid bulk of two or three other châteaux standing in their patchworks of vines. There in the distance were the tiny movements of cars on the vineyard road. Except for the occasional throaty burr of a woodpigeon, the wind in the treetops and Charles's even breathing beside her, everything seemed to be waiting in an enchanted silence.

Charles turned to look at her and before their eyes met Bell let herself look at each of his features in turn. The arrogantly sensual mouth and the aristocratic curves of his jaw and cheekbones. Blond hair ruffled by the wind. Darker brows, slightly raised with a question now, and the searching navy-blue eyes. A formidable, puzzling, enigmatic man. But a man she wanted.

'Why are you here?' he whispered.

Without hesitation she answered, 'Because of you.'

'And will you stay, knowing what you know about me now?'

'I've known it all along. Charles, do you want me to stay?'

'I can promise you nothing, Bell. You know how it is with me.'

'Do you want me to stay?'

'Please stay. Stay until after the vintage. After the vintage,' his voice sank to a whisper, 'I promise I will either ask you to stay for ever, or . . . we will both know that I must let you go.'

His hands closed over hers and they sat, looking into each other's eyes. In the dim light Charles's were almost black. The supernatural silence cloaked the wood as if in assurance that they needed no words.

Then, very slowly, Charles leaned forward. His mouth felt for the shape of Bell's, and then he traced the outlines with his tongue. His hands cupped her face, turning it up to his as he tasted her mouth. Their eyes explored the tiny changes of expression, hungrily, wordlessly.

Bell felt as if her skin had been peeled away, leaving the nerves and muscles naked to his fingers. There was none of the passion that she had felt the first time he had kissed her, and this dreamy certainty was a million miles removed from the swirling currents of longing that she had felt for Valentine.

Just once, Charles looked up and pointed ahead. 'Look, out there. Is this where you want to be? I'm part of it, you know.' Bell gazed down at it, remembering. Château Reynard. Sunny, pockmarked golden stone. Whitewashed *chais* and stone-flagged floors. Vines, bare earth and the seasons – mist, frost, rain and sun. She would have gone with Charles anywhere, but she loved him deeply just here.

'Yes,' she told him. 'I want to be at home here.'

He smiled down at her and the silence lapped around them again.

Then, breathtakingly, a gunshot cracked through the quiet. It echoed crisply through the magical woodland and set up a flutter of wings in the branches overhead. Bell gasped and shrank. Charles's arms tightened protectively around her before he laughed.

'*La chasse*,' he reassured her. 'Farmers after woodpigeons, I should think. We'd better move.' He stood up and helped her to her feet. They turned away back to the long slope, their fingers still laced together.

'I haven't been here since I was nineteen. Jeanne brought me first.' He looked back briefly, remembering. 'Eternal afternoons. Hot, and secret, and bewildering. I used to think of it as an enchanted place. Out of time, out of reality.'

'Thank you for bringing me back to it. Charles, I'm very happy.' He stared at her, surprised and then grateful.

'Happy? I told you, Bell, you seem to bring happiness with you.'

Bell understood that the afternoon they had shared, the secret, silent wood, had been a rare confidence. Charles had drawn her into his life, just as she had hoped.

They were together and she never wanted to be anywhere else.

When they came out of the trees again the sun had moved down to the west and was throwing long shadows behind the tussocks of grass. They had been out for hours. They began to walk quickly, down towards the grey car parked in the gateway.

'Charles, I need to find a job.'

'A job?'

Bell explained, as briefly as she could.

Charles was frowning, kicking out at the rough ground as they paced over it.

'Was that a bad blow for you, losing your place on the paper?'

Bell allowed herself a wry smile. 'Not as bad as the other things that were happening to me just then.'

There was an answering flicker of a smile. 'Yes. Well, you could begin by going to see Jacques Lapotin in Bordeaux. After the vintage, I'll see what else I can do.'

'Don't worry about that now,' she said quickly. 'You're picking tomorrow?'

Instinctively Charles glanced over at the horizon, barred with long pink and grey clouds. It was settled weather in spite of the wind.

'Yes, God willing. My pickers are all ready and I believe it's time to go.'

'It's earlier than usual.'

Charles frowned again, making Bell remember the autocratic baron touring his cellars like a monarch. 'It's the right time, nevertheless,' he told her. 'We're in for a hard autumn.'

They reached the car and he held the door open for her. 'Come over to Reynard and watch the picking,' he suggested, telling her that she was forgiven for her suggestion that he was hurrying his harvest. Bell grinned at him, happy.

'On the last day, perhaps. You'll want to get on with what you're doing, and I have to look for a job. And research an article.'

'That sounds very severe. Must I wait until then?'

'Mmmmm. Perhaps.' They were laughing, a new teasing laughter that was a token of their intimacy.

Charles drove her back to Le Girafe and left her in the cobbled courtyard. He drove away with a wave, and a brilliant smile that Bell was too happy to feel that she had to cling to.

Bell was humming contentedly under her breath as she walked along one side of the tree-lined square in the centre of Bordeaux. She knew that she was lucky, unbelievably lucky, but life seemed to have righted itself again. There were still so many things to be unsure about, but on this brilliant autumn morning it was impossible to feel anything but happy optimism. As she smiled up into the pale blue sky Bell's thoughts flicked briefly to the vineyards at Reynard. She knew that Charles's pickers would be at work by now, stooping rhythmically along the rows of vines, snipping through the stems and tossing the juicy bunches of grapes into the huge waiting baskets.

The vintage was under way. It always made her feel excited, but this year she felt as much a part of it as the pickers themselves.

Bell came to a tall house with elegant wrought-iron grilles at the upper windows. Number sixty-eight. This was it, she thought, and walked up the steps to read the words *Jacques Lapotin. Négociant* on the discreet plate beside the bell.

Monsieur Lapotin had been encouraging when she had telephoned him from the cramped booth at Le Girafe. Now, after a lengthy bus ride in from Vayonnes, Bell was trying to think herself into a businesslike frame of mind for her interview.

She needed this job.

The red-faced man who stood up behind his desk to greet her looked instantly familiar. Bell stared at him and searched desperately for the reason why the sight of him should make her feel so uncomfortable. Then it came back to her. Of course. He had been there on the night of her birthday party, at the moment when she had announced to the gathering that she was off to California to stay with Valentine Gordon. The man looked more businesslike now, but it was definitely him. And he recognized her too.

'Miss Farrer. So you are that Miss Farrer. Do you really want a job here in Bordeaux?'

Bell murmured briefly that she wanted to broaden her experience, see as many sides of the trade as possible. The *négociant* nodded, perfectly satisfied.

'Yes. Well, you couldn't be more highly recommended. Baron Charles spoke very warmly . . .'

So he had already spoken to Lapotin on her behalf. Charles the all-powerful. Gratitude to him flooded through Bell and she caught herself smiling dazedly.

'And so, Miss Farrer, you had better tell me what you can do.'

By the time Bell had finished selling herself, she thought that the *négociant* ought to be impressed enough to give her his own job.

'Very good,' he nodded at her more cordially now. 'Well, you are here at the right time. My own assistant is having a baby. I can't offer you the job for ever, but . . .' He shrugged, expressively, as if to say that there was no telling with new mothers.

'That's fine by me,' Bell told him.

They were shaking hands on the deal when his telephone rang on his desk.

'Send them up,' Lapotin said into the receiver. 'Miss Farrer and I are just finishing our talk.' He hung up and looked across the desk at Bell. Was she imagining it, or was that a flicker of unprofessional interest in his face?

'Friends of yours, I think,' he told her blandly. It must be Charles. Bell turned delightedly towards the door, waiting to see him come in.

Then she heard voices on the stairs, American voices, and a lazy laugh that was as familiar to her as her own. The two men who appeared in the doorway were Bob Cornelius and Valentine.

'Well hello,' said Valentine. 'Jacques told me he was seeing you.'

He was obviously, unaffectedly, delighted to see her. Before Bell could move, or think of anything to say, he was hugging her. Over his shoulder she saw Bob blinking behind his round glasses and murmuring, 'Hi there, hi.' Bell was uncomfortably aware of Lapotin's eyes boring into her shoulder blades. He was undoubtedly watching the little scene with interest. Damn him. Bell felt anger rising inside her. She wanted to keep well away from Valentine and out of the dangerous net that he trawled with him. Yet he kept turning up to threaten her. *You, me, Catherine, Valentine,* Charles had said. *We're all part of something, God help us.*

Well, Valentine wasn't going to be part of it any more. Bell wouldn't let him be. She looked at her watch with artificial concern.

'I must go. And you'll have business to discuss with M. Lapotin . . .'

How silly and stiff and false she sounded. She broke away from Valentine and almost collided with Bob in her anxiety to escape.

'You seem to have useful friends everywhere.' Lapotin suddenly sounded oily.

'Valentine' – he pronounced it in the French way, Vallonteen – 'is an important customer. At least, I hope he will be. Stay and have a drink with us – you can regard it as your first job for me.'

Lapotin was already producing glasses and a bottle.

Bell felt trapped.

When at last she found herself out in the square again, Bob and Valentine were standing on either side of her like warders. Valentine was smiling his relaxed smile and shading his eyes against the sun hanging low in the sky.

'Now, what about lunch? Seafood, Bell? Bob?' He tucked his hand under her arm again and Bell froze. 'You know, I was really surprised when Jacques told me he thought it was you, applying for a job. But it all fits. It seems right that you're here. And why didn't you get in touch with me?'

Why do you imagine, Bell thought. Because I didn't want to see you. Valentine was guiding her along the pavement, gently but firmly. Bell resisted the brief impulse to go along with him and stopped dead.

'Valentine, I've got a lot to do. I must go.'

She turned to walk away. 'Goodbye. I'll ring you. 'Bye, Bob.'

Valentine stopped smiling and looked mock-repentant. 'You're not still mad about that evening in London?' Bob Cornelius was standing a step or two away, gazing with tactful fascination at a torn circus poster.

'No. Of course not.' Bell forced a smile. 'I just need a bit of time to myself. Please.'

'Ah. I see.' Valentine's eyes were searching her face, uncomfortably close. He doesn't miss much. He's too clever, Bell thought. He's going to guess, soon. But he let her go with a little shrug.

'Come to Larue-Grise soon,' he told her quietly. 'I want you to see it. It's at its best now.' He was proud of Hélène de Gillesmont's family home. He glanced up into the thin sunshine. 'There'll be another two weeks of this before we need to start picking. I'm going to have a great vintage.'

Bell opened her mouth to tell him that he was leaving it too late, then thought better of it. Valentine saw it and his confident grin broadened. 'Think I'm pushing it, do you? Don't worry, my love. With my new tractors and the mechanical pickers we can have it all in within four, five days. It's only at crumbling relics of châteaux like Reynard that it takes them a fortnight.'

Valentine reached down and kissed her, hard, on the mouth. 'Come whenever you've had enough time to yourself.' Then, with Bob beside him, he was strolling away under the plane trees.

Bell turned, deliberately, in the opposite direction. She wasn't sure where she was going but she wanted to put as much distance between herself and Valentine as possible. I've annoyed him, she thought vaguely. Not that it matters in the slightest, she reminded herself more firmly.

But Valentine, only outwardly giving all his attention to discussing with Bob where they should eat lunch, wasn't annoyed at all. At the back of his mind he was aware of surprise, and a growing awareness that Bell Farrer mattered to him. Somehow she had got under his skin.

It wasn't just that he wanted her, although he wanted her now as badly as any girl he had ever known. Somehow, obliquely, she challenged him. And she was hiding something of herself, too. After all the women who had fallen, wide open, at Valentine's feet that made Bell exotic. And even more desirable.

Valentine was unaware of the brilliant, complacent smile that always irritated Bell. He was just thinking that it was taking a little time, but he was certain that he would win out in the end. Bell would yield her secret like a pearl coming out of an oyster.

The prospect whetted Valentine's appetite. Seafood, he thought. Definitely oysters.

Bell had gone to a nearby garage and hired herself the cheapest car she could find. She was not due to start work with Jacques Lapotin until the following week, but she needed to be able to get about right away. It would be impossible having to rely on the twice-daily bus that meandered through Vayonnes on its way to Bordeaux.

The hire-car was a serviceable Fiat that reminded her of Edward's. Bell drove slowly out of Bordeaux and turned towards Vayonnes.

Two kilometres out of the village Bell became aware of another car, driving dangerously close behind her. The green Renault kept swerving out to overtake and then having to tuck in again at the last minute to round a bend or let the oncoming traffic pass. At last, as they came up to the sign for Vayonnes, there was a horn blast and the car tore past. Looking sideways in alarm, Bell glimpsed a dark-haired woman at the wheel. Then the Renault was gone, accelerating recklessly through the village with the driver's impatient fingers on the horn. Bell shook her head in absent-minded disapproval and slowed down to a sedate speed that brought her trundling safely into the courtyard at Le Girafe.

Charles stood upright to ease his back. His boots were caked with earth and he was tired from the strain of bending all day. There was no need for him to be out here like a workman, picking, but the ties that bound him to the soil in his vineyards were so strong that he could think of nowhere else that he wanted to be. All around him were the hunched, blue-overalled backs of his pickers. They and their families came from the surrounding hamlets, year after year, to bring in the baron's grapes. That morning, the first day, they had started out laughing and joking as they always did. Now, in the early evening, they were tired and silent. They were all too conscious of the green lines stretching ahead and the back-breaking work of the hours waiting in front of them. Not until the last couple of days would the jokes start breaking out again.

Charles looked up at the sky. Pale grey, now, in the fading light, but still clear. The horizon was a reassuring shell pink although he thought he could smell something in the air that he didn't like. It was a long way off yet, but the savage weather was on its way. He looked back at the pickers again, making sure that each one was hard at work, then beckoned Jacopin over. The little man looked tired and anxious too. It would be another day or so before their muscles became re-attuned to the task. The cellar-master's watch over the work was as vigilant as the baron's.

'Another half-hour now, I think, before the light goes completely,' Charles told him. 'We'll keep going.'

The two men bent to their work again. Charles let the worry of the harvest slip out of his mind. He was thinking about Bell, up in the trees on the long black ridge that reared in the distance, and the translucence of her skin in the dim light.

At last the day was over. The pickers straggled out of the vineyard, rubbing their aching muscles. Hot coffee and slugs of cognac were waiting for them in the *chais*, and then they would disperse, to their homes if they lived nearby or to the dormitory rooms in the kitchen wing of the château.

Work began at first light the next morning, as it would every day until the last grapes were gathered.

Behind the workers Charles and Jacopin were heading for the *chais* too. The first truckload of grapes was already in the old fermenting vat, and the air was thick with the heady smell of running purple juice.

Only when he was certain that everything was in its place, did Charles come out into the darkness and around the jutting wing of the château to the double front doors. He ran lightly up the steps, for once thinking of nothing, and walked into the waiting silence of the imposing hallway.

A bar of light was striking across the floor from the open door of the salon. Charles half-turned towards the stairway, intending to go up and dress, then he shrugged. He would go in and have a drink with his mother and sister first.

What he saw stopped him dead in the doorway.

The three women were sitting in silence, their faces turned towards him. They looked like actresses, carefully positioned for the curtain to go up on the last act. Hélène was half triumphant, half apprehensive, but Juliette was simply pale with anxiety under her freckles. Charles met the third pair of eyes, and saw the question there at once.

Catherine's pointed chin lifted defiantly.

'Catherine,' said Charles softly, then again as a question. 'Catherine? Why are you here?' But he knew already.

Hélène, at her most stately, stood up and beckoned to Juliette.

'We will leave you in private, Charles. Catherine, my dear.'

When they were alone together Charles saw, irrelevantly, that his wife was dressed for dinner in pale silk jersey. Her dark cap of hair was brushed smooth to her head and she was wearing the rope of fine pearls that had been a wedding present. She was as immaculate as ever, and just as determined, he thought. As he put his hands on her shoulders and looked down at her he noticed how tiny she was, after Bell's rangy height.

After Bell.

The fine tension of guilt and foreboding began to shimmer in the room like a gauze curtain.

'Why are you here?' he asked again.

There was vulnerability and sadness as well as defiance in Catherine's face as she whispered back. 'I want to go back over it all, Charles. I want to see why it went wrong and see if we can't make it come right. It's two years since Valentine's party for the vintage. Two years, and now vintage time again. I couldn't stay in Paris any longer. I wanted to be here, here with you when the grapes come in, where I belong. Before it's too late. Please, Charles.'

There was silence in the room except for the ticking of the mantel clock in its porcelain case. As the seconds crept past Charles recognized what she meant. There was, after all, no loophole. No escape from giving hurt and having it dealt back again. The thought of what he must do to Bell hit him like a blow. Then anger and resentment made his face set hard.

'And how do you propose that we start again?' he asked, with the terrifying coldness that Catherine remembered too well. She took his hands in hers and told him, softly, 'First, by not being like this with each other. By being gentle and patient. I'm your wife, Charles, remember? Will you try to help us?'

Charles sighed and then, reluctantly, took her in his arms. As his face sank against her hair he felt the perfect familiarity of her body and smelt the unforgotten scent of her skin.

I am your wife, Charles.

Juliette had gone straight to the privacy of Charles's study. For a while she sat in one of his battered armchairs, thinking, and biting absently on a ragged nail. Catherine was back, and she was still the old Catherine that Juliette liked and admired. But she had acquired a new maturity too, and it suited her well. Juliette guessed shrewdly that it was born out of useful experiences in Paris, but those very experiences must finally have convinced Catherine that she belonged back at Reynard with her husband.

Juliette shifted uncomfortably at the thought. She was wretchedly torn between her loyalty to her sister-in-law and her friendship with Bell. Her responsibility for Bell.

The English girl was sitting out there, alone in her cold little holiday cottage, waiting and believing that Charles would come to her. And she was doing it because Juliette had encouraged her.

It was an uncomfortable dinner at Château Reynard that evening. Juliette was the usual talker, but tonight she was quiet, depressed at the thought of what lay ahead. Occasionally she looked across at Charles, trying to gauge what he was feeling, but his face was expressionless except for the hard set of his mouth. She guessed that he had been drinking before he came to the table, and now he was ignoring his food and drinking steadily. All her life Charles had been too self-controlled ever to get drunk, and she knew that wasn't going to happen tonight. He must be drinking to blunt his feelings instead, and Juliette was afraid that he wouldn't succeed. She felt desperately sorry for Charles, and for the two women – so different, but both in love with him – waiting on either side.

Hélène presided over the conversation, with Catherine doing what she could to dispel the brooding atmosphere. From time to time Catherine also shot a glance at Charles, questioning, almost pleading, but he seemed oblivious. The talk between the three women, about the redecoration of the upstairs rooms, struggled lamely on.

At last the meal was over. Charles pushed back his chair and stood up.

'Will you excuse me?' he said abruptly, looking from Hélène to Catherine as if they were jointly in charge of the grim processes of polite behaviour. 'It's the vintage,' he explained, exaggeratedly. 'I have a great deal to do.'

As she watched him go Catherine bit her lips and her eyes filled with tears, but she blinked them away before the other two could see.

Juliette excused herself too. She went heavily upstairs to get her coat and car keys, and when she came down again she met Charles. He was slipping out of his study like a ghost.

He stared at her, and then caught her wrist in iron fingers.

'Where do you think you are going?'

Juliette caught the smell of cognac. Poor Charles.

'To see Bell. She's got to know . . . *oh*!'

Charles was dragging her towards him, wrenching her wrist.

'Don't you think you have interfered enough?' She had never seen him so angry, never so angry with her. 'Do you think that it's anyone's responsibility but mine, to see Bell now?'

'Yes. No . . . I just thought . . .'

'Then don't think any more, Juliette. Just leave us alone. Leave me alone.'

Then he flung her hand away and crossed the hallway into the darkness outside.

A few seconds later she heard the Mercedes roaring away. Catherine materialized beside her.

'What's happening, Juliette?'

'I don't know,' she told her, truthfully enough. 'I just don't know.'

Bell was sitting in the quietness of her cottage. She had eaten a simple meal with a book, *The Portrait of a Lady*, propped up beside her. She had just been out to replenish the log-basket from the woodpile in the yard when the lights went out. Immediately the dogs started barking hysterically behind the house, and she felt a vague prickle of fear along her spine. The glowing redness of the fire gave her just enough light to see by, but the room was suddenly full of threatening shadows and there was utter blackness outside.

It made her uncomfortably aware of her solitude again, and of the unlocked door that opened straight out into the night.

Don't start to be afraid, she warned herself. It's just a power failure. Find some candles.

She was still groping in the pitch-black recesses of the kitchen when the beam of a powerful flashlight came bobbing across the yard. It was M. Durand with a cardboard box under his arm.

'It's the generator,' he told her gloomily. 'Happens a lot in the winter, usually when we've got a roomful of diners. It may be off for a while, until they can persuade one of the engineers to get up here and fix it. Here are some candles,' he was rummaging in the box, 'and some matches. Now, will you be all right out here?'

'Of course I will.' Bell was reassuring herself as much as the innkeeper. They went round the room together, lighting up the cheap white candles and sticking them in saucers. The soft light made the rustic room look even prettier, but there were still odd shadows lurking in the angle of the stairs, and beyond the kitchen door.

M. Durand stumped off to the inn again, and Bell settled down to try to read by the light of two candles perched in a saucer on the arm of her chair. It was hopeless. After a moment or two Bell let the book slip to the floor and sat gazing into the depths of the fire instead.

Her head and heart were still full of Charles, as they had been ever since yesterday's hours in the magical wood. She was glad to be giving up everything for him. Whether it was after the vintage, or whether it took months, or years, she would wait for him. He would be hers in the end, she had to believe that. And she would gladly exchange the precariousness of her career and the freedom of her own life for the inexorable roll of the seasons at Reynard with Charles beside her.

She was so lost in thought that the car was turning into the courtyard before she heard it. The headlamp beams raked across her windows and the powerful engine was suddenly silenced. Someone for Le Girafe, perhaps.

There she heard a footstep, and a hand falling on the latch of her door.

'Who's there?' Her voice was high-pitched, too obviously afraid.

'Charles,' came the low reply, almost a whisper.

Bell wrenched the door open and he stepped down into the room, having to duck his head beneath the blackened beams. Her dazzled smile of greeting faded when she saw his face. He was very pale, and his eyes were glittering dangerously in the flicker of candlelight.

Charles put out his arms and drew her to him. 'I had to come,' he whispered. 'Do you mind?'

Bell shook her head, pleased, but surprised at the urgency of his manner. She was going to ask him something trivial, but he stopped her mouth with his own. At once his tongue was searching for hers, and he was pulling her against him with an insistence that was new to her. His face against her cheeks felt very hot, but his hands were icy.

When Bell gasped for breath and drew her head back his eyes snapped open. The formidable planes of his profile brooded over hers, immobile for an instant. His eyes bored into the bones behind her face, relentless. Then he asked her, his voice cracking. 'Bell, I have to know something. I have to know you. Will you give yourself to me? Are you ready?'

So that was it. Was that really all? Was it so very much to ask? Bell remembered blindly how different Valentine Gordon's casual reaching out for her had been. This moment, this very moment, gave her a thrill of triumph and excitement that she had never known before.

Of course she would give herself to Charles. Willingly. *Longingly.* Deliberately she raised her head so that their mouths were touching again.

'Yes,' she said. The word whispered in the air between them in the seconds before he put his hands to her throat and, with a single tear, pulled back her shirt and left her shoulders and breasts bare to the flicker of fire and candle.

CHAPTER NINE

Bell reached down to kiss Charles's face. She found that his eyes were screwed tightly shut, and, with a slow shock, tasted the salt traces of tears. Those tears couldn't be her own, could they? She bent over him again, trying to shut out even the glimmer of the single candle with the curtain of her hair.

The intimate point of light made the little room seem even smaller. Bell's world had shrunk even within those confines, down to the high brass bed and the naked man lying tense in her arms. Outside the thin cretonne curtains at the window there was nothing. Even the sentimental picture of the Holy Family over the bedhead was beyond her universe.

It was so lonely here.

Even with the texture of Charles's skin under the palms of her hands, the weight of his body against her and his breath on her face, she felt alone. They were as separate as if a thick sheet of plate glass had slid between them.

Oh yes, it had been fine to begin with. He had half-carried her up the corkscrew stairs and then undressed her in the candlelight. His face had been full of sensual command, but his hands were trembling. Bell had felt so sure, and she had wanted him so much.

For a few wonderful moments the unapproachable baron and the passionate man had been one, and he had belonged to her. Bell frowned, trying to remember. Then something had gone wrong. A flicker of doubt, or something, and she had lost him.

Yet there was no real reason for her to feel so rejected. So cut off from him. He had done what he came to do, expertly, bloodlessly. But it was as if – in the middle of it – he had ceased to be there. Even in the secret seconds when he had stretched and shuddered in her arms, he wasn't hers.

Bell breathed out a long sigh. And now, she thought, he had been crying. Why? *Why*, when it all seemed so simple? With grim pessimism, Bell began to doubt that she would ever succeed in untangling him. Then impatiently she brushed the thought away.

Charles stirred and opened his eyes. 'I'm sorry,' he said. 'It was my fault that wasn't very good.' Then, softly, looking down at her stretched beside him, 'You're very beautiful.'

Bell smiled. 'That's very gallantly French. But it takes two to make an anticlimax. What is it, Charles? Won't you tell me?' There was a shuttered, defensive look in his face again that made her feel apprehensive.

'Go on,' she prompted, trying to sound lighthearted, 'I can take it, whatever it is.'

Charles's face darkened, and he shook his head once so that the blond hair fell over his forehead. Bell waited, but there was nothing to say.

'Shall I get us a drink?' she whispered at last.

'Please.'

Bell padded downstairs to find the cognac bottle and blow out the candles.

Charles drained his glass and then his head flopped back against the hard pillows. His eyes closed, and Bell watched him fall asleep almost at once. He looked drawn and exhausted. The candlelight made the hollows in his cheeks look deeper and threw dark shadows under his eyes.

How vulnerable people are when they're sleeping, thought Bell. To her surprise, back into her mind's eye came the image of Valentine asleep, swathed in pink nylon ruffles in their Las Vegas suite. The vision made her laugh, very softly, out loud.

When her glass was empty Bell lay back and pulled the covers around them both. At least he was here, beside her.

She turned her face to Charles's shoulder and breathed in the warm, male smell of him. It would all come right, she let herself think as she drifted into sleep. She would make it.

The solitary candle guttered in its blackened saucer, and went out.

Charles was already awake when she opened her eyes again. The dirty grey square of light at the end of the bed told her that it was getting light once more. Charles's mouth was at her ear.

'I have to go,' he told her.

'Wait.' Bell reached out for him anxiously. They must make it right before he went away from her. She put her arms around his shoulders to pull him back against her warmth and ran her tongue up through the fair hairs at the nape of his neck. He yielded for an instant and then tensed again. Charles pulled himself away and left her staring up at him.

'Not now,' he whispered. 'Not now.' He dragged on the creased white shirt from last night and the incongruous smooth blackness of his dinner jacket. 'Jacopin will be waiting for me.'

Bell nodded, accepting dumbly. The harvest must go on.

Standing there in the cramped space, with his shirt open and the ends of his black tie dangling, his cheeks unshaven, Charles looked dissipated and more attractive than she had ever seen him. She wished that he would come back to bed.

'Adieu,' he said. What was that in his face? Regret? Guilt? Anxiety?

Bell listened to him going. He brushed down the narrow stairs, let himself out into the cold light of dawn and eased the big car out of the courtyard.

Then she turned over and willed herself to go back to sleep.

At the wheel of the Mercedes, Charles had hesitated for an instant before turning back through Vayonnes, in the opposite direction from Reynard. Beyond the village he started driving fast along narrow byroads until he came to a hamlet in a circle of muddy fields. At the centre of the cluster of shabby houses stood a tiny church. A cracked bell was ringing insistently from the stubby square tower. Charles glanced at his watch. Seven o'clock. Early mass.

He left his car in the shadows of a side road and walked swiftly across to the door of the church. Inside in the incense-laden dimness there was a handful of villagers mumbling through the mass. To one side was the plain, square shape of the confessional. As the old woman in black who had been

222

kneeling with her lips to the grille stood up, crossing herself, Charles slipped forward from the shadows.

The yawning young priest on the other side of the grille stared for a second at the unshaven man in evening clothes.

'Forgive me, Father, for I have sinned.'

The priest folded his hands to listen patiently to the baron's confession. By eight o'clock Charles was in his heavy boots again and was walking with Jacopin to the vineyards.

Catherine had gone to bed in the bare room once occupied by Bell. She got up to see her husband crossing the grass with his cellar-master beside him. She smiled, once, at the familiarity of the sight, and then went calmly into her luxurious bathroom to take a shower.

For that day and the next no word came for Bell from Château Reynard.

She was busy enough.

There was her piece on the vintage to prepare, and she sat dutifully in front of her portable typewriter to rough out some ideas. It occurred to her that she would be better occupied in rubbing the cobwebs off her secretarial skills for M. Lapotin's benefit, but the prospect bored her so fatally that she decided she would just have to manage as she went along.

On the third day, Bell went across to the inn to have breakfast with the Durands. When the breakfast plates were cleared away Madame Durand brought out the flour and mixing bowls and Bell had her promised lesson in making brioches. At the other end of the table M. Durand was filleting fish for the lunch guests, expertly flipping the fringed backbone out of the white flesh and tossing it into the stockpot.

The telephone kept ringing. Each time Bell thought that it must be Charles, or even Juliette, but invariably it was another customer. When the two waitresses arrived and the kitchen began to fill with a delicious mixture of cooking smells, Bell reluctantly decided that she must take herself out of the way. She left her brioches to be baked and went back to the solitude of her cottage. *The Portrait of a Lady* was still lying, face-down, on the floor.

Tomorrow, Bell told herself decisively. Impatience was beginning to break through her self-control. Tomorrow was Sunday, and the work in the vineyards would slacken off. She would call in at Château Reynard to see the progress of the vintage; to visit her friends.

Charles was strange, and distant, but Bell reminded herself that she had always known that. With his careful defences he was not an easy man to draw close to, and it was that challenge that had always excited her. She would break through completely in the end, and the more difficult he proved to be now the more open and natural she would be herself. And so, in the most natural way, she would drop in at Reynard. Nothing would look odd in that.

The inner conversations went on, elliptically.

The truth was that Bell found it hard to think directly about the night she had spent with Charles.

He had wanted her, there wasn't any doubt about that. But he had managed, still, to keep his core of remoteness. She felt a flutter of indignation, remembering how open she had been ready to be for him. He was a strange, mysterious man. Bell shivered a little at the memory of his hands on her.

She was uncertain what kind of game she was being asked to play, and she disliked games anyway. Then she reminded herself candidly that the pull of attraction that she felt for him was as unwavering as ever. And if that was truly the case, she would just have to go on until she won through to him.

She was her own woman, after all. She was big enough and strong enough now.

Sunday was another fine, clear day.

Valentine grinned with pleasure as the shadows of the poplar trees lining the road cast flickering bars over his face. Beneath him the bike purred sweetly and the white road unwound enticingly ahead.

Reynard, he murmured.

He was heading for the de Gillesmonts' home, and the knowledge lent an extra spice of anticipation to the pleasure of the ride. Valentine's smile broadened in enjoyment of the mystery. Seconds later he saw the château on its low hill, and he made the familiar turn to swoop in through the gateway and up towards the house. Gravel sprayed beneath the front wheel as the bike turned in a wide arc and drew up under the windows of Hélène's salon. As Valentine leaned back to stare up at the classical proportions towering above him, a slim figure came out on to the steps. She hesitated for a second and then came down towards him.

Catherine de Gillesmont was as beautiful as ever, Valentine thought, and as determined to have her own way. Why was she back here, and why had she called him with such insistence that he should visit her here, now, after so long?

'Valentine. Thank you for coming so quickly.' Their eyes met. Valentine's found his held by his old friend's level, serious stare. Ignoring her outstretched hand he leant to kiss her cheek and relived for an instant the memories brought back by her perfume. His mouth touched hers but Catherine's body was held stiffly away from him.

So, thought Valentine. Summoned as a friend, not as a lover.

'How could I resist such a mysterious summons?' he answered lightly. 'You look wonderful, Catherine.'

'Come inside,' she said simply, and they climbed the steps together.

Bell drove slowly towards Reynard. The Indian summer seemed set to go on for ever. Valentine might turn out to be right after all, Bell decided. Trust him. For every extra day of sunshine Valentine's grapes would have an extra depth of sweetness inside their purple skins.

On either side of the vineyard road there were muted, Sundayish signs of activity amongst the vines. At the end of one track a huge, garishly yellow tractor and picker combine was squatting on its caterpillar tracks with a couple of blue-clad men peering anxiously into the works. At another intersection she braked to let a wagon-load of grapes trundle across the road. With the luscious harvest gleaming in the pale sunlight, the empty white road and the knot of trees beside it with their leaves beginning to turn gold, the scene might have been a painting entitled 'The Harvest Safely Home' or 'The Perfect Vintage'.

The vintage was well under way at most properties, Bell noticed. After the long, warm autumn that had been blessed with just the right amount of rain, it looked set fair to be a great year. And if Valentine was proved right in his gamble to hang on for just a little more sun, he could have one of the greatest years of all. Well, she hoped so. He deserved that.

There, on the low hill to her left, was Château Reynard. Bell deliberately went on thinking about Valentine and his ultra-modern techniques. She wanted to keep the lightness of her mood intact. She needed to feel casual. There must be no sense, even at the back of her mind, of entering the lion's den.

There was the driveway up ahead. She turned in through the gates, seeing out of the corner of her eye that there were figures at work amongst the vines after all. Charles was a demanding master, she reflected.

Then she pulled up on the gravel sweep under the blank eyes of the classical façade. A sense of something being out of place nagged at her for an instant before she recognized it. A powerful metallic-blue motorcycle was parked under the windows of the salon. The de Gillesmonts had another visitor on this Sunday morning . . .

Behind one of the blank windows Valentine was sitting in a spindly chair with his long legs stretched awkwardly out in front of him. He was watching Catherine sceptically as she leaned forward, talking in a low insistent voice.

At last Valentine interrupted her. 'All this is very praiseworthy, but I still feel like a stray Montagu in the Capulets' hall. Charles will probably cut my legs off when he sees me. Where is he, anyway?'

Catherine gestured with impatience. 'In the vineyards, where else? Please, Valentine. You've got to help me defuse the tension here. You're still very much a part of it, you know. I've come back to Charles, and I want to make it like it was .. before.'

'Mmmm. Easier said than done. Let me see, have I got this straight? We're aiming at an end to the feud between Gordon and de Gillesmont? A manly handshake, a gruff "sorry, old man, for having it off with your wife", and all's well? Jesus Christ, Katie, he challenged me to a duel. Or don't you remember that? We're poison to each other.'

'*Please*, Valentine.'

'Okay. I'm sorry. You want me to be seen to be harmless and likeable, a jovial American from up the road who just happened to be in the wrong place at the wrong time? I can't see what all the fuss is about. I am all those things. Except,' and he broke off to grin at her, 'it may have been the wrong time, but it was definitely the right place.'

But Catherine wasn't interested in joking. Her face stayed pale and stern.

'Listen. I want to show Charles that you and I don't – never did – matter.' She took a deep breath and put her white hands together, finger to finger, as if she was making a difficult point in a classroom. 'And I can't do that if you're up the road there, like some invisible threat to us. Let us be civilized. Let us just all have a meal together. I don't expect you to be friends . . .'

'That's realistic of you.'

'But it would help me to begin to restore things with Charles if we could put a stop to this state of war.'

Valentine watched her face for a moment and then said, with all the laughter gone from his voice, 'You really want to make it work, don't you?' Catherine nodded deliberately. 'I have to try. I've tried not being with him, for two interminable years, and that doesn't work. Nor does being with other people. I miss Charles too much. Now I know that I want him back. Without each other, I don't see how either of us can go any further.' She was quiet for a moment and then added, 'It was hard, coming back here, you know. Charles can be very intimidating. His armour isn't easy to penetrate.'

Valentine was considering carefully.

'Yes. Look, Catherine, I don't like your husband very much. I find his kind of arrogance and blinkered superiority very hard to deal with. But, for your sake only, I will try to

227

bury the chainsaw. Will that do?' Valentine's brilliant smile crept back as he stretched luxuriously in the confines of his chair. 'Tell you what. There's no time like the present. I'll stay to lunch, but only if Charles wheels out a bottle of the Krug.'

Catherine stood up, the determined lines of her mouth and chin softened by a slight smile. 'Thank you,' she said. 'I'll ring through right now for the champagne.'

As she moved gracefully to the bell she caught sight of the little Fiat bowling up the driveway. It came to a full stop at the château steps. A girl got out and hesitated for a second, her eyes turned upwards to the grand front door at the top of the double flight of steps. Catherine saw a luxuriant mass of dark hair, a striking face that might be beautiful in laughter, and a slim figure that carried its height gracefully.

'Well now, who can this be?' murmured Catherine.

Valentine crossed to the window and peered out.

'Don't you know? That's Bell Farrer. A friend of mine, as it happens. And a friend of Charles and Juliette. She's someone rather special.'

'Is that so?' said Catherine in her quiet voice.

Marianne answered the door to Bell. The little maid smiled nervously at her. '*Bonjour, madame.* They are in the salon, if you will come this way . . .'

Bell followed her inside.

The lofty height of the hall, the curve of the stairway reaching upwards under the magnificent chandelier. It was all, everything, just as she remembered it. Even the dim scent of pot-pourri and beeswax polish.

Marianne was holding the door open, and Bell heard her name being announced to the gathering in the salon. In spite of all her resolutions to be casual, Bell had to brace herself. Hélène will be there, she was thinking. And Charles probably hated to be surprised. Well, it was too late to worry about that now. Just let Juliette be there as well.

The first person she saw, standing loosely with his hands in his pockets as if he lived there, was *Valentine*. The motorbike. Of course. It was Valentine's.

But . . .

Then she saw the elegant dark-haired girl sitting in

Hélène's chair beside the marble fireplace. She had a skin like marble herself, but blessed with the same warm glow as the pearls around her neck.

'Bell. It's good to see you.' There was the comfortable circle of Valentine's arm around her shoulder, but he was propelling her closer to the face that she didn't want to recognize. It *couldn't* be . . .

'Catherine says that you haven't met. Catherine de Gillesmont, Bell Farrer.'

She was choking inside, fighting against the iron bands that were clamping around her chest and throat.

'Bell? How do you do?'

The baroness held out her hand. There was a fraction more warmth in Catherine's first greeting than there had been in Hélène's, all those weeks ago, but only a fraction. Charles's wife looked very cool and faintly hostile. Under her gaze Bell felt her own panicky confusion rising inside her as she struggled to find a conventional greeting.

This was all wrong, a terrible distortion. What was Catherine doing here, now, after all this time? And why had no one told Bell?

Oh, Charles. She suddenly saw it. He had known, the other night, and he had said nothing.

Suddenly, overwhelmingly, Bell longed to escape from this chic room and the elegant stranger who belonged in it so perfectly. But she stayed rooted to the spot, tongue-tied and blushing like a schoolgirl caught in some silly deception.

It was Valentine who came to her rescue. He took her hand and led her to one of the silk-covered sofas.

'I've just invited myself to lunch,' he grinned at her. 'I think you should do the same. Shouldn't she, Katie?'

Katie? And what *was* Valentine doing here, in the heart of enemy territory? Bell felt as if all the sensible landmarks in the world had been torn up and then plumped down in the wrong, threateningly wrong, places.

'Of course,' said Catherine courteously. 'I was just going to ring for some champagne, also on Valentine's insistence, but I think it might be quicker if I went myself.' Somehow, she made it sound like a voyage into the unknown. 'And I'd better tell Madame Robert that we'll be two extra for lunch.'

Bell's eyes followed her as she walked across the room, with her perfect French deportment and her discreet trailing scent of lilies and lilacs. Charles's wife made Bell feel lumpy, and slouching, and dishevelled.

Valentine squeezed her hand again.

'What is this? A social call?'

Bell shrugged, with an effort at casualness. With Catherine out of the room she was beginning to recover herself. Valentine must never, ever, guess the truth.

'I was passing, so I thought I'd drop in.'

'Ah. You look upset, that's all. Is anything the matter?'

'No. Of course not. Anyway,' she rounded on him, 'what the hell are you doing here? I thought you and the Baron were sworn enemies.' Bell heard some of the anger and puzzlement that seethed inside her escape in the sharpness of her tone. But if Valentine noticed too he chose to ignore it.

'Catherine wants me to be here,' he said seriously. Bell thought she saw a look in his eyes that startled her. So she still had Valentine, too, did she?

She glanced across to Hélène's work-table, to the treasured photograph of Catherine in its silver frame. The French girl looked like a lily as well as smelling like one, all creamy scented whiteness but with a powerful inner core of strong green sap.

Bell was jealous, bitterly and resentfully jealous. It was an alien feeling and she hated it, and it was indissolubly bound up with the hurt and humiliation of this ugly situation. Bell felt that she had come creeping up to Reynard like some ill-briefed commando on a sneak raid, only to find the invincible general in possession. And not only in possession of her rightful territory, but of all the surrounding landscape too. Oh God, she must get out of here at once.

Valentine was talking again, flippant and teasing once more.

'I feel a little snubbed, you know. You must have just been passing Larue once or twice, but you've never dropped in to see me. Wait till you see what I've done with it. It's the very last word.'

'I know, I'm sorry,' Bell said absently. She could hear Catherine coming back, her heels clicking across the flagged hall. 'I'll come whenever you like. I'm not at all busy.'

There was such desolation in her voice that it made Valentine look sharply at her.

'Over here, Marianne,' the young baroness was saying. There was the misted silver of the ice-bucket and the jaunty clink of glasses. 'Valentine, would you . . .'

He opened the bottle deftly and let the wine sparkle out into fragile glasses. Bell accepted hers and then said, 'Thank you. But I won't impose on you for lunch, Catherine.' She hoped that she sounded composed, when all she really wanted to do was run and run.

Catherine frowned. 'Oh, but you must, mustn't she, Valentine? It's all settled.'

She made Bell feel like a spinster up from the village, being pressed to stay at the Big House for an unwanted treat. Damn her. She would stay, then, and she would hold her own too – come what may.

More footsteps were coming clicking across the hall towards them. Bell had to brace her shoulders to stop herself physically shrinking into the depths of her chair. The step was too quick and light to be Charles's, the shoes too dainty and high-heeled to be Juliette's.

Hélène, of course.

As soon as Hélène came in, Valentine was on his feet, holding out his hands to hers.

'Baroness, it's been far too long. Catherine is quite right. But you look more wonderful than ever.'

Bell, watching him, thought how perfectly charming he could be. There was no insincerity, no self-consciousness, no hesitation. It was quite plain that he was delighted to see Hélène, and the ripples of warmth that he sent out had an immediate effect on the older woman. Before Bell's eyes the frosty correctness melted and she smiled, flirtatiously, like a young girl.

'Valentine! You are very wicked. What are you doing here?'

'Hoping to see you, what else?' The teasing, lazy smile.

231

'What nonsense.' If Hélène had only been carrying a fan, Bell thought, she would have rapped him playfully across the knuckles with it. Clever, clever Valentine.

'Catherine, perhaps you will talk some sense. What is this?' Charles's wife tilted her head, determined.

'It is the best way, Hélène. We have a great many things to put behind us, and the way to do it is without bitterness.'

'Yes, well . . .' The mother frowned slightly, warning her. Not to be discussed in front of strangers. 'And Miss er . . . too.'

'Bell Farrer,' Bell reminded her automatically.

'Bell is a good friend of mine,' Valentine said, drawing her loyally into their circle. 'Isn't it a tiny world?'

'Yes, indeed. I hope you are both staying to lunch? Valentine will, won't you? And you, ah – Bell?'

'Catherine insisted.' Bell allowed herself that, but Hélène was already turning away.

'And now that you are here, Valentine, you had better sit here beside me and tell me what you have been doing.'

Ensconced side by side on one of the sofas they were soon deep in conversation. Valentine's low laughter and an occasional, staccato giggle from Hélène – as if she was just remembering how to do it – told Bell that they were enjoying the reunion. Catherine and Bell were left looking at each other from either side of the marble fireplace.

How perfect she is, Bell thought. Not a blemish, or a crease, or a hair out of place. Nor any of the lines of suffering that showed in Charles's face. Yet her losses had been just the same. Bell guessed that Catherine de Gillesmont was much tougher than her fragile looks suggested. She would be a formidable enemy.

Bell's feelings were in turmoil. Her immediate impulse had been to run away, and part of her still wanted to duck out of the uncomfortable encounter that was to come. Yet another instinct – one that seemed to exist separately, beyond her control – made her long to see Charles. Even here, with his family around him, even with Valentine Gordon at the same table. Even after the failed closeness of their illicit night together, and the dawn of her suspicion that Charles had used her then to escape Catherine's return. Resentment and anger began to prickle in her, but they served only to strengthen her determination. She would go on fighting for him.

'Do you know my husband and sister-in-law well?'

This is only the beginning of the deceptions you are going to have to handle, Bell warned herself. Be calm. You owe it to yourself, as well as to him, to hide your feelings.

'Not all that well. We met in August. Charles was kind enough to ask me to spend a few days here to prepare a profile of him and the château for my paper. The newspaper I worked for then. I'm a journalist.' Bell thought how feeble she sounded, and made herself go on talking brightly. 'Then we met again at the IWC dinner, although I was Valentine's guest.'

The level stare of Catherine's hazel eyes left her face for a moment, flickered to Valentine, and then back to Bell again. Was there a faint lessening of the hostility there, or was that Bell's imagination? She felt lost. She had no idea what was real and what was her own mistaken hope or fear, any more.

'I see,' said Catherine.

It was an awkward moment.

Bell was almost relieved to hear the voices of Charles and Juliette. Juliette was laughing as they crossed the hallway together, and Bell had a sudden picture of the way they would look, their faces turned to each other, different and yet so alike. Hélène and Valentine had stopped talking too. The four of them sat motionless waiting in the last seconds of silence. Bell's eyes were fixed on the empty doorway. Then suddenly Charles was there, and she felt the breath catch in her throat. The brother and sister had come straight from the vineyards; they were work-stained but their faces were bright from the pure air.

Charles's eyes went straight to Valentine, lounging at Hélène's side.

The crackle of tension ran round the room like electricity.

For three, four, five seconds no one spoke. The two men went on staring at each other, Charles's navy-blue eyes unfathomable, Valentine's bright blue ones sparkling with a cold light.

Then Catherine stood up. Calmly she walked over to her

husband and put her arm through his. Bell read the mixture of defiance and apprehensiveness in her face, and understood that she was taking a terrible gamble. Whatever game she was playing, there was obviously everything to win or lose.

'I asked Valentine to come over and see us,' she was telling Charles. 'It is time for us all to be sensible, and forget.'

Slowly, very slowly, Charles let his dark stare switch from Valentine to his wife. 'To forget?' he repeated, his mouth twisted painfully. 'It is you who have forgotten, Catherine. I can't.' He disengaged his arm from hers and turned. In that instant he saw Bell in her chair beside the fireplace.

'*Bell.*' The exclamation was involuntary. There was no mistaking the shock in his voice. Bell was nakedly conscious of them all watching her, somehow waiting to judge the two of them by her reaction. To her everlasting surprise she found it in herself to meet the occasion. Her voice was steady, her smile natural and not too bright.

'I was passing, so I just dropped in. I didn't intend to intrude on something important.' The perfect, casual flutter of her hands took in Valentine, Catherine and Charles himself. And even, still in the background, Juliette. Her friend, mute with misery, couldn't meet Bell's eyes.

The moment was past, and she had deflected it. Charles and Bell were no longer the focus of attention, and she allowed herself to look back at him. He was angry. Whether it was with Catherine, with Valentine, or with Bell herself for her intrusion, she had no means of judging.

Hélène was, for once, her ally. She was marshalling them all into the dignified dining-room, trying to pretend that there was no threat, no unspoken secret, hovering over all their heads.

Hélène herself sat at the head of the gleaming table, Charles took his accustomed place at the foot. Even here, amidst all this formality, Valentine seemed completely at ease. He was attentive to Hélène, and to Bell on his other side. More champagne had arrived, and he held up his glass to his host.

'At least we are in agreement about the perfect champagne.'

'At least.' Charles's responses were the minimum possible, and his eyes remained fixed on his plate although he was eating almost nothing. Bell could only guess at what he was going through, forced to sit at his own table between his wife and the outsider who had just become his mistress. And to listen to the easy, bubbling talk of his old enemy. The strain showed in his face, white to the wings of his nostrils.

Juliette was almost silent too.

To her astonishment Bell discovered that she was able to keep the conversation flowing herself. She found herself talking amusingly about going to work for Jacques Lapotin, and the shrouded typewriter that was waiting for her tomorrow in his secretary's cubby-hole. Catherine and Hélène showed their gratitude by plying her with feed questions about her work, her plans, and life at Le Girafe.

'It's enchanting,' Bell told them. 'The happiest place I have ever lived in. And I have my own little cottage, like a doll's house. All thanks to Juliette.'

'It will be cold, when the winter really comes,' said Juliette, almost in a whisper. At last she brought herself to meet Bell's eyes, and her face was full of sorrow and sympathy as well as silent apology.

Never mind, Bell wanted to tell her. It wasn't your fault. It isn't anybody's fault. And in any case, it isn't all over yet. The realization surprised her. But Valentine was drawling something at her side. He had been drinking steadily, first the champagne and now the impeccable claret, but it was only making him seem witty and warm alongside Charles's remote hauteur.

'Bell, why haven't you asked me to see this wonderful place? A doll's house? I can think of nothing more comfortable than to be in a doll's house with you.'

He put down his knife and took her hand. 'Say when. Tomorrow?'

Bell didn't have to look; she felt the white flash of anger and jealousy flare up in Charles before it was shut away again under the armour of his self-control.

She knew then that it was impossible, that all this tangle of bitterness and jealousy that tied each of them would never resolve itself peacefully. Cold fear touched her, making her falter as she answered.

'I have to work, tomorrow. I told you, for M. Lapotin.'

'Oh, in the evening then. We'll have a dolls' dinner, together.'

Was he doing this deliberately, trying to bait Charles?

'Maybe,' she said gently, 'when I've finished my piece on the vintage. I have to clear that first.'

'Aha, the vintage,' said Valentine. He filled his glass again and lifted it in a toast. 'That's important to us all. To the vintage.'

They drank, in a deepening pool of silence. The women were waiting for the battle lines to be drawn.

Valentine leaned back in his chair, one arm dangling loosely over the carved back as he looked down the table at Charles. 'I saw on my way up. You're almost through with the picking.'

'Still a few more days,' said Charles carefully.

'Yeah, it's a slow job, doing it by hand.'

Charles rotated his empty glass so that it caught the light.

'And you will have to do a very fast job. I don't think that, even with all your machinery, you will be in time. The bad weather's coming.'

Valentine laughed, his low teasing laugh, but with an edge to it now.

'Bad weather? I don't think so, Baron. The met. station and our own equipment at Larue tells me different.'

Charles's voice went very quiet. 'I have lived on this land all my life, and my ancestors for four hundred years before that. In almost every one of those years, there has been wine made at Reynard. Do you think that, with all that in my blood, I can't smell the air and read the skies?'

Valentine laughed again. 'No, I don't think that you are incapable of either of those things. What I don't believe is that your nose and eyes can do a better job than the best technology in the world. But we'll see, won't we? I am confident – no, *certain* – that this year will be the greatest ever for Larue. And I believe that you have thrown away your own chances of a great vintage by picking too early. Simple.'

'I have not picked too early.'

'Oh yes, Baron, you have.'

The silence fell again.

This is what it is all really about, thought Bell.

At the heart of it none of us women is important. They hate each other because they stand on opposite sides of the great divide. The old world and the new, old blood and new blood. And now, facing each other defiantly in the shape of two men from different worlds, the sure slowness against the quick gamble. They were already locked in a kind of combat.

The winner could only be proved by the sun in the calm, pale blueness of the autumn skies, or by the rolling grey clouds riding in from the Atlantic on the savage winds.

Whatever Catherine was trying to do to them all; whatever happened to Bell herself, to her love for Charles and her irrepressible liking for Valentine, were in the end so unimportant. What mattered was the age-old mystery that turned the raw, running purple juice of the grape into miraculous wine.

The air was full of it, and it was nothing to do with love, or sex, or jealousy. What moved the men was their passion for their own worlds, and the rivalry sprang from their opposition.

It was coming, the collision between them, as surely as the existence of the peaceful landscape beyond the windows of Reynard.

Bell shivered, wondering where her own true loyalties lay. The old or the new, she thought, which do I believe in? In four hundred years of Château Reynard, of course, she answered herself, but at the same time recalled the gleaming, efficient technology at Dry Stone and felt a tremor of doubt.

Charles laid down his napkin and said, 'I must get back to my men.'

'And may we come too? It's pure interest, Baron. I'm not out to steal any of your secrets.' Valentine spoke, velvety-polite.

'I have none for you to steal. I do things here just as they have been done in the Haut-Médoc for generations. It was all there for you to see at Larue before you tore it out. But you may come, of course.'

That was the baron that Bell had first seen. Courteous, but distant. Unassailable. She had to remind herself that she knew a different man. She knew the Charles of the magical woodland over on the low hills, but the recollection pained her now. He seemed, once more, after so little precious time, beyond her grasp. They went straggling out into the mid-afternoon light.

Catherine and Hélène had protested that they had too many other things to do to want to spend hours trailing through the vineyards, but Valentine and Bell had followed the brother and sister.

They walked across the grass, dappled with already lengthening shadows, two by two. Charles and Valentine strode ahead in silence, Juliette fell into step beside Bell. Before she spoke she looked ahead to make sure that her brother was out of earshot.

'I feel that this is my fault. I encouraged you to come out here again.'

'How could it be your fault? Did you know that Catherine was coming back?'

'*No*. I thought it was impossible. None of us knew. She just arrived.'

'When?'

'Two days ago.'

Yes. On the same night Charles had come to her at Le Girafe. Had he been trying to escape, or to prove something to himself?

Whatever it was, his resolution had failed him and they had lost each other. They crossed the narrow road that separated the château from the walled vineyards. Charles held open the tall gate and they passed through under the arch that bore a weatherbeaten shield with the de Gillesmont crest.

The pickers had just returned from their meal in Madame Robert's kitchen and they were bending reluctantly back over the vines. The rows in front of the visitors were stripped bare of their grapes and the straight alleys of bare earth between them were trampled flat by the passing and repassing of the workers' heavy boots. The air smelt wonderful to Bell after the claustrophobic tension of the château dining-room. It was so clean out here, so rich with ripe fruit and damp earth.

Jacopin was coming towards them, his wrinkled face alight with pleasure. There was a flurry of handshaking, Valentine having to stoop right down to reach the little man's hand.

'*Bonjour, bonjour.* It goes perfectly. In three, four days – a week at the most – we shall be safe. But, monsieur, they tell me that you have not even begun yet at Larue.'

'You guys hear everything. There's plenty of time yet, you know.'

'Ah, I hope you are not mistaken.'

'So do I, Jacopin, but I don't think I am.'

Charles turned to talk to his men, and Juliette had already slipped away. Bell saw her with her basket, already bent to her work, and she longed to join her. She envied Juliette her involvement, her belonging to Reynard. She couldn't forget that she was only a visitor here. She would only ever be a visitor, now.

With Valentine beside her, she followed Jacopin to the vines the pickers were working on today. The capacious wheeled trolleys stood at the end of the rows, waiting to be filled from the individual baskets. Then the trolleys in their turn were wheeled to a wagon which trundled the grapes across the road and up to the *chais*.

Valentine was stooping, letting the gravelly dirt run through his fingers, just as he had done in the blazing sun at Dry Stone. The bright blue eyes missed nothing. He saw the dark, knotted wood of the old root-stock, pruned brutally to the stumps from which this year's luxuriant growth had sprung. He reached out and plucked one of the bunches of fruit, and rubbed the dark bloom with his fingertips as caressingly as if it had been a woman's neck. His sigh was barely audible, but Bell caught it.

'What is it?' she asked him lightly. 'Losing your confidence?'

Valentine leaned over and dropped the bunch of grapes into the nearest basket.

'No, Princess, nothing like that. I'm just thinking that if we

239

had all this time behind us, this much solid growth, we'd be the greatest in the world.'

'If we had . . . ?'

Valentine looked up at her, squinting against the light, serious for an instant before the smile flooded his features.

'I didn't mean you and me, necessarily. I mean that people like us aren't part of this world.' He waved his arm to take in the patient pickers, the ancient pattern of the vineyards, the golden stone of the château beyond the low walls. 'We're parvenus, you and me. We may not have the advantages, or the right names, but we do have the brains, and the guts. We win out in the end.'

He straightened up again and brushed the earth from his fingers. Then, surprising her, he reached out to touch her cheek. 'That's why I like you. Brains and guts. I'm not sure what you're doing out here, but you're being brave in some way. Perhaps,' his voice dropped to a whisper of intimacy that was instantly familiar to Bell, 'I did mean you and me.'

What did he mean? Bell felt herself stupidly blushing again, and then she saw the arrogant, conquering smile that had once angered her so much. She stepped away from him, protecting herself, not knowing what to say that would deflect him. All the flippant full-stops that came into her head sounded cheap and wrong. At last Valentine looked away. The moment was past.

Bell dared to glance back and see whether Charles was watching them. No, she was safe. He was intent on his orders to a little knot of pickers. But Valentine had followed her eyes and now a flicker of surprise showed in his face.

'I'm not sure what you're doing out here,' he repeated, almost to himself, 'although something has just occurred to me.'

Bell's heart lurched. The vineyards suddenly settled into stillness. There was no sound, except the full-throated song of a blackbird in the poplar trees.

'Doing?' she said lightly into the listening air. 'Trying to earn my living. Escaping from London. Does it matter?' She wondered if her voice really sounded as artificial as she thought it did.

'Not in the least. But I wouldn't enjoy seeing you get into a mess.'

'No chance of that.' *I'm in a terrible mess already.*

'Good.' He touched her elbow lightly. 'Shall we turn back? Everything out here convinces me that the Baron is doing a thoroughly sound job.'

He hasn't guessed, she thought, going limp with relief. If he had guessed, he wouldn't be able to resist sliding the knife in just a little deeper.

Dangerous Valentine. Bell couldn't forget the antagonism that boiled beneath the surface of the fragile truce. Whatever game Catherine de Gillesmont was playing, it would be best for them all if the two men stayed in their separate worlds. Her relief at her escape was enough to leave her off-balance for his next casual-sounding question.

'Are you still so busy? Why not have dinner with me on Wednesday? I'll pick you up straight from Lapotin's and take you somewhere amusing.' Bell groped for her excuses, and then stopped herself. She was aware of liking Valentine as much as ever, and it would be a welcome diversion in an otherwise empty week to have dinner with him.

'Well – yes, all right,' she said uncertainly. He patted her shoulder, satisfied, and smiled his brilliant smile.

Charles left his men as Bell and Valentine walked up to him.

'I have to get back to Vayonnes,' Bell told him.

Their eyes met for a brief, troubled moment before he answered. 'Of course.'

Nothing else.

'Goodbye,' Bell said, and turned to go. Charles made no move to stop her, and anger with him swelled up inside Bell. She had been shut out, as firmly as if a steel door had swung to between them. Charles had said nothing, and Catherine's presence at Reynard was inexplicable, but it made it impossible for Bell to stay too. As she walked away she felt that she was leaving her whole world there in the vineyards of Reynard.

At the arched gateway she turned back for a last look. She saw Charles's blond head and beaked profile, intent once more on what he was doing. The vines arched around him, looking to Bell in that instant like the green stockades of a prison compound. The wheeled trolleys trundled to and fro, the blackbird sang on in the trees.

Goodbye. Goodbye.

Then Bell saw Juliette running towards her along the rutted track. Her fair hair bounced in thick waves over the collar of her overall. She waited until Juliette bumped against her, and then the French girl's arms went around her in a fierce hug.

'I want to come and see you,' she whispered. 'Can I?'

Bell smiled at her. 'Yes. Please come. Don't worry, Juliette. I'm all right. Or – at least – I will be all right.' Juliette saw determination and a hint of healthy self-mockery in the depths of Bell's eyes. Her friend would be all right, she understood that. Survival might cost her something, but there was no doubt that she would survive.

Valentine was strolling up the track too. His hands were in his pockets and Bell could hear him whistling. The sound brought back sunny mornings at Dry Stone, and the sun reflecting off the blue water of the pool. A long, long way away from here and now.

Juliette waved as she ran back to her work.

Keeping up a casual front for Valentine's benefit made it easier for Bell to turn and walk away.

'Won't you come to Larue soon?' he asked her, as they crossed the road and strolled up the curving driveway.

'Soon, yes,' Bell answered, not caring.

'Saturday morning, then. Come and watch the start of the picking.'

At the château steps, he opened the door of the little Fiat and helped her inside. Bell fumbled absently for her keys, unconscious that she was staring up at the immaculate façade above her, trying to print the image of it on her mind's eye for ever. It was so beautiful. So achingly beautiful. She felt that she loved it with a love that was almost physical.

Reynard . . . Charles . . . and Reynard.

Her fingers closed on the hard circle of her key fob and she leant forward to the ignition. Valentine stood back, and she was too intent on her secret farewell to see the darkness in his face.

'Be careful with yourself, Bell,' she thought he said.

Then Catherine appeared like a slim, dark wraith at his side.

'Come and see us again, one day, won't you?' she asked Bell. Bell found one last smile in response, and then spun the wheel. The car jerked away. The last sight Bell had was of Catherine and Valentine together, going up the steps and in through the heavy double doors.

Jealousy and bitterness stabbed through her all over again.

CHAPTER TEN

Interminable days. Days that were leading nowhere, meaning nothing.

Bell felt out of tune with the whole world as she made her dull journeys to and from Bordeaux. All around her were people enjoying the fruits of their year's labour. Slowly the vineyards had been stripped, and the heavy lorries had brought in their loads. Evening after evening as she passed by she saw the little knots of pickers in the gateways, gathered together to celebrate the bringing home of the last grapes. Bottles of wine were passed from mouth to thirsty mouth until only the lees remained. And those last drops were emptied liberally over the exhausted earth in a symbolic giving back of fruitfulness for the next year. After the gatherings in the vineyards there would be parties in the châteaux, jovial affairs where the red-faced pickers danced with the proprietor's wife and daughters, where the tables were heaped with hearty food, and where wine flowed and flowed to the music of fiddles and accordions.

The climax of the year.

The wine trade was jubilant. A wonderful vintage, the *négociants* murmured to each other in the city's restaurants. A classic year.

Bell felt as if she was the only person in the world who couldn't rejoice at the harvest home. She was all wrong for it, squeezed dry as she was of everything. She couldn't even find it within herself to cry, or even feel any anger after the moment when she had driven away from Reynard. Instead she was gripped by a dull ache of disappointment, and the sourness of frustration. Sometimes, alone in her office cubicle or her silent cottage, she thought back to the days of the early summer. She felt that she had changed so much that it was difficult to remember the old, vital Bell. After Edward had gone she had felt sad, but certain too, and full of the

244

excitement of a new life. And what was left of that now? She had her independence, yes, but it felt more like loneliness. She had calm, but it was dull isolation instead of serenity. Charles had taken all her certainty away, and left her empty. It was difficult not to feel resentful, and impossible that she wouldn't, somehow, go on fighting for him. But, for the moment, she could think of nothing that she could do, and so the meaningless days ground on.

Jacques Lapotin was busy. Huge orders and begging requests for more were beginning to flood in from his clients in France and the rest of Europe.

Bell sat at her typewriter completing shipping documents and customs forms with five carbon copies, and typing Lapotin's letters to customers on his thick, cream-embossed stationery. It was boring, anodyne work but she worked hard to try to forget herself. She began to field the *négociant*'s telephone calls, dealing deftly and tactfully with queries from all sides of the trade. Lapotin began to look at her appreciatively, murmuring 'Good, good. Sensible girl.'

Then, true to his promise, on Wednesday evening Valentine had turned up to take her out to dinner. Jacques Lapotin had already gone home, and Bell was putting the cover on her hated typewriter for another day. She had deliberately shut Valentine's invitation out of her thoughts, she realized with a little shock, as she went reluctantly down to answer the insistent shrilling of the front doorbell.

Valentine was outside, lounging against the wrought-iron railings. The collar of his black leather jacket was turned up over a thick silk scarf, and his hands were deep in the pockets of his jeans. Above the dark clothes his eyes shone very bright blue.

'Oh, good,' he grinned challengingly at her. 'I'm glad that you haven't dressed to kill either.'

In spite of herself Bell's hands went up to the neck of her red sweater and she glanced down at her corduroy trousers and the toes of her leather boots, but before she could think of a quick enough retort, Valentine had wrapped her in a leathery bear-hug. She felt too grateful for the warmth that emanated from him to want to resist, and for a moment she let herself be smothered in his arms. Her face was pressed against his shoulders, and his face was buried in her hair.

'Come on,' he reminded her gently at last, 'get your coat. And you'll need to put this on.' The black motorbike helmet, twin of his own, dangled in his hand.

'No,' she said weakly, but Valentine was not to be denied.

'First we have to work up a really impressive appetite, then we can go and satisfy it. I'm talking about food, of course.' The old arrogant grin came, but there was friendliness in it too. Bell found herself laughing back at him.

Valentine drove so slowly through the thin evening air that Bell had no reason to be anxious. They took the road east out of the city, and wound into the quiet countryside beyond. Once out of the traffic they turned into smaller and still smaller roads, until they seemed to be the only moving things in the landscape and Bell felt herself relax completely against Valentine's back. The clean air blowing into her face was bracing, and she realized that he was right – the ride was giving her an appetite. A little of her unhappiness lifted and her arms tightened around Valentine's waist. At once he flung his quick, dazzling smile back at her.

At length they stopped in the unremarkable *place* of an unremarkable village. *Les Trois Canetons* said the crooked sign tacked to the peeling stucco of the single inn. Bell looked around, puzzled, but Valentine was giving nothing away.

'I'm not quite hungry enough yet,' he told her. 'Let's have a quick walk, first.'

Setting a breathlessly brisk pace he led the way up a little road, barely more than a track, that curved up the hillside away from the village. The walked in companionable silence for a while until Valentine stopped to lean against a low stile. Bell perched beside him and they peered into the thickening dusk together. The lights of the village were blinking on one by one, and there were the smells of woodsmoke and, faintly, cooking, drifting in the air.

'I love all this,' Valentine said simply. Bell looked sideways at him and saw that his face was intent, his eyes fixed on somewhere beyond the unspectacular view below them.

How like Charles, she thought, remembering the still

afternoon in the enchanted woodland above the Médoc. You have that in common. You love the land as much as you love people. Even the people closest to you. More, sometimes.

Suddenly Valentine's arms came round her. She could feel his breath warm on her face.

'Bell, will you . . .'

Apprehension, defensiveness and fear gripped her and she was startled by the vehemence with which her interruption came.

'No. Don't ask me for anything, Valentine. I can't, now. I just can't. Please.'

At once Valentine's hands dropped and his face went blank. For a long moment silence hung between them, and in it Bell could hear the church bell in the next village tolling flatly. Then back came Valentine's smile, at its most cynical.

'Okay. Let's go and satisfy at least one appetite, then.'

He took her hand and with one accord they ran full tilt down the gentle hill. With every plunging footstep, relief pounded in Bell's head. She didn't want to know what Valentine had been going to ask. He wouldn't ask again, and that was enough. She must keep him at bay, at all costs.

As they arrived, flushed and panting, at the door of Les Trois Canetons, Bell saw that the *place* was crowded now with cars, all kinds from big, sleek Citroëns to dusty 2CVs. Then Valentine was steering her inside. The big room was brightly lit, steamy, and crowded with diners at long tables. But the plump waitress showed Valentine and Bell to a tiny table for two, half-hidden from the rest of the room by a wooden partition. They must think we're lovers, Bell thought sadly. How easy it would be, if only things had happened differently.

Well, if only was no use to her now.

Bell refocused her attention forcibly on the immediate present, and glanced around the room.

'No menus?' she asked Valentine, with an effort at normality.

'No choice at all,' he told her, raising his eyebrows in mock-surprise. 'Just take every mouthful you are given, and offer up thanks for it.'

It was, indeed, a wonderful meal, in the best tradition of Bordeaux peasant cooking. There were none of the artfully-arranged little platefuls of colour and texture so beloved of the smart city restaurants. Here the food came in workman-sized portions, in thick white plates, served without ceremony or reverence. There was creamy vegetable soup, each separate flavour distinguishable, magnificent gamey pâtés, fish in a sauce of capers, pink and gold duck unadorned except for its own juices, the biggest array of cheeses Bell had ever seen, and a melting *tarte* of late-summer fruits.

'See what I mean about needing an appetite?' Valentine smiled at her.

They ate everything, voraciously, and washed it down casually with *cru bourgeois* claret. The talk was unremarkable, the conversation of old friends relaxed in one another's company.

'They're right, the old doom-sayers,' Valentine told her. 'The bad weather's coming. We start picking this weekend.'

'Why not before?' Bell asked anxiously. 'Better to be safe than sorry.'

'I'm a gambler, Bell, not like you. Remember Vegas?' Valentine's teeth showed white in his tanned face as he attacked the bones of his duck with obvious relish. 'I said it wouldn't be until the weekend, and it won't be. Every day of sun counts, you know, and my information tells me that I've got plenty of time yet. You'll see that I'm right,' he said, and laughed easily.

Only once did they come close to shattering the thin ice that kept the evening clear of the dark currents beneath their determined cheerfulness.

'You'll come to watch the picking start on Saturday?' Valentine asked.

Bell, in her present mood, was reluctant to commit herself to anything. Besides, the faint hope still lingered that Charles would come to her again, and she couldn't bear the idea of not being there for him.

'No,' she said as gently as she could. 'I don't think so.'

Valentine gripped her arm, suddenly angry.

'Why not? You were at the bloody baron's picking, weren't

you?' He stared at her, his eyes blazing with something like contempt. 'Don't tell me. Are you imagining you're in love with him or something, like a half-assed kid? Is that what all this mystery is? If it is, you're a bigger fool than I'd have thought possible. Can't you see him straight? Can't you see him there with his château and his codes of behaviour, his four hundred years of goddam heritage to live up to, and his wife, for Christ's sake? Where do you imagine that you're going to fit into all that lot?'

Bell withdrew her hand. Her face was white but her voice rock-steady when she answered.

'Be quiet, Valentine. You're quite wrong, and it's no business of yours in any case. All right, I'll come to Larue on Saturday if it matters that much.'

Valentine sighed, exasperated.

'It doesn't matter a jot, Princess. Do just as you like. Oh, shit, let's have another bottle of wine and talk about something else.'

Together, determinedly, they had drawn the threads of the evening tight again.

It was late when Valentine slowed the bike to bring it purring quietly to the courtyard entrance at Le Girafe. Bell swung herself down from the pillion and stood uncertainly with her hand on Valentine's arm. He pulled her roughly to him and as their mouths met Bell knew that she wanted him still, and that he would always excite her just as he did now.

'Let me come in,' he whispered urgently.

'No.' She hoped that she sounded more certain than she felt. 'Goodnight, Valentine, and thank you.'

With a jerk he pulled away from her and the bike swooped away into the darkness.

Slowly, Bell crossed the cobbles to her door. She liked Valentine, liked him more and more, and she found it no easier to resist him now than she had in California.

And yet, and yet. He was only Valentine. Charles stood apart from him as he did from every other man she had ever known. It was Charles she wanted, and everything that he stood for, and it was the thought of Charles that Bell clung to in every long hour of the day. While she was still here, and for as long as she was important to Charles – and she was certain that she was important – there was still hope.

The cottage seemed emptier and lonelier than ever that night.

Another evening Juliette had come. The tentative knock at her door reminded her of the evening when she had found Charles standing there. Even now it gave her a little shock to see his bone structure under Juliette's freckled cheeks and the familiar colour of her hair.

At first, the two women had been awkward with each other.

Juliette was subdued as she sat in the armchair with her legs drawn up beneath her. Bell made coffee, fumbling in the kitchen as she tried to think of something cheerful to call out through the open doorway.

'Valentine asked me to dinner,' she said at last. 'We went to Les Trois Canetons. I quite enjoyed it.'

She put the tray down on the low stool beside Juliette.

'Oh, Bell,' the other girl put out her hand impulsively to grasp Bell's wrist. 'It must be so lonely for you here.'

'Not so lonely, really. I'm working hard, and the Durands are always just across the courtyard.' There was a little silence before she asked, unable to stop herself, 'How is he? What's he doing?' She bit her lip at once and frowned at her lack of control, but Juliette nodded in quick complicity.

'Working. Working all the time. He has been out in the vineyards from dawn until dark, and then sitting alone at night in his study. But tomorrow is the last day, and when he doesn't have the picking to immerse himself in any longer, he will have to confront what's happening.'

'What is happening?' Bell hated to feel that she was prying, winkling the news of Charles's marriage out of his sister, but she had so little pride left. She ached to hear. Juliette watched her friend's face for a moment, and then put her hand over Bell's.

'Catherine wants him back. She's fighting to put things right again.'

'I know that.' Bell's voice was a whisper. 'And Charles?'

'I don't know. I can't see inside him any more. I think he's fighting too, but whatever it is, it's within himself.'

Fighting. What, or whom?

Suddenly Bell's eyes filled with tears. She felt them burning under her eyelids for an instant and then rolling unstoppably down her cheeks. It was a relief to cry.

Juliette started to say something, her concern showing in her face, but Bell shook her head through the blur.

'Best on my own. Please.'

Juliette went away. The door swung to behind her with a long creak and a final, isolating click.

Bell went slowly up the stairs into the darkness and lay across the high bed. Somewhere, lingeringly, she thought that she could still feel the warm closeness of Charles.

When she had cried herself out she fell asleep.

As soon as she woke Bell knew that something had changed. She lay under the blankets for a minute, trying to work out what it could be. Then she realized. Of course, it was the light. There was no sunlight filtering through the thin curtains.

When she sat up and swung her legs out of bed the flowered linoleum struck cold to the soles of her feet. The bedroom was cold; she could see the faint mist of her breath hanging in the air.

With a sweater over her nightdress Bell went downstairs to look at the sky. It was purled from horizon to horizon with light high clouds, and there was an unfamiliar piercing wind blowing from the north-west. As Bell stood in her doorway tasting the cold air Madame Durand came out into the courtyard.

'Winter's coming,' she called. 'You will need oil-stoves in your house. Durand will bring them across.'

Bell went back indoors to search out a thick sweater and socks. She felt muffled up and constricted in the heavy clothes after the long freedom of the summer. Valentine, she was thinking. I hope that you haven't left it too late after all.

As if he was coming to answer her, she heard the motorbike throbbing in the street outside. A second later Valentine swung into the courtyard. It was the same metallic blue machine that she had seen at Reynard, and he sat astride it as he looked up at the windows of the auberge. Bell could see him from the safety of her cottage, sitting there calmly in his leather jacket with his black hair blown into a peak by the wind.

She realized that she was half-hiding, and simultaneously thought that it was foolish. She was glad that he had come. Bell doubted that she would have had the energy to go to Larue alone today, even though she had promised to be there.

Bell came out. Her dark hair was still unbrushed and tumbling over her navy-blue sweater. Valentine looked up at her in open appreciation.

'You look like you used to do in Napa,' he told her, and kissed her quickly on the corner of the mouth. 'I've come to take you away to my château.'

Bell settled her arms around his waist and the bike swooped away. The fear she had felt in California was all gone. Today's ride felt to Bell like a bird in flight, skimming over the vineyard road and cutting through the bends in a series of effortless arcs.

Before she had time to remember that it was coming, Reynard loomed ahead and then dropped behind them. Like a coward Bell kept her face turned away, but she saw that the vineyards were deserted and still. Charles's vintage was safe.

The thought made Bell turn her face up into the rushing air to see the sky again. It was greyer now, with a threatening yellowish tinge. Instinctively Bell tightened her grip on Valentine and ducked her face behind the protective wall of his shoulder.

They rode on through the empty vineyards and past the châteaux where all the attention would now be focused on the great vats inside the *chais*.

Up ahead was the square shape of another château. Valentine tilted his head back so that Bell could catch his words.

'There it is,' he shouted. 'See?'

The road swung away to the right here, leaving the house nestled in the midst of its vineyards instead of being separated from them. Valentine slowed at the intricately wrought gates and they bumped between the stone pillars and into the vineyards of Larue-Grise.

There were men in yellow oilskin jackets moving to and fro amongst the vines. Then beyond them the glistening paintwork of a brand-new mechanical picker caught Bell's eye. The machine was rumbling in neutral at the end of the long rows.

'Come on.' Valentine grinned at her, his face alive with enthusiasm. 'See the first grapes being picked.' He waved his arm in a wide arc to signal to the driver, and with a rumble that rose to a deafening roar the machine began to inch forward on its tracks.

The silvery columns of the rotor arms, shining with their coating of viscous oil, began to move closer and closer to the hanging grapes. With a flutter of foliage and the crackling of twigs the luscious bunches started to plop down on to the moving belt that swept them backwards, grapes and wood and debris all together, into the yawning hopper. There, still out in the vineyard, the grapes would be shaken out ready for crushing.

Bell watched fascinated. She had seen machines like this in action before, but it had never looked so smoothly automatic. A movement at her side distracted her from the spectacle, and she turned to see Bob Cornelius.

'It really works.' She smiled at him and looked back at the machine. Valentine was riding beside the swarthy driver, calling instructions as the metallic monster prowled forward.

'Oh yes, it works,' Bob said. 'I just hope to God it works fast enough.'

'What?'

'The weather's turned faster than we thought. There's a storm coming.'

'Oh, *no*.'

'Yes. We've got one hell of a lot of work to get through.' The little scientist looked unusually grim behind his round spectacles. Valentine had jumped down from the picker and was running towards them.

'Forecast's bad,' Bob shouted into the rising wind. The three of them looked north-westwards to where the clouds were banking up, heavy grey coils of them, and then back to the picker blundering between the vines. Suddenly it seemed much smaller, a toy machine nibbling at the threatening expanses of vineyard. Valentine's dark eyebrows were knitted together, and his face was sombre. Bell knew what he was thinking. Heavy rain and high winds would be a disaster now.

'Nothing we can do,' Valentine shrugged, with an attempt at cheerfulness, 'except keep going. It may still hold off.' He glanced over to assure himself that the grapes were tumbling down on to the conveyor belt and then beckoned over one of the men in yellow oilskins who were attending to the machine's progress. It was the foreman picker, a dark, tautly-knit Spaniard with a magnificent El Greco face.

Bell noticed as Valentine gave a stream of terse instructions that his Spanish was as good as his French, heavily accented but fluent and idiomatic.

'And now,' he turned back to them, 'let's go and have some coffee.'

With the evil wind beginning to pull more greedily at them they walked up to the house in silence.

Bell saw that Larue-Grise was smaller than she had imagined from the only picture she had seen of it – the water-colour, she remembered wryly, that hung opposite the foot of Valentine's bed at Dry Stone. It was less perfect than Reynard but somehow warmer, like a laughing woman with a lined face beside an unsmiling beauty. Bits had been added on here over the years; the house had obviously grown to fit the needs of the family who had owned it, with an extra wing tacked on here and another pair of windows let into a wall there. It had been Hélène de Gillesmont's family, Bell recalled, without emotion. Her ancestors had evidently been more relaxed than she was. The stone of this house was the same colour as Reynard, and the tall windows in the main façade were arranged in the same way, but the two buildings were as different as their owners.

'What do you think?' asked Valentine. 'It's not quite Versailles, but I like it.' The pride was audible in his voice.

'So do I,' Bell said simply. She was looking at the late-flowering mass of scarlet geraniums in the stone urns beside the front door. They looked incongruous in this cold light, and there was already a drift of bright, torn petals on the paving.

'*Season of mists and mellow fruitfulness*' she quoted softly, meaning that it was gone. The autumn had been snatched away from them, and they were left staring into the thin face of winter.

Valentine's eyes met hers, with a smile in the depths of them.

'*Close bosom-friend of the maturing sun;*
Conspiring with him how to load and bless
With fruit the vines that round the thatch-eaves run' he finished for her.

'Not a bad epigraph, that. We've had our maturing sun, and now let's pray God that the fruit isn't smashed to pieces by the storm.'

Bob was staring at them with blank incomprehension in his face.

'Keats, Bob. An old favourite of Bell's and mine.' His arms came round her and for a moment Bell let him pull her close. As they stood there they were both remembering the dark beach, the salt air and the Pacific pounding ahead of them, and the single bright star hanging in the sky above. In the end it was Valentine who moved away. 'Coffee,' he reminded them. 'And then back to work.'

Inside there was the same lofty hallway as at Reynard, and the curving stone stairway on a less grand scale. Somewhere a clock was ticking steadily. Valentine threw open the doors of the drawing-room for Bell to see inside. The room sparkled with fresh gilding, polished wood and the shafts of light struck from tall mirrors. In one corner stood a little spinet, in another an armoire that must have been a spectacular item in any saleroom.

'All very perfect,' murmured Bell. Valentine's collaboration with Hélène in restoring the house had evidently been a success. Yet somehow she couldn't imagine Valentine sitting here in the evenings, his jeans and sweatshirts against the figured silks of the chaises longues.

'I know what you mean,' he grinned at her. 'If I put the red ropes up I could charge people a couple of bucks a throw to come in and have a look.' Bell followed him back across the hall and down a passage. 'Bob and I live on hamburgers in here.' The kitchen belonged to a different world. It was comfortably dishevelled, with a welter of coffee mugs and bottles on the table, and a well-used frying pan on the range. Amongst the clutter was a transistor radio, already switched on.

'*Shush!*' Valentine held up his hand urgently, but there was no need. All three of them froze into silence as the French announcer began to read the shipping forecast.

'. . . with winds gusting up to force eight . . .' Bell heard, '. . . followed by prolonged rain. Visibility poor to moderate.' Valentine moved tensely and flicked the switch off. He looked grimmer than Bell had ever seen him. The ominous silence that filled the kitchen stretched on until Bob broke it with a murmured apology and the savage rattle of the coffee grinder. Valentine was standing at the window with his hands in his pockets, gazing out. The stance was casual but every line of his body gave away the tension inside him.

'Already?' he said at last, in a low voice. 'I knew it was coming, but all the rules say that this weather should still be days away, out over the Atlantic. Where's this damned wind sprung from? It's not *possible*.' Yet outside, for all of them to see, it was more than possible. The wind was tearing down the leaves and sending them scattering over the grass, and with it it was bringing the rain in from the sea.

Neither Bell nor Bob could think of anything optimistic to say.

Not knowing what else to do Bell began to stack mugs and plates in the sink. She realized that she was ravenously hungry. She had eaten no breakfast, and no supper the night before.

'Shall I make something to eat?' she asked Bob.

'Sure. Eggs, bread, everything's in there.' There was an old-fashioned pantry, stone floored and lined with stone shelves. It would be deliciously cool in summer but it felt icy now.

Bell made them platefuls of creamy scrambled eggs and

poured coffee into blue and white mugs. Then they sat round one end of the chunky oak table, listening to the wind. Somewhere at the front of the house a shutter had broken loose. It flapped to and fro; every time the sound came the frown deepened between Valentine's eyes. At the outer corners, fine lines showed.

When the meal was finished Valentine pushed his plate aside and looked first at Bell, then at Bob.

'I think,' he said softly, 'that I may have screwed it up this time. But I want to try and get in every grape that I can. Will you help, Bell? Every pair of hands . . .'

Bell stood up, looking steadily back at him.

'You know I will.'

'Let's go then, Bob?'

Hanging on pegs in the lobby beyond the kitchen, was a row of yellow oilskin jackets identical with the ones that the pickers were wearing out in the vineyards. Bell took the one that Bob handed to her and pulled it on.

'You'll need these, too.' Thick, unwieldy gloves to protect her hands against the tough tangle of vines.

Outside, the sky was even darker but the wind seemed to have dropped for an instant. In its place was a brooding stillness in which every sound was eerily magnified. As Bell stood there she heard the distant drone of a jet descending through the clouds and, from somewhere a long way off, the rhythmic clunk of a mallet driving in a fence post.

'The wind . . .' she breathed, beginning to hope, but Valentine didn't even look round.

'Haven't you heard of the calm before the storm?'

Even as he spoke, the first drops of rain spattered black on the paving stones between the fading scarlet petals. At once, together, the three of them were running.

Valentine's pickers were spread along the first row of vines. The sight of them stooped to their slow task reminded Bell of the same scene at Reynard. But here the baskets were still empty and there were too few men. Far, far too few. They were dwarfed by the waiting acres.

No one was watching the mechanical picker now. It inched along unattended to except by its impassive driver. Every other pair of eyes was turned downwards to the vulnerable grapes and the slow hands that were fighting to save them.

Panting from her run Bell snatched up a basket and a pair of the small sharp shears used for snipping the bunches off the vine stalks. Here. She would start here. She bent down and her fingers felt for the firm stalk bearing the first cluster of purple fruit. The heavy gloves made her fingers feel thick and useless so she tore them off, dropping them without a glance. The sharp twigs ripped her skin as she groped, found the stalk, snipped and laid the precious fruit in the basket. Then another bunch, then another; reaching, snipping and bending to the basket. Again, and again, and again. Grimly Bell made her mind go blank, filling it with the rhythm of her work and letting nothing else matter. Once, and only once, she glanced up to see the distance she had travelled and the length of the row she still had to work along. Beyond that she couldn't even imagine. The world dwindled as she worked to the inches of bare, trodden soil at her feet, the vicious clawing fingers of the vine and the endless fruit. Pain began to stab up her back from the unaccustomed bending and her shoulder muscles ached. But none of that mattered. If only the rain would hold off.

Dimly Bell heard Valentine shouting something, '. . . *as fast as you can* . . .' and then realized that he was shouting over the wind again. The wind rising, springing from nowhere, colder and more insistent, and here with it was the rain. It wouldn't stop now.

Faster. Work faster.

Bend, cut, turn to the basket. Bend, cut, turn again. Listen to the wind howling, and feel the rain cold in her face. It was driven at a cruel angle by the wind, biting into her neck and plastering her hair in heavy coils that she struggled to put out of her eyes.

When at last her basket was full, she heaved it up, surprised at her own strength, and half-ran to the waiting trolley. Strong hands snatched the basket and emptied it, then she was running back to her place. The dry earth was drinking in the rain and already clods of heavy mud were clinging to her boots. Valentine was just ahead of her, black hair sticking to his forehead with a mixture of rain and sweat. As he bent and straightened again, grimly, never looking round, Bell caught a glimpse of his face. The fury in it shocked her.

He won't forgive himself, she thought.

Then the treadmill of the work again, every muscle in her body crying out in protest now.

No stopping yet. No rest. Don't even think about it. Just keep going.

Immersed in her own struggle, Bell didn't hear the roar of the cars until they were in through the vineyard gates. Then when she looked up she saw the grey Mercedes burning to a stop beside the vineyard track. Behind it came a little column of dusty trucks. Bell watched, rooted to the spot, as Charles leapt out of his car. Leaving his door swinging and the engine still running he began to race towards them. Unnoticed, the icy mud spattered over the glossy leather of his shoes and clung in ugly blobs to his perfect clothes. His hair was streaked dark with the rain. Behind him came Jacopin with his blue overall flapping in the wind and a knot of swarthy pickers, all running.

Charles was barely in earshot before he was shouting urgently to Valentine.

'Extra pickers. Where shall we start?'

In Valentine's face anger, pride and desperation fought briefly. Then another glance at the sky told him that he had no choice.

'Over there,' he shouted back. 'Baskets at the end.'

Charles's men fanned out with practised movements and bent to their picking. With so many hands at work Bell dared to hope that they might yet beat the storm.

Before she went back to her own stretch of vines Bell was rewarded by a greeting from Charles. It was no more than a brief nod, but there was no surprise in his face. To Charles it was right that she should be there amongst the workers, struggling desperately to save the fragile grapes. Bell stooped to work again.

Was she imagining it, or was the wind shrieking into a gale? The leaves that she was bending over were whipped cruelly back to leave the knotted stems bare. The bunches of grapes as she lifted them were wet and slippery, all the precious bloom scoured away. A single glance at the sky showed Bell that it was almost black with huge, racing clouds.

Then, into her upturned face, something flicked like a whiplash.

Not that. It couldn't be. It wasn't cold enough. Then Bell felt the icy blast of the terrible wind and knew that it was indeed cold enough.

There it was again. It was the savage bite of hailstones.

Rain during the harvest can turn the finest vintages into poor ones. But hail is the one thing that every vineyard worker prays to be saved from. The little, freezing bullets slash through the tender grape skins and the pulp within is lost. Hail is the destroyer, bringing in a matter of moments the destruction of the vintage and the ruin of a long year's work and hope.

Slowly Bell stood upright. Instinctively she crooked her arm to her face to protect it from the stinging hailstones. Already the ground at her feet was grey-white with melting ice and the hail was still pelting against the fruit with the force of thrown gravel.

Ahead of her she saw Valentine straightening too, turning his face to the sky. His arms dropped limp at his sides and he looked quickly down again. The fury was all gone. In its place was the exhaustion of defeat.

Bell was already moving forward, unthinking, to put her arms around him when she remembered Charles. The baron's hand went to his face too as he felt the bite of hail and then he saw the melting grey slush at his feet. Beyond him Valentine's handful of grey-faced pickers stood dejectedly between the vines, the mechanical picker slewed motionless in the mud at the end of the vineyard.

Beside Charles Jacopin stared aghast at the devastation. For a moment they all stood in stunned silence. The two bands of pickers faced each other, empty-handed, encircling Charles and Valentine.

When Charles spoke, shock and sympathy vibrated in his voice. The autocratic manner was all gone.

'If only we could have helped. We could have beaten the

rain. But hail . . .' It was strange, to Bell, to hear him sound so helpless.

At last Valentine moved. He turned to his rival, dazed, and then frowned in an effort at concentration.

'Nice try, Baron,' he said tonelessly, 'but as a noble gesture it came too late.' As he spoke he reached for a bunch of grapes that still hung on the vine. With a savage twist he wrenched it away and held it up like a trophy.

Moving like robots, the pickers, Charles and Jacopin, Bell herself, gathered around Valentine to look. The grape skins were torn and tattered and the juice oozed from the pulpy mass like blood.

There would be no wine made at Larue-Grise this year.

In the silence that spread around them the two men stared at each other. Bell saw their faces in the livid light and her skin crawled with fear. Charles. Proud once more, his face chiselled with arrogant lines. The born aristocrat, used to the lordly giving of help, certain of gratitude. A man sure of his place and his rightness for it.

Valentine, with his own kind of fierce pride, reeling from the terrible blow. There was a look in his face now that Bell had never seen before. It was shuttered, blind, defensive. Yet there was danger in him too.

'I think you win,' he said, through white lips.

'It's not the kind of victory I care for.' Charles's voice was like a whip. He had recovered from his shock at seeing the broken vineyards. The sympathy was gone and he was dismissive now. The recognition of that drove Valentine to the attack as surely as if Charles had threatened him.

Valentine's bright blue eyes were glittering. 'Then what would you care about?' he whispered.

Bell stared down at the churned mud, breathlessly waiting for the cold stab of Charles's answer.

But no one spoke.

She raised her head then and met Charles's eyes at once. There was no need for him to speak. In his face, in that moment of startled clarity, she read the passion – hopelessly tangled with doubt and fear – that she felt herself.

And Valentine was watching them too. A spasm that might

have been pain passed across his dark face but it was gone before Charles wrenched his eyes from Bell's.

'Why should that interest you?' Charles's answer came too late, but the dismissal was no less abrupt. Without even waiting to hear Valentine out, Charles turned away and began the walk back to his car.

'Oh, but it does matter to me.' Valentine had to shout after him.

Charles went on walking. He motioned Jacopin into the Mercedes, and drove away without a backward glance. His pickers straggled up the vineyard path after him. Bell felt Valentine's stare like a burn on her face. When she steeled herself to look at him she saw the dawn of understanding and a wave of sadness, and she knew how much he needed comfort.

At least she could try to give him that. As his friend. She couldn't give him that love he demanded, but she could comfort him in his defeat. Everything else might be despoiled, like the ruined harvest around them, but there must be something she could do to help him here and now.

The violence of the storm was past. It was lighter now but the rain had settled into a steady, grey curtain that would be drawn across the sky for hours to come. Valentine shrugged wearily. He dropped the wreckage of the bunch of grapes into the mud at his feet.

'There's nothing we can do here now,' he said dully. 'Come inside, everybody.'

The pickers had been fed and filled with warming cognac. They had gone away in a silent little crowd after murmuring to Valentine their awkward attempts at consolation.

Now Bell was sitting at the kitchen table amongst the litter of plates and cups. Valentine and Bob were beside her, passing the brandy bottle to and fro between them in silence. Valentine's dark head was buried in his hands, and he moved only to lift his glass or to stretch out and refill it. The château was utterly quiet around the three of them. Bell thought it was as if the stone itself had been stunned by the disaster. The loose shutter was still, even the clocks seemed to have stopped ticking. Only the rain, pattering against the windows in a monotonous blur, seemed to have any life left in it.

When Valentine lifted his head at last Bell's heart went out to him. He looked as grief-stricken as if he had been bereaved. Laughing, cocksure Valentine had been bowled over.

'I love this place,' he whispered, not looking at either of them. 'And I've let it down. Let it down so stinkingly badly . . .'

Bob Cornelius stirred uncomfortably. 'That's all bull,' he said gruffly. 'You couldn't have known. A freak hailstorm . . .'

'*I should have known*,' Valentine hissed back at him. 'The goddam Baron did, didn't he? Over there with his half-assed tribe of family retainers and his bloody four hundred years of history, his grapes are safe and mine are hanging out there . . .' Valentine jumped to his feet, overturning his chair with a clatter that shocked through the quiet. He stumbled over to the window and leant against it with his forehead pressed to the misted glass. 'Mine are hanging out there with all their sweetness pouring away.' His voice sank to a whisper. 'My fault. My own fault. I should have known.'

'You didn't know,' Bob told him gently. 'And there's nothing we can do now except never let it happen again.'

Valentine turned back then to look at them both.

'Yeah. I know that. You're quite right, Bob, and thanks. But,' he shrugged, 'you know me. Not too hot at being beaten.' He smiled, crookedly, a rueful smile through his defeat that made Bell smile straight back at him. She liked him more for that than for all the playboy charm that he could wield with such unthinking ease.

'I haven't thanked you,' Valentine went on. 'Either of you. Both of you. But you especially, Bell.' He came back to the table and stood beside her chair, then bent to pick up her right hand. He turned it over to look at the deep red scratches on the tanned skin, and at the raw tips of the fingers. The nails were rimmed with black vineyard dirt.

'What a funny girl you are,' he whispered. 'What a strange, secret girl.' Now it was Bob's turn to blunder to his feet.

'Guess I'll get over to the *chais*. We got one truckload in before the rain came, remember.'

Valentine's laugh was short and bitter. 'One truckload. Enough to make a couple of dozen cases.'

Bob was on his way. 'Sure. Well, think of the rarity value. Those bottles will be worth a bomb.'

Valentine nodded. 'Yeah. Let's think of something. Anything.'

Then Bob had gone and they were alone in the untidy kitchen warmth. Valentine perched on the table edge where he could look straight down into Bell's eyes. She found herself wanting to look away, and then not wanting to. Her heart was thumping.

'You strange girl,' he said again. 'You know what? Out there in Napa, I thought we were so alike. Fixers. Winners. The bright people. But now . . .'

Bell winced inwardly, waiting for it. 'But now, I'm not sure you're quite such a cool customer after all.' He was looking at her too hard, too appraisingly.

'You don't know much about yourself, do you? Or about men, Bell?'

She buried her head defeatedly in her arms. Anything to escape the clever light in those blue eyes. Valentine had seen Charles looking at her out in the storm, and seen her own eyes locked in his.

No secret, any more.

'No,' she murmured into the thick sleeve of her sweater. 'But I'm learning the hard way.'

Valentine's hand rested lightly on her shoulder.

'Want to talk about it?'

'No. No, there isn't anything to talk about.'

'That isn't true, is it?'

Bell seized the tattered remnants of her determination and sat up.

'Leave it.'

He looked at her for a long, cold minute and then shrugged.

'Okay.' He poured two huge measures of brandy into their glasses.

'Let's just drown our sorrows like two old friends.' He raised his glass. 'Here's to it. *Season of mists. And mellow fruitfulness*, God help us.'

He tilted his head and poured the drink down his throat.

Bell stared dully down at her own glass.

What a Godawful mess. Charles. I know now that you love me, and I know just as well that we can't have each other.

Drown our sorrows? Your lost grapes, and my lost hope. Why not?

She drank half her own brandy at a gulp and fell back coughing as Valentine slopped more into her glass with an ironic flourish.

Season of mist. And hurt, and loss, and pain.

Cheers.

Hours later Bob Cornelius came back to find them still sitting in the kitchen. The brandy bottle was empty but its contents hadn't helped either of them to forget anything. Valentine was back at the window, dejection showing in every loose line of his body.

Bell, with her fingers knitted round a mug filled with the bitter dregs from the coffee pot, was frowning through the beginnings of a pounding headache. She felt blankly incapable of saying anything to help either of them. The best thing would be to go back home and try to sleep. Forget it all for a while, perhaps. Then back to Jacques Lapotin's office tomorrow, back to the customs declarations with five carbon copies and the endless letters to be typed.

The sudden futility of it all made her laugh, a bitter laugh that didn't suit her.

'C'mon, Bell, it isn't that bad. There'll be other years for all of us.' Simple, cheerful Bob.

No more like this one, I hope.

'I must get back to Le Girafe.' Her own voice sounded stupidly blurred in her ears. Valentine turned to look at her with a brief flicker of animation in his face.

'Won't you stay here?'

She shook her head.

'No.' There was a finality in it that silenced them both.

'You'd better not drive,' Bob told her authoritatively. 'Here, come on. I'll run you over there.'

She had pulled on her coat and was following him out of the

kitchen when Valentine's sharp voice stopped them both in their tracks.

'You'll be coming to the party?'

Bell and Bob both swung round to gape at him.

'The party?'

'Sure. I always have a party for the vintage. A real big one. Don't I, Bob?'

'Not this year, you don't.'

'Oh yes, this year especially.' Valentine picked up the brandy bottle, then pushed it away irritably when he remembered that it was empty.

'A great big party. We'll ask everyone. Even the Baron. Especially the Baron. He really enjoys parties, and mine are his favourite kind.' Valentine was hunting for a piece of paper. At last he unearthed an old envelope and began scribbling busily on the back of it.

'It's a lousy idea,' Bob told him flatly.

'Thanks for the support. You'll come, won't you, Bell?' he repeated. 'All your pals will be here.' There was a deliberate little barb in that. Bell's heart sank. It was a doomed, disastrous scheme but she shrank from telling Valentine so in his present mood. Perhaps he'd think better of it tomorrow.

'I'll come,' she told him without enthusiasm, and he shot her a smile that was almost the old Valentine. Her own smile came naturally in response.

'That's more like it,' he said.

We are alike, Bell thought inconsequentially as she followed Bob out of the dim château and into the rain. It's just that it isn't the real me, the person who's been living inside here for the last few weeks. *Brains and guts*, Valentine had said, remember? If I truly have got those things then I haven't been using them much lately.

Somehow the realization cheered Bell. She lifted her chin out of her coat collar and straightened her shoulders. There had been too much unhappiness. It was time – time to be in command of herself again. If it was going to take brains and guts – well, Valentine believed she had them, didn't he?

Bell became aware that Bob was looking sideways at her.

'Bad day,' she said, wanting to break the silence.

Bob smiled a little. 'Mmmm. You know, Valentine made a bad mistake before. Our second year at Dry Stone. Tried a technical shortcut that resulted in an undrinkable, enormous batch of wine. Lost a lot of money that he couldn't afford in those days. But he learned a lot from that. My God, he learned.' Bob laughed softly. 'That's his real strength, you know.'

Bell stared at the serious little scientist with new eyes.

Yes, she thought. That's just it. Just how Valentine is, and I've only just seen it. And how I admire it, the way of learning from loss.

If only I can do the same.

CHAPTER ELEVEN

The front of Château Larue-Grise was brilliantly lit. Even from where she sat, in the darkened safety of her car, Bell could hear the music.

Footsteps crunched past the Fiat and incurious faces turned briefly to look at her. It was a woman swathed in furs and a man in a bulky overcoat. There was a low laugh and they moved off towards the lights of the house.

Instinctively Bell reached up to smooth her hair. She had made herself ready with care in the primitive little bathroom at Le Girafe. The violet and gold blazer was the most festive thing that she had brought with her for her winter in Bordeaux. It reminded her of the other doomed party, the one that Juliette had given for her birthday at Reynard. A hundred years ago. It would remind Charles too, perhaps of the vanished seconds when they had waltzed together, alone, across the wide shining floor.

She wanted to be here tonight to see Charles. Even after everything, she still needed to see him.

It was a long walk up the cold driveway, but still not quite long enough for Bell. She hated going to parties alone, hated the moment of stepping into the bright lights where everyone knew one another, and where the laughter was a threat. It was a moment of loneliness more intense than any of the others, and tonight Bell felt it fourfold.

Come on.

She lifted her hand to bang the heavy knocker but the door was already swinging open from her gentle push. The hall was crammed with people. Bell squared her shoulders and slipped inside, a smile already prepared.

Then, relief. There was Bob Cornelius almost beside her.

'Hi! Great that you could come.' As ever, he was blinking from behind the owl glasses. 'Bell, you know, you look fantastic. Valentine's asking for you.'

'I'll just go upstairs and . . .'

'Oh sure, but come right back.'

Bell pushed through the crowds of people and up the curve of stairs. She found a bedroom, and the long mirror that was lacking at Le Girafe.

Yes, she was all right. The stare she gave herself was long and critical, but she was looking fine. The blue-green eyes were a shade too bright perhaps, but no one could have guessed at the apprehension and perverse excitement that were creeping up inside her.

Out on the upper landing again Bell leant on the rail to look down at the heads below. No one she recognized. Not yet.

But wait – there was Valentine. Open white shirt, jeans and sneakers. He looked about eighteen. Impossible that he could really own this grand house, be the host to all these people. As she watched, Bell saw him meet Bob Cornelius and ask a quick question. Bob was nodding vigorously and pointing to the stairs. Valentine was asking for her.

His eyes followed Bob's pointing finger and then flicked upwards. He had seen her. He was pushing his way towards the stairs, laughing and greeting people as he went. Then running lightly up the steps towards her. In a second he was at her side, swinging her round so that he could look full into her face.

'I'm sorry you had to come alone,' he said seriously. 'I'd have come to get you, but . . .' A wave, dismissive of all the noisy crowd.

How nice he can be when he wants, Bell thought, for the hundredth time.

'I'm quite independent,' she smiled back at him. *Liar*.

Valentine was still serious; he was so familiar, looking down at her.

'I wish there was no one here but you.'

No, this isn't how it should be, Bell caught herself thinking. I mean, I mustn't let him talk like this.

'Bob and I tried to talk you out of it the other day.' She made her voice sound light. 'But you wouldn't listen.'

For a moment he went on looking at her, then his hands dropped from her arms.

'Shall we go downstairs? You'll want to meet some people.'

Bell bit her lip. From his voice she knew that he was disappointed in her. Whatever she did, caught in this tangle, she couldn't hope that it would be all right. Couldn't hope to escape without causing hurt to someone. Her eyes were on Valentine's shoulders as she followed him down the stairs. She knew his shape so well.

Not Valentine, she hoped

And please, not Charles.

It would be Bell herself, of course. She deserved that, for not seeing more clearly from the very beginning that she was playing with fire. It was all on her own head. Bell and Valentine stepped down into the heart of the clamorous room. Music began to swell louder around her as Bell found herself a smile and turned to face the world. She was ready for it.

A party, just like so many others. Valentine had steered her into the middle of a group of flushed, animated faces and then he had gone away. Well, she could manage now. There was plenty to talk about.

'Appalling bad luck, that freak hail,' somebody said.

'Well yes, but he had left it far too late, of course,' another proprietor chipped in.

'Dreadful for darling Valentine, all the same, when everyone else has done so well.'

A striking woman talking this time, waving her hands tipped with long scarlet fingernails.

Poor Valentine, Bell thought. He must be hating the idea that they're all feeling sorry for him, gossiping about his failure. She stood there for a few more moments, listening to them talking about how talented, but how stubborn, they believed their host to be. Then, when the topic was exhausted and they were beginning to turn to her for a contribution, she looked down at her empty glass and murmured an excuse. It was easy to slip away into the crowd.

Bell longed for anonymity tonight. She wished that she could be invisible, could skirt round the edges of the party and search out the faces that mattered to her without having to meet those eyes with her own.

If only she could see Charles and Catherine together. If she could watch them look at one another as they did when they were alone, it might help her to understand them. Help her to know whether she should creep away, or go on hoping.

Odd, she thought, that she had driven out here with the conviction that tonight would bring some kind of solution. Now she was here she felt, dully, that it was just another social gathering. A lot of polite talk and mechanical laughter, one or two tipsy indiscretions, and then everyone trickling away again to the thick-walled houses of their private lives.

Bell wandered from the hallway into the drawing-room. The music was coming from in here and it met her at the doorway like a wall. The carpets were rolled back ready for dancing. A girl in a mini-dress and a man in khaki fatigues were – incongruously – jiving. Bell thought she caught the smouldering smell of grass. There were glasses on all the polished surfaces and cigarettes hanging dangerously out of ashtrays. Hélène must be shuddering, Bell smiled to herself, and then, I wonder if she is here?

It suited Bell's mood, this wandering and watching. In another, smaller room beyond the big one there were leather chesterfields and green-shaded side lights. Much more American. There were men in dark suits in here, sheltering from the crush, and Bell spotted Jacques Lapotin amongst them. To her astonishment he blew her a kiss and then raised his glass. Not wanting to be trapped she pointed at her own empty one and waved.

Then, as she turned away, she saw the de Gillesmonts. Even though she had been expecting it, the shock still jolted her. They were in the far doorway, looking in at the dancers, just as she had done herself. Charles, with his wife on one side of him and his sister on the other. He looked very tall and fair, across the thronged room and, with his hooded eyes and strongly curved features, just a little disapproving. No, it wasn't the kind of evening he could be expected to enjoy.

Catherine was wearing a slip of a short black dress with frivolous, floating feathers at the neck and hem. She turned her calm oval face to watch the people, secure with her husband beside her.

Bell tasted bitterness in her mouth and swallowed hard to dispel it.

Juliette knew the dancers. They had grabbed her by the arms and were pulling her between them on to the dance floor. She was laughing – she was amongst friends, too.

It was bitter. Bell turned away, knowing that it was weak to feel sorry for herself. This was all, all of it, of her own doing. Self-protectiveness hardened around her. She didn't want them to see her. Not yet. Deliberately she went across to Jacques Lapotin in the furthest corner of the room.

'May I join you?' she murmured. 'So crowded out there.'

'Of course, of course. You know Michel Lebegue?' A great name in Bordeaux. This must be the grandson or great-grandson of the house, a young man with dark brown velvety hair and dark brown close-set eyes. He had a narrow, clever, whimsical face, a little like that of a small intelligent animal.

'*Enchanté.*' He leaned over Bell's hand to kiss it. 'But you don't have a drink. Let me get you one at once.'

Jacques was smiling and shrugging, proud of his compatriot's dazzling way with the ladies. Well, why not? She would sit here and talk a little, probably flirt a little, with young Monsieur Lebegue. She wasn't busy.

The evening began to melt harmlessly away. Michel was amusing. He brought her a carefully arranged little plate of supper and unfolded her napkin for her. He kept her glass well filled and as they ate he told her witty, spiky little stories about the people who passed their corner.

Valentine came in once and spotted them immediately. Did he look relieved, she wondered, or did she just want to think that he did?

'I might have known that I'd find you with the most dangerous bastard in the house.' He was laughing, not drunk but a little high, enjoying his own party. Bell was glad to see that.

'Bugger off, Vallon-teen,' said Michel.

Evidently the men were old friends. 'I'm quite safe,' she smiled up at him.

'Don't be so sure,' Michel told her, settling an arm around her shoulders. Valentine went away again.

272

Later Michel steered her into the next room to dance. The lights had been dimmed but the dancing was still at the exuberant, bouncing stage. Bell kicked off her shoes and let the rhythm swallow her up. It felt good. Good to be alive and, just for a moment, oblivious.

A hand touched her elbow, lightly.

Bell whirled around and came face to face with Catherine. 'I thought we might see you here,' Catherine said. She looked luminously calm, talking quite naturally to an acquaintance met by chance at a party. I must be the same, Bell warned herself, resisting the impulse to back away like a rabbit from a snake. Michel was standing at her side, listening. He had nodded courteously to Catherine. Of course they would all know each other.

'May we have our dance later?' Bell asked him.

'I'll make sure that we do.' He smiled at them both and strolled away.

'Perhaps we could find a quiet corner,' Catherine suggested tranquilly. 'Valentine has a little sitting-room upstairs.'

Catherine would know all about that. What a dense, ugly tangle this was. The feathery fronds on the baroness's dress floated as she walked. Perfect deportment, perfect chic. Bell dug her hands deeper into the pockets of the blazer and gritted her teeth. Whatever was coming wasn't going to be easy. There were diamonds in Catherine's ears, and a diamond and sapphire bracelet around her wrist. *What does she want with me?* Bell's fingers felt for the shape of her own ivory bangle. She was wearing it pushed well up her arm, hidden under the cuff of her shirt like a talisman.

Catherine knew the house well, all right. In this little upstairs room were all the trappings of ordinary life – a portable television, piles of magazines, squashy chairs and a chessboard with the pieces poised in mid-game. This must be where Valentine spent his time, here and in the kitchen downstairs. Not within the invisible red ropes that set off Hélène's elaborate domain.

Catherine had arranged herself in one of the armchairs. She plucked gently at a feather and then turned her face to Bell. Pure steel, someone had said, Bell recalled. Juliette?

Valentine? That pointed chin, and the determination in the wide-set hazel eyes. How extraordinary that so many things should connect her to a woman so different from herself. Two men. Valentine and Charles. Bell felt that her breathing was uncomfortably loud.

'I hoped you would be here,' Catherine was saying. 'We should know one another better.' She was speaking so slowly, each syllable as clear as a little crystal bell. 'Valentine says you are special, Juliette talks of you as a dear friend. The only person who never talks of you is Charles.'

A long, long pause through which the dance music thumped, extinguished but for the throbbing bass line.

'Strange, that.'

You know, then. Bell's thoughts were racing. What are you going to do . . . threaten me? Challenge me? Or just warn me off?

'Charles has helped me a great deal. I would like to think of him as a friend.'

Bell sounded just as cool. It was a game that two could play.

Catherine's eyes were turned downwards, shadowed by the long black eyelashes. She looked just as she did in the photograph on Hélène's work-table. Yet when she started talking again her voice was low and throaty. She sounded as if every word had suddenly become a struggle. Her lovely face was tense now, unmoving but rigid.

'Help. Friends. I need both of those too, and I'm finding that they are rare currency.' She paused again, seeming to wait for something, but Bell gave her no sign. In truth she had no idea what was expected of her. Catherine ducked her head even lower and her voice sank to a whisper.

'I did a terrible thing, Bell. I betrayed my husband, and with a man I didn't even love. I was looking for something, and – like a fool – I was looking in all the wrong places.'

From somewhere a long way off, it might have been the other side of the world, came a shout of laughter and the crunch of breaking glass. Dimly Bell remembered that there was a party going on down there, yet there was nothing, anywhere, but the shadowed profile of Charles's wife.

'When my baby died I wanted to die too.' The words were being wrenched from Catherine now. 'The innocence. Perfection of his hands, and hair, and laughter. Then, suddenly, too much pain and he was gone.'

Stop it. *Please*, Bell wanted to say.

'After that, nothing. Then slowly came the need for help, and company. Charles couldn't give me either, and I should have understood, and helped him too. Instead, I turned away. To your friend. Valentine Gordon.'

Bell sat stiffly. She didn't want to hear this to the end, but she knew she must.

'It meant that in the end I had to go away from Charles. But we belong together, Bell. Even in our failures, we belong together. I am Charles's wife, you see, and because of the beliefs we share I know that he can never forget that. I am his wife,' Catherine repeated, 'and I am the only one who can make him recover from his grief, and guilt, over our loss of Christophe. Because he was my child too. Charles can never escape that shared failure, and it binds us closer than any happiness could. Closer, and more painfully. I know that now because I have tried to live without him. Tried it alone, and with other men, and I have failed. Just as he can only go on failing without me. I know that now.'

Bell saw, shocked, that there were brilliant tears, shining brighter than her diamonds, on Catherine's lashes.

'Why are you telling me this?' There was no answer. 'How can I help?'

The hazel eyes met hers directly now, and there was a hard glitter in them behind the tears.

'I think you know how.'

Yes.

When Bell looked up again Catherine was gone.

Disconnected impressions seethed for a moment in her mind, behind the clear picture of the pale oval face, then began to coalesce into logical thoughts.

A formidable enemy, she had judged Catherine to be on their first meeting. That was quite wrong. It was more than formidable of Charles's wife to have shown her own wounds to Bell, and to have called for her help.

It was brilliant.

It meant that there was no contest. Bell saw herself, spotlit, as the real enemy. She wanted to take Catherine's husband away.

Still did. But that would have to stop, here and now. Poor Charles. Poor me. Clever, clever Catherine. Bell knew that they were too different ever to have liked each other, but she could feel admiration for her. More than that – Catherine's words m..de her see what she had been wilfully closing her eyes to for so long. Charles never would find happiness with anyone else. All the traits in him which drew Bell so strongly, his heritage and his rigid morality, his unquestioning acceptance of the strictures of his code, all meant that he could choose only one partner. And he had chosen her already. Catherine, from the same race and background and raised in the same faith, had become his wife. That was unalterable, and Bell – so stridently from the wrong world – saw at last that she could never hope to change that in the future. Nor, more importantly, could she ever succeed in obliterating the past that tied them. Catherine and Charles did indeed belong together, in their failures as well as in the possibility of success. The certainty and the taste of defeat came to Bell together, bringing with them a suffocating wave of misery.

No time for self-pity now. Things to do.

Bell went back to the party.

The noise level had gone up by several decibels, the smoke had thickened and there were dancers and drinkers everywhere. It was a good party. A real big one, just as Valentine had wanted. Juliette and Valentine were dancing together now, both laughing uproariously. They saw her and waved. Bell wanted to be laughing too. She was beginning to tire of being frozen and apart, but there was somebody she had to see first. As she turned away in search of him she felt another hand at her elbow. This time it was Juliette. Suddenly Bell felt that she didn't want to go on being the object of her sympathy and concern.

'I'm okay, Juliette. Catherine and I have been talking.' The questioning expression, Charles's but yet not Charles's, watching her. Bell went on, deliberately. 'I know where I

stand. Don't stand, rather. Do you know where Charles is?'
Juliette pointed. There he was, at the head of the stairs,
leaning over to watch them just as Bell herself had done
earlier. Then he was walking lightly down, coming through
the tangle of people, half a head taller than the crowd. Bell felt
a pain that threatened to stifle her.

There was pain in the depths of Charles's eyes too.

'I want to tell you something,' Bell said, her voice sounding
fierce.

'Here.'

Behind a heavy closed door was a dim room, brown and
restful. There were leather-bound books behind metal grilles
and sombre wood panelling. In the stone fireplace a log fire
was flickering out in the midst of its own downy grey-white
ash. When the heavy door closed again they were quite alone.

Bell felt so tired. She leaned her head against the stone
mantel and stared down into the dying embers, then stirred
the lazy ash with the tip of her toe. What was there to say,
after all?

Nor did Charles speak. Instead his arms came around her
and his mouth moved over her hair, against her wet eyelids
and at last over her mouth.

Bell sighed, a long drawn-out breath. She was so tired, and
it was so peaceful here. If only she had come home safe,
instead of having to fly away again for ever after these
borrowed seconds were gone. She would never feel him close
again like this. Never know the beating of his heart against
hers, his breath warm on her skin.

Charles drew back so that he could look at her once more.
Bell knew that he was memorizing her face, feature by feature,
and she ached for him. At last he smiled, a sad smile that made
his fine-drawn face look infinitely vulnerable. In all his
moods, she had never seen him look like this. The gold flecks
in the depths of his eyes were luminous.

Bell heard the soft, soft whisper of falling ash on the stone
hearth.

'I love you,' Charles said.

The words should have been the sound of perfect happiness
but instead they had a dying fall.

'I love you too.' Bell breathed it. 'If only . . . ' but the words were stopped by Charles's fingers on her lips and she was glad. There were no words that could have made any difference. She knew that there was no point in fighting any longer. She would never truly break through to him, any more than Charles could ever really hope to escape.

Resolutely Bell unbuttoned her cuff. The creamy circle of ivory slid back to her wrist and she closed her hand over it to slip it off. For a moment it lay in her cupped hand and then, slowly, she held it out to Charles.

'I can't keep it,' she said, simply. She knew that there was no need to explain why. That she could never look at it again because it would hurt too much. Charles took the beautiful thing and turned it in his fingers, touching the swollen grapes and the intricately carved leaves. Bell saw that his hands were work-roughened from the vineyards and scarred with long scratches. Just like her own, from Valentine's land.

The land. The seasons. And so it all goes on. What does it matter?

Slowly Charles turned the bracelet once more, then folded it away. Like people in a dense mist they reached blindly for each other and their mouths met hungrily once, just once, more.

Then, as they clung together, the protecting door swung open. Framed in the square of light stood Valentine, the intruder. It was too late. There could be no guilty springing apart. Instead their arms unwound with painful slowness and Bell stumbled back against the wall. Instinctively her fingers crept out from her sides, then encountered and laced in the cold metal lattice of the bookshelves. She clung there, helplessly.

There was a long, long silence as Charles and Valentine measured each other. Then Valentine let the door close softly.

They were trapped, the three of them, together.

Valentine came prowling round the room, restless as a caged tiger, but Charles stood stiff and motionless, looking nowhere. Bell felt a prickle of anxiety run over her scalp, and the fluttering breath of reawakened fear. From the moment when he had first seen them Valentine hadn't even glanced at her. All his attention, the aggression that frightened her so much, was focused on Charles.

Valentine picked up a silver box from the table and flipped it open. Charles shook his head impatiently as he offered it but Valentine simply shrugged, took a cigarette for himself and lit it with exaggerated care. He breathed in deeply.

'You're not so very perfect after all, then, Baron. It's a relief to know that.'

His voice was silky. 'Do you remember, just two years ago? When you saw me with Catherine? In this very room, wasn't it?'

'Valentine, stop . . .' Bell's voice was pleading, but he wouldn't let her.

'No, Bell, not you. It's Charles I want to talk to tonight.' He was still pacing to and fro as if the tension inside him quivered too high to allow him to stand still.

'Do you remember what else happened that night?'

Charles stood unmoving, not giving the American the satisfaction of an answer.

'Perhaps you don't remember?' The drawling voice rippled on. 'You challenged me. To a duel, of course. How quaint, how European, how romantic.' He sounded dangerously quiet now. 'Do you know, Baron, ever since that night – I've regretted not fighting you? Not fighting you every bloody inch of the way?'

'No. You're crazy.' Bell was almost sobbing in her anxiety. He didn't even look at her.

'Be quiet.'

At last Charles melted from his frozen silence.

'You can still fight me if you feel so strongly.'

Valentine smiled briefly. 'Oh, I know I can, Baron. And I'm going to. With the greatest, greatest pleasure.'

As Bell looked from one man to another her fear crystallized. These were bitter, angry words. They were angry, yes, but it was cold, slow-burning anger. Not the kind that flames up overnight and is gone with the light of morning. They would fight each other; not the quick struggle that it would be if they leapt at each other now, but a deliberate, destructive battle. No one could stop them now. A little sound escaped her, like the whimper of a child, but neither of them heard it.

Valentine turned sharply and threw his cigarette into the dead heart of the fire.

'I dimly remember,' he said in a new, ominously businesslike voice, 'from books in which this kind of thing happens, that it is the privilege of the challenged to choose the weapons.'

Charles inclined his head. 'You are surprisingly well-read. Yes,' he sounded indifferent, 'you can choose the weapons.'

Valentine straightened up sharply.

'In that case, Baron, we race my motorcycles.'

Charles's face didn't betray even a flicker of surprise. Bell listened with a slow horror rising around her. One of them would be killed on those vicious machines. Valentine went on reciting the conditions, efficient and deadly.

'. . . at first light tomorrow. From the gates of Larue to the gates of Reynard. No other rules; who gets there first, wins. There should be no traffic then. And it's a fine, straight road.'

He's been planning this, thought Bell. Working it out. Biding his time.

'I know that it is a straight road.' Charles's voice was biting and there was contempt in his face. 'Until tomorrow, first light, then.'

He was already halfway across the room when he remembered Bell. Deliberately he turned back, looked down at her for an instant, and then kissed her lips. His face felt as cold as marble.

'Goodnight.' The farewell, with surprising gentleness, included them both. The door opened, and then closed once more.

Bell searched for words, feeling her own anger mounting inside her. Valentine was smiling a remote, satisfied smile that looked beyond the library to the vineyard road.

'Why?' she asked at last. 'Why risk yourself, and Charles? Those bloody bikes. Don't do it. Don't be a reckless fool. It's not too late – it would be braver not to do it, for God's sake.'

Valentine's face didn't change but at least he was looking straight at her.

'I think, Bell, out of all of us, that it is you who are the biggest fool.'

There's truth in that, Bell thought bitterly. If I have played a part in all this, however small, I hope I may be forgiven.

'It's not what you think . . .' The classic words of the age-old excuse came out involuntarily, but she faltered even before Valentine turned away.

'Don't flatter yourself that this is because of you. It was bound to happen, as surely as Charles and I both exist. It was bound to happen in the end,' he repeated softly, 'and it's happening according to my rules. For God's sake, it's only a race. No crap with guns. What can happen? Nothing.'

Bell closed her eyes. What could happen? She remembered the terror of the ride through the California night, the brutal nearness of the road and the fragility of their bodies crouched above it. She knew, all too terrifyingly well, what could happen.

'Shall we get back to the party?' Valentine looked as handsome, fit and full of energy as he always did. 'No point in going to bed, is there?'

Bell looked at her watch. Two a.m. Only a very few hours left until dawn.

'No point at all,' she countered, forcing a smile. She wouldn't let him see just how afraid she really was. Bob. Bob Cornelius. That was it – she would find him and get him to help. Between them, somehow, they must stop this race.

Bob was sitting in the chaos of the kitchen with a glass of vodka in front of him. He had lost his earnest, blinking stare and was smiling vaguely instead.

'Everyone's going,' he said, 'mush too early.'

'I'm still here,' Bell said urgently. 'Listen, Bob, I need your help. Do you remember the duel? Valentine and Charles de Gillesmont?' She saw the vagueness chased out of Bob's face by listening alertness.

'Yeah. I remember the duel.'

'They're going to fight after all. Tomorrow. No . . . this morning. At dawn. They're going to race Valentine's bikes from here to Reynard.'

Bob rubbed his hands wearily over his face. Bell was infuriated to see that he looked relieved.

'Well, that's not so very terrible. Val's idea?' Bell nodded briefly. 'Surprisingly sensible, then. I thought you meant a real fight. It's only a race.' Valentine's own words exactly. Bell reached out and fiercely gripped his wrist.

'We've got to stop them. They could kill themselves.'

'Stop them? Stop *Valentine*?' He laughed, really seeming to be amused. 'Haven't you noticed by now that when he decides to do something, he does it?'

'Yes. I've noticed. But must he decide to go out and maim himself? Or maim someone else?'

Bob looked at her briefly, then put his hand over hers. 'Don't worry. They'll be all right. Where is he?'

Bell waved towards the main part of the house. 'Enjoying his party to the very last.'

Bob chuckled. 'Of course.'

There were a few guests still left out there. Valentine was standing in the doorway, waving to a departing crowd of noisy revellers. When he saw Bob he smiled his bright, confident smile.

'Bob! I need you to be my second. I can't recall what a second is supposed to do, but no doubt the Baron will be able to fill us in on tricky points of etiquette.'

'Oh sure,' said Bob. 'It's just a question of picking up the pieces, I think.'

He's enjoying this just as much as Valentine is, Bell thought, despairing.

What can I do?

'You'd best get home to bed,' Valentine told her curtly. 'Will you be all right on your own?'

'Yes.' Bell turned away, defeated.

'I'm going out to look at the bikes. A little fine tuning, I think . . .'

He was actually rubbing his hands in gleeful anticipation.

'And I'm going to get some kip'. – Bob, yawning and stretching, looked quite unconcerned – 'before the big race.'

In a couple of minutes Bell was alone. Alone, that is, except for the last few guests and they were in no condition to matter.

She wandered absently through the turmoil, picking up a glass here and righting a chair there. She found a rumpled man asleep on one of the sofas, and there were two or three couples still murmuring in corners or hidden in the sanctuary of a curtained window seat.

No one paid any attention to Bell.

It saddened her to see the lovely, formal rooms in such disarray. There was something very sordid, she reflected, about the aftermath of a party. But no doubt Valentine would organize an army of workers to swoop in tomorrow and restore it to perfection. If, that is, he was capable of organizing anything. Bell shut off the thought abruptly, furious with herself for permitting it. It was unthinkable to go home. What could she do in her empty cottage at Le Girafe, but sit and wait for the news to come to her? If she stayed here at least she would know as soon as it happened.

Back in the kitchen she made herself a cup of thick black coffee and sat down to watch the slow fingers of the clock, and the dark square of the uncurtained window.

The hours trickled painfully past.

Just before half past five, Bell thought she saw the first, ominous grey smudge. Minutes more passed before the light intensified, so long that she began to think that her tired eyes were tricking her. Then she saw that it was no trick. Dawn was breaking.

For a second she sat, undecided, wondering what to do. The thought of it frightened her, but she knew that she must watch the start of the race. There was still the faintest chance that she could persuade them to call it off.

Wrapped in her thin evening blazer and clutching the inadequate black silk square of her bag, Bell slipped out of the house. The new day was raw under a dull, clouded sky. A thin, sour drizzle was relentlessly falling. There was not a sound or a movement anywhere. The vineyard road was deserted, Larue-Grise itself was shuttered and silent. Perhaps it wasn't going to happen.

Perhaps she had imagined it all. Perhaps . . .

No, there was no hope of that. The uneasy silence was ripped apart by the splutter and then the mounting roar of powerful motorbikes. There were two of them, bursting round the side of the house. Valentine, sleek in his black leathers, was perched on one. Bell saw him lean forward anxiously to catch the note of the engine as it rose and fell, one gauntleted hand caressing the throttle. Bob, less obviously at ease, was riding the other machine, the gleaming metallic monster familiar from the morning at Reynard. As the riders swooped forward Bell shrank involuntarily, but they slowed again when they saw her and the menacing note of the bike engines dropped away to a purr. Valentine raised a black-gloved hand in a wave, and Bell saw the white flash of his smile. His face was glowing with excitement. He's revelling in this, Bell thought.

With a swerve that crunched the wet gravel Valentine brought his machine alongside Bell.

'Ready for the off?' He grinned at her as if they were setting out on a picnic. Bell grabbed the unyielding leather of his sleeve. 'Please, Valentine, don't do it. You can still call it off.'

'Call it off?' He laughed at her in disbelief. 'I haven't looked forward to anything so much in years. You surprise me, Bell. I thought you were a girl of spirit.' He shook her hand off his arm and reached for the throttle again.

'Nobody will be hurt. I'll just cream the smug bastard. Jump on, ride with me to the gates. I'll show you nought to sixty in five seconds.' He was laughing, delighted with himself and the prospect of the race. Even Bob, evidently hung-over, was smiling behind him.

'I'll walk,' Bell shouted over the din, and Valentine shrugged. The two bikes flashed past her in a blast of fumes.

Bell saw them reach the gates and stop. They hung there side by side in the wet grey air, poised and ready. Waiting for the battle.

Heavily she followed them and took up her position under the dripping trees at the roadside. Valentine bounced in his seat and revved his bike impatiently.

'Where is he?' he muttered. 'Not going to chicken out, I hope.' No one answered, but the three of them stared fixedly up the road that stretched away to Reynard. Then, as she stood there shivering, Bell saw what they were waiting for.

It was the grey Mercedes, coming on through the rain like a shadow.

Charles was at the wheel; while he was still too far away for her to see clearly Bell could imagine the cold set of his features. Beside him was Jacopin – the baron had brought his second too. As Bell strained to see the men's faces, the bikes went on ticking over threateningly in the thick air and sending blue clouds idling out behind them.

The car slid to a halt, and Charles got out. His face was pale and expressionless, and when his glance flicked over Bell she could read nothing in his eyes. He went at once to Valentine. Bell saw to her surprise that they were almost the same height. Strange, that. She could have sworn that Charles was much taller.

'Well?' Charles's monosyllable was curt. Valentine went on smiling, but anger sparkled in his eyes.

'Just you and me, Baron, the bikes and the open road,' he answered. 'Like in all the songs. Shall we go?' Charles turned his face away from Valentine's taunting smile.

Bob surrendered his bike to Charles and then held something out to each of them. It was the pair of black helmets with their heavy visors. Valentine slipped his on and secured it with practised ease, but Charles fumbled with the strap of his for a second. Helmeted, the two men looked like clumsy creatures from another planet. At last they were ranged side by side in the roadway, astride the thundering bikes. As the revs mounted the exhaust fumes thickened and coiled lazily away.

Bell found that her throat was as dry as sand. She must do something now, or it would be too late. She stumbled forward into the middle of the road. Dimly she thought that somehow she could block their path.

'Please stop it,' she implored, her voice barely more than a croak. 'Don't. Charles, Valentine, listen to me.'

Valentine's smile was lazily confident now, sure of getting what he wanted.

'Move, Bell,' he ordered briefly.

Bell turned to Charles. He looked like a stranger in the unfamiliar helmet but in the second that they looked at each other his face softened. Then a roar from Valentine's bike reminded him, and the stony stare returned.

'Let us pass.'

Bell stepped backwards at once, defeated. Her legs were numb, and as heavy as lead.

Bob was fumbling with something at the roadside, then handing it to Jacopin. It was a white handkerchief. The starting signal.

Ahead of the racers the road stretched away, slick and black and threatening. It was patched with gaudy wet-yellow leaves from the poplars, and it was shiny with grease.

A treacherous road and treacherous weather.

Jacopin was holding the handkerchief aloft. It fluttered bravely like a pennant, and in that split-second Bell saw Valentine's mocking smile whiten under the black mask of his visor.

Then Jacopin's arm dropped, there was a rending scream of tyres and a stench of rubber, and the bikes were gone.

Bell was biting so hard into the back of her own hand that the pain made her cry out. The cry hung in the air, and over it she heard the din of the racing bikes drop in pitch from a scream to a dwindling whine that was swallowed up in seconds by the muffling air.

The silence that followed terrified her even more.

There was nothing, nothing to be heard. Not a bird, the snap of a twig or even the wind in the branches.

Panic engulfed Bell like a tidal wave. Bob and Jacopin, not looking at each other, stood with their heads cocked to the emptiness.

Bell heard herself scream at them.

'Don't stand here. Follow them.' She dragged wildly at Jacopin's arm, trying to pull him to the Mercedes, but the little Frenchman stood his ground.

'I am to wait here,' he said mulishly, not admitting the possibility of doing anything else.

'Bob. You come, please.'

'No, Bell. Don't interfere.'

Oh, God. Bell looked wildly up the driveway to her own car, gauging the distance, imagining the run to it in her stupid high-heeled shoes or in bare feet. Too far. The powerful Mercedes was right here, the ignition keys dangling their invitation.

Without a second thought, Bell vaulted into the driver's seat and set the engine purring into life. Struggling with the heavy steering and with the unfamiliar gears, her wet shoes sliding on the pedals, Bell wrenched the car into reverse, swerved it out into the road and then shot forward.

How far? Where would they be? Her breath was coming in short painful gasps and the blood pounded in her head. With her knuckles white on the wheel Bell drove on. The road unwound in front of her, reassuringly empty. Nearly at Reynard now. Could they be safe?

Relief was already warm inside her as she swung the Mercedes towards the corner that obscured her view of Reynard and the end of the race. Then, with a sickening screech of tyres, she had to swerve to avoid what lay in front of her.

One of the bikes was lying slewed across the road, at the apex of the single right-hand bend before Reynard. One wheel, still spinning, pointed drunkenly at the arch of trees. The other bike stood, silent and innocent, at the roadside. Bell jammed the brakes and the heavy car skidded into the verge. Ahead of her was one body sprawled in the road and the other – unrecognizable, black against the skyline – stooped over it.

Please God, Bell prayed as she ran, don't let it be Charles. Not Charles. Not Charles.

When she reached them Bell dared not look down at the crumpled figure. Instead her eyes went to the other visor, still not knowing who it was. Then a gloved hand lifted the mask away and she was staring into Charles's white face.

Valentine? Lying down there?

Ah no. No. No. Not Valentine.

Bell was on her knees in the road, her stiff white hands helpless over his body. There was blood in the grit and blood on his tanned face.

Not dead. Oh, please, not dead.

His eyes were closed and he was utterly motionless. Bell dared not undo his clothes, feel for the wounds. Keep him still. Bad bleeding? No. Her fingers, patting over the black road, showed only rainwater. Just grazes then, this redness here.

Get help.

Bell threw another glance at Charles. He was very white, stunned for a moment by the shock. For one terrifying moment Bell recoiled from him, imagining him to be the Angel of Death as he stood there in his black clothes. Then, with a visible effort, Charles shook himself into life. He took command unthinkingly, as he had been born to do.

'Stay here with him,' he ordered. 'Don't touch him or try to move him.'

He glanced briefly at the Mercedes with its wheels buried in the soft earth of the verge. 'I'll go for help. Don't panic. I don't think he's that bad.' He was utterly collected now, as detached as if it was a stranger's body at his feet.

Bell stared up into the familiar, aristocratic face, and to her eternal shame something snapped deep down inside her. Uncontrollable tears poured down her face and she had to clench her teeth on the hysterical scream that rose in her throat. Pure, urgent fear for Valentine mingled with her sudden, terrifying realization that for months she had been wrong. She never would have broken through to this chilly Frenchman. Because now, here in this horrible roadway, she was seeing the real Charles. Cold, commanding, and just a little disgusted by the messy, brutal and undignified realities of life. She had turned away from real vitality, and now it was ebbing away on the wet ground in front of her.

Tears blinded her and the screams came out as a low-pitched moan.

Charles snatched her arm and shook her.

'Stop that,' he commanded. 'You are hysterical.'

The moaning trailed away and Bell looked down again at Valentine. His eyes were open, moving, and he was trying to speak through bruised lips. He was alive, and conscious. Strength flowed back into Bell through magic floodgates.

'Don't move. Don't talk, Val. You'll be safe. Help's coming.'

Charles was still standing over them. To Bell he seemed very far away, and very unimportant now.

'Go then,' she shouted at him. He turned away at once and ran for the car.

The quiet returned. Bell sat in the road with Valentine's heavy head cradled in her lap. He was watching her, the bright blue eyes dim with the coming of pain, but there was the ghost of an unquenchable smile tugging at his mouth.

The tears were wet on Bell's face. *Valentine*. Painfully he turned his head. There was blood on her blazer, dimming the bright colours with its ugly spread. He whispered to her. 'Sorry. Another . . . screw-up.'

'Don't try to talk. Help's coming.'

Falling leaves came spinning around them like confetti.

Then, suddenly, there was a mosaic of noise and faces.

Charles came back, grim and silent. Then Bob and Jacopin, running. After them came a low white French ambulance with its siren shrieking. White coats were bending over the man in the road and hands were touching him where Bell had not dared to. Then they were lifting him on to a stretcher. With the heavy helmet taken off Valentine's hair looked very black in a tumble on the thin white pillow.

'Let me go too,' she begged them as the stretcher slid inside. They stood aside to let her climb into the ambulance beside him.

Before the doors closed she looked back into Charles's face and was shocked to see the remoteness of his eyes. Then the doors were slammed shut between them. Although she couldn't see him any more the expression in the Frenchman's face stayed with her all along the endless road into Bordeaux.

The smell of antiseptic engulfed her. There were harsh overhead lights here and hard wooden chairs, and a long vista of people passing to and fro . . . not looking at her. Bell sat in the hospital waiting room stifled by her own impotence. It felt like hours since Valentine had been wheeled away on a tall white trolley. His eyes had closed during that long agonizing drive and he had drifted away somewhere inside himself.

'You are the patient's wife?' the registration official in the casualty department had asked her.

'No.'

'A relative?'

'No. Just a friend.' The woman had been impatient. Bell had realized that she didn't know Valentine's full name, his date of birth, next of kin, date of entry into the country – or any of the things that sounded so important but which didn't really matter at all.

'Wait in there,' they had told her. So she sat in her bloodstained clothes, her eyes gritty with the lack of sleep and with the ribbon of her thoughts for company. Don't take him away. The words became a litany. *Don't take him away.* Not now. Not after all this. Bell kept seeing the accident as she had first glimpsed it. The sight was fixed on her brain, and each time it returned – newly vivid – she felt the same sick fear and panic.

Why did nobody come? What were they doing to him, behind those closed doors? Down at the end of the corridor, just inside the entrance, there was somebody not dressed in white. It was a girl in a duffle coat, asking anxious questions of an orderly. Bell saw that it was Juliette, squeaking towards her along the polished green tiles. The anxiety in her friend's face mirrored her own. Their hands reached out for each other and Bell clung to the warmth of Juliette's fingers. Her own felt like ice.

'Thank God you've come. I can't bear just sitting here. Oh, *God*.' Bell was angry at her tears but it wasn't for herself. It was all for Valentine. Juliette put her arms around her and whispered comforting, meaningless words. Then she made Bell sit down again and rummaged in one of her deep pockets. 'Here,' she said. It was a flask, full of hot coffee and generously laced with brandy. Bell warmed her hands around the plastic cup with gratitude.

'Charles told me the bare story,' said Juliette. 'This stupid, stupid race. What happened?'

'I don't know any more than that,' Bell told her wearily. 'I saw the beginning. And the end. That's all.' But it wasn't all. There was something else that she couldn't forget. 'Juliette,

I've been so wrong about everything. Charles was so far away. He seemed not to care. As if we were all nothing to do with him.' Bell's voice sounded like a tired child's, bewildered.

'Oh, he cared,' Juliette said gently. 'He cares, all right. He just can't let it show. It's just like he's always been. With Catherine, and Christophe.'

She looked away, down the long tunnel of the hospital corridor.

'I love him. More than I love anyone else in the world. But I know that his defences are so solid – well, they become offences. Can you understand that?'

Yes, Bell could understand it. But here, so real and close to hand, it was not easy to forgive. Especially in Charles, who she had come so near to loving very much. Bell knew that she would never forget the way he had looked down at Valentine; as if he was offended by the undignified sprawl, the mess and vulnerability. As if – and she shivered at the idea – the rules of rightness had somehow been vulgarly broken.

Poor Charles, she thought. Trapped inside his life, and his role, and his sad inability to let himself bleed and cry and sweat like other people. And so, even though he was lying somewhere behind those doors, lucky Valentine. He was as free as air because he allowed himself to be, and he was free to smile although he had been beaten.

The two women went on waiting in silence because there was no more for them to say.

Bob Cornelius came in and took the hard chair next to Bell's.

'Any news?' He looked grey with anxiety.

'Nothing yet,' they told him. Bob slumped back in his seat.

'I had to see the police. My French is so lousy. In the end Charles dealt with them.'

Yes, Bell thought, Charles would be good at that.

At last the French doctor appeared from behind his stalwart doors. They shut again with a hiss of air, not allowing even a glimpse inside. The doctor was short and simian with ridged grey-black hair. Bell noticed as she stood up to face him that there were hairs in his ears and nostrils. Her eyes mechanically took in the row of pens in his breast pocket, the plastic name badge pinned to his lapel and the stethoscope dangling just like a medical student's in revue . . . but now he was talking, and she couldn't ward off the moment any longer.

'You are the friends of Mr Gordon?'

The three of them nodded dumbly. The doctor was scanning his clipboard as if to remind himself of whatever news he had to break to them.

'Your friend has concussion. Slight. A bad break of the upper femur. Now re-set. Three cracked ribs. Extensive bruising. Some cuts, one deep, and superficial grazing.'

He stopped. That was all. No more; nothing else?

'Will he be all right?' The question at last, dared to be asked.

'Oh yes, madame, he will be quite all right. He just will not be riding a motorcycle for a few more months.' The doctor sounded pleased about that.

It was Juliette and Bob who were saying thank God, smiling at each other and the doctor. Inside Bell the surge of relief was so huge that she could do nothing. Nothing mattered. He wasn't going to die, that was enough.

'May we see him?' Juliette asked.

'One minute only. Just through there.'

Valentine was lying in a white bed in a curtained cubicle. His chest was bare, tanned under the thick dark hair, but halfway up it was strapped with heavy bandages. His head was bandaged too, and there was a cage to keep the bedclothes off his right leg. Amongst all the whiteness his blue eyes shone intensely. Bob and Juliette went quickly to him but Bell hung back. She felt – of all things – oddly shy of him.

Valentine was dazed. Bob touched his hand and Juliette bent to kiss his cheek. When they turned away they left Bell standing in her place at the foot of the bed. She was watching his face intently, and she saw a glimmer of the old smile. 'Thanks,' he whispered. She knew that he meant for following the race, for being there when he needed her, and for coming to the hospital.

'Hush,' she told him.

Valentine said painfully, 'He really wanted to win, you know. Your baron.' Then his eyes closed and Bell saw that he was exhausted. She left him there in the little cubicle.

Of course. Charles could not have borne defeat, especially by Valentine. But to Valentine himself it didn't matter; only the race mattered. Like the vintage, it was just another lesson to be learned. Yes. She admired him for that – a lasting, powerful admiration.

Bob and Juliette were waiting for her. After the relief had ebbed away tiredness overtook Bell like a powerful drug. She found that she was stumbling as Bob guided her to the car.

Home, she thought. The sanctuary of Le Girafe, the high brass bed and the holy picture, and the soothing emptiness of sleep.

CHAPTER TWELVE

Madame Durand was making pâté. Her blunt fingers worked the cream and pink marblings of fat pork through the mincer. Beside her on the table were nutmegs, cayenne pepper, brown eggs still with the farmyard dirt on them, and the floury kitchen cognac bottle. Fragrant truffles lay in their juice ready to be chopped and added to the mixture.

Bell let herself simply sit and watch, marvelling at the calm deftness of the cook's movements. No rush, no flurry, and never a wrong move. Not like me, Bell thought. And then, *I don't want to think about me any more.* I'm tired of myself. I've made too many bad mistakes.

Madame Durand looked across the table as Bell sighed. She pursed her lips and wiped her hands on her ample aproned front.

'I think you aren't enjoying it here as much as you had hoped,' she said shrewdly.

Bell answered quickly. 'I'm very happy here. I love Le Girafe. But no, you're right. Perhaps I shouldn't be in France at all.'

'*Chérie*, why don't you go back home? Back to your own family?'

Bell shook her head sadly.

'Well then, back to your friends. Your own people. We will miss you, all of us, but it is not right for a young girl to be all alone here in winter in that little summer house.'

Bell picked up a head of garlic and turned it in her fingers, then sniffed the heart of it. The very essence of France.

'I think,' she said slowly, 'that that is good advice.'

How many more evenings did she really want to spend in the battered armchair in front of her cottage fire, trying to read? How many more days in Jacques's office, stifling her impatience with the tedium of life?

Even Valentine didn't need her any more. He was getting better fast – displaying superhuman vitality, just as in everything else. For the first few days Bell had gone in to visit him on her way home from Jacques Lapotin's, for a tentative few minutes at a time. He had been lying in a small, square room with grey slatted blinds at the window. Even though he had a regular stream of visitors who brought him flowers, precious bottles of wine and teetering piles of glossy books, he had been impatient with boredom as soon as the concussion passed. He would lie propped up against his pillows, demanding to be diverted with news of the outside world, his blue eyes sparkling bright with restlessness. Bell felt that she had nothing to offer him; she was wrung dry with the strain of the past days. All she could do was slip in to reassure herself that he really was there, and getting better, and then drift away again. She left him to the company of the bright young Bordeaux people, the jolly businessmen and elegant French matrons, all of whom seemed to know him much better than she did herself.

On the fourth or fifth day Bell had found the little side room empty. The crackling ward sister told her that Monsieur had had himself transferred to the public ward. And there she found him – with two rheumaticky old men perched on his bed and with the admiring stares of all the road-accident victims and post-operative convalescents fixed firmly on him. Valentine revelled in it. The nurses loved him; the nuns who swept up and down the wards in their long creamy robes and starched white coifs came to visit him again and again. How like Valentine, Bell thought, to make a party out of the pain and boredom of hospital life.

To her surprise, on one of her visits she found him alone. Bob had just been and had brought with him a pile of accounts, letters and print-outs from Dry Stone. Valentine was flipping through the paperwork with an exasperated air.

'Look at this,' he greeted her. 'If I don't get out of this dump instantly my entire empire will collapse.' He was only half-joking. She knew how much it must chafe him to be confined to his bed while the world went on without him.

'On recent showing, they'll do better out there with you

safe in here,' she teased him, and he acknowledged that with a crooked smile. Bell sat down on the edge of the bed.

'Valentine,' she asked suddenly, 'what happened? In the race? What made you crash? I know you ride that hateful bike as if you were born on it.' Valentine was watching her carefully, his black eyebrows knitted together.

'What happened?' he repeated at last. 'I just fell off. Skidded. You saw, didn't you?' Then he frowned and looked away. 'It doesn't give me a great deal of pleasure to talk about it, as it happens.' He touched her hand, but it was dismissive. No more questions, then. But still the tiny doubt nagged on inside Bell's head. Would she ever know what had really happened, that wet ugly dawn on the vineyard road?

'Valentine! Coo-eeee!' Two pretty girls in dizzy clothes were waltzing down the ward towards them. Between them they were carrying a giant blue nylon-fur teddy bear, its chest and leg bandaged just like Valentine's. Bell thought she saw the shadow of impatience in his eyes as he glanced up at her, but it was gone before she could be sure of it. At once he was greeting the girls who bent over him to murmur their sympathies and kiss his cheeks. Valentine reached out for the champagne bottle that was standing ready in an improvised ice-bucket for the entertainment of his visitors.

'Don't they mind you treating the place like a night-club?' Bell asked him cheerfully.

'Mind? They adore it,' he had grinned back at her. 'Come and see me tomorrow, won't you?'

'Oh, perhaps,' Bell said airily and went away with a wave and a smile. The teddy bear was in the bed beside him and the pretty girls were giggling over their champagne.

Bell's thoughts circled back from the bustling hospital to the winking warmth of the auberge kitchen. She saw that Madame Durand was still looking at her, concern wrinkling her round face. Her hands were still smoothing the front of her apron.

'Yes, Madame Durand.' Bell could only agree with her. 'Perhaps it would be for the best if I went home.' But to do what? Where?

Later, Bell crossed the cobbled yard to her cottage. It was very quiet, and bone-chillingly cold even with the oil heaters that the *patron* had produced for her. The pervasive mist seemed to slide unstoppably in through the windows and the damp glistened on the dark stone floors. Bell stood in the middle of the room with her hands thrust deep into the pockets of her woollen jacket. Her eyes were looking far away, back to the blue light of her Californian summer and the heat that had radiated down from the constant skies. She shrugged, hopelessly, and then her eyes caught the calm stare of Juliette's sculpture. Little Laure, gazing down at her as she always did from the centre of the mantelpiece. The same circle of thoughts, round and round, and always the same blank wall that loomed to confront her at the last turn. She had made too many mistakes, and now, was it too late? Bell was afraid that it was. She had chosen, chosen wrong, and so how could she ask for all that to be wiped away . . . and after all that had happened?

It wasn't possible.

Bell bent to the logs in the fireplace. Painstakingly she began to build a fire, watching the first little blue flames lick reluctantly upwards. When they grew stronger and the crackle and flare began to warm the patch of hearth she sank back on her heels. Her eyes, wide, stared into the fire's depths.

Back home? To London, pouring wet and winter-shiny? To piece some life together again, somehow? What else was there? Who else? One man, only, and she had turned away from him like a pouting schoolgirl in pursuit of a daydream.

No, nothing else.

Bell stood up stiffly and lifted down the little sculpture. The reddish stone felt warm in her hands. Slowly she went up the narrow stairs and found her suitcase tucked under the brass bed. She dragged it out and then wrapped the little head in a long scarf before laying it in the empty case. Back downstairs the space on the mantel looked much bigger than the real size of the piece. Bordeaux was over, then. Bell's eyes flicked round the room. There wasn't much, really. Hardly any packing to do. Odd that she had felt so at home in this tiny house.

when now she came to look around there was so little of herself in it.

Yet still she procrastinated. Two more days slipped by. Bell promised herself that she was waiting for the right moment to tell Jacques Lapotin that she must leave.

Then among the dozens of telephone calls that came for the *négociant* one morning was a single one for Bell herself. She listened in puzzlement to the velvety French voice on the other end of the line, knowing that she recognized it but unable to place exactly from where.

'Michel Lebegue,' he repeated into her split-second of silence. 'At Valentine Gordon's amusing party?'

'Of course. Of course. What can I do for you, Michel?' Bell asked pleasantly, assuming that his call must be to do with her work.

'You could agree to have dinner with me,' he said softly. 'I have a proposal to put to you. And you still owe me a dance, remember?'

Bell was about to tell him crisply that she was not in the market for proposals – of any kind – and that she would be on her way to London soon. Then she saw that Jacques was watching her, sharp-eyed, and knew that she must wait to tell her employer first.

'We–ell, thank you,' Bell said into the receiver.

'Good. Tomorrow night, then? When shall I pick you up, and where?'

'Don't worry,' Bell answered quickly. Somehow the idea of suave Michel Lebegue did not fit in with Le Girafe. 'I'll go in and see Valentine in hospital first, and then perhaps I can meet you in town?'

They made their brief arrangements and Michel rang off. Bell evaded Jacques's interrogative stare and went back to her typing.

Valentine's bed was surrounded with visitors the next evening, just as it always was. Bell was later than usual, and his eyebrows went up when he saw her at the edge of the crowd in her dark silk-crepe dinner dress.

'All this splendour just to visit me?' he asked sardonically, holding out a glass of the inevitable champagne. Bell felt a pang that he should treat her just like all the other girls who trooped past his bed, and then reminded herself that she had no reason to expect to be treated otherwise.

'Not at all.' She matched her tone carefully to his. 'I'm having dinner with Michel Lebegue.' If she had hoped to see a give-away sign of anger or jealousy in his face, she was disappointed. Valentine laughed merrily.

'Take good care of yourself, then. He's the sort of man your grandmother would have written off as Not Safe in Taxis.'

'Oh, I expect to be able to cope,' Bell told him coolly, but inside she was stinging. He was making her feel just like his wayward younger sister. Or like Joannie.

'Goodbye,' she said carefully. Another cork popped and glasses clinked around them. 'Have another good party.' The sadness in her voice was more apparent than she knew, and Valentine watched her swing away with a tenderness that would have startled her.

Michel was waiting for her at Le Vendange.

The restaurant was small, dark, chic and expensive. The reputation of its food stood almost as high as that of Chez Lestoq, but the ambiance was light-years away from the formal austerity of the other dining-room. Here there was a dance floor at the heart of the cluster of tables, candlelight and soft, soft music. Michel kissed her hand in greeting. Even though Bell shut off the memories with brutal determination, the evening – an evening she hadn't wanted anyway – was starting very badly.

But Michel's clever, close-set eyes saw her mood at once and he devoted himself to charming it away. Without demanding any response from Bell he coaxed her with a stream of stories, Bordeaux gossip and wry, deprecating jokes.

Wine came, and so did the food – flavours overlapping, beguiling and disarming her. At last she felt herself relax. She smiled back into Michel's narrow face and raised her glass once more.

Bordeaux, she pledged silently. Goodbye, but – in a way – thank you. With their coffee came armagnac, forty years old, and petit fours arranged like a posy of pink and green flowers in a nest of lace and silver.

'And now,' Michel said, 'my proposal.' Bell waited, calm and amused. 'You know that at Lebegue & Fils we are expanding?' She nodded, turning her glass to and fro so that the golden brandy caught the candlelight. 'Expanding, we hope, into the English-speaking market. The United Kingdom, of course, and also America.' He paused for a moment, turning his words, and then said, 'Would you like to join us? I know your work, and I'm impressed by how much you know. You have your languages, of course, and you have something else, too. You have style.'

Bell smiled.

It was a wonderful, flattering, tempting offer. Lebegue & Fils was a great house, with a name that was known throughout the wine world. To work for them, Bell realized with regret, would have given her a fascinating opportunity. It was impossible, after what had happened, to think of staying in Bordeaux – especially in the small world of a job where she would have to meet Charles, and Valentine, so often. But it was heartwarming to have been asked. Confidence, missing for so long, began to flood back into Bell like a charm.

She weighed her words carefully too, before she spoke.

'Thank you, Michel. I'm pleased – flattered – that you've asked me. But I have to go back to live in London. Very soon. For personal reasons,' she added firmly. 'I'd have liked nothing better than the chance to work for Lebegue & Fils,' she went on, truthfully, 'but I'm afraid it isn't possible. I'm very sorry.'

He smiled back at her regretfully. 'I'm sorry, too.'

Michel Lebegue, Bell thought, you've done me the biggest favour possible. What's been the matter with me for so long? I may not have a job to speak of right now, but I know I'm good. I can go back to London and find myself another job whenever I like. A better job. I know I can and what's more, *I damn well will*.

'Then what about my dance?' Michel was murmuring.

'With pleasure.' There was more happiness in her smile

than there had been for days. Michel's arms came round her at once and his cheek found hers as they moved to the gentle music.

'Mmmmm,' he whispered. 'I think, after all, I'd rather have you here than in the office.'

Bell stiffened as his hand slid down her back, then she laughed inwardly at herself. If she was going back to London alone, alone into a world she understood, then this is what it would be like. Of course there would be men who would take her out to dinner and then try to kiss her afterwards.

It wasn't so very terrible.

She was lucky, after all. Except for one thing, she had everything she needed in the world. And there was no use in spilling any more tears, even if without that single thing the world looked grey, and sounded empty of teasing Californian laughter.

Later, safely back with their table between them, Michel asked her, 'Can't anybody persuade you to stay in Bordeaux?'

'One person could.' The wine and brandy had mellowed Bell, and she answered without thinking. 'But I don't think he will want to.'

'Valentine,' said Michel shrewdly. 'Oh. I see . . . Well, if I must compete with Valentine, then I suppose I must. But really, you would do so much better with me. Valentine is such a cowboy. Those endless jeans.'

Bell was laughing, in spite of herself.

'Must I have either of you?'

The suave little Frenchman entered spiritedly into the battle. Bell soon discovered that Valentine had given her no idle warning. Michel wasn't safe in taxis or in restaurants, with or without a table in his way. Yet even through all his importuning, he was amusing. Bell liked him very much.

At last she made her escape. Complaining comically to the last, Michel held open the door of her Fiat and leant over it.

'Goodnight,' he said, 'Valentine should be made to make you stay. Does he know how lucky he is?' Michel kissed her, quickly, and then stood back to let her drive away.

Thoughtfully Bell followed the familiar road back to Le

Girafe. With the return of her belief in herself came the determination not to put off the break any longer.

It was time to go.

Back in Vayonnes the windows of the auberge were already dark. Bell trod softly across the cobbles then groped for the latch at her cottage door. The side door opened with the familiar creak and Bell blinked as she turned on the light. The little room already looked unlived-in. No, there was not very much of herself here.

She moved quickly around the room, gathering up the tattered paperbacks and lifting the photographs down from the shelves. Then she went upstairs and laid the bits and pieces in her suitcase alongside the carefully-wrapped sculpture.

She was doing it; the withdrawal was beginning.

'Jacques, I have to tell you something.'

Bell put the latest sheaf of forms down on the *négociant*'s desk and waited.

'And what is this you want to tell me?'

There was a pause. Bell glanced out at the wrought-iron decorative balcony outside the long window and then back into the room.

'I'm going to have to leave Bordeaux,' she said slowly. 'To go back to London. I'm sorry to let you down.'

The *négociant* peered over the top of his spectacles at her, then took them off his nose and began to polish them.

'You haven't found what you wanted in Bordeaux.' It wasn't a question. Bell smiled sadly at him.

'No. I suppose I haven't.'

'You haven't been very happy, either.' Nor was there any point in arguing with that. Had it really been so obvious to everyone? Jacques settled his spectacles back into place before leaning over to pat her hand.

'Don't worry. You will give me a week's notice?'

'Of course I will. Jacques – thank you.'

Bell was standing in the cramped phone booth at Le Girafe, listening to the ringing tone again as it burred into the air at

Reynard. Even at this distance her heart was beating uncomfortably, audible in her ears as she waited for someone to answer.

'*Oui?*' The voice, thank God, was Charles's. They hadn't spoken to one another since they had stood in the vineyard road with Valentine's body lying between them. Bell's words came tumbling out.

'Charles, I . . . I'm leaving Bordeaux. I want to come and say goodbye.'

'Ah, Bell, I've wanted so much to see you. But, as it is now . . . what is there for us to do?'

'I know.' Bell interrupted him, to save them both the pain of saying any more.

He was still Charles, the voice still with its patrician accents and the undertone of sadness.

'When may I come?'

'You want to come here?'

'Yes.' She was quite sure of that. She wanted to make her farewell complete.

'Tomorrow, then,' Charles said. 'We'll hope to see you in time for lunch.'

We, Bell thought bitterly. 'Yes, I'll be there.'

It would be almost her last day in Bordeaux. Her plane ticket was already bought and was waiting on the empty shelf in her room. There was no thought of economizing now. What point could there be in that?

First, before Reynard, she had to go and say goodbye to Valentine. That would be the hardest part of all.

Deliberately Bell chose a time outside the normal hours of visiting. If the staff were all so fond of him perhaps they wouldn't mind a single visitor slipping in to catch him at a quiet moment. How could they talk to each other with so many other faces crowding round the narrow bed?

Bell had no idea what she was hoping for; nor even any real belief that she should hope at all. Yet she clung to the wish that even now, in these last few minutes that were left to them before she exiled herself, Valentine might say something – give even a sign – that would make her stay. The truth was that all of her determined preparation for departure had been carried out in a dream world, where nothing was real but the fierce hope that Valentine might stop her going away from him.

Bell pushed open the swing doors and stepped back into the smell of antiseptic, rubber and dry heat. The soles of her shoes squeaked as she walked down the green and white corridor to Valentine's public ward. She paused at the doors and looked in through the circular windows to his bed. Valentine was talking and laughing over a game of cards with one of the old men.

A nurse passed by behind Bell. To her relief it wasn't the crackling sister, but one of the giggly younger nurses who argued between themselves over who was to have charge of Valentine.

'May I go in and see my friend? It's something . . . private, and visiting times are so hectic.'

The nurse smiled, conspiratorial. 'Of course. Just pull the screens a little, if you like.'

Bell went into the ward. Valentine smiled his relaxed smile, pleased to have company, and the old man shuffled off regretfully.

'Come and sit down and tell me something to make me laugh,' said Valentine, patting the edge of the bed.

'It's not all that funny,' Bell answered. Their English, in the ward full of Frenchmen, gave them as much privacy as thick stone walls. 'I've come to say goodbye.'

He looked straight back at her, the smile gone now. Even after his accident and long days in the hospital, he still looked fit and tanned, incongruous in the middle of the airless ward.

'Goodbye?' There was nothing in his face; no regret, not even a ripple of surprise.

'Yes.' Bell's voice was very low, the blankness of bitter disappointment already beginning to take hold of her. 'I can't stay here. Not after everything that's happened to us all. I must go back to London. Start work again.' She stopped, waiting for him to say something, but to her sharp discomfort Valentine seemed to be waiting too. The long seconds stretched out as his blue eyes, more piercing than she had ever seen them, searched her face. 'I have to go,' she repeated, 'unless . . .'

His black eyebrows went up a fraction, and still he was waiting for her.

But Bell failed to find the words to tell him what she wanted. What was there for her to say, after rejecting him so harshly? That she was sorry, she had misjudged her own feelings? After their sun-washed month together . . . the night of the Ball . . . after he had found her in Charles's arms, and after the vileness of the race?

Shame crawled over her skin and drained the colour from her face and lips. The chance was gone. Once again, Bell found herself in the wrong place. Valentine could have no time for her now, even if she found the courage in herself to ask him. And why expose herself to more humiliation?

After all, he was giving her no flicker of encouragement now. He didn't care whether she was here or not.

'Yes,' Bell went on, making her voice come louder to give it some conviction.

'I'm going back almost at once.' She longed to let the hot tears roll down her face, but fought to keep them back until she could escape his sight.

The silence froze between them on and on. Valentine looked up at last, but it was to say no more than, 'You must do whatever you believe is best.'

'Yes, yes.' Bell stumbled to her feet. 'It's for the best. I'm sure of that.' She leaned over to kiss the warm roughness of his face for the last time, and his hand brushed her cheek lightly. 'Get better quickly, won't you?'

He nodded. 'You bet. They won't keep me in here much longer.'

'Goodbye, Valentine.' *Was she really saying this?*

She knew from his eyes that he was disappointed in her, but there seemed no way to change that now.

'Goodbye, Bell.' His voice was steady and his eyes already on the air behind her head.

Bell turned away and fled the agonizing length of the ward to the loneliness of the corridor beyond. Bleak waves of loss and disappointment washed around her, threatening to carry her away with them. The tears stood out on her white cheeks in tracks of shiny wetness.

I've been such a fool. The refrain beat in her head like a sentence to servitude.

Out in the car park Bell met Bob Cornelius. He was carrying more piles of paperwork for Valentine, but when he saw her, he put it all down on the wet tarmac at their feet and stretched his arms out to her shoulders.

'What's wrong? Something bad's happened. Come on, tell me. Just let me help.'

How kind he is, thought Bell, seeing the worried, short-sighted eyes blink at her, and how I wish that he really could help me.

'I've been to say goodbye to Valentine.' She was sobbing now, great bubbling sobs that took her breath and strength.

'Why's that?' asked Bob, all gentleness.

'I've been so wrong, Bob. And now he doesn't want me any more.' Her voice was muffled, but there was no mistaking the pain in it.

'You'd like him to?'

'Oh, yes. But it's too late. Everything is gone.'

'Bell, listen to me.' Bob's fingers gripped her harder, almost shook her. 'Have you told him this?'

Bell breathed in hard to stop the flood of tears, then scrubbed her eyes with her handkerchief. She was here, standing in the middle of the car park at a city hospital, feeling a greater sense of loss than at any moment in her life. She was full of gratitude to Bob, but there was nothing he could do. And she longed, with a fierce, protective longing, to be alone. To lick her wounds, alone. She breathed in once more, then stared back at him through the mist of tears.

'No, Bob. What would be the point of that? You didn't see the indifference in his face, back there. Look – thank you. I'm stupid, and I'm sorry, and I need to be on my own. I'm going back to London.'

Bob let her go and she hugged him quickly. 'Goodbye. Thank you, for everything.'

Bell stumbled to her car, groped for the controls and backed away. Bob watched her for a moment with his familiar frown puckering his face, then shook his head, picked up his mass of papers and went in to see Valentine.

They would be waiting for her at Reynard. Bell pressed the cold sponge to her eyes, then stared into the square of dim mirror again. Her face was dead white except for the swollen, scarlet rims to her eyes. Anyone could tell at a glance that she had been crying. Well, that didn't matter. With fingers that were still shaking Bell dabbed some blusher on her cheeks and twisted the spiral of the mascara wand to her eyelashes. Now she just looked as though she was trying to put on a brave face to cover her grief. That didn't matter, either.

As a final afterthought Bell pulled a vivid red sweater over her plain skirt. Perhaps that would be bright enough to take their eyes off her face.

Now, for the last time, she eased the car out of the courtyard and turned it towards Reynard. The road unfolded steadily in front of her. The vineyards were all bare and stark now, the long summer shoots of the vines cut back. Soon the ploughing would begin, turning the blankets of soil over the exposed wood to protect it from the frosts of winter. Then, through the long, cold months the vines would be lying dormant until the sap began to rise again with the first warm breath of spring. Bell turned her head away. Spring seemed an impossibility now.

There was Reynard, up on the rounded hill above the river. Bell recalled her first glimpse of the imposing château. Before all this began. Life had seemed so promising then. And now – well, life would just go on. But she had missed the chance to fulfil that promise.

Don't cry again, Bell warned herself. Just get over this last hurdle, and then you can go home.

On impulse she left the car at the roadside just outside the château gates. Ahead, around the single bend, lay the treacherous stretch of road where Valentine had had his accident. Even now Bell felt a shiver of delayed shock as she saw the scene – the dark, wet road, the clump of trees, and the overturned bike with its wheel still spinning at the sky.

Wordlessly, as she had done a thousand times since that dawn, she thanked God that Valentine was still alive.

Bell lifted her head and began to walk up the driveway under the arch of trees. She had been quite sure that she was right to come here to make her farewell. She wanted it to be seen by all of them, unmistakable. But now she felt afraid – and sad, and vulnerable.

Keep on walking.

When she came under the shadow of the house she hesitated. In front of her was the double flight of steps, the weight of the great doors and the massive bell-push. But she could hear voices – Juliette's, Catherine's, and perhaps Charles's low murmur. They would be sitting in the salon with the tall french windows open on to the lawns and the last dappling of October sunshine. Bell walked quickly round the corner of the house to the open windows.

She stood there for only a second before they saw her, but the scene froze like a tableau in Bell's consciousness. Hélène was sitting in her straight-backed chair beside the fireplace, watching with more serenity in her face than Bell had ever seen before. Catherine and Juliette were side by side on one of the sofas, Catherine's dark head bent over the pages of a photograph album. Charles was leaning behind them with his face in shadow.

Bell's brief impression was that the room was full of cultured French voices, at ease with each other in the absence of strangers. They were sitting there amongst their beautiful possessions, in the château that had been their family home for endless generations. They were closely united by the ties of culture, the nuances of their nationality, and even by the iron bands of tragedy. How could she, Bell Farrer, an Englishwoman without family or place in the world, an outsider to their tight-knit society, ever have hoped to belong to this?

Or even to understand it? Valentine was right. They were parvenus, the two of them. She had loved Charles, yes, a misbegotten love nourished on hopelessness, but it could never have won the solidity of truth.

Bell lifted her hand to tap lightly at the glass.

'Am I interrupting? I heard voices, so I came round outside.'

At once they were looking up, smiling, greeting her. For a second Charles's hands were gripping her own cold fingers, but she didn't look back into his eyes.

'Come and sit here with us. We're looking at the family pictures.' That was Catherine, moving to give Bell room to sit beside her on the sofa. Juliette greeted her with a hug and a kiss on the cheek. Even Hélène smiled and held out her ringed fingers.

Bell sat sown beside Catherine and her eyes fell on the open pages of the album.

'These are the pictures of Christophe,' said Catherine gently. 'It's been . . . so long since any of us looked at them.'

Bell saw an oval portrait photograph of a little boy. His colouring, the baby-gold hair and deep blue eyes, was Charles's, but the shape of his face and pointed chin were Catherine's. A little child, the perfect amalgam of two people, now lost to them. Bell felt a wave of pure sorrow for Catherine and Charles. Theirs was the saddest loss of all, against which her own paled into nothingness. Bell longed for them to find each other again and make another child – a child who might go a little way towards filling that aching gap yawning between them.

'How like you both he is,' Bell said softly.

Charles reached over and took the album out of her hands, then placed it in the long drawer of an inlaid table.

A shadow lifted from Hélène's face as she looked from Catherine to her son and then said briskly, 'Charles, what about a drink for Bell?'

My name at last, Bell thought. Generous in victory, Hélène.

Lunch was a meal much like the others that Bell had eaten at Reynard. There was sparse, simple, excellent food served on the finest china, and exquisite wine in fragile glasses. The talk was restrained, polite, running evenly from one to the other of them and back again.

'The vintage,' said Bell, over the rim of her wine glass. 'Will it be as good as you hoped?' For the first time in this their last meeting her eyes locked with Charles's and she saw the flash of pride and pleasure in them.

'Ah, yes. Better even than we had hoped. The first signs are that it will be a classic year. Even Jacopin is optimistic.'

The new wine would be fermenting now in the great wooden vats across the way in Charles's *chais*. Poor Valentine, Bell remembered painfully. His own gleaming vats would be empty, the rows of temperature and pressure dials reading zero.

'That's good news,' Bell told Charles quietly. 'I'll be watching out for Château Reynard in next year's tastings, then.'

'So you are going back to your work in London?'

'Oh yes. Almost at once. Back to work, although I'm not sure where, yet. Something interesting will turn up, I'm certain.'

'I'm certain too,' Charles answered softly.

After lunch, and after the formality of coffee in the salon, Bell looked deliberately at her watch and then stood up. The ordeal was over, without even having been too testing. She was glad, after all, that she had done it.

'I must make my way back home. I still have all my packing to do.'

They followed her out into the magnificent hallway. At the door Catherine took Bell's hand and held it for a moment. The glance from her hazel eyes said everything, and among those things were 'thank you', and 'I'm sorry'.

Hélène found it in herself to kiss Bell on either cheek, bringing a waft of expensive flowery scent, before following her fat dachshund back into the salon.

'Goodbye, Bell,' she said before she disappeared. 'It's been so interesting to meet you.'

Juliette's farewell was the warmest, and she insisted that it was only au revoir.

'Next time I'm in London, I'll be turning up on your doorstep again.' They kissed each other, remembering. Bell knew that she would be glad to see Juliette again. But not yet. Not yet.

'Where is your car?' asked Charles.

'Down by the gates.'

'I'll walk with you.'

Together they walked down the curve of stone steps and away from the proud height of Château Reynard. Bell kept her eyes fixed on the tunnel of trees and on the empty, open road waiting for her at the end of it.

'I want to tell you something, Bell,' Charles said when they were alone in the afternoon stillness. Bell looked up to see that the branches were almost bare now, except for a few rags of leaves clinging defiantly on.

'What is it?' she asked.

Charles's face was partly turned away from her but she could see that he was frowning. Lines of tension were etched around his mouth and into his cheeks. He looked older; she had a sudden image of how he would look as an old man.

'The race,' Charles said in a hard voice. 'I wanted to win it. It was important to me, not being beaten by Valentine Gordon. Yet I was trailing behind him almost all the way, even though he had given me the more powerful machine. Then, when we were coming to that bend up there,' Charles waved through the trees towards it, 'I knew that it was my last chance.'

Bell listened tensely, counting the even pace of their footsteps on the gravelled drive.

'And so,' Charles said, 'I accelerated and sliced inside him just as we reached the crown of the bend. But I miscalculated. There wasn't enough room for me to get through and the bend was sharper than I thought. Valentine had to swerve to give me space, and in saving me he . . .'

'Nearly killed himself,' Bell finished for him in a dead voice. Now she understood. And Valentine – reluctant at the last to tarnish what he must have seen as Bell's gilded image of Charles – hadn't wanted her to know.

How blind and crass she had been.

'And what did you tell the police?' Bell couldn't stop herself from sounding cold and bitter.

'Just that. They didn't really even want to know that much. Because of who I am.'

And who are you, Charles de Gillesmont? A lonely man in

your luxurious world, tortured by your own guilt; set apart by your rigidity and fear even from the love of your wife. Once more sympathy and sorrow swept over Bell and she stopped walking so that she could turn and look full into his eyes. They were dark with hurt, and held hers with a kind of imploring question that made her want to turn away to spare his vulnerability.

'Don't worry, Charles,' she murmured. She took his hands in hers and rubbed them gently. 'Don't blame yourself any more. Valentine never will suffer like you. He doesn't care as much as you, nor does he set himself such rigid rules. It means the world can deal him fewer knocks. He wins, in his own way, whoever passes the finishing post first.'

Bell couldn't help showing the depth of her feeling for Valentine in her voice and in her brief smile; Charles saw it and understood.

In unison they turned back towards the gates and walked on. Beside Bell's car they stood close to each other for the last time.

'Go back to her,' Bell whispered. 'Make it right.'

Charles groaned, and then his arms came round her like dead weights.

'I loved you.'

She barely caught the words, they were spoken so low. 'But it couldn't be.'

'I know.' *I loved you too, but I'm glad it's over now.*

He kissed her once on the lips and then turned away. He walked back through his tall iron gates with proud shield and motto, back through the richness of his vineyards to his family and home.

Bell watched his tall figure going away from her; he looked defeated and so alone that the tears sprang back into her eyes. It has to be like this, she told herself. And then, he won't let himself be defeated. They will win through, the two of them, in the end. They have too much to let it slip away.

Bell climbed into her car, started the engine and rode away from Château Reynard without allowing herself a backward glance.

*

The sheltered cobbled yard at Le Girafe was warmed by the late sun. Bell stood for a moment and looked up at the crazy slopes and angles of the auberge roofs, then let herself into the sanctuary of her cottage. Her suitcase lay open on the high bed upstairs. She had nothing to do but fold her clothes and put them inside. *The Portrait of a Lady* still lay, face-down, on the arm of her chair. Bell sat down in the shabby depths of the armchair and began to turn the pages. There was nothing all around her, silence and emptiness, until she heard the sound of a car on the vineyard road. It came closer, slowed, looking for somewhere. Then there came the crunch of stone beneath the tyres as it turned into Le Girafe. It was a Bordeaux city taxi, yellow, with its number on a shield above the windscreen.

Someone was struggling to get out, moving awkwardly. A tall, lean man, black-haired, leaning against the side of the taxi to swing a pair of crutches into place.

Valentine.

Bell's heart lifted with the music of pure happiness, and the sun poured into her little room with the gentleness of a benison.

He came limping across to her door. Bell saw how unwieldy the new crutches were for him, and loved the fierce lines of determination in his face. Her fingers felt thick and flaccid as she fumbled at the latch, and then the door swung open and they faced each other.

Valentine's face was grave as he looked down at her.

'I came as soon as I could,' he told her.

'Why did you let me go, then?' Bell asked him the first words in her head. She felt limp with bewilderment and the fear of daring to hope all over again.

'Let's go inside.' He swung the crutches and levered himself down the single step into the room. Bell's hands fluttered about him, anxious to help but incapable of doing anything.

With a gesture of irritation Valentine dropped the crutches and hobbled to the table, then from the table propelled himself to the armchair. He had to stoop beneath the low beams, too tall and suddenly ungainly in the little house.

313

'Doll's house is about right,' he said drily, looking around it with raised eyebrows. 'Why, Bell? Hiding in this little place, all on your own.'

'*Valentine!*' Bell could bear it no longer. She ran her hands feverishly through her hair and over the contours of her face, trying to make sense out of what was happening. 'What are you doing here – out of hospital – after we said goodbye?'

He silenced her with a single commanding gesture. 'You said goodbye, remember? I've come to say something to you. It's something that I couldn't say in that ward full of sad old men and cripples. So will you listen to me now, Bell?'

She nodded dumbly, her eyes no longer on his face.

'I want you to be honest with me,' he said, and she waited, counting the seconds, for what was to come. 'And with yourself. And in return, I'll tell you the simple truth. Is that a deal?'

Again she nodded. If she could have seen his face the tenderness in it would have reassured her, but she kept her eyes averted, poised to defend herself.

'Well then,' his voice was low, 'the truth is that I love you.' He said it so simply that it cut into her. 'I should have told you long ago, but it wasn't until I saw you in my library with Charles that I realized it would kill me if I lost you.'

Blindly Bell turned to him and buried her face against him. In the incoherent avalanche of thought there was one clear thing. *So lucky. I'm so lucky.*

Valentine's fingers tangled in her hair then he lifted her and stooped, painfully, to kiss her eyes and forehead.

'Wait.' It was a command. 'It's your turn to be honest, Bell. Tell me.'

She searched for words and then, not caring, plunged in haphazardly. 'I didn't understand. Not you, myself, or Charles. Especially Charles.' Valentine smiled crookedly at his name. To both of them, it sounded so irrelevant now. 'I thought I wanted the perfect man,' Bell went on, 'and Charles had all the right ingredients, on the outside. I went on making excuses for his reserve because it challenged me. I told myself that I would win through to the warm, private inside of him, and that would be my reward. But I had got it all wrong, and I was imagining a man who didn't really exist. Only in the second when I came to the accident, still praying all the way that Charles would be safe, did I understand it all. I would have died if you were dead. Nothing else mattered. Not me, not Charles, not anything.' Valentine held her face in his hands, not letting her turn her head away.

'And so,' he said softly, 'not Charles de Gillesmont after all, but me.'

Bell understood the triumph in his voice. 'Bell, you have known this all these days, all the time I have been lying there in that hospital bed. Why couldn't you have told me? I was waiting for you to. Waiting, interminably.'

Why couldn't I have told him, Bell thought helplessly.

'Listen,' he said. 'You could tell Bob. You even told that rich man's Sacha Distel . . .'

'Who?'

'Michel Lebegue. And so they both came to tell me. But not yourself. Why, Bell?'

The bright blue eyes held hers, demanding. Bell peeled away the last of her defences and let him see her terrifying weakness.

'I was ashamed,' she murmured. 'And afraid.'

'Bell, darling, we are all afraid. And shame has to be lived with. Like mine, after the vintage.'

'I know, I know,' she blurted. 'And I loved you for that, too.'

He was watching her now with a queer, intent look in his eyes.

'Say that again,' he commanded.

'I love you.'

This time his mouth found hers and he bent her head back painfully with the weight of his kiss.

'We need each other,' he said against her bruised lips. 'As equals, one to one. I am your counterweight. No father-figure, and no boy next door. Nor a Prince Charming with ice running in his veins, but a real man, flesh and blood. We are two perfect, matching halves.'

Bell let herself fall against him, into his warmth and strength, closing her eyes on the avenues of the past weeks.

When they stirred again it was Valentine who said, 'Marry me. Will you have me, knowing all my faults?'

Bell took his hands and her eyes were brilliant as she answered.

'Yes. And will you take me, with mine?'

He laughed aloud in pleasure. 'Ah, Bell. Where shall we go? Choose anywhere you like. America . . . Paris . . . London, if you like. Or no, what about Burgundy? I'll buy you one of those old stone houses in a fold of the Côte d'Or . . .'

Bell drew herself away from him and put her fingers to his lips.

'I don't care where we go. I just want you to make love to me. Here, and now . . .'

Valentine's eyes flickered, then his arms dropped and he groaned through his laughter. 'Undone! How can I, with this?' He pointed to the heavy plaster on his leg. 'I couldn't even climb the stairs.'

Bell was laughing now too.

'I think you could, I'll show you how.' Her hands were gentle on him. Together they conquered the narrow stairway, ducked under the low doorway into the bedroom and climbed to the refuge of the high brass bed.

Their mouths and arms and bodies found each other, hungry, and took strength. This is my true celebration, thought Bell. A celebration of the truth at last. It hurts to learn, but there is such joy in knowing.

There in the little house at Le Girafe Bell and Valentine unlocked the secret rooms and walked through them together. There were no hours there, no walls or sky, and no destinies but their own.

At last, exhausted and at peace, they lay tangled in each other's arms to listen to the silence in the dim room. Valentine's mouth moved against Bell's hair.

'There's something else I've got to tell you.' She stiffened, half afraid again, but he laughed into her eyes.

'The night of the party, when I found you with Charles . . .'

'*No.*'

'Wait . . . listen. I told you that it wasn't because of you that I wanted to race him.'

Bell nodded. The sound of their words and the sight of the two men, poised, was vivid in her head.

'Well, it was a lie. It was because of you. That he should have you, and not me – I knew in that instant that it was impossible.' Valentine laughed his lazy laugh and tightened his arms around her. 'I should have taken the sabres. Or the flintlock pistols, perhaps. Who knows, I might have won with those?'

'Be quiet.'

'Come closer, then.'

Bell closed her eyes in the realization of pure happiness. This was here and now, a perfection to be savoured and saved up. There would be difficult times, she knew that. Bell would never again be looking for a fairy-tale come true, not with this man whose faults and strengths she knew and loved as much as life itself. But now, tonight, they had come through their season of mists in the vineyards of Bordeaux. They had come out into the clear, bright light, together.

'I love you, Valentine.'

Again that low, half-mocking laughter. Valentine leaned over her so that his bright blue eyes were hypnotically close.

'*Prove it.*'

Yes. The mist had lifted and the sun shone in the broad skies overhead.

Also available in Arrow

THE POTTER'S HOUSE

Rosie Thomas

Olivia Giorgiadis has left her English roots far behind. She lives on a tiny Greek island, married to a local man with two small sons. Year on year, island life has followed an idyllic but unchanging rhythm...

Until now. An earthquake ravages the coast, its force devastating the island. In its aftermath comes a stranger, an Englishwoman, destitute but for the clothes she wears.

Olivia welcomes the stranger into her home, the potter's house. But as Kitty wins over her family and the village community, Olivia begins to sense danger from the visitor with no past...

'Beautifully constructed and written ... a treat'
Marie Claire